Also by Miki Starr Martin

Well Runs Dry

Broken Promises

blueprints

a miki starr novel

A REIGNSTORM PUBLISHING

PUBLISHED BY REIGNSTORM

A division of Starr Eclectic Concepts

Los Angeles, California

Copyright © 2008 by S Michelle Martin

ISBN: 0-9721246-2-4

Printed in the United States of America

Book design by Starr Eclectic Concepts

www.mikistarr.com

blueprints

Mike & Nate Meet

"Thanks cuz."

Nathaniel Lee Marshall was minding his own business, strolling down his street, bouncing his basketball that his grandmother had given him for Christmas when he happened upon a group of young neighborhood boys traveling in the opposite direction as he was. He recognized most of their faces, most from school, some from the neighborhood. He'd never spoken to any and was quite positive that they had not even realized he existed up until this precise moment when the one with the appearance of being the leader of their little thugged-out pack snatched Nate's basketball mid-dribble.

Nate stopped short as the gang of seven eleven and twelve-year-olds continued forward laughing in joy of their mischief. Basketball was Nate's life, his whole world revolved around the game. He was terribly shy and quiet and thus had no true friends. His father, a strict disciplinarian, had no interest in being buddies with a child. His mother had given birth to six children. Nate was her first and only male child. Needless to say with all the mouths that had to be fed there would be no extra money in the budget to buy Nathaniel Lee Marshall a new basketball.

Nate turned on his heels and reached toward the ground before pushing his way through the crowd of delinquents, his mind focused on getting his ball back and not the potential ass whopping he could be setting himself up for. He wasn't too worried about it however because what his peers were not aware of was his level of determination and that in his hand he held a large rock, was cocked and ready to throw. Yes, maybe he would get his ass kicked out here today but he was taking somebody down with him. Before anyone had a chance to react Nate had already swung the ring leader around and pushed him onto on his back on the earth below. He was poised above him with the rock aimed at his skull.

"Give me my ball back!" Nate spat out.

From behind he could hear the young boys yelling out threats and profane statements of disbelief as they honed in on him. The young man beneath Nate simply laughed and called his dogs off. He handed Nate his ball.

"Well you can't just leave me here," he said.

Nate reached out to help the young boy to his feet. He didn't see the blow coming. He felt the kicks in his side but was temporarily blinded and couldn't tell where they were coming from. From his position sprawled out on the concrete he could hear yelling and cheering. He felt around, again his ball was missing. He began to panic. He managed to dodge another kick and stagger to his feet.

"Where's my ball?" he yelled at his tormentor.

"Where my ball? Where my ball? What choo a l'il white boy uh sumthin'?" another of the kids passed the ball off to the boy, "You won't cho ball, come get it den!"

"Aaaargh!" Nate yelled out as he charged at the boy. The two exchanged blows as they rolled around in the dirt. Nate quickly began to get the best of the young boy. As soon as his crew recognized the potential defeat they dove in on top of Nate. He fought strong and hard and landed several good blows before he was imminently overcome.

"Git y'all l'il bad asses away from the front of my house wit' dis nonsense! Git up offa dat dere l'il boy, wuss wrong wit' ch'all?" Ms. Muriel Johnson shouted as she beat the boys off of Nate with a broom, "Gone nah, fo' I call y'alls mammy's, ya hear?"

Like roaches when the lights came on the boys scattered in different directions. They all knew old Ms. Johnson and thus knew that she was not one to be played with. Nate was balled up in pain in the dirt that should have been a lawn. Ms. Johnson pulled him to his feet and gave him a once over. He was filthy and his long lanky body was battered. His shirt was torn and one of his sneakers had come off. His nose was bleeding and there was a gash over his left eye. He was a very fair-skinned boy despite growing up in the blazing Florida sun and thus his arms had black and blue bruises. Ms. Johnson held his cheeks firmly between her thumb and fore finger and turned his head in both directions.

"Aw boy you gone be alright. Nah gone on home to ya mammy so she can clean ya up. Go on nah," and with that Ms. Johnson disappeared into her little yellow house and locked the screen door behind her.

Nate dropped his head and limped over to his missing sneaker. His head pounded as he struggled to bend down to tie it. He looked up and around to see the streets was empty, his ball gone. He sighed and resisted the urge to cry. His father had taught him that only girls and sissies cried and he had enough girls and didn't need one with a dick. He vowed if he turned out to be a sissy he'd surely kill him with his own bare hands. So Nate swallowed his emotional pain and limped toward home. When he arrived he was surprised to find his very own bully sitting on his front stoop as if nothing had happened. Even worse, between his legs he bounced Nate's basketball. Nate walked inside his gate and glared at him. His face became heated as the blood rushed forth.

"Catch," he said, passing the ball to Nate who instinctively caught it, "Yo' name Nate ain't it?"

"Yes," Nate answered clutching his ball in fear that this may be a set up.

"My name Mike but the bitches call me Romeo."

"I know who you are," Nate tucked his ball safely under his arm and walked past Mike to his front door. Mike rose from his position on the concrete and headed for the gate. He called out to Nate without stopping or turning around.

"Ay you wanna roll wit' me an' my homies to da 'Plex t'nite?"

"Sure."

"Meet us at the corna o' 193rd at six o'clock. Frenchy momma gone drop us off."

"Okay."

"Lata."

1 Nate

My parents, four out of five of my sisters, their spouses, and Sierra were all gathered at the table with excited wonderment. I'd called them all here to my childhood home and had mother prepare a hearty meal so that I could make the announcement. The wonderful meal my mother had prepared awaited their salivating mouths. They were anxious and hungry, hungry and anxious as the aroma from Mother's infamous baked beans circulated the air and filled up their nostrils.

Mya was at my side watching me...watching her man as he stood before his loved ones looking good as always. Yes, I was clean. Navy blue tailored pants and light blue and white pinstriped button down Perry Ellis shirt and tie. On my feet I wore square toe Ken Cole's. My hair was cut low and faded to perfection, my lining and sideburns sharp. My mustache ideally trimmed. I'd had a manicure done early that afternoon so you know my nails were right. And oh yes, when I raised my wineglass to commence my announcement that was a Rolex you saw hanging onto my wrist. I keep it clean and always have. Even when I was a young man running the streets of South Dade County with a young thug named Mike (oh, but the bitches call him Romeo.)

Mike, now that's my homey. The two of us have been down since we first scuffled back in uh, hmm, what was it like '87? Damn time flies. But yes, we whipped each other's ass and have been tight ever since. Got-damn we were terrible together. Running the streets, starting fights, in and out of JC. My mother, who has never actually hated anyone, came real close when it came to Mike. See you have to understand something. Before that fight over my basketball, my mother's son was a good son. I did my chores; I went to class and even made good grades. I kept my mouth shut and did everything that was expected of me or shall I say everything my mother expected. But that loyalty kept me from being popular with my peers.

Raising me with five sisters it often became difficult for my mother to differentiate her behavior. What does that mean? Well simply put she didn't know how not to treat me like she treated the girls. I learned to cook, I learned to clean, I was taught to play the piano and much to my father's dismay I was even taught to sew. I was often treated like one of the girls and I was comfortable with that as it felt natural...normal. That is until I was about seven. My dad was hardly ever home and when he was he was too tired to teach me how to be a man. One day he came home from work early and I was in the tub taking my bath only instead of bathing I was playing with toys as children do. My father entered the bathroom with an overloaded bladder. He didn't pay much attention to what I was doing until he finished what he was doing. *"You playin' wit' them GI Joe's I bought you son?"* he asked me as he zipped up his workpants. *"Uh uhn Daddy. Barbie."*

Wrong answer. I remember him having this...this horrified look on his face. It was as if someone had told him that his best friend was dead. He yanked his big black leather belt off so quick if it could have it would have caught whiplash. He grabbed me out of the water by my wrist and beat my soaking wet seven-year-old ass. I screamed and I hollered and then he beat me for crying. That's the first time I remember him saying to me that men don't cry, only girls and sissies but with the way my mother was raising me it wouldn't be the last. He drilled his theory into me throughout life, that and the promise that if I turned out to be a sissy he'd kill me with his own bare hands.

But anyway back to my story. Naturally all the commotion attracted the attention of a crowd. My mother rushed to my aide and attempted as best as she could to pull my daddy off of me. *"James Nathaniel Marshall you let him go!"* she cried. He obliged but paused long enough to blame her for the situation and turned with an open palm and struck her down to kiss the linoleum tile floor. He dropped my battered bleeding body beside her and pushed his way past my sisters. His footsteps faded to nothing as he made his way to the front door and out into the streets. That would be the first and last time my father would ever hit my mother, I'd see to it. If it weren't for her he would have killed me for certain.

My mother nursed me back to health. She kept the incident within the confines of our immediate family. She advised school that I had the flu and would be out for a few days. My pops, angry and embarrassed at what he'd done to my mother I suppose, stayed away for a week. When I'd fully recovered from my "whoopin'" I steered clear of anything that could have possibly been deemed "girlie". I ceased to engage in games with my sisters and rather kept quiet, kept to myself. My mother, who had always been terribly feminine, unaware of how to teach a boy to be a man left me be. School days I would come home, sit on my bedroom floor and pick at my toes between homework and dinner until one day I paid attention to an old worn basketball in the corner of my room. I took it under my arm and carried it out to the back of the house and there shot my first basket.

From that day on all of my time was divided between school, homework and shooting hoops. My mother had given up on culturing me not wanting to risk enraging my father and my father began to look at me differently than he had in the past. Though he and I still did not communicate verbally I would feel the difference in our relationship when he'd allow me to sit with him while he sipped a cold Bud and watched sporting events. But the ultimate breakthrough came when I began to hang out with Mike. Mike was the ultimate man-child and my pops loved him. He loved him so much that I didn't want to be like Mike, I wanted to be Mike. Everything that Mike did, I did. If Mike cut school, I cut. If Mike picked a fight, I finished it. If Mike stole a car, I stole two. Yes, my grades slipped and my juvenile rap sheet was beginning to read like a book but it was a small price to pay to get your father to like you.

Yes everything Mike did, I did and when for Mike snatching purses and jacking sneaks began to become overshadowed by pussy I remained hot on his trail. Now believe it or not this was the biggest feat for me. I'm going to share with you something about me that no one; I mean no one else is aware of. I'm homosexual. Yes gay, queer, a faggot, whatever you want to call it. Shocked? Well, you remember that saying? The biggest trick the devil ever pulled was what? Pretending he didn't exist. So yes I am gay. I am not proud of it; I am not ashamed of it. I just am. And don't go blaming my mother for it either. Pay attention. When we began all of this I told you what? It felt natural. You may think something is normal but it doesn't mean you're comfortable with it. It's when you think that it's natural that could be cause for concern. If my pops had not been so hard on me, so homophobic I'd still be who I am today except I'd probably be making this announcement tonight with a boyfriend instead of my girlfriend.

Ok, okay, I gotcha, I gotcha. Your next question is if I'm gay why I even have a girlfriend. Well, I'm going to address that now. Like I said in order to keep Pops satisfied I needed to in a sense "be" Mike. Well, girls and pussy became an intricate part of who Mike was. I was an actor in a staring role which was my life. I couldn't back down. So I bit the bullet and fell into character. Soon, it went from being a chore to being a mission. With all the women I slept with, allowed to perform oral sex on me, and a few other sexual deeds I'm not very proud to confess to, I hoped that one of those coochies would have the secret cure for my curse. Of course none of them did. When I was alone I felt guilt. I hated what I was doing to these women and as I aged the tougher it became, the more emotional distress I experienced but alas I had to keep up with Mike aka Romeo.

When my 25th birthday rolled around Mike was still lovin' 'em and leavin' 'em. I could keep it up no longer as my conscious would not allow it. At the same time a fear of disappointing my father kept me trapped in the lifestyle that I'd emulated for so many, many years. It was around that time that I met Mya Engles, a gorgeous Black woman from Great Britain. At the time she was a waitress at a little café I patronized on South Beach. I became fascinated with not only her lovely accent but her demeanor as well. She was so refined and gave the presence of being highly intelligent and extremely cultured. The striking similarities to my mother stimulated my mind and I'd hoped to have an opportunity to converse with her. Opportunity finally knocked. A meeting had run late and Mya was nowhere to be found when I arrived at the café. I thought to ask for her but not wanting her to get a misconstrued impression of me I kept quiet. I decided to skip lunch and head back to the office to go over some paintings when I spotted her (I'm the H.N.I.C. now but at the time I was a junior art buyer). I'm not clear as to how but fortunately I did. She was sitting across the street on a blanket reading James Baldwin's *1 Day When I Was Lost*. Being cast as a player and smooth talker most of my life I felt no intimidation as I walked in her direction.

"Excuse me, Miss." Her beautiful eyes met mine though seemingly unfazed by my charming good looks. Her brown curly hair was wild and pulled into a haphazard ponytail. She peered at me over the stylish eyeglasses that sat on the brim of her nose. She was wearing the apron that was a part of her uniform and so I correctly reasoned that she was on a break. It was clear that she was annoyed with me for disturbing her reading but recognizing my face and being the person she is she offered me a slice of pineapple from the bowl she was snacking from. As it turned out she was just the woman I thought her to be. I didn't go into this situation with the intent of having a more intimate relationship with her. She intrigued me and I wanted to know her as a person. Over the years we became close but when she confessed that she was falling in love with me my first instinct was to stop her in her tracks quickly. But then I realized that she was what I needed, who I'd been looking for. No I wasn't "in" love with her and realized that I may never be but I did love her as a person. I was sure she would be as close to true love as I could ever expect in my lifetime and it would keep the role going. So I professed to love her when in reality I did not though I foolishly hope someday it will be true and that's what brings us to this announcement today.

"Ladies, gentlemen, I suppose you're all wondering about the reason that we are all gathered here today. Well, besides the pleasure of partaking in this wonderful meal which Mother has prepared for us, I have a special announcement to make," I took Mya's hand in mine and pulled her to her feet beside me. At a petite 4'11" tall beside my 6'4" we make quite the odd couple. She was just as lovely as ever on this occasion with her honey brown complexion and bright green eyes. She'd had her naturally curly hair dyed a light golden brown and straightened so it hung to her elbows. Normally her choice in style was in direct contrast with mine but for this evening she wore a simple yet elegant backless red dress just to please me. I leaned forward and kissed the back of her hand before I turned to face her. I looked at Mya; her hand still in mine but directed my words to the group.

"Mother, Father, family. I've asked you all here to announce that I've asked young Ms. Mya Rene Engles to be my loving wife."

"And I said yes," she finished in her beautiful British accent.

I eased the engagement ring with the 1-carat princess diamond set in platinum onto her small finger and pulled her into a warm embrace. The group applauded, my mother cried, my sisters all gathered around Mya trying to check out their brother's generosity. Sierra congratulated me and kissed my forehead. My father beamed, the ultimate victory could now be achieved; an Oscar could now be won. Caught up in the moment and opportunity I continued to stand after most of the commotion had calmed.

"And that's not all," I continued, "We're also working on having a baby."

I lied. Just like that I lied but being a good sport Mya didn't let me slip; she jumped into character as my supporting actress and went right along with it. We hadn't yet discussed having children but to be perfectly honest I knew I did not want any – ever. I wasn't sure if Mya did or not but I got the feeling it didn't much matter to her one way or another. The question was whether or not I'd set myself up to work on it now? Either way I didn't care as I'd just received my Oscar.

"Congratulations son, I'm proud of you," my old man said, shaking my hand.

"Thanks Pops," it was done, locked and sealed. I'd never have to worry about my father wondering whether or not I am a man.

Dinner was consumed through mouthfuls of excitement driven chatter, which was mostly courtesy of the women. They were curious about everything from what style of dress Mya wished to wear to what we'd name our unborn, unconcieved, unagreed upon child. After dinner I took a seat on the sofa. My father sat beside me and handed me one of his prized Cubans. He pat my back and smiled with pride.

"Good job son," he said before he stood and went to join the other men. My Father was satisfied, I'd done well.

"Is this seat taken?" that was Sierra, my best friend in the world surpassing even Mike. I'll get back to her momentarily.

"Never," I answered.

"Wow, so you and Mya are finally going to do it right."

"Yep."

"Congratulations baby. You know I'm happy for you, Mya is a beautiful woman. But uh, how are you gone break this news to your friend?"

"I'm going to tell him. I didn't want to invite him here. You know how ignorant Mike can get."

"Mmhm."

"Really though, it shouldn't come as such a surprise to him. We've been seeing one another for almost three years now."

"I know, I know but you know how your boy is. It's enough for him to deal with you being involved in a long-term relationship, now you're going to tell him you're getting married? Tying the knot? Jumping the broom? God I'd give nearly anything to see the look on his face when you break to him his biggest fear and worst nightmare. Oh no I'm sorry, second worse. His worst is him getting married!" the two of us laughed together, it felt good. It always felt good.

"Well he's just going to have to get used to it. How long does he expect we can play the field? On up into our 70's? Yea right, when I get old and decrepit I want to know that I have someone that can bury me. Not wonder how long I'll sit and rot before someone sniffs me out."

"Eeew Nate that's nasty!" Sierra laughed, "Well baby just remember that I love you and no matter what I got your back."

That's why Sierra's my best friend. She's true and honest, real. I could tell her any and everything and I did just that with the exception of the truth about my sexuality. It is not as though I did not trust her with that information or thought I'd loose her behind it, it's just that if I told anybody it could compromise the portrayal of my character and I could not afford for that to happen. And Sierra being the devout Christian that she is would try to convince me to come to church and ask Jesus to purge it from me. She'd want me to speak of it and how could I deny it if I was dealing with it?

Sierra and I met when we were juniors in high school. We were sixteen years old and for the third consecutive year we occupied space in the same classroom, Señor De La Cruz's Spanish class. I suppose one would assume that after spending two years in the same class we would have met long ago. Those people don't know Sierra Douglas. As I stated Sierra is a devout Christian, daughter of a Pastor and perfect Pastor's wife. She only spoke when spoken to and focused deeply on actually learning the foreign language unlike myself. I was content to simply learn just enough to maintain the C average which kept me staring on Varsity basketball. At the time I was all about playing ball and fucking to put it bluntly and I knew that would not happen with a girl like Sierra and so there was no reason for me to approach her. It's likely that I would have allowed four years of high school to pass by without so much as saying "excúseme" to her. But on that very first day she sat beside me and mumbled *"Oiga que vamos otra vez"* which I later found out was 'hear we go again' in Spanish. It was a sweet effort and so I entertained a conversation with her before class. What I was unaware of throughout that brief exchange was that it was just the start of a lifetime friendship. Over the years that passed she was there supporting me in every positive and during the repercussion of every negative endeavor. I know for certain there is nothing in this lifetime that Sierra wouldn't do for me as there isn't a thing in this world that I wouldn't do for her.

"Honey, it's getting quite late. I think we should be getting home now," Mya interrupted our conversation. She was correct; it was getting quite late into the evening and we both needed to get up early the next morning, "Sierra darling, thank you so much for joining us."

"Of course sweetheart. Congratulations again," the two embraced and then it was off for Mya and me. I said my goodbyes to the family and graciously accepted their repeated congrats as we headed outside to my brand new Mercedes Benz CLK320. Both Mya and I were silent on our drive back to our six-bedroom home in Weston, Florida. Chopin played in the background setting a relaxing mood for the two of us. I parked inside the three-car garage beside Mya's silver Porsche 911 Carrera 4. I think you're beginning to grasp the idea that together Mya and I were set financially. Neither of us wanted for anything. I was senior art buyer for a large local firm and Mya was a CPA with her own accounting firm not to mention the fact that she was born with a silver dish set in her mouth. So the idea of starting a family at her age 26 and my age 28 was not too farfetched, not too farfetched at all.

It had been a long day and I was very tired. Mya led me up the stairs to our bedroom where she helped me out of my evening attire. She's not ever been a chatty woman but I noticed that she was unusually quiet this evening. I figured it may have had something to do with my little addendum to our announcement. I recognized that at some point she would voice her opinion and so I left her to her thoughts. I stepped into the shower and cleansed the daily dust from my body and washed my short hair. When I was done I wrapped a towel around my waist and stood before the sink to brush my teeth. Mya was making some notes in her journal when I rejoined her in our bedroom. I grabbed a bottle of Aloe Vera lotion and sat on the edge of the bed. Mya closed her book and slipped it inside the top dresser drawer that was filled with all of her womanly accoutrements. She walked to me wearing nothing but the bra and thong that she'd worn beneath her gown and took the lotion from my hand. She oozed the creamy substance onto her hands and rubbed it down my legs and to my feet.

"You must really be tired," she joked as she rubbed my inner thighs.

"What? Oh yes," I responded once I caught on to her jest regarding my penis which was as limp as a cat with a broke leg. She climbed onto the king size bed and sat on her knees behind me. She began to massage the lotion into my shoulders.

"So," she began, "what exactly is this about us working on having a baby? Is that what we've been doing here? If so I really wish you would have told me Nathaniel as it would have saved us plenty money on birth control pills."

"Sorry sweetheart, I know I should have discussed it with you first. It's just me getting caught up in the moment and not thinking. If you're not ready I'll understand. We can wait as long as you need to," secretly I hoped she would decide that we should wait.

"Well what do you want Nathaniel? If you're second guessing your decision we don't have to go along with it."

"No, no, I'm not second guessing anything," I lied; I'm second-guessing everything.

"Well in that case my darling, I say let's go for it."

"Are you sure?" are you sure, you're sure?

"Darling I'm as certain as I am going to get. Nathaniel Marshall I love you more than life itself and I would be honored to carry your child."

I turned to look Mya in the eyes. Happiness was there, certainty, love, "Well let's go for it my love."

Mya squealed and wrapped her arms around my neck. She kissed my lips over and over as she repeated her vow of love to me. She eased away from me and in a sexy manor unsnapped and removed her red lace bra allowing her B-cup breasts to spill forward. She teased her nipples with her fingers and slowly ran her tongue across her lips.

"Nathaniel," she spoke in a low husky voice.

"Yes darling?"

"I've already taken my pill for the day so I can't get pregnant tonight but how about a practice round?"

"Sure, why not?" her hand slid down her body and inside the center of her red lace thong panties. I watched as she stroked momentarily before sliding her hand back up her body and slipping those naughty fingers inside her mouth, "Okay darling, let's practice," I took her 98-pound body in my arms and slammed her onto the bed. I climbed on top of her and instinctively my "young man" downstairs did what he was trained to do.

2 Sierra

Sierra waved good-bye to her best friend Nathaniel's family as she jogged out the front door and to her old 1993 Chevy Caprice that was parked in front. She reached down and gathered her ankle-length purple cotton dress and climbed into the driver's seat. She put the car in gear and drove in the direction of Fort Lauderdale to her parent's home. It was past time for her to pick up her three children before her parents nine pm bedtime. No one understood better than Sierra how dull the lives of church officials could be. Sierra, also known as Si-Si, grew up as the older of two girls and naturally spent most of her childhood in the church. She was raised to be a very obedient young lady, an ideal preacher's daughter far from the wild, outgoing, sex-driven stereotype. She studied hard with aspirations of being an attorney when she became a woman. She was an attractive young girl coming up, men recognized that but she did not allow that to influence her lifestyle. She had plans for her future and she was very determined to bring those plans into reality when she reached her prime.

Sierra's father had other plans for his girls. He allowed his eldest to attend college more for the purpose of meeting a spiritual, intelligent husband with a promising future than to establish a financially secure future of her own. For him, his daughter becoming anything more than a housewife with a degree was out of the question. Taking after her mother the "perfect pastor's wife", Sierra caved into her daddy's wishes as a child should honor thy mother and father. During her senior year she met Darryl Douglas, a law major. As Sierra could not accomplish her mission of becoming an attorney herself out of respect for her father, she decided that involving herself with one was the next best thing. After two years of dating without any sexual involvement, Darryl proposed. He'd established a solid repor with Pastor Mitchell and was well on his way to becoming a prosecuting attorney and so even though she wasn't in love, she accepted his proposal. This decision pleased her father greatly therefore Sierra did not second-guess it. She supposed that she would fall in love with Darryl eventually.

They were married the Spring of Sierra's twenty-third birthday and had since given birth to three beautiful children, the eldest child Michele was four years old. She resembled Darryl with her brown skin and round brown eyes. Though she was very intelligent, quick-witted and talkative, it was her behavior that most bothered Sierra's father who felt she talked too much for a young girl. He would constantly chastise Sierra about her daughter's mouth. As much as Sierra scolded her child about her ways there was no way to readjust the young girl's personality.

Sierra and Darryl's son Lee, named in honor of Sierra's friendship with Nate, was three years of age and a spitting image of Darryl. He was a quiet and obedient child. Being his father's only son one would think that they would be close but they were not. As a matter of fact Lee behaved as though he did not like his own father. The baby was two-year-old Jennifer, Sierra's pride and joy. She bore the most similarities to Sierra in terms of personality as well as physical features. But no matter whose physical attributes the children inherited it was clear all three children held a greater affection toward their mother than her husband. As a matter of fact Darryl had no bond with their children at all.

Sierra and Darryl had less than an ideal marriage. They had much less than even a decent one. The two had barely spoken and had no physical contact since the birth of Jennifer. Most of their problems stemmed from Sierra's tainted childhood. Her uncle, her father's brother and the church Deacon Myron Mitchell was very popular not only within the family but the church as well. He was a handsome gentleman but he'd never married and never had children of his own. Sierra and her younger sister Lillian spent a great deal of time around their uncle Deacon Myron Mitchell but of the two it seemed that Sierra was his favorite. He regularly provided her with money and treats and in return for his supposed generosity he made her give him her innocence. He touched her in places and ways that only a husband should; he made her do things to him that only a whore would. These rituals carried on for seven years of Sierra's childhood, only ceasing when a fed-up Sierra began to "loose control" of her teeth at the most inopportune moments. Realizing that his power over her was diminishing, he soon ceased touching her in that way.

Sierra hid the sad experience from her family. With her uncles popularity she was certain that no one would believe her if she told them anyway, so what would be the point? The only time she'd ever spoken of it was to Nate. He encouraged her to speak up to her family about it. She promised that she would do so but she could not bring herself to disgrace them and the church in such a way. She assumed by the time she was a married adult she would have a much better handle on things. She could not have been more wrong. When the time came to consummate her marriage it was emotionally as well as physically painful for Sierra. Going into the relationship Darryl was fully aware that Sierra was a virgin; unfortunately she'd never filled him in on her family secret. He assumed that as time passed the sex would improve but Sierra never felt comfortable with it. She would lie beneath her husband stiff and tense and secretly afraid. She would never try to make it better; she would never display a desire to experiment.

Although the two decided to wait until Darryl finished his education and obtained a secure position with a solid law firm before they had children, Sierra decided early into the marriage that she needed to stop taking her birth control pills. From her point of view if she became pregnant she would not have to make love to Darryl for at least nine months. Her plan succeeded but upset Darryl. As a cover for her deceit Sierra lied and stated that her pills were not strong enough. She promised to have her gynecologist prescribe her a more powerful dosage after she gave birth.

Michele LeAnne Douglas was born and Darryl accepted the child. Sierra recovered and Darryl attempted to resume a normal marriage, a normal marriage that included sexual affinity. Sierra quickly became paranoid and again felt the only way out was to again become pregnant. Darryl was incensed. The last thing he needed was another mouth to feed. There was no way that he'd believe that the pills were still not strong enough and so after the birth of Lee Darryl Douglas, her husband began to monitor her usage of her birth control pills. He required Sierra to take the pill in his presence every morning and to Sierra's dismay he wanted sex from her most every night. Sierra became frantic, dreading the idea of going to bed at night. She did not want to participate but he was her husband, how could she tell him no? After the years that past she could not muster courage to confide in him about her history and Darryl never bothered to try and find out just why his wife was so intimidated by intimacy. He instead was determined to force her involvement in their sex life. In a frantic effort to escape it, Sierra replaced her birth control pills with pills of the same size and confidently popped one every morning in front of her husband.

It was when she became pregnant with Jennifer Leenette that her marriage was essentially over. Being against the idea of needing to use condoms with his wife, Darryl ceased having sex with her altogether. Sierra was relieved yet concerned that if he'd ceased trying with her that he was achieving it elsewhere. Since he never introduced the prospect of divorce she allowed the thought to slip to the back of her mind and continued on accepting things as they'd become. Naturally Sierra did not want her marriage to be that way; she just did not know how to make it different. She did not know how to be what Darryl wanted and needed for her to be. But with all the love that was expressed between Nate and Mya tonight, Sierra began to become hopeful that she could somehow turn her marriage around. It was 9:10 pm when Sierra knocked on her parent's door.

"Si-Si, honey you know what time me and your father go to bed," her mother stated as soon as she opened the front door.

"I know Momma, I'm sorry."

"You can't be leavin' these babies like this Sierra."

"Mom, I'm sorry."

"'Specially that Michele. You had betta nip that little personality in the bud before she turn out like your sista," Mrs. Mitchell turned on her heels to gather up her grandchildren. Sierra swallowed her comments. What made her mother think that she could nip Michele's behavior if she could not nip Lillian's?

"Mommy!" Michele called out as she ran into Sierra's arms. The two embraced, "Mommy, Mommy, Granpa yelled at me."

"He did not yell at you little girl, quit being so sensitive," Sierra's mother defended her husband.

"Uh huhn, Granny he did!"

"Michele!" Sierra snapped, "You don't talk to your Grandmother like that."

"But-"

"Michele," she said again firmly. She felt bad inside as her daughter sat on the edge of the bed in the guestroom holding back the tears in her eyes.

"What I tell you? She too sassy for her own good. I got the sista's prayin' over her mouth, you should try it too."

Sierra listened to her mother lecture her about how to raise and pray for her daughter. Some things her mother said disturbed her but she was respectful enough to respond only with an occasional "yes ma'am" or "no ma'am". As her mother spoke she finished preparing her babies and took a sleeping Jennifer into her arms and led them to the front door with her mother close behind. Once they were standing outside of the house she calmed. She kissed Jennifer on her cheek and hugged and kissed Lee who was not too thrilled about leaving his grandmother. Michele stood by her mother's leg more than ready to go.

"Come give your Granny some sugar," Sierra's mother told Michele, her arms extended. Michele looked up at her mother for her approval before she stepped forward. Mrs. Mitchell shook her head and tsk-ed as she stood upright, "I love you baby, you drive safe," she said as she hugged Sierra.

Once Sierra tucked her children into bed she went to her room and took a brief hot shower. When she finished she returned to her bedroom, her husband had still not come home. She didn't expect him for a while. Although his work day ended at 6:30 he rarely came home before ten at night. Tuesday's and Thursday's were the only days she could count on him being home by a reasonable time. She removed her bathrobe and pulled a long cotton nightgown over her head. She sat on the edge of the bed and thoroughly lotioned her body before slipping beneath the comforter. Two small lamps lit up the bedroom. Sierra picked up the book she had been reading, *In His Image*. A half an hour into her reading Darryl entered the bedroom. She curiously peered up at him. She wanted to speak but respecting their established ritual of silence she returned her gaze to the words on the page she was reading and kept quiet.

Darryl crossed the room without looking in Sierra's direction. He ran himself a shower and washed the day's dirt and fumes and fragrances from his body. He felt tense each time he came home. He did not want to be there; he hated this life and regretted making Sierra his wife. He blamed her for his inability to finish school and become the attorney that he dreamed of becoming. Instead he was forced into taking his knowledge of law and using it to become a legal secretary. In his opinion it was a woman and a sissy's job and he was no damn sissy. But with three extra mouths to feed it became increasingly difficult to study and pay for school.

He should have met Victoria first. Victoria Hart was the woman he'd been having an affair with for the past three and a half years of his marriage. He had to admit that Sierra was attractive at 5'5" with her bright skin tone and big brown eyes. Her long thick, natural non-chemically treated brown hair hung past her shoulders. But she was plain and the babies left her out of shape with a pouch for a belly and stretch marks etched her thighs. Victoria was sexy. She had long muscular legs and nice perfect breasts. Unlike his wife her waistline remained visible even though she herself had a son and a daughter. And though her hair and nails may have been store bought she kept them well maintained. He would leave Sierra in a heartbeat to be with Victoria if it weren't for those money guzzling rug rats she'd tricked him into having. He made just enough to comfortably support his family and his mistress. Thus he adopted the aphorism, "It's cheaper to keep her."

The only reason Darryl married Sierra was to be the first she'd ever had sex with and because of her parent's apparent wealth and her father's connections. The pastor embraced Darryl and wanted to make him happy by providing invitations to important social events and tickets to sports games and more. He'd never planned to have children with Sierra though he'd allow her to believe that. He never expected to remain married to her long term. But this was the life he'd foolishly chosen and he had to accept it.

Darryl stepped out of the shower and dried his feet on the bath rug. He dabbed his body with the large towel and stepped into a pair of blue and white striped boxers. He brushed his teeth and returned to his and Sierra's bedroom. Sierra continued reading when he climbed into his side of the bed and turned the lamp off. He pulled the sheet over his head and tossed a couple of times.

"Can you read that someplace else?" he asked, a hint of attitude in his voice. Quietly Sierra set her book on the table and turned her light off. She turned her back to her husband and stared into the darkness, thinking.

It was a Tuesday afternoon and Sierra had just returned home from grocery shopping. She stood in the kitchen removing items from the shopping bags. Her girlfriend Pam Thomas was assisting her as Sierra's three children and Pam's twin girls Alexus and Porsche played together in the backyard. Sierra and Pam had been friends for a couple years. The two met at a coffee shop only to find out that they were neighbors. What attracted Sierra to her was the fact that she spoke her mind on most every subject, this day was no different.

"So what do you think this dinner is going to do?" Pam asked Sierra as she handed her a box of powdered milk.

"I don't know what it'll do but I have to try," Sierra answered taking the box from her girlfriend's hand.

"Why do you have to try? Because Nate and Mya are getting married? That's some bullshit Sierra, what you need to do is leave his sorry ass."

"Watch your mouth."

"I done told you about trying to censor me Sierra. Those kids ain't hardly thinkin' about us right now, anyway," Pam folded the paper bags and stacked them on the counter, "He cheatin'. I know it, you damn sure know it. Leave him."

"You know I can't."

"Why not? When I found out the girls daddy was fuckin' that trick Betty, I kicked his sorry ass to the curb with the quickness."

"We done been through this before Pam. I can't divorce Darryl. I took a vow before God. I can't just break that. It said for better or for worse."

"That nigga breakin' it by committing adultery. I don't believe your vows allowed for that."

"We don't know he's cheating, you're assuming that."

"Don't be naive Si-Si, we know. A nigga get off work at 6:30 but don't get home until 11 at night had done picked up some extra-curricular pussy," Pam took an apple from the fruit bowl on the table and bit into it, "Now girl, what you need to do is take that fine friend of yours Nate away from that European bitch. You know you like him."

Sierra rolled her eyes and smiled as she continued to put food in the refrigerator, "I never said I like him."

"You never said you didn't."

"Well, I don't, not like that anyway. He's just my friend."

"Gurl please! Who you think you talkin' to? Shit you named all your kids after the nigga! Give me a break, friend my ass."

Pam hopped from her stool and headed out the back door to check on the children. Sierra shook her head. Nate was her friend, her very best friend and he was happy with Mya. She would never try to come between them. Besides, she didn't think she was Nate's type anyway. Even if she did have a slight crush on him it wouldn't be worth pursuing. She was a married mother of three. So it may not have been a happy marriage but it was a marriage none-the-less. Not to mention that involvement with a good friend was not always healthy and she would not wish to possibly compromise her and Nate's friendship.

Sierra cooked a fine meal for her and her husband's enjoyment. She set the dining room with their best dishes. Two candles in the center to set the romantic mood she was hoping for. It was nearing 6:30 and Darryl would soon come. Sierra left the children in Pam's care who was reluctant to take Sierra's three home with her. Reluctant not because she did not enjoy Sierra's children but rather because she disagreed with her friend trying to revitalize a useless marriage. Sierra took a hot shower and shaved the excess hair from her legs and armpits. She oiled her frame and put on a black bra and her only pair of black satin panties. Her hair she pulled back into a bun. Gold earrings dangled from her ears. A long navy blue sleeveless sheath dress was laid across her bed.

She dressed and slid her eyeglasses back onto her face then took a seat in her living room waiting for her husband to come home. At ten to eight o'clock she heard Darryl's car pull up. She quickly jumped up from her seat on the sofa and returned to the kitchen to prepare. Darryl's key turned in the door and seconds after the sound of his footsteps faded as he walked to the bedroom. The sound of movement traveled on the air from the rear of the house followed by footsteps in Sierra's direction. Despite the tempting aroma he continued past the kitchen and into the living room where he turned on the television.

In the kitchen Sierra's nerves were frazzled. She practiced breathing techniques and touched her hair to be sure it was still in tact. "Hear goes nothing" she mumbled to herself as she walked out of the kitchen and to the living room. She stopped at its edge nervous and afraid to continue forward. Darryl sat slouched on the sofa surfing channels. He wore his store bought work slacks and black dress socks. A standard white button down shirt was open revealing a slightly dingy wife-beater. His tie had been removed. Sierra took a deep breath and continued on until she stood beside him.

"I cooked, would you like to eat?" she asked timidly.

"I'm not hungry," he responded without looking at her.

"The kids are with Pam. We have the house to ourselves for awhile."

Darryl remained unfazed, his gaze affixed on the television. He began to feel annoyed. Curiosity engaged his senses and he wondered what incited her to suddenly strike up a conversation with him. Relief set in when she appeared to give up as she began to turn away but she instead stopped and turned back to him.

"I cooked your favorites. Pork chops and homemade mashed potatoes and gravy and green beans. I even made a peach cobbler," she tried again.

"I said I'm not hungry," he said staring Sierra directly in her eyes before returning his attention to the television.

Sierra gave up and swallowed her pain. She didn't cry though she wanted to, she instead chewed her bottom lip. She'd long lost her ability to cry. Sierra left him be in the living room but paused directly outside of it. She leaned her back against the wall and stared at the ceiling as she came to terms with what had just happened, how she'd been so terribly rejected by a man who vowed to dedicate himself to her happiness. From where she stood Sierra could hear Darryl pick up the telephone receiver. A brief moment passed before his voice tapped against her eardrum.

"Yea what up dawg?" he spoke into the receiver, "nothin' just flippin' through bullshit on TV.... oh yea?.... when?.... I'm down, shit nigga my ass starvin' like Marvin...hell yea, let me just get out these plantation clothes and I'm on my way.... aiight."

Darryl replaced the receiver and turned the television off. Not wanting him to be aware that she was spying on him, Sierra rushed into the kitchen and out of visibility. As Darryl changed out of his make money clothing and into his spend money attire to wear out to dinner with his friends, Sierra put away the dinner she'd put on her evening gown to eat with her husband in.

3 Mike

Michael Romelle Toussaint left the plans on his desk in his office and rushed to the elevator. He was supposed to meet his best homey Nate for lunch but was running late. With their hectic schedules every minute they could manage together mattered. He stood with his briefcase in hand in front of the elevator amongst a small cluster of employees on their way to lunch. Mike looked beside them to Samantha Falls, an attractive blond who was the secretary for Bradley Klein, one of Mike's associates. He instinctively licked his lips, mesmerized by her creamy white cleavage which was peeking at the world from the insecurity of a gold silk blouse. Samantha smirked and attempted to divert her eyes but she couldn't help looking back in Mike's direction. When they caught eye contact for the third time Mike winked and Samantha diverted her eyes again.

The elevator dinged and the doors opened allowing the employees to pile in. Mike made certain he stepped in ahead of Samantha so that he could stand behind her. Mike looked down at Samantha's well-toned rear. With his free hand he grazed across its curve. The couple was against the wall so no one else on the elevator was aware of the goings on. He reclaimed his hand and paused for Samantha's reaction. She did not behave awkwardly so Mike became bolder. For the ride down the next seventeen flights Mike fondled and caressed. When the doors opened at the first floor Samantha reached back and stroked between Mike's legs before the two stepped off the elevator and grinning went their separate ways.

Mike headed up the street to the good parking spot he often managed to find coming into work in the morning. He saw his Lexus SC 430 parked a few steps up the block and pointed his keyless remote to start his engine. He stepped off the curb and walked to the driver's side. His heart dropped when he looked at his prized possession. Rage had his face hot and his fists clenched as he looked at the long scratch along his doors. It was clear that someone had keyed his car; the question was which bitter bitch did it? Pissed and in a hurry, Mike climbed in behind the steering wheel and tossed his briefcase into the back seat. He checked his rearview mirror before peeling out into the afternoon traffic. He took the remote for his stereo in his hand and pumped up the volume on the *Yukmouth* CD he was listening to. He sped through traffic dangerously cutting off cars until he made it to the South Beach area a short time later. It was a struggle to find parking but he soon managed to steal a spot some sucker was waiting to back into. The older white gentleman whose spot had just been jacked yelled out profanities before he sped away. Unfazed, Mike turned off his engine and stepped out into the Florida sunshine. He slipped on a pair of sunglasses with blue tint to protect his eyes and headed up Ocean Drive toward the TGI Friday's at the end of the block.

Mike walked with his head high. He was a handsome young Haitian-American man, 5'11", dark complexion with round coal eyes. He kept his head shaved bald as he preferred the look and feel of it. He strutted down the street in black tailored slacks and black satin shirt with a silver tie. He wore a diamond ring set in platinum on his pinky finger and Bulova watch on his wrist. Appearance was of top priority for Mike; he was extremely materialistic. He considered those who could not afford to live life on his level to be inferior to him. He aspired to catch up to those who could afford a better lifestyle than he. Mike was hot on their trails. He was one of few black architects in Miami and was in high demand. Thanks to Nate, he'd invested money in stocks and bonds and owned a couple of duplexes in Miami and Fort Lauderdale and one in

West Palm. He and Nate were putting the final touches on a deal and were well on their way to becoming club owners.

Anyone that knew Mike growing up found it difficult to accept his current success, it was so unbelievable to them considering the way he'd behaved as a child and the fact that he'd hated school. But Mike knew exactly what motivated him to achieve his great successes. To prove to his grandmother, his aunt and all those people that said that he wouldn't be shit…that he'd be dead or in jail…he wanted to prove that when he became a man that they would all kiss his black ass.

Nate was seated at a table outside the restaurant sipping on a Margarita. He tapped the face of his watch when he saw Mike walking toward him. Mike threw his hands up in defeat to indicate that he knew he was wrong. He took a seat across from Nate in front of a slightly watered down Long Island Ice Tea that had been ordered on his behalf. He sipped it and turned up his nose. He signaled for the waiter to come and replace the alcoholic beverage.

"So what's going on man? How's the building design business treating you?" Nate asked before taking another sip of his drink.

"Same ol'. It's straight y'know, I'm feelin' my job but I gotta keep competin' wit' these damn crackers."

"I hear you man."

"Listen to dis my nigga. Some bitch done keyed my got-dman Lex, can you believe that shit?"

"You've got to be kidding me."

"I wish I was. Bitch bet' not slip and let me find out who she is, ya heard me?"

"Hell yea."

"Damn that broad is fine," Mike said looking at a waitress from a distance.

"Yea, she's nice," Nate agreed.

"So wassup my nigga? You talkin' but you ain't sayin' much, what's goin' on wit' you?"

"You know, same ol' same ol'. Working and things. I have to start taking these renaissance art refresher courses. Oh and Mya and me are getting married."

Mike choked on his drink and coughed hard before he spoke, "What did you just say my nigga?"

"You heard me, Mya and me are getting married."

"What the fuck is wrong wit' you? You seriously phenna marry dat hoe?"

"Ay man, watch your mouth about my woman."

"Nigga-"

"Come on now Michael how long you expect for me to be running the streets man? Me and Mya are in love-"

"Love."

"Yes man, love, something you obviously don't know nothing about."

"Like I give a damn about love. Nigga pussy make my world go 'round and I ain't phenna stop the ride for no bitch, ya heard?" Mike turned his attention back to the attractive woman waiting on a couple at the far end.

Nate shook his head and finished up his drink. Their waiter returned and set a plate of fresh wings and fries before them. He set two clean plates and napkins on the table before taking the empty glasses away.

"Nigga I don't understand why the hell you wanna get married," Mike said to Nate as he took a wing off the appetizer plate, "There's so much pussy out there that we ain't conquered and you wanna waste yo' dick on one broad. I ain't feelin' it. Dat's some stupid shit nigga, fo' real tho'."

"Whatever man," Nate responded sticking a fry in his mouth.

"Yea exactly, whateva. Ay I'm phenna get that phone numba. Shorty fine as hell."

Knowing that was the best he'd get out of Mike, Nate left it at that and focused on snacking on their chicken wing lunch. Mike leaned back in his seat and watched the mysterious waitress exit with the couple at the end's food. He looked her body up and down and enjoyed what he saw. Her bright skin was speckled with brown freckles and her long hair was pulled into one braid. Her body appeared full and curvaceous in her uniform. Mike patiently waited for her to finish with the couple before he signaled her over.

"I'm not your waiter," she mouthed.

"I know who our waiter is, just come here for a second!" he called out to her.

The waitress rolled her eyes before walking to Mike's seat, "May I help you?"

"Damn l'il momma, what's yo' beef? I'm sayin', a nigga just thought you was fine as hell and wanted to know yo' name."

The young waitress began to blush. Nate cringed at Mike's blatant ignorance and disregard for women. He never could understand how this behavior got women in bed with him. But it did and here he was working his magic again.

"Lisette."

"Lisette, mmmm. That's a sexy ass name," Mike pulled the chrome colored Nokia out of his suit pocket and handed it to Lisette, "Why don't you put yo' phone numba in here Lisette."

"Alright," she said. She took the phone from Mike and keyed in the info before handing it back him.

"I'mma hit you lata," he said smiling.

"You do that," she told him as she turned to go back to her job.

Nate had witnessed Mike at work before but nothing amazed him as much as the simplicity just displayed, "You're kidding me right? Just like that?"

Mike watched her rear move from side to side as she walked away, "Just like that. See that's what I'm sayin'. And you ready to give this shit up?"

"Yes I am," Nate answered with certainty.

"Whateva nigga," Mike leaned back in his seat and sipped on his fresh glass of alcohol and watched Lisette work.

After lunch, Mike called his Lexus dealership and advised them of the scratch. They had a loaner waiting for him upon arrival. He slid *Trick Daddy* into the CD player before opening his phone and calling Lisette. She answered on the second ring.

"Ay l'il momma, what time you get off?" Mike asked without greeting her or announcing himself.

"Who is this?" she asked.

"You know who dis is shorty, now what time you rollin'?"

"Oh dude from earlier. As a matter of fact I'm about to be out right now. Why whassup?"

"I want you to meet me somewhere."

"I can't, I don't have a car."

Mike rolled his eyes to the back of his head and blew frustrated air from his lungs, "I'm coming to get you, just stay there."

"You're what?" Lisette asked but it was too late, Mike had already disconnected the line.

Lisette sat waiting at one of the tables when Mike arrived. She tried her best to contain her excitement at the sight of the car he was driving but she could not deny the broad smile that was breaking out across her face. Mike noticed and his level of confidence increased. He unlocked the door and Lisette climbed in. The two rode speechlessly to Coconut Grove and caught a movie before having a couple drinks at Wet Willie's bar and making small talk. Mike was pleased with Lisette's ability to consume liquor; he knew it would not be long before she was tipsy and her rationale out the window. And just as soon as Lisette became giggly and chatty and revealed too much information for a first date, Mike invited her back to his home.

Lisette was fascinated with Mike's South Beach condo. She could not take her eyes off of the breathtaking view of the ocean. Mike poured Lisette a glass of Perrier-Jouët and popped in his infamous homemade lovemaking CD. He stood behind Lisette as she enjoyed the view and handed her the wineglass as he kissed and nibbled on her neck. Mike stepped back and licked his lips as Lisette downed the alcohol. He took the glass from her hand and set it down. He took her hand and eased her to the floor, laying her on her back on his plush cream carpeting. He kissed her exposed flesh as he unbuttoned her blouse. He slid her skirt off and sat up to take in the curves of her body. Mike stood and went to retrieve the chilled wine bottle. He filled his mouth before sucking one of her nipples inside. Lisette moaned and clawed. As he sucked he slid his fingers inside the wetness between her thighs. Mike traced his tongue from between Lisette's breast and down to her waistline. He teased and she squirmed in anticipation. He skipped her spot and bit her inner thighs. Finally Mike licked her clitoris sending waves of pleasure throughout Lisette's body.

Mike participated in the giving of oral sex not as an act of love but as a way to control women. If he worked his tongue properly he'd have power and that was what was important to him. He licked and nibbled and caressed her spot with his tongue until Lisette exploded in pleasure. She was sprawled about the carpet panting and smiling. Mike stood and stepped out of his clothes. Lisette was thrilled at the sight of Mike as he stood above her. His skin was milk chocolate and muscles protruded from every possible inch of his frame. But it was the unusual length and girth of Mike's manhood that caused waves of intimidation to sweep through Lisette's weary body.

"You like this?" Mike asked, Lisette nodded, "Come kiss it then. Show me you want me."

Lisette pulled herself to her knees before Mike. She teased the head of his penis with her tongue before stretching her jaws to take him inside her mouth. She tried to confidently consume Mike's massive manhood but she occasionally choked and gagged. Mike grabbed Lisette by the hair and pulled her back and forth but her gagging annoyed him. He yanked her away and calmly helped her to her feet. With *Gerald Levert* singing in the background, Mike led Lisette to his bedroom and onto his king size bed. He removed a condom from his nightstand and rolled it on. He propped Lisette's legs open and thrust himself inside of her. She was briefly winded as he thrust in and out of her body. Mike placed Lisette's legs on his shoulders but not being able to handle the pressure of his size she squirmed to take her legs down.

Mike became flustered by Lisette's inability to handle him but he tried to remain calm. He instead flipped her over and pushed inside of her from behind. Lisette, sensing Mike's annoyance, bit down on her lip and dealt with the pleasurable pain. Mike moved in and out faster and harder until he finally collapsed on top of Lisette's sweaty naked body. Mike caught his breath and rolled away. He walked to the bathroom and dumped his wasted sperm and brushed his teeth spending extra time on scraping his tongue. Lisette was still passed out on the bed when he returned. He sat on the edge of the bed and turned the television on. He flipped through channels until he found ESPN.

An hour passed and Lisette awoke to Mike's voice. She did not move, just lay there looking at the wall in silent irritation as she listened to his telephone conversation.

"Naw, I told you ain't nobody important girl, quit trippin'…So you gone come through or what?…Please, ain't no bitch mo' important than you…I ain't gone beg yo' ass…Yea, that's what I thought…Aiight then shorty, I'a see you in about forty-five. Holla."

Lisette rolled her eyes in disgust but embarrassed she didn't let on to Mike that she was awake. She felt him rise from the bed, she heard him go into the bathroom and run shower water. Lisette continued to lie in his bed thinking and hoping she'd misunderstood. There was no way he'd take her home so he could fuck some other bitch. When he was done he returned to the bedroom and turned on the light. The bed dipped under his weight. She listened to the sound of him sifting through drawers.

"Ay shorty time to raise up," Mike spoke out. Lisette didn't move right away, "I know you heard me. Quit frontin', yo' ass ain't sleep. I got company comin' thru, you got to raise up."

Lisette sighed and rolled out of Mike's bed, "Can I take a shower at least?"

"We ain't got time for all that. Gone and get yo' shit baby, you got to ride."

Lisette huffed and stormed out of the bedroom and into the living room. Hurriedly she put her blouse and skirt on. She grabbed her purse and sat on Mike's sofa waiting for him. Five minutes passed before Mike exited his bedroom.

"You still here?" he asked.

"What? Y-yea, I'm waiting for you to take me home," Lisette answered panicked.

"Bitch please, I ain't 'bout to go nowhere. I told you I got a guest comin' so you gotta get da hell out."

"Bitch?"

"Oops, m'bad, hoe get the fuck out."

"Oh hell naw, you gone take me home."

"Oh you wanna get sporty? I ain't phenna do shit. Now you can raise on up outta here or I can put you out and you don't want me to do that. It'll get all ugly and embarrassin' an shit."

"How am I supposed to get home? I don't even know where I'm at? How can you just do me like this?" tears rolled from Lisette's eyes.

"That's what happens when you go home with strangers. Call yo' ass a cab and git the hell up outta my crib."

"I don't have money for a cab," Lisette lied.

"Aww, well you pretty much fucked then. Shorty, you tryin' my patience. You 'bout five blocks from ya job, quit frontin'," Mike lit a freshly rolled blunt before he walked to the door and opened it. He stood waiting for Lisette to walk out, inhaling the drug. Reluctantly she grabbed her purse and picked up her heels on her way out. Mike exhaled the smoke purposely as she passed him. She gave him her most spiteful look as she choked on the fumes, "Bitch always chokin'," he said as he slammed the door in Lisette's face.

4Nate

I'd enrolled in an art renaissance class at the local college. I felt that if I wanted to remain ahead of the game and further lock down and secure my position that I needed to keep up with my knowledge of all art. Being a black man in this field you have definitely got to do twice as much just to keep up.

"So tell me what you know about Sanzio Raphael. Uh, Diana?" the professor asked the class.

"He was a great artist but further into his career he had a tendency to assimilate new techniques of Leonardo and Michelangelo when it came to the creation of his Madonna's. It's like he couldn't figure out his own style. First he started out imitating Perugino and then them," Diana answered. It was a decent answer but not very insightful in my opinion. I raised my hand.

"Mr. Marshall."

"While it is true what Diana said, that some of the faces and figures could have easily been painted by Perugino, Raphael can elsewhere be seen to introduce elements which reveal his interest in the achievements of the new age. For example, in his *Sposalizio*, the domed building in the semicircular upper half of the picture may be derived from Bramante's contemporary ideal of architecture, as expressed in his round tempietto at S. Pietro in Montorio in Rome."

"Very insightful Mr. Marshall."

See, what did I tell you? I know my art very well. I took an interest in it back in high school when I began messing around with a young lady named Carrabelle. She was in the honor society and deep into art and classical music. She would always ask me to take her to openings of cultural events, to the local art museums and jazz clubs. At the time I thought it was a bit odd as we were but sixteen years old. But I suppose Carra was ahead of her time. With her I learned about artists like Sandro Botticelli, Leonardo Da Vinci, Rosso Fiorentino. I never told my boys about the type of dates she and I went on, especially not Mike. Back then it would have been embarrassing to admit that it began about the booty but I wound up actually enjoying it. I never slept with Carra; I respected her too much to take advantage of her in such a way. I never thanked her making me go.

The class was in its second hour going over the works of Benozzo Gozzoli when the door was opened. As a natural reflex to hearing noise I glanced up in its direction. A young man walked into the room and directly to the professor. He was a decent height with dark olive skin and dark hair. He wore a street messenger bag strapped across his body. He was wearing a pair of small wire framed glasses on his face. On his body he wore baggy jeans with a white button down shirt and Birkenstocks on his feet. I returned my attention to the book of paintings before me.

"Excuse me class, may I have your attention?" Professor White began, "Class, this is Anthony Montoya a new student who will be joining us today. Can I get a volunteer to help Mr. Montoya catch up on the material he's missed from last week?" Half the women in class raised their hands, "Mr. Marshall, would you mind? The two of you can get better acquainted after class."

"No problem," I said again returning my attention to my studies as Anthony took a seat beside me. I could feel the eyes of my female peers burning holes in the back of my head but I didn't care. It didn't matter to me if I helped the guy or not. Mr. White only chose me because I was hands down the best student in the class.

I began to pack my bag before the end of class. I was ready to get out of there and go home to Mya. Anthony was re-packing his bag when Tanisha Rhodes stopped by my desk. I looked her over and rolled my eyes to the back of my head. She was ridiculous. She'd already hit on me several times despite the fact that she knew about Mya. She'd seen her and me together a few times. Tanisha leaned across my desk in her V-cut blouse allowing her breasts to spill forward. She wore a mini jean skirt and when she leaned like she was doing now you could almost get a perfect view of her rear end. I had to admit that it was a nice ass but it didn't interest me.

"Hey Nate," she said.

"What's going on, Tanisha?" I replied.

"Nothing much. Hi, uh, Anthony? I'm Tanisha, it's a pleasure to meet you," She introduced herself as she leaned past me with her arm outstretched.

"Hello Tanisha, the feeling's mutual. Nice skirt," he commented. I thought I'd be sick listening to the two.

"Thank you. So what are you guys up to?"

"Well, I was sort of hoping that Nathaniel here would fill me in on what I missed last week. Y'know, I'd like to be ready for class on Wednesday."

I turned awkwardly at the sound of my proper name being used by a perfect stranger. I was reluctant to agree. Of course it was not very late at night, it was just past 8 pm but I'd rather go home and relax with Mya. I was caught between Anthony and Tanisha. She was anxiously awaiting my response. If I turned him down he'd be forced into getting to know Tanisha, she's very persistent. If I agreed I'd get to see the disgusted look on Tanisha's face as she stalked away and get this tutoring thing over with.

"Sure, we can go up the street to Benny's Tea Spot and go over it. You didn't miss very much so it shouldn't take too long," I answered, "You don't think it will take too long, do you Nish?"

"No, not long at all," Tanisha answered with attitude in her tone, "It was nice meeting you Anthony, maybe next time you'll be free."

"Maybe," Anthony answered with a smirk. Tanisha's smile broadened with hope as she turned to walk away.

"I'll meet you there," I said.

I threw my bag on my shoulder and left Anthony behind in the classroom. I made my way down and out to the parking lot and into my car. As I drove up seventeenth to the strip mall I flipped open my cellular phone and called Mya and advised her I would be tutoring a classmate and would be home a little late. No complaints. She told me she'd be waiting for me when I arrived. She was a good woman.

I was sitting at the small table by the window when Anthony entered. I waved him over and he took a seat across from me. If I were still trying to follow in Mike's footsteps this young brother would and could give me some serious competition. The young waitress who served my mochaccino returned to take Anthony's order. Lust was in her eyes and she could not stop smiling. It was pathetic. The longer I sat there enduring it the more anxious I was to leave.

"We haven't formally been introduced," he spoke as soon as he sat down extending his hand to me, "I'm Anthony Montoya and I hate to be called Tony."

"I'm Nathaniel Marshall and Nate is just fine with me," I said shaking his hand, "So are you ready to begin?"

"What, you have something to do? What's the rush?"

I was becoming annoyed. I wasn't in the mood to spend too much time with this pretty boy. Besides his east coast accent was beginning to irritate me, "No rush, none at all."

We made small talk for a little while before I cracked my book open and began to go over Melozzo Da Forli and Giulio Romano, the artists we'd covered the week prior. I got the impression that he really did not need my assistance. I could have given him the names and he would have been okay but I played along. He was an interesting person and as it turned out this wasted tutoring was not a total waste. I was able to watch him flirt shamelessly with our waitress only to turn her down at the end of the evening. It was clear to me that he enjoyed leading fast women on and shooting them down just because. I figured it was due to him having some young exotic woman waiting for him in his bed but I didn't bother to ask. It wasn't any of my business. Besides I was too excited about his inviting me to a Heat/Bulls game with courtside seats as his way of thanking me for sharing my knowledge. I'd have to keep pretty boy around if he kept this type of activity up. We shook hands outside of our cars, which were parked side by side and went our separate ways.

Mike was less than encouraging when I shared news of the invite with him the next day, "Man what kinda faggot shit is that?" he asked obviously trying to hold a cloud of smoke in his mouth.

"Mike are you smoking in your office?" I asked.

"Naw, why you ask?" he asked blowing smoke into the receiver.

"Lying ass. Whatever, anyway why does it have to be faggot shit Mike?"

"'Cause dawg, nigga's don't do nuttin' like that. They don't take no 'nother nigga who they don't know to no basketball game 'cause he told him who some painter is. I don't think you should go, he might try to feel your booty."

"Aww man please. You're just mad because you're not going. If it were you you wouldn't have turned it down, would you?"

"Well, naw dawg but that's me!" we laughed, "Ay nigga you need to see if ol' boy can get a extra ticket for yo' boy."

"Yea, I'll see. Hey man I have to go. I promised to take Mya to this African Art Festival in the Grove."

"What kinda bullshit y'all be doin'? Nigga y'all weird but aiight, holla."

I grabbed my briefcase and went downstairs to the parking garage. I drove to Sierra's house to pick up my oldest godchild Michele before heading home to pick up Mya. Most every time Mya and I decided to partake in a cultural event, Michele went along with us. It was a ritual that Mya began.   She felt children would be better off if they experienced a broader range of education outside of the classroom. Michele was rather young but Mya admired her level of intelligence and therefore felt the time was perfect to begin teaching her.   It would be awhile before we imposed our will upon Lee and Jennifer. But I got the impression that Michele actually enjoyed the time the three of us spent together at these events.

Mya stopped at nearly every display and explained them to poor little Michele. With Mya's accent I doubted that Michele could understand half of what was said to her. It is my belief that she was more fascinated with the way my fiancé spoke than anything that she actually said.   I began to feel bad for our future child. Michele was getting off easily because the time Mya had to spend with her was so limited. But Mya was highly educated and broadly cultured. She'd spent time in Paris, Italy, Japan, and Spain, not to mention her home in London, England. She was fluent in French, Japanese, Spanish, Italian and Greek. The woman could even speak Pig Latin, it was ridiculous the things she'd been taught. Like my mother, she was a classically trained pianist as well as violinist and was an alumnus of Julliard. At times I wondered what she saw in me. To the average woman I was irresistible, something special. But Mya was clearly far from average. She didn't need me. With the money she grossed she could take care of herself easily. She honestly did not have to work to survive if she did not want to. The only reason she ever worked to begin with was as a way of educating herself on survival should she ever somehow find herself without. It was apparent that when she told me she loved me she meant it.

Michele was exhausted by the time I returned her to Sierra. To my surprise Darryl was home. Mya and I discussed just how trifling he was as we drove home that evening. The man was barely ever there. He was blatantly cheating on Sierra but more a fear of her father than the words of the Bible kept her from divorcing him. I did not like Darryl and I probably never would.

I was thrilled to finally be in my own home, running behind a four-year-old all day could take a lot out of a person. I picked up my remote control and collapsed on the sofa in front of the television.   Mya followed me into the living room and sat on the sofa beside me. She lifted my legs and laid them across her lap in order to remove my shoes. She sat them on the floor and massaged my feet.

"Would you like a beer honey?" she asked.

"No thank you darling, I'm fine."

"Well, I may have something else in mind that you can't say no to."

"Oh really?"

"Yes really," Mya loosened my belt and undid the button on my slacks. As she slid my zipper down, I rested my head on one of the couch cushions. She reached inside of my boxers but stopped and grabbed her handbag off of the table. I looked up to see what she was up to. She eased a breath mint into her mouth and returned her attention to me. I relaxed again and waited. My body tensed from the cool heat I felt when she put her mouth on me.

The game was excellent. It's no secret that I have an undying love for basketball but to watch my two favorite team's battle it out on the floor directly in front of me was amazing. I had never before enjoyed such a fantastic experience. It was safe to say that as our Miami Heat beat the Bulls by merely one point in overtime I was happy that I'd been volunteered to tutor Anthony in renaissance art. After the game we agreed to stop off at Hooters to have a couple of beers before we retired for the evening. I determined that he was a decent intelligent guy. We shared more over a couple of Corona's than I'd expected.

"I hope this doesn't sound too ignorant but what are you? Ethnically speaking I mean?" I asked.

"Part Black and part Italian. My pops is from Rome. Oddly enough so is my mom's. Rome, Georgia."

"Heh, heh. So where did you come from as if the accent doesn't give it away."

"New York, of course. Bronx baby, where else? What about you, you from Florida?"

"Technically no. I was born in Colorado, raised there for about a year or two before we relocated to South Florida. The rest of my years have been spent in Dade. Hope to have some time to visit someplace outside of the United States and Caribbean in the near future."

"Oh yea? Well when are you going to have some free time? Me and a couple of my friends are planning a weekend trip to Dublin, Ireland for later this year. I just so happen to be able to get my hands on an extra plane ticket if you'd like to go. And hey, don't get weirded out or nothing. I just have pretty sweet connects."

An extra plane ticket? Who in the hell just so happens to be able to get their hands on an extra plane ticket? What kinda "connects" did he have anyway? I was beginning to think that this conversation was becoming a bit odd or maybe it was all in the beers I'd consumed, "Yea, I'll remember that. So, uh let me ask you a question. I see you flirting with all these beautiful women; you get them going and then just shoot them down. What's up with that? Not to pry or anything but you must have some fine ass woman at home that you're crazy in love with because goodness knows you could have damn near any ass you wanted," I laughed. He blushed.

"Actually, uh Nathaniel, I don't. I'm not exactly interested in women."

"Not interested in women? What do you m-? Oh, ahh," courtside Heat tickets, extra plane tickets, suddenly it all began to make perfect sense. Mike was right; this really was some faggot shit!

"I hope that doesn't make you uncomfortable but, well, I just assumed you knew."

"Uncomfortable? No, naw," my voice began to crack as I spoke. I was uncomfortable, I was very uncomfortable. I downed the rest of my beer and wiped my mouth with the back of my hand.

"That's good. So what about you? Are you seeing anybody?"

"Who? Me? Nah," *Nah?* "I mean yes."

"No, yes, which is it?"

"Well yes but it's not too serious," *not too serious?* What the hell am I saying and why the hell am I saying it?

"Not too serious huh?"

"Umm, well it is but... So uh, why-why umm did you miss the first week of class?" I could feel beads of sweat on my forehead.

"I see you want to change the subject. Okay. Well, my mother passed suddenly. I had to go home for the funeral and I couldn't get a flight back until first thing Monday morning."

"I'm sorry to hear that," I could feel beads of sweat forming under my armpits. It felt as though someone put a brick on my chest, I couldn't breathe. I had to get out, "Hey Anthony, I uh, hate to cut this short but I have to get up early. You understand."

"Yes, certainly. So I'll see you in class Wednesday."

"Yes, of course. Hey Anthony, uh thanks for the game. I appreciate it."

"Anytime," he said to me.

I stepped down from my barstool and rushed out to my car.

5Nate

"If you're not screwing around then why are you spending so much of your time out all of a sudden and who are you spending your time with? It isn't Michael and it isn't Sierra. Who is she?"

Mya was beyond angry with me and she had every right to be. For the past eleven weeks I'd hardly spent any time at home and no I was not with Mike or Sierra all of those times. But I of course was not with another woman. There was no woman in the world that could take Mya's place neither in my heart nor in my mind. I hadn't told Mya anymore about Anthony. She knew I tutored him the first night we met and she knew that he'd invited me to attend the game with him. As far as she was concerned outside of class, that night at the bar was the last time we'd hung out. I wished I could say that were true but it was not. All of my available time was spent hanging out with Anthony. We went to basketball games, movies, shot pool, had dinner, and hung out at bars. I wasn't cheating on my woman, not by any means. Anthony and I were friends, nothing more. I'd never engaged in anything physical with him nor had I intended to. Yes, Anthony wanted more from me, that I was certainly aware of. I'd drawn that conclusion not based on anything that he had specifically said to me with regards to it but it was quite obvious. I allowed all of his advances to blow with the wind, as I did not want to lead him on. Ironically I still had not told him about Mya and was not too sure why I hadn't. I just did not have the urge to.

I leaned my back against the kitchen counter and sighed. I was not sure just how to explain things to Mya. I could barely rationalize things in my own mind. Why was I keeping my outings with this man a secret when I had absolutely no romantic involvement with him?

"Well," she pressed.

"Well what Mya?"

"Are you going to tell me who she is? Do I know her? Do you work with her? Which is it?"

"Mya!" I yelled out becoming frustrated with her incessant questioning. She jumped at the unexpected pitch in my voice, "Mya, Mya, Sweetie, stop it, please. Believe me when I tell you that I am not cheating. I've just had a lot on my mind; a lot I'm dealing with at work and trying to have a baby with you, planning our wedding. I'm just needing some me time, baby, that's all."

"Do you not want to marry me baby?"

"I didn't say that."

"You don't want to make a baby with me?"

"Mya stop that, please. Baby I want to marry you and I want us to have a child. I love you and I don't want anyone but you."

Mya's arms were still folded across her breasts but her expression softened. Her mind was working, assessing everything and wondering if she should believe me and accept my words as truth. She stared into my eyes long and hard. I had to break the silence. I grabbed my keys from the counter.

"I have to go."

"Figures. Going to see her?"

"If by 'her' you mean Sierra than yes. If you can stop bitching at me for two seconds you may recall me telling you that the Chevy broke down again and she needs to get to the grocery store."

"And why can't her husband take her to the grocery store? We're talking here," I simply looked at her like she'd surely lost her mind. She realized she had and changed her tone, "Sorry. I didn't mean any harm. Go on and help Sierra, I'll be here when you return home tonight. We will talk then."

"Thank you," I kissed Mya's lips, "I love you," I told her looking directly into her eyes.

"I love you baby, I love you more than words can express."

"I know," I whispered. I kissed her again and turned to head out of the door.

I was surprised to see Darryl open the door when I arrived. It was a Saturday and he was never home on a Saturday. He looked comfortable in a pair of boxers and flip-flops without any shirt. The exposed course chest hair irritated me. I turned up my nose but was ridiculously polite when I greeted him. He simply grunted and strolled back toward their bedroom scratching his ass along the way. I shrugged it off and stepped inside the house. I called out to Sierra.

"In here," she called from the girl's bedroom in the rear of the house. She was leaning over Jennifer's narrow bed placing her sandals on her small chubby feet. Michele ran from her mother's side and into my arms when she saw me enter the room. I picked her up and held her in my arms as I kissed her mother on the cheek.

"What's up with your husband? I've never seen him home on a Saturday afternoon. What's going on?"

"I don't know, guess his girlfriend is busy today," Sierra mumbled.

I was shocked to hear her say it. For so long so many of us tried to convince Sierra that a man that never stayed home long enough to make love to his own wife was definitely fooling around. But she would not hear of it. She would continually deny that Darryl could do her that way. I knew better but I didn't want to force my thoughts and opinions about Darryl upon her. Sierra was an adult and was capable of making her own choices. If she and Darryl wanted to carry on in a marriage in this manner then that was their prerogative. What I did not appreciate was the way he dealt with his children or better yet the fact that he did not deal with them. He'd never spent time with any of them. When Michele was six months old Sierra left her with Darryl for twenty minutes while she went to the local store to buy formula. Michele cried and Darryl never spent time alone with her again. He'd never spent time with Lee or Jennifer.

Michele pulled my sunglasses from my eyes and smashed them onto her face, "Where is my little man?"

"In his room sleep. Can you get him for me?"

I nodded and put Michele down at my side and with her hand in mine walked to Lee's room to get him ready. When all three were dressed we loaded into my secondary vehicle, which was an SUV (okay it was really Mya's but what's hers is mine) and I drove my extended family to the local supermarket to shop. Midway through Sierra's spending Darryl's money my cell phone vibrated, it was Anthony. He extended an invitation for me to meet him at Hooligan's bar that evening. I debated, as I was well aware that Mya was upset with me and wanted to continue our discussion about who I was spending my time with. Reluctantly I agreed to meet with him.

I ate dinner with Sierra and the children while her so-called husband ate the pizza he'd ordered in their bedroom though he was well aware that she'd prepared a plate for him. After dinner I headed out to Miami Lakes to meet with Anthony. I should have called Mya and told her but I did not feel like arguing. He was sitting at the bar watching a sports game on one of the many televisions that were located around the bar sipping an Ice House. I climbed up on the bar stool beside him and he automatically ordered another for me. There were no words shared among us as we rooted for the players running up and down the court. During half time was the first moment we exchanged words and made eye contact. Initially it was small talk about stats and coaches and players but Anthony soon got to the point of this little get together. The point that I'd been dreading would come for months now.

"So how's your 'kinda' relationship going?" he asked.

"It's okay," I answered before downing my beer.

"So when do I get to meet this lucky person?"

"Huh?" I nearly choked on my beer. *Meet Mya? Why?* "What for?"

"Well, we've been hanging for months now. Doesn't he wonder who you've been out with? I mean if your relationship means that much then I'm sure he's wondering."

He? Why did Anthony keep saying-? *Aaaaw shit!* He thought I was seeing a man! Damn, what was I getting myself into here? I had a good woman at home who was in love with me and who I loved. Then there was Anthony. It was clear that he wanted more from me than simply the time we spent watching sports and drinking beer but I could not stop seeing him. What was with me? Who was he to me?

"Nah, Anthony I don't think it's a very good idea."

"Well why not Nathaniel? We're friends right? You say you can cook, so how about a good Sunday dinner? Then I can meet your significant other, assure him that there's nothing to be concerned about."

"A-alright, fine. Um, how 'bout tomorrow night, about eight."

"What's his name?"

"Anthony."

"C'mon just asking."

"Can we please not talk about this any longer, the games back on."

"Oh okay, sure."

I could feel his smile and eyes lingering on the side of my face moments before he finally returned his attention to the game.

My throat was tight. My breathing was ragged. I could feel tiny beads of sweat form on my forehead as I drove home. It was two o'clock in the morning and I had not called Mya to explain that I'd be coming home late. I also had to cook a dinner for Anthony and Mya the very next evening, had to endure Mya's realization that I'd not been seeing a woman but a man behind her back. I had to let Anthony see that I was not involved with a man but actually a woman. Fortunately Mya was asleep when I arrived home that morning. I didn't want to disturb her and I wasn't in the mood to argue so I instead pulled a throw blanket out of the closet and rested my head for the night on my sofa.

"You are such a typical Negro and that is something that I never thought I'd think about you but it is true," Mya screamed at me as I smeared sleep from my eyes.

"I'm sorry," I grumbled in my early morning voice.

"Yes, yes that you are," she turned away from me and headed toward the stairwell.

"Mya," I called to her but she started up the steps, "Mya! Listen to me darling, I am not cheating. As a matter of fact I want you to meet the person I've been hanging out with that way you can see for yourself that it's all innocent."

"Innocent? You expect me to believe that you're innocent?"

"Yes baby," I rushed up the stairs to meet her. I stopped when we were eye to eye, "I love you Mya. I'm not cheating. I've been hanging out with a former classmate, Anthony."

"Anthony? The guy you tutored?"

"Yes honey."

"So why would you keep it a secret, Nathaniel?"

"I don't know. I guess I just needed to have a personal life for a while. I think I was just afraid…y'know getting married you sort of give that up. Look, I'm sorry baby I was wrong. But you'll meet tonight, see that I am not cheating and I swear honey I will never mislead you again."

I had to clear this up with Anthony, make this right with Mya. Her expression eased as she looked in my eyes. I leaned forward and kissed her lips, she reciprocated. Mya gently traced the outline of my jawbone as she looked lovingly into my eyes.

"I love you Nathaniel Marshall, I just…love you," she whispered before kissing me again. I lifted her into my arms and carried her upstairs to our bedroom.

Sweat dripped from beneath my armpits. Intense perspiration suffocated me. It felt as if the air passage to my lungs was blocked. Dinner was ready, angel hair shrimp and lobster pasta in a buttery wine sauce, garlic bread and an aged red wine. I invited Mya to prepare it as my nerves were too frazzled to do dinner justice. It was ten to eight when the doorbell rang. I swallowed hard and pulled myself to my feet. Mya seemed to float down the steps. She was beautiful in her black satin evening gown with her hair pulled up into a bun and held together with two silver chopsticks. We met at the bottom of the stairwell and greeted Anthony at the door together.

"Hello, you must be Anthony. I'm Mya, Nathaniel's fiancée but I'm sure you know that already."

"Uh yes, yes of course. He uh, talks about you all the time," Anthony lied, his eyes locking briefly with my own. I wanted to bury my head in a pile of sand. He extended his hand to hers and kissed the back of it, "It's a pleasure to-to... finally meet you."

I endured the most awkward dinner ever. I sat eating yet not tasting my food, listening to Mya and Anthony try to outdo one another with their intellect. They'd both traveled around the world and spoke a multitude of languages; they both knew countless, pointless facts that I did not comprehend.

"So of all the places in the world that you've seen, what possessed you to settle on Florida?" Mya asked. She tilted her head sideways and locked gazes with Anthony. Neither flinched nor fell victim to the social pressure that each was impressing upon the other.

"Same as you, I suppose. Miami possesses such a rich and affluent culture that one is hard pressed to experience in other places. It's the diversity that I find so captivating."

"Oh. Culture. Yes, that makes an awful lot of sense I suppose. Yes, that is what I appreciate most about Miami. I find its allure to be quite sexy if I may be honest. But now Anthony, darling, please correct me if I'm wrong-"

"Go on."

"I shall. New York, well isn't that a place just as entrenched in culture and diversity? Certainly Florida is not the only place where this type of void can be filled."

"Certainly not but it is however the only place that I have found that can serve it with the beauty of a palm tree."

Mya twisted her lips and smirked. Thoughts were brewing and she seemed ready to take him down. I stepped in.

"Mya darling, dinner was absolutely delicious."

"Oh why thank you Nathaniel. I'm so glad that while you picked over the two forkfuls that you managed to force down, it did not mean that I'd disappointed you."

"Sorry, I just don't have much of an appetite," a fresh bead of sweat popped up on my nose. I cleared nothing from my throat taking advantage of the opportunity to sweep it away.

"Mm, breakfast will do that to you won't it? So Anthony, where's your lady friend?"

"Excuse me?" Anthony answered with widening eyes. I choked slightly on the wine that I was sipping.

"Certainly a man as handsome as you mustn't be unattached."

"Mya," I intervened.

"Well, you of course have nothing on my sweetie but-"

"Mya."

"It's unimportant. Anthony, it's been a great pleasure. And please never mind me, I'm hard on any mind that I respect. Isn't that right darling?"

"Yes, yes you are."

"No harm, no foul," Anthony replied.

I was relieved when it finally ended and Mya retired herself to our bedroom for the evening. She extended her dainty hand to Anthony then left me with a soft peck on the cheek. As Mya glided up the stairwell and out of view, I carried the dirty dishes from the table and to the sink. Anthony and I stood alone, quiet inside of the kitchen. I rolled my sleeves back and began to rinse dishes and place them in the washer. Anthony sat at the breakfast table watching me.

"Do you mind?" he asked pulling a cigarette from his dinner jacket.

I shook my head no and returned my attention to cleaning. I could hear Anthony push his chair away from the table and walk toward me but I refused to look his way. He stood beside me and inhaled the smoke from his cigarette. I handed him one of Mya's ashtrays. He turned his head away and exhaled. He set the cigarette in the tray and placed it on the counter. He took the dish from my hand and sat it inside the washer.

"Nathaniel, talk to me. What are you doing?" he asked.

"What are you talking about Anthony?" I tried to divert my attention but he gently grabbed my arm and turned me to face him.

"A woman Nathaniel? What are you trying to prove?"

"Man keep your voice down. What the hell are you talking about anyway? Just because you want me doesn't make me gay."

"You are gay; I don't have to make you that way. Yea Nathaniel I want you, I will not deny that but you're the one that's denying who you are."

"What the fuck makes you think I'm gay?" We spoke in hushed tones so that Mya would not hear.

"We have been seeing each other for how many months and I'm just now finding out that you're involved with a woman. Not only that but you downplay the relationship, tell me that it's not that serious but shit, you're engaged to her. Nathaniel you are fucking gay and you know it just as well as I do and I'll prove it," Anthony stepped forward and with great passion kissed my lips. I did not reciprocate but I did not stop him either. A tingle went through my spine, a chill like I'd never before known. It was as though I'd never been kissed before. He pulled his mouth from mine and stepped away. He took his cigarette and put it back to his lips and walked to retrieve his sport coat from the chair he'd previously occupied, "I'll see myself out," he said as he walked to the front door.

I leaned my back against the counter and slid down to the floor. I sighed and rubbed my temples with my hands.

6Sierra

It was a Thursday afternoon and Sierra sat in her mother's kitchen awaiting the feast of fried chicken wings, cabbage and cornbread to be complete. This ritual existed for the previous twelve years of her life. Banquet Thursday's had been in place in her parent's church for just as long and each week on that day Sierra assisted her mother in preparing their contribution to the feast. It was always over-the-top, a big to do. Each church wife trying to outdo the next by over extending herself and creating new twists and turns to perfectly good old family recipes. These meals were eaten at a long banquet table in the church hall, intentionally reminiscent of The Last Supper. Old black women in tall flashy hats and floral dresses prepped their husband's plates while making sure that the fellow sisters and mothers knew who prepared the potato salad or that fine pot of collard greens. It had been nearly a year since Darryl joined the family for the church dinner so it should not have surprised Sierra's mother the least bit that he would not be in attendance yet again.

"So will your husband be joining us for church this evening Si-Si?" Mrs. Mitchell asked.

"No ma'am, he's got to work late," Sierra cringed. She hated the idea of lying, especially to her mother.

"You wouldn't be lying to me chile now would you?" her mother asked setting her iced tea on the table and looking her daughter directly in the eyes.

"No ma'am," Sierra's voice was low.

"Mmhm," she sipped her drink, "I don't know what done got into that husband of yours. It's like he's runnin' from the Lord all of a sudden. Somebody need to lay hands on that boy, bring him back home."

Sierra nodded and took a brush to Jennifer's head. She was quietly lying across her mother's lap trying to fall asleep but Sierra continued to disturb her intended slumber by parting and oiling her scalp and brushing her hair. Everything had changed and so quickly. When Sierra and Darryl were first married he attended service with her every Sunday, Monday night and Thursday evening. There was no stopping his praise. But as time passed and their marriage failed Darryl attended church less and less. Now it was a miracle to still see him there on Sunday's. He rarely ever missed that day. Maybe he felt he needed to repent for all the commandments he'd broken throughout the week. That was the closest to a true family Sierra could get. Though he arrived separately he sat with his wife and children with his daughter Michele, the only one he somewhat knew, on his lap. It was all a show of course, a front for the benefit of the elders but Sierra did not care. She was happy on Sunday's; she smiled on Sunday's. She pretended that they were in love with each other and mutually in love with all three of their children on Sunday's. But after the service was complete and lunch had been eaten with the Pastor and Mrs. Mitchell, Darryl disappeared and Sierra was returned to her reality of being a single parent living with her husband.

Sierra braided her youngest daughter's hair while listening to her mother hum church hymns as she listened to the message of the Reverend Creflo Dollar on the small black and white television that sat upon the kitchen counter near the sink. Lee stumbled as he ran into the kitchen followed by Michele who was chasing behind. Mrs. Mitchell scolded them for running indoors and sent her grandchildren back into the living room to play with their toys after swatting Michele on the behind for supposedly encouraging Lee to misbehave. Sierra cringed again. She saw her mother treating Michele differently, singling her out just as she'd done her sister Lillian. Fortunately Michele was seemingly just as strong as Lilly.

"I got a postcard from Lilly, Mama," Sierra said.

"Mmm, where she at now? What kinda mischief is she getting herself into?" the sarcasm in her voice was thick.

"She's umm, she's in Utah, Salt Lake City, Utah. She's working for their telephone company. She says it's okay, better than you'd expect."

"So what man she follow behind this time?" Mrs. Mitchell stood from her chair and walked to the stove to check on her chicken.

"I don't know Mama. Maybe she's on her own this time."

Mrs. Mitchell looked at her daughter and rolled her eyeballs to the back of her head, "Chile please, don't go and get naïve on me Si-Si. Has she ever jumped ship alone?"

Sierra shook her head "no". Her mother was of course right, Lilly had moved to Utah with her new boyfriend Steve. It wasn't anything new of course. Over the past ten years she'd lived in Alexandria, Virginia with Lucas, in Dallas, Texas with Joseph. She'd lived in Portland, Oregon with Phillip and in Santa Ana, California with Derek and even spent some time in Vancouver, British Colombia with Jarumai but the cold sent her running. Over the years Lillian returned home but she never stayed long, she'd been running ever since she was fourteen years old, shortly after she'd been forced into having an abortion.

"Mama, I need some advice," Sierra mumbled.

"Yes chile?" she answered still focused on the television.

Sierra patted Jennifer on the behind to signal that she was done. She tried to help her down but she fought against it so Sierra allowed her to stay, "Mama, I'm thinking about leaving Darryl."

"What do you mean you're thinking about leaving Darryl?" Mrs. Mitchell directed all of her attention to her daughter.

"I mean divorce-"

"Divorce?" Mrs. Mitchell's voice was raised. She could barely believe she'd truly heard what she'd just heard.

"Yes ma'am, divorce."

"No."

"What?"

"No you will not even consider such a thing! You were raised better than that. You stood before God and vowed to love this man forever, you will not break that vow, do you hear me?"

"But Mama just hear me out-" Sierra pleaded.

"Sierra Diane, look at me and listen to me, hear me good. I'm gone let you in on a little secret about men. Men do not stray, do not act a fool, do not neglect their women if they are happy at home. If Darryl is doing any of that then he is lacking something and I'm sure if you think for two seconds Si-Si you will figure it out. You need to give whatever it is your husbands' needing from you but divorce is not the answer. Now I'm gone pretend you didn't even suggest that," and with that Mrs. Mitchell returned her focus to the televangelist.

Sierra sighed while wishing she'd never told her mother of her thoughts. She should have known that there was no way a deeply religious Pastor's wife would accept *any* excuse her daughter had to break one of the Lord's commandments. Sierra put a drowsy toddler on her shoulder and carried her with her as she checked on her mother's cabbage. The back door opened and Pastor Mitchell hobbled in. At the sight of him Jennifer fidgeted in her mothers arm. She was just as crazy about Sierra's father as Sierra was. Her eyes grew as big as saucers as she reached out to him. Pastor Mitchell smiled as he hobbled over to take his grandchild in his arms. He kissed his daughters cheek before taking a seat at the table across from his wife. Sierra listened to the two discuss the Reverend on television. She so wished to have as close a relationship with Darryl as her parents had with one another. But her mother was right about one thing and it didn't take her as long as two seconds to figure it out.

Sierra made the decision that she was going to save her marriage; she'd give her husband what he needed. Sex, all he desired was sex. Yep, she'd just do it, just like that. Shouldn't be too hard. After dropping Michele to pre-school she gathered up Jennifer and Lee and dropped them to her parents for the afternoon. With her free time she shopped at Publix and picked up a few magazines, Cosmo, Glamour, Mademoiselle and Vogue. This was the only way she knew to start. She picked up a sub and juice and sat in the park flipping through her magazines and highlighting ideas and pointers. One of the magazines directed her to purchase sexy lingerie. Sierra drove to the local mall where she found Victoria's Secret.

She was intimidated by the large selection of skimpy, lacy, silky garments. She didn't know what to select and was furthermore unsure if she'd even have the courage to wear any of it. A saleswoman offered assistance but feeling very self-conscious about even being in the store she declined and backed away. Sierra took a seat on a bench near the store and pulled a bulky cellular phone from inside of her purse. After two rings her girlfriend LoriAnne answered.

"Wassup l'il momma?" she answered sounding as if she had a mouthful of food.

"Hey L.A., what you up to?"

"Nothin' girl, just watching my soaps and eating some Cap N' Crunch. Why wassup?"

"I need a favor; can you meet me at Pembroke Mall in front of Victoria's Secret?" Sierra asked timidly.

"Victoria Secret? Hello? I'm sorry who is this? I thought I was talking to my girl Si-Si," LoriAnne joked.

"Girl stop that now. Look this is important. I'm trying to save my marriage here and-"

"Save yo' marriage? What marriage?"

"L.A. don't start that now I need your help. Are you going to help me or not?" Sierra waited impatiently for her friend's response.

LoriAnne sighed before answering, "Girl, give me fifteen minutes."

Twenty-five minutes later Sierra spotted LoriAnne waddling through the crowd. She was a sizeable sister though very attractive in the face. Despite her size she'd never experienced any difficulty when it came to connecting with the opposite sex. Sierra had known LoriAnne since right after she graduated from high school, she knew her well enough to know that she could trust her judgment however not her timing.

"Fifteen minutes huh, L.A.?"

"Shoots girl, I had to finish watching my soap."

It took LoriAnne an hour to convince Sierra to purchase a red lace teddy and matching thong. It was a painful experience for LoriAnne but she was determined not to allow Sierra to walk out of that shop without the sexiest item they carried. Sierra's cheeks were flushed from embarrassment when she walked to the counter to pay. She felt that loud red was screaming, "Whore!" and she shared that opinion with LoriAnne. But LoriAnne simply discounted the harsh assessment commenting "Every man wants a lady on the streets, a chef in the kitchen, a maid in the bathroom and a hoe in the bedroom." She attempted to add a garter to the ensemble but Sierra would not budge on that matter.

She plotted her comeback for that same night, the sooner the better. She knew that if she stalled she would loose her courage and soon disregard the idea, tossing it to the back of her mind as she tossed the sexual undergarments to the back of the closet. When their shopping was done LoriAnne advised Sierra that she needed to go home and let her two boys and her daughter into the house but she would meet her at her home later in the afternoon to give her some pointers.

After Sierra picked up her three she headed home and phoned Pam. She advised her of her intent to have sex to save the marriage and asked her if she'd come and support her. After enduring Pam's comments and strong opinions she was finally relieved to hear a "yes". Sierra had not shared with Pam and LoriAnne the fact that she'd barely had sex with her husband not to mention the reason why she had not. They were not aware of just how important sex was; how huge a factor it was in possibly saving her marriage. They were aware that sex was not a regular routine between Darryl and Sierra. She did not have to share with them what was painfully obvious. They were also quite certain without her saying anything that she was not very sexually experienced. Secretly they agreed with Darryl's cheating as they assumed that their goody-goody girlfriend Sierra was very boring in bed. What they disagreed with was the obviousness of it.

Sierra prepared a small meal for her girlfriends and their children of baked chicken wings and tatter-tots as she chatted with Nate on the phone. She wasn't sure if she should mention to him her plans. Since he was aware of her secret she knew that he would encourage her to speak on it and after all these years she did not want to deal with it anymore. She wanted to go on with the rest of her life pretending that the memory was unreal; that the pain she'd carried in the back of her mind had not ever really happened.

"Why didn't you just tell Mya that you and this guy Anthony were hangin' out? I just don't get that Nate, you don't keep secrets from Mya," Sierra questioned, "Lee get down from there!"

"I realize that Si-Si but damn, I just wanted to have a personal life. You know me and my past, you know I have never before her answered to any woman. Since we've been together I have to share everything with her. Well, I'm sorry but I didn't want to share this, not immediately."

"Okay, so she forgave you?"

"Yea she forgave me but I think I'm going to cut out Anthony since it's interfering with my time and relationship with Mya."

"Why? If he's a good friend and you get along then I'm sure Mya can respect that. She won't care as long as she's not being left in the dark about what you're doing and who you're doing it with. Get down!" Sierra yelled again at Lee. He did as instructed and sat on the kitchen floor in front of his building blocks.

"Nah, he's not that important. Besides my spare time needs to be open to you and Mike not some Italian nigga from NY with an irritating east coast accent because he can get me good seats to the games."

"You sound bitter, did he do something?"

"No, no. Just trying to be honest."

"I guess. Well, hey baby I'm going to get back with you. I think Pam and the girls are at the door."

"Okay honey, enjoy your ladies night," he kissed into the phone and waited for Sierra to return it before they disconnected the line.

Sierra opened the door to allow Pam and her daughters inside. Alexus and Porsche squealed and ran through the house to search for Michele. Shortly after the two women sat to chat at the kitchen table the doorbell rang once again. She opened it for LoriAnne and six-year-old Renesha who behaved as if she were twenty-six. She'd always tried to sit under the adults and they would have to force her to play with the younger girls. This day was no different.

After dinner was done and the children were full, the women retired to the living room. Sierra kept a bottle of wine on hand at all times. She herself did not indulge but she knew that those that she entertained did. She grabbed the bottle of bubbly and two glasses along with a bottle of sparkling water. She turned on the stereo and allowed Hot 105 to play softly in the background. She curled up on the carpet with her legs crossed. LoriAnne was seated in Darryl's recliner while Pam sat on the carpet with her back rested against the sofa. The women poured their drink into a glass and sipped. LoriAnne smiled at Pam before reaching on the side of the chair and picking up a lone grocery bag and handing it to Sierra. Confusion swept over Sierra's face as she peeked inside. She pulled out a container of Cool Whip and a tub of strawberries. She shrugged her shoulders.

"What's this for L.A.?" she asked.

LoriAnne and Pam looked at one another before breaking out into hysterical laughter. Sierra felt embarrassed and uncomfortable. Pam noticed her changed expression and crawled to her side and wrapped her arms around her.

"Oh honey, we're sorry. Listen baby girl, the berries and whipped cream are for… y'know."

"What?" Sierra asked still dumbfounded.

"Sex girl, sex," LoriAnne mumbled as Pam doubled over in laughter.

"Sex? What? How can I use this for sex?"

"Damn girl, no wonder your marriage is in trouble," LoriAnne blurted out unintentionally hurting Sierra's feelings.

"LoriAnne!" Pam scolded. LoriAnne's laughter ceased, "Sierra baby you gonna have to be creative with this-"

"And freaky," LoriAnne added.

"Yes, the freakier the better."

"Freaky?" Sierra began to feel shy.

"Yes," Pam continued, "Think about it now Si-Si, how could you combine sex and these common refrigerated products?"

Sierra looked at the Cool Whip and fruit before her. She felt embarrassed even considering this especially in front of other people, even her best girlfriends. She twisted her mouth as she thought long and hard about Pam's question.

"I guess...I guess I could put it on him," Sierra answered awkwardly.

Pam giggled, "Good answer. Spread it on his body, take a strawberry rub it off and sexily suck the strawberry right from the stem. His ass would be so fucking turned on!" Pam and LoriAnne slapped palms.

"Or," LoriAnne began, "My favorite. Slather that shit on his dick and suck it right off!" she applauded herself as Pam rolled her eyes.

"You can do that but you don't want to cheapen the experience. We're trying to make love here, save the dick sucking for later on in the evening," Pam said looking at LoriAnne. She turned her mouth up at her, "But Sierra my darling, do not forget to slobber the dick!"

"That's what I'm talkin' about!"

"Hold, hold, hold on. You want me to put my mouth on his private?" Sierra asked with a concerned expression. Pam and LoriAnne nodded, "The mouth I kiss my kids with? No way!"

"Si-Si, that's what men care about, that's about all they care about baby girl. Tell it L.A."

"Lemme tell it Pammy-Pam. Head, head and mo' head. Lick a man right and his ass will give you damn near anything you want. I'a slob dat knob in the bedroom, in the shower, in the car, in the Jacuzzi-"

"She gets the point L.A. Bottom line Si-Si is that at some point you're going to have to do it if you want this sex thing to work out. If tonight is so important to you, well you know."

Sierra wanted to end the discussion so she nodded as if she agreed, "Okay, okay, what else do I need to know?"

Together Pam and LoriAnne shared sexual exploits and ideas with Sierra. Told her how to talk, what to say, what to do and as best as they could, how to do it. By midnight Sierra was as ready as possible and waiting. The children were tucked in bed and Sierra had showered and dressed in her new lacy undergarments feeling self-conscious. The Cool Whip and strawberries and a fresh bottle of wine were placed on her nightstand. Pam had given to her what she referred to as a "Do-It CD" and Sierra played it softly, trying to set a tone. She experimented with lying in various positions as she was told to look "longing" when Darryl came in. So Sierra laid her body on her side across the bed and tossed her head back so her hair could touch the center of her back. To an outsider the view would be comical but she knew no better.

Sierra looked at the clock; it was 12:48am. She spied the Arbor Mist bottle and considered it. She shook her head no but her attention was drawn to it again. She sat on the edge of her side of the bed and took the bottle in her hands. She whispered a silent prayer for forgiveness before turning the bottle up at her lips. Her face contorted as she held the weak alcohol in her mouth. She jumped from the bed and ran to the bathroom to spit it into the toilet. She coughed and gagged and spit to rid her mouth of every trace of the drink. She stood and wiped her mouth with the back of her hand while flushing the toilet. When she turned Darryl was standing in the doorway watching her, a disgusted look on his face. Sierra felt humiliated but she tried not to let it show.

"What are you doing?" he asked frowning.

"Um, w-waiting for you," Sierra answered. She was so nervous that her hands began to shake at her side.

"For what?" he asked pushing past her to get to the tubs faucet, "Why you dressed like that?"

"I-I was hoping…I mean I wanted to…to m-make love to you tonight," her voice was barely audible.

Darryl stood upright and turned around to face his wife. He had to admit to himself that she was damn sexy in that lace teddy. He fought against a smile, "Bullshit Si-Si. Don't play wit' me, you don't want this. You scared of this here."

Sierra swallowed hard, "I-" her voice cracked, "I'm ready for you Darryl."

Darryl looked her up and down. The bulge in his pants said he wanted her but he'd make her suffer like she'd made him suffer. He waved her off and went back to preparing his shower.

"You still a little girl, Si-Si. Twenty-eight and scared o' dick."

"I'm for real," she practically whispered. She tried to ignore his harshness, not let it hurt her. She summoned the courage to tell him what LoriAnne had told her to say, "Let me taste you," her breathing was rapid and she wanted to cry from the embarrassment.

Darryl stopped playing hard to get and turned to face Sierra. He was shocked but intrigued by her offer. For the first time that evening, for the first time in years he paid attention to her. He noticed the ruby red painted on her lips and the spiral curls in her hair. Silently he pulled his clothes from his body until he stood naked before her. She was tense but she tried to relax. Darryl signaled for her to follow him back into the bedroom. He laid her on her back and proceeded to kiss her body. Sierra awkwardly rubbed his back. He moved away and sat with his back against the headboard and pulled her to him, guiding her head to his stiff penis. Sierra began to hyperventilate but Darryl rubbed her hair and whispered for her to "come on" and "it's okay". She calmed some. She took as much in her mouth as she could but she gagged and coughed and her teeth would scrape him. Darryl however remained unusually patient with her.

"You ain't ready for all that. Come here," he whispered, "lay down."

To Sierra's surprise he began to kiss her inner thighs. She began to panic; she hadn't been warned that he'd do that. When his tongue touched her opening she jumped.

"What are you doing?" she asked in horror.

"Just relax, you'll like it."

"Stop it Darryl, no. Only whores like that," Sierra was outraged and insulted.

Darryl sat up and pursed his mouth as he chewed the inside of his bottom lip. He was mutually insulted and becoming increasingly angry, "Just lay on your back."

Reluctantly Sierra did as she was told. Darryl climbed on top of her and attempted to shove his not as hard penis inside of her body. Sierra jumped. Darryl struggled to get a stroke but Sierra was too jumpy to allow him to get his rhythm. He was angry. He yanked himself from inside of her and saying nothing more rose from the bed and went into the bathroom. He dressed and walked out of the bedroom without any explanation. Sierra curled in the corner of the bed with her blanket drawn to her chin. She heard the front door open and slam closed. Moments later she could hear Darryl's car peel from the driveway. Sadly Sierra rolled from the bed to her feet and removed what remained of her sexy ensemble. She climbed in the shower that Darryl had left behind and harshly scrubbed away the memories of the evening.

7 Mike

Mike rubbed the crust from his eyes as he whacked the alarm with his free hand. "Shit, not again," he mumbled beneath his breath. It was a Sunday and his alarm sounded at five o'clock in the morning because he'd forgotten yet again to turn it off the night prior. He gently pulled the sheet, which had slipped from his almost naked body, and settled his head back into the feathery down pillow. He tried his best to relax but movement from his rear jarred him. A warm arm slowly eased around his body as a head full of silky hairs nestled into his back. *"Shit! Why won't this bitch ever fuckin' go home?"* he thought to himself. Too tired to fight, he opted to let things be. But the constant rubbing and curling quickly became an unbearable annoyance.

"Sam. Sam!" he said pulling free from her grip.

"Yes baby?" she grumbled in an awful, early morning voice.

"Woman could you quit movin'? Damn. Just move over there, shit. Let a nigga breathe."

Samantha Falls sighed and rolled to the left side of the bed. She wasn't upset; she was used to Mike's harshness. In truth it excited her, turned her on. So she did as she was instructed, after all as far as she was concerned he was her man and she loved him just as he was. She knew that Mike loved her as well; he was just having difficulty expressing it.

Naturally Mike's view of the situation contrasted greatly with Samantha's. He did not love Sam, he did not like Sam but she was tolerable. She was a very sexual woman and that was the one quality he did appreciate about her. The fact that he could speak negatively to her all day and still have hot, raunchy sex with her that very evening was a thrill. She had her own in this world and if nothing else he respected that. She was unselfish when it came to "her Mikey". Never would she shop for herself without thinking to purchase an expensive gift for Mike. In addition she shared his passion for partying and had V.I.P. connections to nearly every club on South Beach. She supported his drug habit and kept him stocked with the alcohol of his choice. Regardless, her existence in Mike's world all came back to her bedroom etiquette and her performance of oral sex. Fallatio. In the car, in the shower, at the ocean, the back of the bar, it didn't matter where, she didn't mind. She made no excuses not to oblige and that, if anything, was what Mike was in love with.

Indeed Samantha gave a great deal but it was not enough to stop Mike from contemplating cutting off the relationship once and for all. Five days a week he regretted his decision to become physically as well as socially involved with Samantha. But two nights a week was all it took for him to forget those thoughts ever lived inside his mind. What concerned Mike was the fact that he worked with her and he knew better than to mingle business with pleasure. But he could not resist. Temptation was a blonde bombshell with a golden tongue. Curiosity killed him. Samantha was sexy and exotic with a body similar to a sister though not quite the same. And besides that fact, of the many women he'd been involved with, a white woman was never apart of that experience. If only Samantha could stop being so got-damned clingy it was highly probable that Mike could be satisfied in their arrangement.

Mike tossed and turned several times before rolling on his back, his eyes open and staring at the ceiling, "Why yo' ass don't go home no more?"

"Sweetheart please, you don't mean that," Samantha rolled over onto her side and rested her head on her palm. Her beautiful tresses hung low, grazing the sheets. She stared sweetly at Mike.

"Yes the hell I do," he was serious but intentionally unconvincing.

"Whatever, you know you would miss me. You and 'Big Mikey'."

Mike rolled his eyes to the back of his head. He was confused and anguished and ready to call it off but her body was soft as she climbed on him and her lips felt good on his chest. Her golden locks tickled his flesh and beckoned his arousal. Her warm tongue aroused him as it made its way down the path to his manhood that she referred to as 'Big Mikey'. And when she shoved a hardening 'Big Mikey' toward the back of her throat he forgot what he was ever stressing over.

It was late in the day when Mike finally decided to roll out of bed. He was relieved to see that Samantha had found her way out of his condo but disappointed that she hadn't bothered to toss out the empty beer cans that were strewn around and dump the ashtrays that were spilling over onto the coffee table. That was the beauty of the sista. Sherika never left a mess behind and she respected his space. His eyebrows arched upon the discovery of a half smoked blunt in one of the ashtrays. He dug it out and put a flame to it. He inhaled deeply and held the smoke in his lungs before blowing it into the air.

He decided to straighten up his home. He picked up the cans turning a half-full one up to his lips and tossed the others into the trash. Tired from a slight hangover, Mike decided that he would clean later. He instead poured himself a glass of Remy Martin and curled up on his sofa in front of the television. He surfed through hundreds of cable stations in an attempt to find something worthwhile to watch. He picked up his cordless phone and dialed Nate's home but there was no answer. He began to dial his cellular number but noticing the time he instead set the phone down. Nate and Mya attended Sierra's family's church on Sundays and though he knew the service was over, the couple joined the family for lunch and spiritual conversation afterward.

Sierra had often attempted to engage Mike. She'd openly shown disapproval of his lifestyle. The women and his disregard for them, the drugs and what she considered to be alcohol abuse. She was genuinely concerned for his soul. Mike behaved as if he did not give a damn but deep down he was touched that she displayed such an honest concern for him, though he would not ever admit such a thing. Sierra did not need his words to validate that appreciation for her concern. She was the only female that he was decent with and respectful toward though their relationship did not begin that way.

Sierra and Nate had been spending time with one another for a few weeks before she was introduced to Mike. Nate knew how rude and arrogant his best friend was with women and didn't want to scare Sierra away. Nate warned her about Mike and Mike unfortunately lived up to those expectations. But over time he began to see that Sierra was in fact different than the other females in their environment just as Nate had tried to convince him. The two were never as close as she and Nate and probably would never be. They argued often but it never became unmanageable and the two were typically amicable in one another's presence.

Besides Mike's issues with women, Sierra as well as Nate had a bigger more pressing concern with him. Though he'd grown up to become quite successful, finally proud to be a Haitian American man when as a youth you could not pay him to confess to it, he tended to abuse drugs an alcohol. If he was not in the office he was in a bottle of Remy or Tequila and in the midst of a cloud of weed smoke sprinkled with cocaine. He was what Nate liked to call a functioning addict. He could get high and drunk all night and still be in the office on time in the morning.

Mike inhaled the last of his blunt as he stretched his body across the sofa in front of the 52" color television screen in his living room. Bored, he closed his eyes and dozed back into sleep. After two and a half hours of quiet slumber the persistent ringing of the telephone awakened him. He felt around on the floor for the cordless. His fingers finally grazed it and he picked it up and pressed the TALK button.

"Hello?" he asked in a groggy voice.

"Ay wassup my nigga? What you sleep?" the woman on the other line asked, "Want me to hit you back?"

"Naw nigga I'm straight. Wassup wit' you doe? Nigga ain't smell dat pussy in ages," Mike struggled to sit up straight but sleep and impure intoxicants weighed him down.

"Nigga please," Sherika retorted, "you been to busy sniffin' dat pork fat you ain't got time for a true bitch no mo'."

"What you talkin' 'bout?"

"That white bitch that got yo' nose wide open."

Mike sat upright in the corner of the sofa, his face flushed with anger, "What the fuck you talkin' 'bout Sheri? What you doin', watchin' me now?"

"Nigga you done got me fucked up, I ain't even on no bullshit like that playa, know what I'm sayin'? Naw bwoy, the trick answered yo' phone."

Mike was dumbfounded, "What?" he asked in disbelief.

"Yea, I was straight trippin' cause I know Mike don't let no broad mess wit' his tele and then I'm hearin' this dis ol' grammer-champ broad on the other end. I hung up on her ass cause I knew I musta had the wrong number but when I called back the hoe answered again. I'm like, damn what da fuck? What's really goin' on?"

"When was this?"

"Just this mornin'. I'm like ay who this is, where Mike at? She was like this his woman and that you was in bed and gone *ask* me not to call anymore. I'm like yo' this bitch done got me twisted an' I told her to watch hu' muthafuckin' yappin' fo' I come thru there and make the shit happen got-damit. Chic hung up me after dat. I figured you ain't know that hoe was answerin' yo' phone."

"Why you ain't call my cell?"

"I did but you ain't answer."

"See that hoe gone make me beat dat ass, that's what's gone fuck around an' happen. Anyway though, lemme me handle that. Wassup up wit' you gurl? What you getting into tonight?"

"Awww nigga you know I'm hittin' up Levels, y'heard me! You wanna ride out?"

"Why not? I ain't doin' shit else. Who you rollin' wit'?"

"Bebe, Reesie and Pookie and I think Farrah might go but her nose be stuck so far up Choo-Choo's ass that she probably stay up in Fort Lickadale."

"Who driving?"

"I'm is! Pookie ain't got no ride and I ain't phenna be seen in Bebe and Reesie piece o' shit ass cars. I got Boobie's Diamante and the shit is gleamin' playa, gleamin'!"

That was what Mike found attractive about Sherika. She technically wasn't on his level as he saw it. She held down a part-time job at PRC but she found ways to live like she was in a higher class than she really was. She was a hustler. She played men, that was her full-time gig. She had an average face but what was considered a banging body. She was great in bed and used sex and her body to obtain jewelry, manicures, pedicures, hairstyles, rent money, use of expensive cars and she was never caught with less than one-hundred dollars in her pocket. Of course none of her tactics worked on Mike, she knew they never would and thus never considered trying.

"Ay why don't you scoop me so we can just roll in one car?"

"Aiight baby, I'a see you 'bout eleven,"

"Yea," Mike disconnected the line. He set his fingers to dial Samantha's cell phone number but he changed his mind. He didn't feel like arguing. He would deal with her in his own time, in his manner. This situation simply clarified the fact that he needed to stop dealing with his co-workers assistant. He decided he would end their relationship and ignore her at the office. He would try to avoid a confrontation with her as to keep peace in the workplace. He determined that that would be the only professional way to handle it. Samantha Falls would be the first and last white woman that he would get himself involved with.

Sherika did not arrive until a quarter past midnight. That did not bother Mike as it had taken him about that long to get ready. At the car he kicked Bebe to the back and claimed her passenger seat. She was annoyed by this figuring he should have taken his own car but she knew better than to open her mouth about it. Sherika would have cussed her from Miami to Albuquerque if she thought to insult her man that way. So she sulked quietly in the backseat feeling as if she were somehow missing out on major action in the front.

The brief ride was filled with lively chatter amongst the women, Bebe not wasting too much time before chiming in. All the gossiping annoyed Mike a bit but it was a small price to pay for a free ride. He didn't like driving through the area at night, as it was much too crowded for him and increased the possibility of his baby being involved in a collision. So he tuned them out as best as he could until they reached the Municipal Parking Garage. The group walked up the street to the nightclub. The line waiting to get in traveled up the block but thanks to Mike's time spent with Samantha he'd developed connections, which allowed himself and his small entourage to gain immediate access. Mike shook hands with the two bouncers that stood guarding the entrance and flirted with Yvette, the young woman at the box office, getting himself and those with him free VIP bracelets.

Sherika and Reesie, grateful to have been spared the twenty-dollar cover sashayed onto the dance floor, swaying their hips to Busta Rhymes hot rhythm. Mike immediately made his way to the bar followed by Bebe. He ordered himself a bottle of Cristal and paid for Bebe's Vodka and cranberry juice and strutted to the VIP section feeling somehow more important than the idiots that paid to scrounge for an open space to stand or dance on the sticky floor. He lay back on the velvet sofa and watched free young women grind to the DJ's beats in their tight skimpy outerwear. He licked his lips at the sight of a young brown skinned club hopper in a long semi sheer dress and high heels. He appreciated the ice that dripped from her wrists and neck and sparkled in her ears. The cornrows she wore in her hair extended to her backside and swayed when her head moved. Mike could see that she was making deliberate moves to gain his attention. He was fascinated with her but alas Sherika was very jealous and enjoyed showing out and she was headed in his direction.

"Wassup baby?" she said taking a seat next to him, "Lemme hit that."

Mike nodded toward the bottle and Sherika poured herself a glass. She gulped it down and jumped up again when the DJ switched up the songs. Mike wasn't one to dance and Sherika was fully aware of that fact. She never tried to pressure him into doing it but she'd always stand in front of him and roll her hips. She knew he enjoyed a good lap dance. Sherika was standing between his thighs gyrating with his hand on her rear when a familiar voice cut through the blaring music. He leaned left and looked past Sherika to see Samantha and a small black woman heading in their direction. Sam was fuming. Mike fought a loosing battle at remaining calm. He knew that if Samantha said anything that seemed as if it could be out of line Sherika would snap and attack and he contemplated tossing his hands in the air and allowing it. But no matter how sick of her and angry with her he was she was still a co-worker and a white female one at that. He had to be smart about how he handled her. He would have to play this as cool as possible although he was not sure if his and Sherika's temper would allow it.

Sherika spun around; fists clenched and ready to beat down the hoe that was talking to her man. Mike grabbed her by her waist and quickly sat her on the modern chaise lounge. Sherika fought to get back to her feet becoming more and more enraged as it dawned on her that this must have been the female who had spoken to her that morning. The look in Mike's eyes as he looked at her told her that it may be in her best interest to obey Mike's demand. She sat back fuming as she watched her girls rush to her aide.

Mike stood and grabbed Samantha by the arm and pulled her aside. He was furious with her behavior but he reminded himself yet again to stay calm actually surprising himself with his ability to do so. He pulled her near the exit so they could speak better.

"What is yo' problem?" Mike blurted out, his visible anger exciting Samantha.

"What do you mean Mike? You're the one showing up here with that thing, embarrassing me. How could you do that?" her face contorted as she spoke but she remained sexy standing there in tight blue hip hugging jeans and a leather halter-top. Even still, *"Bitch please...."* was the first thought to come to Mike's mind but he suppressed that thought.

"You know what Sam, you trippin' and I ain't even gone go off on you right nah. I'mma holla at you lata."

Mike walked away and returned to the section to advise the women that it was time to go. Initially they resisted understandably as they'd barely been inside the club for an hour. But Mike knew that Samantha wouldn't leave it be, she got off on conflict. If they stayed any longer he and Sherika would probably wind up beating her down before the night was over and he didn't want to speculate how she'd explain her black eye and cracked ribbed to the powers-that-be in the morning.

The four mobbed toward the exit expressing their anger through profanity. Mike was impressed and Samantha's ballsiness intrigued him as she boldly stepped up to him in front of Sherika, Bebe and Reesie and told him that she would call him.

"Uh-uhn, no that bitch did not-" Sherika raised her fist but Mike quickly stopped her and pulled her forward, "Naw damn that shit Mike, I wanna fuck that hoe up, quit trippin'!"

Mike pulled her away swearing and screaming threats at Samantha, still ranting even after they'd dropped Bebe and Reesie at their Southern Miami homes and returned to Mike's South Beach condo. He allowed her to vent. He knew just as soon as they were settled inside and he'd gotten her undressed she'd forget what she was so angry about in the first place. And he of course was proven to be correct. She continued to fuss as he undid her blouse and bra but as soon as his tongue touched her erect nipple the only sound from her mouth were moans of intense pleasure. The two escaped to his bedroom and enjoyed wild animal sex on his bed before collapsing into an exhausted sleep.

"Who is that?" Sherika asked sitting up wide-awake and annoyed in Mike's bed.

Mike angrily tossed the sheets from his semi naked body and charged out of the bedroom and to the front door in response to the loud banging from the other side, "It betta be a got-damn fire," he muttered as he crossed the living room, "Who is it?"

"Sam!"

"What the fuck?" heat permeated from Mike's face. He quickly undid the locks to open the door, sure he must have misunderstood. A drunken Samantha Falls was standing in front of his opened front door sucking on a bottle of hot beer.

"Hey baby, I came by so we could work it out," she slurred stumbling toward him.

"Bitch how you get up here? What you doin' here, tryin' to get yo' shit split?"

"Screw you Mike, stop tripping. Listen I forgive you for bringing that cheap whore to the club tonight but don't push it."

"Fuck-….hoe…," Mike tried to remain calm. He resisted the urge to harm Samantha though it was becoming increasingly difficult, "Samantha take yo' ol' fuck ass home. We gotta work in a few hours."

"That's okay honey, I'll just ride with you. I always keep a spare change of clothes in my car. Besides baby you know you sleep better after you've had some good head."

"Bitch he already had it. Now I'm gone give you a five second head start fo' I beat the dog shit out yo' ass!" Sherika was standing in the living room in one of Mike's tee shirts ready to pounce.

A look of horror crossed Samantha's face. She quickly escalated to an anger of her own, "Michael Toussaint, what is she doing here?" she asked but Mike was speechless. He couldn't believe what was happening, "Answer me got-dammit!"

Mike quickly, instinctively grabbed Samantha by her long blond hair and pulled her head to him. His voice was low and deep when he spoke into her ear, "Bitch don't you ever disrespect me again or I *will* fuck yo' dumb ass up," a huge part of him wanted to sic Sherika on him but no matter how upset he was he simply didn't want to risk Samantha going to work bruised and battered and blaming him. So he instead pushed her back out into the hallway and slammed the door.

"I loved you Michael and this is how you treat me?" she called from the other side of the closed door, "You'll regret this Michael Toussaint! You'll regret that you ever messed with me motherfucker!"

"You just gone let that tramp get away wit' that?" Sherika asked jumping in Mike's path.

"Sheri get out my face wit' this bullshit," he responded as he pushed past her.

"Oh uh-uhn, I know you ain't phenna stand here and get sporty wit' me afta you let that heffa holla at you like you was a bitch. What cause the hoe white that bitch got you fidgety?"

"Sheri shet yo' dumb ass up. You don't know shit, you'se a silly hoe pimpin' silly ass nigga's wit' yo' battered ass coochie. You don't know about business bitch!"

"I know if that bitch was black you'da let me stomp a hole in her ass a long time ago, that's what I know."

"I ain't phenna argue wit' yo' dumb ass. As a matter of fact what the fuck you still doin' here? I shouldn't even be seein' you right now."

"Oh you puttin' me out?"

"What you thank?" Mike opened the door and waited beside it while an aggravated Sherika gathered her belongings. She didn't allow herself to get too upset as she knew how Mike was and what he was truly capable of. Rather than pick a loosing battle and get her feelings hurt even more she opted to shut her mouth and go home. She exited without speaking a word but hoping to run into the brazen white girl that wanted her man so badly, on the premises. Mike slammed the door behind her and locked it, "Fuckin' hoes need to learn some manners."

"Michael may I see you in my office for a moment?" Reginald Tuttle asked sticking his head into the hall as Mike passed.

Mike turned on his fancy heels and walked into his superior's office. Subconsciously he knew that it must have something to do with Ms. Samantha Falls. Despite that feeling he kept his head high as he walked inside and to Mr. Tuttle's desk. He'd simply keep his mouth shut and deny everything. The two men shook hands before taking a seat.

"What's going on Reginald?" Mike asked adjusting his tie.

"I'm going to get straight to the point Michael. I have a couple of questions for you."

"Okay shoot."

"Do you know Samantha Falls, Brad's assistant?" Mr. Tuttle asked lighting a cigar. He offered one to Mike but he declined.

"I know of her, yes."

"Do you find her attractive?"

"What?" Mike asked startled.

"Simple yes or no question Michael. Do you find her attractive?"

"I guess but to be honest Reginald, I'm not really into women outside my race."

"But she is pretty."

"Yea she's pretty," Mike was becoming annoyed but he checked his emotions.

"Have you ever expressed that to her in any way?"

"No I have not. Look Reginald, what's with the interrogation? What are you getting at?"

"Okay Mike, bottom line is Samantha Falls has gone to the board and accused you of sexual harassment."

"Sexual harassment? Ain't dis some shit," Mike muttered loosing character.

"Yes, sexual harassment. Now I respect you as a man and as an architect, you're one of my best and I'll back you wholly but you've got to tell me everything. Have you ever hit on her? Did she maybe ever hit on you and you turned her down?"

"No. We made small talk in the hall once or twice but that's it."

"You're sure Michael? There is nothing that you can think of, honestly, that could have prompted this."

"I mean, we've spoken but nothing out of the ordinary."

"Okay Michael, I'm going to take your word. Go on back to your office, relax, and don't let this bother you and I will keep you informed as to how things are going to proceed."

"Thank you sir," Mike shook Reginald Tuttle's hand before disappointedly and angrily walking back to his office.

Parkin' Lot Pimpin'

"Bitch betta have my money! Aaawww shit! Here we go on the one y'all...-" Mike sang out along with the voice of AMG which was beating through the stereo speakers of Nate's hand me down Impala. He inhaled the cigarette, which was held between two fingers. He leaned his back against the car and with his eyes closed bobbed to the beat. His jeans sagged halfway down past his waist, his Hanes underwear in plain view to the public. He wore a brand new pair of Jordan's, which he did not pay for on his feet, his muscular chest bare as he'd tossed his tee shirt inside the car.

Nate sat on the trunk of the car, which was parked in the high school parking lot. He tapped the hood with the rings on his fingers to the beat of the music. He sat in his varsity basketball uniform anxiously awaiting the end of the lunch hour, ready to get to Phys Ed. Several young ladies smiled and waved as they passed the two eleventh graders. Nate nodded. Mike adjusted his penis.

"Ay nigga, who dat is?" Mike asked Nate.

"I don't know her but I think her name is Sandy or Carmen or something like that. She's the new chic in my Science class I was telling you about. "

"Dat hoe finer than a muthafucka. I'm phenna holla at her. Ay! Ay gurl! Ay redbone come here! You hear me callin' yo' ass!"

The young fair-skinned girl was very pretty with long brown hair and bright sparkling brown eyes. She was buxom for a teenager and the boys loved it. She walked beside two of her girlfriends in her mini skirt and blue "Jodeci-style" boots. She knew Mike was referring to her, she'd transferred to this high school only six weeks prior and it seemed every young boy wanted a piece of her. She was excited by Mike's expressed interest but she had to keep the appearance of control in front of her girlfriends. So she pretended as though she was unaware as to what was going on around her.

"Fuck you den bitch!" Mike called out before returning his attention to the lyrics he'd been reciting.

"Why you have to be so got-damned ignorant?" Nate asked.

"Why you got to act so got-damned white, nigga?" Mike retorted.

"Fuck you nigga."

"Fuck them hoes. Yo' nigga ain't that yo' girl ova there wit' Jenny Johnson?"

"Yea, that's her."

"That bitch is phat! You gone lemme hit dat?"

"Whatever."

"Hook it up then, nigga!"

"Aaaww hell, look out Mike. Here comes Thalia's fat ass."

"Damn," Mike muttered as he scrambled to climb inside Nate's vehicle. He was too late, he'd already been spotted.

"Hey Romeo!" Thalia called, "How you doin' Nate?" She asked changing the tone in her voice to obvious attitude. Nate nodded and returned his attention to tapping.

"Whut up Thalia?" Mike asked surrendering.

"Shit. Whut up wit' you nigga? When me and you gone git down?"

"Come on nah, Thalia you know good an' well a nigga can't fit in between yo' thighs," Mike commented leaning toward Nate for dap.

"Aaww forget you Mike! Once you go fat you neva go back, nigga! Haha! Gone 'head and keep screwing wit' dem skinny hoes if you want to. You don't know what you missing out on but when you ready to find out, holla at me."

The bell sounded and students scrambled inside the building. Nate slid from the trunk and headed to lock up his car. Mike complained about being a slave to the school bell but Nate was able to quickly convince him as usual to go back. It wasn't too difficult, his next class was Calculus and though he hated school and the discipline of it, he loved the challenge that math provided.

Mike pulled his shirt over his head. He grabbed a toothpick from the glove compartment and twirled it around with his tongue. Together Nate and Mike strutted toward the building. They found themselves behind the young bright-skinned woman that Mike had displayed interest in earlier that hour.

"What you can't hear or sumthin'?" Mike asked stepping closer to her rear than what was socially acceptable.

"Huh?" the girl asked trying to pretend as if she did not know what he was talking about.

"If you can huh you can hear. So I guess you gone play stupid right since yo' girls ain't wit' you now."

"Naw my bad. What's up?"

"Ay what's yo' name?"

"Candy."

"Candy? Git outta here! Straight up?"

"Mmhm."

"Got-damn dat's sexy."

Nate simply laughed to himself as he followed the two inside the building.

8Nate

"Nathaniel darling, are you about prepared?" Mya called to me from below.

"Almost sweetheart, I'll be down in a minute!"

I slipped my feet into a brand new pair of tan sandals to match my linen shorts suit. I walked over to the dresser and picked out a Movado watch and clasped it onto my wrist before spritzing myself with cologne. Sierra had invited us to a BBQ that she had put together on Fort Lauderdale beach. My life was beginning to get back on track over the past few weeks. I'd told Sierra that I would step away from Anthony and I'd meant that. He was causing too much friction in my world, undoing everything I'd worked so hard to put in place and I couldn't have that. At the same time I knew Anthony was a good guy and I didn't want to hurt him. I didn't have the heart to come out and say to him that I didn't want to see him anymore so I instead avoided him. Yes, I realize that my behavior could be viewed as childish but I knew no other way to handle the situation.

Anthony reached out to me the very day following our little encounter. He asked if I'd meet with him to talk, just to talk. I lied and said that I was busy that day but would get back to him. I never did but he was persistent. He continued calling, wanting to connect and each time I'd piece together another untruthful excuse not to oblige him. He'd called me as recently as two days prior and I'd denied him yet again. See what Anthony did not understand was the staring role that I'd been cast in and how I'd trained for twenty-eight years less childhood to perfect my performance. And since I'd stopped spending time with him I had more time to devote to my fiancée, my family and best friends. Any potential suspicion had immediately been diverted. Besides, Mya did not particularly care for him anyway. Though she told me that she could not put her finger on it there was something about Anthony's demeanor that made her uncomfortable.

I grabbed my cellular phone from my bureau and jogged down the steps to meet Mya. She was sitting on the bottom step in her adorable ankle length spring dress and a large sun hat that appeared slightly too big for her small head. She tapped her foot, which was encased in stylish burgundy colored sandals. I knelt down behind her and tickled beneath her armpits.

"Stop that Nathaniel," she laughed, "Stop it!"

"You know you like it girl."

"You know I do baby," she replied turning to face me.

"Bring your sexy European ass on," I kissed her lips before we stood and headed out of the front door.

The oceanfront was packed when we arrived. I struggled to find an empty parking spot but was eventually successful. We climbed out of the car carrying a large bowl of Mya's delicious homemade potato salad. Mya slipped her tiny feet out of her sandals and struggled to cross the hot sand. I snickered at her as she tried to pretend that her feet were not burning. Her smile was beautiful. Sierra was setting out napkins and paper plates while her cousin Junior flipped burgers and chicken on the grill.

"Hey y'all! Glad you could make it!" Sierra called. She jogged over and embraced Mya and kissed my cheek before taking the bowl from my hand.

"Damn y'all have a lot of food!" I said rubbing my stomach, "Hey Junior, what are you doing on the grill? If I get sick I know where to send my lawyer!"

"Heh, heh! Ol' Nate-Dog, wassup young blood?" Junior and I shook hands and embraced in a half hug, "Where's that l'il black ass friend of yourn?"

"Who? Mike?"

"Yea, yea, that's him! Where he at? How he doin'?"

"He's well. He's supposed to come through here today but with Mike, hey, you never know."

"I hear he done made sumthin' outta hisself. That right?"

"Yea Cousin Junior, you know Mike is an architect."

"Oh yea? I know'd that already huh? Hmpf, well I'm getting on to be an ol' man, what can I say? Well you lookin' good son in yo' ol' fancy duds. You always was an ol' clean, smart young boy. Shole wished you'da ended up with my Sierra 'stead o' dat dead beat Darryl."

"I know, I know but she's my very best friend and I wouldn't have it any other way. There's my future wife right there. Right there in the burgundy dress, the little bitty one."

"Oh now that's a pretty l'il thang. Dat you?"

"Mmhm, sure is," I answered with pride. Junior patted my back and returned his attention to the meat. He was happy for me but I knew deep inside he wished that I'd sweep Sierra off of her feet and take her away from *Deadbeat Darryl*. Her family loved me as much as they knew I loved Sierra but I could never make them understand why I could never be with her romantically without overexposing myself. In another lifetime she'd be my one and only true love. I would sacrifice myself for Sierra. But in this life we would have to settle for true friendship.

Mya handed me a plastic cup filled with ice and ginger ale. I took a seat beside her on the dirty wooden bench. She smacked my leg and instructed me to stand so that she could spread a towel on the bench for me to sit upon. I reached into an aluminum pan and placed a few grilled chicken wings on a paper plate. Sierra plopped a spoonful of potato salad on the side and a scoop of red beans and rice on the other side. The sun was warm as usual but for the first time in a long time humidity was down which was refreshing. The breeze off the ocean felt cool against my damp and sweaty skin. The children were chasing one another across the hot grainy sand with loaded water guns. The men were gathered together arguing about sports while the women gossiped about each other to each other, about fashion and how fat they thought they had gotten. It felt good to be able to kick back and relax and just simply enjoy life for a change.

"Hey, who wants get in this volleyball game?" Pam called out.

"Girl I shole don't wanna be running 'round in this hot ass sun with my big ass," Lori Anne protested.

"That's what the hell you need to be doing."

"Aawww hell forget your ol' bony ass Pam."

"I would love to play," Mya chimed in, "Come Nathaniel."

"Oh no-o. I'm with Lori Anne, y'all are not about to get me in that hot ass sun running around," I protested.

"Aawww baby, don't be such a stick in the mud."

"You know I'm in," Sierra piped up, "Come on Cousin Junior."

"Chile yo' Cousin Junior too old for that jumpin' around and stuff," Junior waved his hands and backed away.

"Come on Nate-Dog," Sierra's much younger cousin Germel joined in, "Skins and shirts though, skins and shirts. I want e'ry female that ain't blood kin to me bouncin' in they bikini's, y'heard me!"

"Aawww boy please!" another relative called out, "Come on y'all, I'm in."

"Don't worry Germel, I'm convinced," Mya pulled her dress over her head to reveal a sexy red two-piece.

"Oh hell yea!" Germel exclaimed.

"Whooo-wee! Aawww sookie-sookie nah!" Junior commented.

"Ay, ay, ay, this is my woman now, don't y'all forget that," I joked.

"The rest o' y'all gone head on and take it off. Be like this young lady here, don't be shy."

"Junior please," Lori Anne responded, "That chile ain't bit mo' than 75 pounds soakin' wet!"

We all harmlessly laughed at Mya's expense and watched her blush. After a bit more poking fun and sweet-talking we got a game going of testosterone versus estrogen though I felt with the way Lori Anne spiked the ball her estrogen level was questionable. I had to admit that it was a good idea. Mya for the most part carried her team. She used her sexuality and half naked body to distract my teammates and score some points, a good tactic though quite underhanded. I nudged Germel who nodded to his friend before I served the ball. At once the three of us removed our shirts revealing well-toned, muscular frames.

"Now what?" Germel called out to the women as I served and earned us another point.

"Cheaters!" Pam called out, "Oh forget this!" Pam shimmied out of her shorts and pulled her shirt over her head revealing a shapely frame in a multi-colored one-piece swimsuit. Our players were distracted momentarily however it did not stop us from winning thirty-seven to twenty-four. The women conjured up lame excuses for their loss as we teased and taunted in celebration of our victory.

I was surprised to see Mike approaching in the distance as I prepared Mya and myself another plate of food. I nudged Sierra and pointed. She nearly dropped the corn on the cob she was eating when she caught Mike in her line of vision carrying a bowl.

"Can you believe this?" Sierra asked in shock.

"Hey, he can surprise us at times," I responded.

"Oh my goodness, it's Michael," Mya reacted as Mike approached the picnic table, setting his bowl beside Mya's potato salad.

"Yea, yea l'il nigga, wassup l'il momma?" he kissed Mya and then Sierra on the cheek. He and I shook hands and half hugged, "Nate-Dog! Whut up playa?"

"Man, not a thing. We just finished whipping these females in volleyball."

"Right-right. Ay y'all ain't got no card game goin'? No dice, no dominoes? Wassup my nigga?"

"Ay I'm wit' that," Germel said.

"Who got some cards?" Mike asked.

"I'on know."

"Y'mammy got some. She over there playing Spades with Felice an' nem but you know she always keep an extra pack," Cousin Junior instructed.

"Aiight then. Ay nigga, I'll be right back."

"So Mike, how ya been?" Sierra asked, "Been staying out of trouble?"

"Aaah gurl, you know me. Just workin' hard, tryna keep shit together."

"Still ain't met that special lady?"

"Nah Si-Si, you know a nig can't be tied down. Besides you already taken y'know," Mike playfully flirted.

"Whatever boy!" Sierra laughed, "Anyway though, thank you for coming and thank you for bringing this lovely fruit salad that you obviously worked so hard on going to Publix for."

"Aawww forget you nigga," Mike retorted while accepting Sierra's peck on the cheek.

"Got the cards baby! What they hittin' fo'?" Germel called out upon his return. The men gathered at the table for a good game of Poker and after a while Spades. It was a wonderful day, which came to an end around 10:30 that night when we could no longer handle being bit up by God's most annoying creatures. I kissed Sierra and thanked her for a good time before Mya and I found our car and headed home exhausted.

"Baby!" Mya called to me, sticking her head out from behind the bathroom door.

"Yes honey?"

"Would you like to join me in the shower?"

"Of course," I began to peel my sweaty, dirty clothing off when my cell phone rang. The caller ID displayed the phone number of Anthony. I finished removing my clothing and joined my beautiful soon to be wife in our shower.

I took a seat at my usual table at Ocean Café, the same café where I'd lunched at for years, the same café where I'd met Mya. I placed my order with Claude and began to flip through a book of paintings and determine which my firm should purchase. I'd been there all of three minutes or less before an uninvited guest took a seat across from me at my table. I sighed and leaned back in my chair, closing the book before me. I was face to face with Anthony.

"It's surprising running into you here," he said.

"Yes, I'm sure. What are you doing here Anthony?"

"How else could I get in contact with you? You don't return any of my calls and you bullshit me when we do speak. So why don't you give me a better way to reach you."

"Anthony, what do you want with me? Why are you stressing me?"

"It's not *what* I want from you Nathaniel, I want you. I don't sweat men like this on a regular basis, shit look at me dammit, I don't have to. But there is just something about you, about us I should say and I'm not about to let it go that easy."

"Could you keep your voice down?" I semi-whispered.

"Why are you so ashamed of who you are? If you want me to leave you alone then explain that to me. What's going on with you Nathaniel? Huh? Inside of you, inside your head, your mind, your heart. Why are you denying yourself of who you really are and why are you depriving yourself of real happiness?"

I shifted uncomfortably in my seat. Anthony was strong, Anthony knew who he was, he knew how to make others see and appreciate him for who he was. He wouldn't ever understand my inability to be as he was. I am sure his struggle hadn't been easy hence the use of the word "struggle" however he obviously had the inner strength to able himself to deal with his genetic flaw. How could he understand? He would never understand. And so I made him aware of that,

"Anthony, you wouldn't understand."

"Then make me understand. As a matter of fact I'll make a deal with you. Indulge me one dinner – now hear me out. Meet me tomorrow night at the Blue Door at 8 pm. I know you know of it. We'll have an innocent dinner and you can explain to me your position. After that whether I get it or not if you want me to leave you alone, then I'll leave you alone. Alright, can we do that?"

"I apologize for interrupting sir, may I take your order?" Claude asked.

"Don't worry about it Claude, he was just leaving."

"Yea," Anthony said rising from his seat, "Thanks anyway. Nathaniel, please don't let me down."

Whether or not I should go through with dinner with Anthony weighed heavily on my mind as I entered my home. I'd finally gotten my life back on track, was finally able to get that incident in my kitchen out of my mind and my immediate thoughts and now he wanted to get together for dinner. For what? Didn't he get the fact that I didn't want him, didn't need him? I was happy with Mya and with my life. But if I didn't show up at this dinner he wasn't going to set me free. I had no one to turn to on this; it was up to me to make the decision.

I sat eating a salad without tasting, staring blankly at the television screen mentally debating my issue. What was there to be afraid of? I'd handled myself for nearly two decades-

"Honey are you alright?" Mya asked.

"Huh?"

"Are you feeling okay?"

"Yea, sure baby, I'm good."

"You certain? You've been awfully quiet. You know you can talk to me about anything. That's what I'm here for."

I paused and looked at her before I spoke. There was sincerity in those hazel eyes and that I truly appreciated, "I love you," I simply replied followed by a kiss on the forehead. She reluctantly accepted and returned her attention to the television. Now where was I? Oh yes, after all the years of training myself to be normal there wasn't anyway that could be undone now. What the hell? I decided that I would go through with it and meet Anthony for dinner, what harm could it really do?

As much as I hated to do it, I lied to Mya that morning while we were both getting ready for work. Told her that I had a lot of work to catch up on and more than likely I'd be late coming home. In keeping with the spirit of dishonesty I called home while on my way to the Blue Door to meet Anthony and re-confirmed that I'd be late. I detected no suspicion in her vocals and thus relaxed. I showered in the bathroom in my office and changed into one of the three emergency dinner suits in my closet before actually making my way to the restaurant. He was of course there when I arrived. The waiter seated me at his table and poured a glass of Chablis. I gulped it down hoping for some sort of buzz that would help me get through this. I sat silently through Anthony's charming smiles. I was anxious to get this over with but I could see he was in no hurry to move things along.

"Very nice," he opened.

"Huh? What?"

"You look very nice."

"Oh, thank you," I answered while nervously scratching my temple.

I sat and endured what I viewed as an uncomfortable silence until our waiter arrived and took our order. After he retreated to the kitchen Anthony relaxed as I again tensed.

"Calm down Nathaniel, I won't bite," he smirked.

I shifted and attempted to relax. I shifted around a few more times under his gaze and sly smile.

"Thank you for coming."

"You're welcome."

"So how was work?"

"Listen Anthony, this isn't a date so skip the niceties and get to the point please," I was becoming anxious.

"Okay, okay. Allow me to get to the point. Why can't I be with you?" I felt as though I'd been smacked in the stomach with a steel bat, "Don't bullshit me either Nathaniel. I have real feelings for you and I need to understand exactly what's stopping me from acting on them. And don't tell me Mya because I know that relationship is based on some bullshit."

For the first time I allowed myself to see the sincerity in his face as well as hear it in his tone. I relaxed some and sipped from my refilled champagne glass.

"Okay you really want to know my history Anthony? I'll give it to you."

"Yes, Nathaniel I really want to know. Help me understand you."

I sighed and assessed the pleading look in his eyes. I decided to spill everything. I told him about my relationship with my father and my father's harsh attitude toward homosexuality. As we spoke I became overwhelmed with a strange sense of comfort and revealed even more about my life over dinner than I'd originally intended. Anthony was much more compassionate and understanding than I'd thought he'd be. He shared his life experiences with me and I began to realize that his struggle hadn't been so easy after all. He'd struggled for acceptance the same as I have. By the end of dinner I'd completely relaxed and opened myself up to him. When the dishes were cleared away I was not ready to depart and neither was he. We spent the night talking and laughing until we were forced to find some place else to socialize.

9Darryl

Heat, sweat, funk and the musty scent of sex permeated the air circulating around the entangled couple. Grunts and moans echoed throughout the bedroom. The headboard crashed against the wall repeatedly awaking the children that had only minutes ago been sleeping ever so soundly in their bedroom. It didn't matter to the couple; nothing mattered except each other and the moment. Their satisfaction was priority and not the two young children who found the act going on on the other side of the door to be vile, disgusting and just plain "nasty".

"Damn yo' pussy feel good!" Darryl groaned in her ear. The stench of stale alcohol on his breath did not phase her as she was simply too thrilled to have him inside her body. She wound her hips in tune with his rhythm. Darryl grabbed her by the waist and roughly flipped her over to her stomach. She pulled herself onto all fours as Darryl held her by her hips and pulled her to him. He thrust himself in and out as she yelped under the pressure of his penis. Moving faster and faster, smacking her rear end as he did so.

"Oh Darryl....oh baby..." she whispered.

"I'm 'bout to cum! Oh shit...oh shit!"

Darryl thrust himself as deeply inside as possible and held his position as he exploded inside of the condom he wore to prevent the creation of a new mouth to feed. He tossed his head back and enjoyed the moment. He then slid from her body and removed his condom. Darryl walked wearily across the hall to the bathroom and dumped his potential children and flushed. When he reentered the room, Victoria was sitting upright on the bed; her back against the headboard, her legs cocked open, smoking a cigarette. Darryl took a seat on the edge of the bed and slipped on his boxers and pulled his t-shirt over his head. He reached back and Victoria handed him the cigarette she'd been puffing on. He took a few long drags before handing it back to her. He reached for his slacks and began to step into them.

"You're leaving already?" Victoria asked.

"Come on now baby, we always go through this. I have to go home, I have to work in the morning," Darryl answered buttoning his shirt.

"And like I always tell you, you can just as easily get to work from here."

"Like it or not Vicky, I have to go home to her."

Victoria, frustrated, ran her fingers through her mane and rolled her eyes, "Fuck her. Oh wait, that's the problem, you can't!"

Darryl glared at Victoria. He pushed his body up from the bed and reached for his shoes. He grabbed his keys from the top of the television and in silent anger headed toward the bedroom door. Victoria swiftly moved from her bed and ran to him pushing the door closed and blocking it with her still naked, sweaty body.

"Baby, I'm sorry, I'm sorry. I should just keep my mouth shut. Come back baby, don't go yet. Please? Baby, please?" she begged.

Darryl sighed and returned his keys to their previous position. Truth told he did not want to leave however he did not want Sierra to know that he was cheating. He figured that deep down she had an idea that he was but he would never be foolish enough to outright confess it to her and not coming home at night was as good as a confession. He allowed Victoria to take his hand and lead him back to her full sized bed. He sat on the edge while Victoria massaged his shoulders and nibbled his ears.

"Darryl honey, when are you going to leave her? She doesn't make you happy; she's a little girl. I love you and there ain't nothin' I won't do for you."

Darryl did not reply. He dropped his head and enjoyed the massage he was receiving. He heard her words but alas in his mind it was a hopeless situation. He had three children with Sierra and if he left her he'd not only have to pay her alimony but child support as well. He'd also need to pay into the home that he'd create with Victoria and her three children. It just couldn't work, there was no way.

"Darryl, please honey just leave her. We can get married and be happy together," Victoria continued, trying not to sound too agitated.

"How many times are we gone have to go through this? I told you Vicky, bottom line, it's cheaper to keep her."

"I'm so sick of hearing that ol' 1960's bullshit Darryl. Leave that tired bitch alone and come home where you belong," Victoria pushed away and slid from the other side of the bed. She snatched an old thinning dingy yellow robe from a chair in the corner of the room and wrapped it around her body. She pulled another cigarette from the pack and lit it. She took a long drag and sat on the opposite side of the bed as Darryl, "This ain't right Darryl."

"Well what you want from me Vicky? Huh? You want me to divorce Sierra, leave my kids, pay all my money to them and still take care of you?"

"Don't exaggerate honey."

"Exaggerate? Vicky that's what's gone happen! And all them pretty l'il hair do's and shoes you want you ain't gone get from me! Don't be stupid."

"Fuck you Darryl! There's a way, if you really wanted to you could find a way."

"You just don't get it do you? It's not that easy! Now just drop the shit Vicky, I ain't phenna put myself out there like that."

"Aaarrrgh!"

"Shet up fo' you wake up the damn kids!"

"Don't tell me how to speak in my own home, remember you don't want to be with me, you wanna stay with your so-called wife!"

"You got-damned right and I'm phenna go home to her right now!"

"So! Fuck you Darryl!"

Darryl charged from the room and out of the apartment into the night air, Victoria in tow. He jogged down the steps and to his car. Victoria watched him climb inside his vehicle.

"I love you!" Victoria called down.

Darryl slammed his door and peeled out of the parking lot, heading home. He sped across Highway 195 twenty minutes north until he arrived. He was reluctant to get out of his car and go inside. He wanted to be with Victoria as opposed to Sierra but didn't see how he would be able to take care of her if he divorced his wife. He would be in a financial rut if he tried and he knew it. He felt that it would be foolish of him to even humor the idea. He'd already made the mistake of marrying Sierra, he wanted to be conscious, careful and aware of every life decision he made from there on out. He wasn't about to make the mistake of divorcing her.

He crept from his vehicle and slow dragged to the front door, unlocked it and went inside. His first stop was the kitchen. The clock on the wall read five past midnight. He poured himself a glass of juice and stood by the sink while he gulped it down. He rinsed his glass and reluctantly walked down the hall to the bedroom he shared with Sierra. He wasn't surprised to see Sierra still awake and reading her Bible. He went into the bathroom to shower before climbing in bed being sure to keep as much space between him and her as possible without rolling out of the bed. He turned his bedside lamp off and waited for Sierra to turn hers off but she did not. He grew agitated quickly. She knew the routine; he'd never had to tell her to turn off the lamp before. He gave her more time to catch on but she still did not budge. In a dramatic motion, he flung the comforter from his body and sat upright. He glared at Sierra who'd already closed her Bible and was obviously not using the light.

"Your hand broke or sumthin'?" he asked viciously.

"Of course not," she answered timidly.

"Then when you plan on turning the got-damned light off?"

"In a minute. Can we talk?"

"Talk? About what?"

"About us, about our marriage, our family."

"Ah shit. Damn Si-Si can we just go to bed? Huh? I work hard all day. I don't wanna come home and listen to you naggin'."

"But Darryl I think this is important. We have three little ones in there witnessing our family falling apart. Doesn't that mean anything to you?"

"Sierra I told you I ain't phenna deal wit' this, what you can't hear now? I'm tired!"

"You don't have to cuss at me and if you weren't so busy sleeping wit' another woman you wouldn't be so tired!" Sierra immediately covered her mouth. She'd never spoken to Darryl or anyone for that matter in such a tone. Darryl wanted to let her know that if she'd sleep with him he wouldn't have to sleep with anyone else but he was too shocked from her unexpected outburst to say what was on his mind. He sat staring at her trying to get a grip on things.

"Sierra, it's late," he spoke calmly, "I gotta work in the morning. Can we talk about this some other time?"

"But Darryl-"

"Si-Si turn off the got-damn light!" he yelled. Darryl pulled the blanket back over his body and closed his eyes. Sierra reached over and turned off her lamp. She chewed her bottom lip as she waited for sleep to set in.

10 Sierra

Sierra and Nate sat silently in the back of the room watching Michele kick and chop along with the other pint sized Jackie Chan wanna-be's in her karate class. She felt proud watching her baby girl learn how to defend herself, something that she did not know how to do. As a little girl she'd been raised to be just that, a little girl. She'd been taught to be clean, respectful, mannerable and feminine. Fighting was out of the question. She did not fight with her sister less known strangers. No, unlike other children she and her little sister Lilly never fought in any form whether physical or verbal. Her parents would not have allowed such mannish behavior.

When the instructor announced a brief break in the routine, the room livened with chatter amongst the adults and sounds of children thrilled to be able to play. Sierra turned in her seat to face Nate.

"So how is everything between you and Mya?" Sierra asked.

"Great and getting better," Nate lied.

"That's good to hear. Mya left me a message saying she wants Michele on Saturday for another one of her crazy artsy gigs."

"Yea, yea she mentioned it to me. How is your relationship going as if I have to ask?"

"I don't know what to do. I know you gonna say eff him, whatever, whatever but he's my husband. We've got kids and I want my marriage to work. I tried everything I could think of to please him," Sierra said with frustration in her tone, "I tried to make love to him but he's so impatient. Tried to cook up a romantic dinner but he turned me down. Tried to talk to him but he blew me off. What is left to do?"

"Leave him," Nate said bluntly.

"There you go."

"Look at me in my eyes and see how serious I am. Leave him. Si-Si, pack your shit and your kids and go."

"Where would I even go with three small kids Nate? Please."

"Si-Si don't start this shit. You know damn well you and the kids are welcome to stay at my home as long as you need."

"I am not about to invade on you and your soon to be wife because I can't keep my relationship together."

"Sierra you got more excuses than a brother in jail."

Sierra shook her head and picked at her fingernails while the small children gathered to the center of the room once again. Noticing the downtrodden look on her face Nate reached over and wrapped his arm around her shoulder and pulled her into his chest. Part of her was beginning to believe that he was right. She'd even considered it but she couldn't help thinking of how it would disappoint her parents, especially her father. It was enough that they already had one child gone astray; she didn't want to further break her daddy's heart. It was a dilemma but she was certain that there must be a way around separation or divorce.

Naturally things weren't always bad in her and Darryl's relationship. She could recall the first time she'd gone out with him. He was so handsome when he showed up at her dorm room. It wasn't all about his smooth caramel complexion, full lips and freshly cleaned navy blue suit. It was the small bouquet of daisies in his hand, the determination in his eyes, the obvious ambition in his heart. She didn't melt right then and there, she was not overcome with excited joy from his presence yet she was extremely flattered by his expressed interest in her and desire to impress her. He helped her into his old 1982 Toyota Camry. It wasn't a flashy ride by any means. All blue with the exception of the driver's side door, which was painted a dull red. There was a crack in the windshield and the left taillight was busted. The interior of the car smelled like pine oil. None of that bothered Sierra and Darryl was aware that it would not. He knew that she was neither judgmental nor superficial unlike the other women he'd encountered during his stay in South Florida. The women were different than the ones from his Nebraska roots. Much more materialistic as well as extravagant and he wasn't going to get one until he at the least upgraded his ride. Sierra wasn't so naive as to believe that he didn't want one but alas he was not up to their standards and thus had to settle for the closest he could get to that world which was Sierra.

The date, besides the uncomfortable drive, was lovely. He took her to a small mom and pop restaurant where they had stew and the best buttered rolls ever. They shared their dreams and their ambitions over that inexpensive meal. Afterward they strolled along the oceanfront and Sierra experienced her first real kiss. They spent nearly every day together after that. Sierra did not realize that Darryl was still such a child and intrigued by her unusual virginity. His goal had become to be her first. Marriage was the only way to ensure such success. Unbeknownst to Sierra, Darryl had never intended to stay in the marriage long term. Just long enough to fulfill this goal, reap a few benefits from her father, and have some stability for a while. Just as soon as he was able to pull someone better or maybe once he was bored with Sierra he'd divorce her and move on with his life. He never planned on the children but this Sierra was unaware of.

After the meet was complete, Sierra and Nate kissed and parted ways. She loaded an exhausted Michele into the backseat and headed toward her home to relieve her mother of her babysitting duties. Michele was sound asleep in the backseat when they arrived. Sierra lifted her out of the car and carried her into the house and in the back to her bedroom. She removed her clothing and gently replaced them with pajamas, trying not to stir her too much. She then laid her little girl beneath the blanket and kissed her soft brown cheek. Sierra pulled the door to and walked down the hall to the mouth of the living room where her mother sat on the sofa reading her Bible and listening to soft gospel music in the background. Sierra took a seat beside Mrs. Mitchell.

She rubbed her mother's knee gently; Mrs. Mitchell set her Bible on her lap.

"So you're back from teaching my grandbaby to be violent?"

"Ma," Sierra whined.

"Don't 'Ma' me, you know how me and yo' daddy feel about that nonsense. So we may as well just drop it. Now how's Darryl? You do what I tell you? Your marriage going better?"

"Yes momma. I did what you told me to do. Things are getting a bit better," Sierra fibbed.

"See, I told you. Just listen to your mother sometimes and everthang'll be okay."

"That's right. Momma you hear from Lilly yet?" Sierra asked changing the subject.

"Your daddy talked to her 'bout a week or two ago but I wasn't home."

"She tell Daddy she coming down here next month?"

"I thank so. I know she told daddy she pregnant and she ain't married."

"Well Momma please don't be so hard on her. She's entitled to make a mistake or two, we all are," Sierra spoke softly while staring in the direction of her and Darryl's wedding picture. Mrs. Mitchell was oblivious to her daughter's sorrow.

"Well she already made her fair share of mistakes. Sierra honey, I'm phenna get on up outta here and get home to your daddy."

Sierra and her mother rose from the sofa simultaneously. Mrs. Mitchell gathered her Bible and sweater and headed toward the front door followed by her eldest child. At the door the two women kissed on the cheek before Sierra closed and locked the door behind her mother. She slow strolled back to the living room and lifted a photo album from the coffee table. It was her wedding album. She sat back onto the sofa and flipped it open. She smiled at the photos of her family. She was happy on that day, so filled with hope for her and Darryl's future. Sierra chewed her bottom lip as she stared at a picture of herself in her beautiful white gown, which represented her purity, standing beside her new husband in his black tuxedo. They were hand in hand in front of the flower filled gazebo in her parent's large backyard. Sierra heard a key turn in the door and quickly closed the album and set it back on the table. She listened to Darryl's footsteps head toward the back of the house. She wanted badly to call out to him and make another effort at working things out but she was sure that it would prove to be a waste of time. She reached behind the couch and pulled out an old throw blanket she'd crotched as a teen and wrapped it around her body and lay back on the couch chewing her bottom lip.

"No as a matter of fact, I haven't heard from him," Sierra spoke into the telephone receiver, "I don't know what's up with Nate. I ain't talked to him since Michele's last karate meet and that was over a week ago. He usually calls me at least every other day but nothing."

"Damn. Sumthin' goin' on wit' him," Mike spoke in a concerned tone, "I called the crib and don't nobody answer. He barely even answering his cell and when he do he too busy to talk. His ass don't never call back no mo'. C'mon Si-Si, I know he tell you everything, what's up wit' him? Him and Mya havin' problems or sumthin'?"

"I swear Mike I don't know. He's been acting real weird and distant. When I call the house if I get an answer its Mya and she barely says two words before she cuts me off. Something's up Mike but I don't know what it is."

"Aiight Si-Si. If you find sumthin out hit me up."

"Okay baby, same for you," Sierra disconnected the line and turned back to the homemade chili she was cooking. She looked down at Lee who was sitting on the kitchen floor stacking building blocks while Sesame Street played on the television for him above. Jenny was nodding out in her high chair with a soggy cookie between her fat fingers. Sierra returned her attention to the boiling pot and chewed her bottom lip. She was beginning to become truly concerned about Nathaniel. She'd not spoken to him for more than two minutes in over a week now. She thought possibly that he just had a lot going on and needed some space but if Mike was worried then it was more to it than just being busy. And Mya had been very short and distant with her the couple times she did answer the phone when Sierra called. But what sent signals was that she went back on her word and did not pick Michele up, which she had never before done, at least not without some sort of an explanation.

Sierra picked up the cordless and dialed Nate's cellular phone but it rang without any answer. She decided against leaving a message. She ran to her bedroom and retrieved her address book and darted back to the kitchen to supervise her dinner and children. She called Nate's office and waited on hold while his secretary rang for him but she promptly returned stating that Mr. Marshall was in a meeting and would return her call. She thought to call his mother but she did not want to put undue worry upon her. She instead tried to convince herself that her best friend was fine, just under a lot of stress and strain right now. That wasn't unlikely as he was always under pressure to prove himself as a Black man in his profession. And with planning a wedding and trying to create a life, it wasn't too farfetched an idea. Sierra's thoughts were halted when she heard her doorbell sound. She wiped her hands on her apron as she went to answer it. It was Rosemary Perkins; her next-door neighbor bringing Michele home from school. Her daughter and Rosemary's little girl were in the same pre-school class. The women took turns picking up each other's child.

"Thanks Rose," Sierra said after kissing Michele on her head.

"Oh of course hon. See you tomorrow Shelly," Rosemary spoke in her thick Boston accent.

Sierra locked the door and helped her daughter out of her backpack.

"How was your day mom?" Michele asked.

Sierra giggled, "It was fine honey. You hungry? I'm making chili."

"Mmmm. Can I have a cookie?"

"A cookie? I say I made your favorite chili and you want a cookie?"

"One cookie first, please?"

"Okay, okay but only one."

Late night after the children were fed and tucked into bed, Sierra ran herself a hot bubble bath. She lit a couple candles and set them around her tub. She tuned into late night slow jams on the radio. Sierra took her Bible from the nightstand and slid into the tub amongst the bubbles. She laid back and relaxed as she re-read Matthew. She reminded herself to say a prayer for Nate, her best friend. She truly loved him and felt that she'd always loved him, even before she knew him. It was instantaneous and would last forever. They shared everything with one another but Sierra felt like this time Nate was hiding something from her and she couldn't keep him on the phone long enough to find out what it was.

When she felt that she was going to doze off in the water she set her Bible down and quickly bathed. She climbed out of the tub and wrapped a large bath towel around her dripping wet body. She picked up her Bible and blew her candles out before exiting to the bedroom. She turned the radio off and grabbed her housecoat from the edge of the bed and wrapped it around her body. Sierra searched through her drawer for a tattered, worn bra and panties to wear beneath her nightgown, which was slung over the back of a chair. She removed her robe and shimmied into her gown. She was making herself more comfortable beneath her sheet and quilt when the telephone rang. It was just after midnight and Sierra assumed it to be Nate and quickly answered but was instead greeted by an unfamiliar feminine voice.

"Who is this?" Sierra asked timidly.

"Sierra my name is Victoria Hart and I'm a friend of Darryl's."

"A friend? Is something wrong with Darryl?"

"No, no Darryl is fine, just fine."

"Then I don't understand, what do you want?"

There was a long silence as if Victoria didn't know what to say, Sierra waited patiently, "Okay Sierra, I don't know you and you don't know me but I'm going to be very blunt. I want your husband."

"What?" Sierra felt as if her stomach had reached up and grabbed her heart and was strangling it.

"Look, you don't really want him, you can't possibly."

"What would lead you to believe that?"

"C'mon, you know as good as I do that your marriage ain't working. Hell if it was he wouldn't be sleeping me. Or maybe if you gave him some him he never woulda started"

"You don't know what you're talking about."

"So you and your husband make love at night?"

"Well no but-"

"But nothin', you keep your nose buried so deep in your fucking Bible you can't make time to screw your man!"

"You don't understand and it's none of your business anyway."

"Listen Sierra, just do us all a favor and divorce him. Move on, you're married to Jesus anyway, let Darryl be happy at least."

"You bitch!" Sierra clasped her hand over her mouth and slammed the phone back into its cradle. She sat fuming, chewing her bottom lip, reflecting on the conversation she'd just had with Darryl's mistress. Darryl's mistress. There was no longer any denying it, he was definitely cheating. Sierra sat feeling dumb and inferior. She wanted to cry but she could not. She instead picked up her Bible and quickly flipped through the pages seeking scriptures to console her.

11 Mike

The expression on Mike's face portrayed that of sincere interest in what Reginald and Bradley were advising him about the case Samantha Falls was trying to build against him. In reality his thoughts were outside of the office and further away. They were deep, deep in South Dade. They were revolving somewhere around the Liberty City projects and some of his childhood homegirls and their violent behavior. Visions of a battered blond bimbo danced in his head.

"So you understand? Michael?" Brad spoke.

"Huh? Yes, yes sir. I understand," Mike answered.

"And you maintain that Ms. Falls' allegations are unfounded?" Brad asked.

Mike's cheeks became red hot instantly with anger and irritation. He knew the real reason why Bradley Klein was pressing this so hard. Rumor around the office had it that Bradley and Samantha had been sleeping together. Bradley Klein was an undercover racist and Mike realized that. He knew Brad hated the thought of this big black Haitian nigger touching Sam's pure white flesh. The thought that Brad was discomforted at the thought of Sam's precious little mouth being wrapped around Mike's Mandingo penis caused Mike to snicker inside but he kept his expression stern when he replied to Brad.

"Brad, those allegations are unfounded."

Bradley leaned back in his chair and folded his hand atop his knee. He maintained direct eye contact with Mike who refused to blink. Bradley would not believe Mike's story. In his mind he felt that if Samantha said he did something then it must be true. Black men were like that, they lusted after white women and a foreign nigger was worse than a domestic nigger. Reginald, sensing the tension between Mike and Brad, cleared his throat to get the two men's attention.

"Okay gentlemen, we will end it here. Brad if I may have another moment of your time. Michael I suppose you're done for the day so I'll see you in the morning and I'll be sure to keep you posted, okay?"

"Sure," Mike answered trying hard to continue to fake an upbeat attitude, "You gentlemen have a good evening."

Mike walked back to his office calmly and softly closed the door behind him. He roughly snatched his jacket off and threw it across his desk. He sat in his chair fuming, tapping his foot vigorously. He thought to call Nate but he'd been behaving so shady lately that he didn't expect he'd be of any assistance. He turned in his seat and gazed out of the window and at the world below. He counted the cars driving Southbound. It was a practice of his since childhood, it soothed him and he needed soothing right now. If not he was afraid that he would hurt someone and that someone would be Bradley Klein or Samantha Falls, whichever he caught first. He felt the tension in his body begin to dissipate, his muscles relaxed and he leaned back into the chair. He tapped his fingers on his desktop and stared at the clear sky searching for some sort of settling thoughts or memories. He wished for a quiet place in his mind where he could retreat when his life was turned upside down. All he could ever find was chaos, the same chaos from his tainted past that spilled forward and affected his present life. Feeling himself slip into the depressing vibe of his childhood he quickly shook it off and returned to his tough "thugged-out" exterior.

Mike turned back to face his desk and the blueprints on top of it. He stared at the plans sinking back into his personal sorrow. He considered the blueprint of his own life and how if the person in charge had made just a few minor adjustments he may have turned out to be a more stable and secure person who made much wiser decisions. He shook his head back and forth a couple times and reached for the telephone on his desk. He dialed Nate's phone number and waited not expecting him to actually pick up.

"What's up man?" Nate asked from the other end hastily.

"Aaawww nigga do know how to work the phone, ha?"

"Man don't start with me please."

"Don't start? Nigga what happened to you? We was supposed to meet for lunch yesterday," Mike instantly felt like a punk after he made his comment.

"I'm sorry, I was busy. You know how it is."

"Yea, whateva nigga. So what's goin' on t'nite? Let's hookup at Hooters or sumthin'. I need a drank, a nigga stressed over here."

"I'm sorry Mike, can't do it. Not tonight."

"Man wassup wit' you? You ain't got time for nobody no mo'?"

"There's nothing up, I just have a lot of work to do."

"Bullshit man, you ain't even-"

"Look Mike I'm sorry, I gotta go," Nate disconnected the line.

"No dis nigga didn't," Mike mumbled.

Mike slammed the phone down, his anger returning. He pushed away from the desk and jumped to his feet. He snatched his suit jacket from the desktop and vigorously put it back on his body. He gathered his plans and briefcase and car keys and headed out the door. He paused and rolled his eyes to the back of his head when he saw Bradley Klein waiting for the elevator. Mike strolled to the elevator and stood beside him being sure to look as intimidating as possible. He and Bradley nodded at one another and waited. Out of the corner of his eye Mike witnessed Bradley looking around. He knew that Brad was hoping that someone else would come along and join the two of them on the elevator. Unfortunately for him it was well past normal business hours and though it was quite possible it was highly unlikely that anyone would be joining them.

The doors opened and the two men stepped inside. Mike stood upright, his back straight with a look of insolence on his face. He was sure to stand within arms length of Bradley. He chuckled inside at Brad's obvious discomfort. When the two men reached the parking garage they nodded once again and parted ways, Bradley moving at an unusually rushed pace. Once he was out of sight, Mike laughed out loud. He was proud of the terror that he'd inflicted in one of his superiors without needing to lay a hand on him. He pushed the button on his keyless remote as he approached his car. Mike stopped suddenly only steps away from the vehicle. His plans and briefcase slipped from his fingers. He ran to his car and looked it over. There were no signs of keying this time though his passenger window was shattered and a brick had landed in his seat.

"Got-damn!" Mike exclaimed at the top of his lungs. He slammed his hand on the hood of the car in a rage of fury. He muttered incoherently under his breath as he leaned against the car. Realizing how hopeless the situation was he pushed off of the vehicle and gathered his belongings from the filthy ground and climbed behind the steering wheel. He peeled out of the garage and sped toward home, as it was too late in the evening to take his car into the dealership. He was forced to hold off until morning.

Mike slammed the door of his condominium and tossed his things onto the sofa. He jerked his tie loose and went into his bedroom to undress. He unbuttoned his shirt and sat on the edge of the bed, his face in his palms. He wondered who could be responsible for damaging his car repeatedly. Samantha flashed through his mind though he was positive it could not be her. It just wasn't her style. Suing him for sexual harassment was her style. Still and all she had become a thorn in his side and he had to do something to make himself feel better. He picked up the phone and called Sherika.

"Wassup my nigga?" she answered.

"Ain't nuthin'. Whut you into right now?" Mike asked between sucking his teeth.

"Nuttin', why wassup?"

"I know you remember that white hoe I was dealin' wit'."

"Yea, what about that bitch?"

"I want you and Reesie an' nem to whop that hoe ass."

"Whut? Mr. Biniss man ready to mix a l'il mo pleasure wit' his biniss?"

"Man fuck that shit, where them bitches at?"

"You know I'm down black but my girls ain't back from Tampa yet. I'a stomp a hole in that bitch by my lonesome tho', wassup?"

"Nah, nah, playgirl, chill out. When they gone be back?"

"In the mo'nin' sometime."

"Aiight when they get back organize that shit and hit me up an' I'a tell you what to do."

"Aiight then holla."

Mike was out of bed and on his way out of the door bright and early on Friday morning. He needed to drop his car at the Lexus dealer. He'd asked his cousin Jean to meet him there to drive him to Alamo to pick up a rental car. He declined the Lexus loaner. He wanted to drive an inconspicuous vehicle to see if the culprit was stalking him or if she just knew his car and where he worked. He parked on the streets in plain view of the general public. If he were being followed he'd clearly be seen exiting a red Ford Taurus. He bumped into Samantha as he headed for his office. His first thought was to grab her by her pretty blond hair and throw her against the wall and pummel her but he denied that desire. He had plans for Ms. Falls. He enjoyed the fear that was vivid in her eyes at the sight of him, he relished it. He smiled and said a simple "good morning" not stopping long enough for her to respond. Once behind the security of his office door he laughed viciously at Samantha's fate.

It was a quarter past two when Sherika called Mike's cell phone. She informed him that the women he'd requested were back and awaiting instructions. Sick excitement was clear in her voice. Mike instructed her to gather the women and be in front of his office no later than 4:30. He described to them Samantha's car and advised that she should follow her as soon as she pulled out of the parking garage. The rest required no instructions. After they'd finished plotting their devious plan Mike set down his cellular phone and picked up his office line and called Nate. There again was no answer.

It wasn't until after six when Mike left the office for the day. Though he wasn't actually busy and could have easily gotten out much earlier he chose to stay later than necessary. He made sure that his presence in the office was known as it became later in the evening particularly after Samantha had left for the day. He did not want her to be able to connect him with the ass whipping he was sure she'd received by now. He hoped that Sherika had done her job; he was still awaiting her phone call. As he walked to his rental car, which remained unscathed, his phone finally rang.

"What's up dog?" Nate greeted.

"Oh you didn't forget a nigga phone numba!"

"Come on now Michael, don't start."

"Michael?" Mike mumbled dumbfounded. At that moment his call waiting signaled, "Ay nigga hold on and don't hang up."

"Alright, alright."

"Hello?" he answered the second line.

"It's done," Sherika said out of breath, "You won't be seein' that bitch for awhile."

"Straight, you did good l'il momma. She didn't see you did she?"

"Naw, naw I got up in there but she ain't see my face."

"Ay Imma hit you back."

"Aiight."

Mike switched back to Nate, "So wassup my nigga, why so distant?"

"Just got a lot going on right now, man you have to forgive me."

"Ay well why we don't hook up t'nite, hit da G-spot or sumthin'?"

"Naw man I don't know about that."

"Aawww nigga c'mon. We ain't chilled in damn near a month. I'm in a good mood; all I need is a few dranks in my system and some new pussy by my side."

"I don't know-"

"Bump that nigga you ridin'. Just got paid, it's Friday night, my dick hard and there plenty bitches ready to choke dis mu'fucka. Meet me at my crib at about twelve. Oh but you gotta drive 'cause my Lex in the shop."

"Again? What happened this time?"

"Shiit, long story. I'a tell you tonight tho."

"Alright Mike, later."

"Ay Nate dog, don't play me my nigga."

"I will be there."

"Yea," Mike disconnected and climbed into his rental. He turned his nose up disgusted at the idea of having to be seen in such an average vehicle.

He was anxious to hear the details of Sherika's fury. Mike phoned her as soon as he made it home. As she described how she beat, kicked and scratched Samantha's pretty little face Mike rummaged through his sock drawer until he found a small piece of folded aluminum foil. He sat at the kitchenette table and poured himself a glass of Remy Martin and began cutting the cocaine he took from the tin foil into lines. He snorted the three lines and leaned back in his chair sipping his alcohol as Sherika spoke. Mike's spirits continued to increase as the drug took its effect and the conversation carried on.

After the two finished Mike staggered to the bathroom, a lit joint dangling from his lips. He made a stopover at the toilet to cleanse his colon before putting out his Black & Mild and climbing into a warm shower. His penis began to stiffen under the warm water. He needed sex but didn't want it from Sherika or anyone he'd ever been with previously. He was anxious to get into the streets. He dried his body and stood naked with the exception of the towel that was wrapped around his waist while looking through the massive amounts of clothes hanging inside his closet. He found a pair of black jeans and an unworn brand name black tee. He dangled a platinum cross around his neck and slipped a large platinum and diamond ring onto his pinky. He was fully dressed and puffing on the remains of his drug when the doorman rang announcing that Nate was in the lobby. Mike smashed the joint into an ashtray on the coffee table, grabbed his keys and wallet and headed downstairs to meet him.

"Wassup my nigga?" Mike said as he climbed in the passenger side of Nate's car.

"Nothing much."

"Wassup wit' you and Mya?" Mike asked as if he really cared.

"We're doing alright. Why's your car on lockdown again?"

"Man, some bitch bust my passenger window."

"Damn, you know who it is?"

"Nigga if I knew who that bitch was I probably wouldn't even be free to tell you this shit!"

The club was packed, hot and musty when Nate and Mike arrived which was normal for a Friday night in a Miami club. The two men shared a couple words with a familiar bouncer and were allowed inside without needing to wait in the ridiculously long line. Mike walked directly to the bar and bought himself and Nate a bottle of Courvoisier. The two had VIP accessibility but due to the structure of the club they chose to get comfortable on the second level. Mike sat back on the sofa and lusted after a young woman dancing nearby. He watched her round rear wind to the rhythmic beats of the reggae music playing. He reached over and gently took her fingers and led her to him. She willingly moved her winding to between his legs to entertain him. It didn't take long for them to go through their bottle especially with a third party assisting. Mike tried to convince Nate to go back to the bar for another bottle but he was too relaxed and refused. Drunk and high, Mike excused himself from the young woman and walked to the bar. After he'd ordered and received a new bottle he walked back toward the small sofa he'd previously occupied with Nate. He was looking down at the change in his hand when he accidentally bumped into another man.

"Pardon me, my nigga," he said not looking up.

"Motherfucker," the man said stopping in Mike's path.

"What the -?" Mike looked up at a man who must've been at least 6'5" and 300 lbs. He tilted his head for a better view. He recognized him to be the husband of Erin Washington, a young woman he'd spent time with occasionally, "Aawww, you Erin's nigga huh?"

"Erin's husband."

"Aw my bad, Erin's husband. You say that shit like you proud. Well, Erin's husband you wanna step outta my way?"

"Fuck you nigga!"

"You wanna do sumthin'?" Mike challenged, bravely stepping closer to the large man.

Noticing something wasn't quite right, Nate jumped from his seat and charged to Mike's side, "Ay what's going on here?"

"Mind yo' own biniss nigga less you wanna get da same beat down, dis nigaa phenna get," the man spat at Nate.

Nate looked him over and sucked his teeth. He turned his back to him and faced Mike, "Come on dog. I don't know what happened but let it go," Nate tried to reason.

"I'a tell you wassup my nigga, this bitch trippin' 'cause a nigga hit his ol' girl. You know the rules of pimpin' nigga, I gotta school you?"

"Nigga what?" big man swung his fist but Mike ducked and pulled the champagne bottle from the ice bucket and slammed it across the side of the man's head.

"Fight!" someone called out as Mike and Nate tried their best to take down a man at least twice their size. Every ounce of frustration in Mike's being he pounded into the husband of one of his previous encounters. Security made their way through the crowd and began the painstaking task of separating the men. They were successful in getting them to the first floor with fists and blood flying. However two men who'd come to the club with Erin's husband recognized him as being in the center of the brawl and stepped in instigating it further. It was quite difficult and nearly impossible but security managed to get the men outdoors where backup police were pulling up. The bouncer who'd let Nate and Mike inside quickly pulled them aside and out of view of the police and their interrogators.

"Man what the hell is going on?" the bouncer asked angrily.

"That nigga a hoe man, fuck that punk ass nigga," Mike answered blowing off the situation.

"Nate?"

"I gotta back my dog Greg, you know how that goes."

Greg the bouncer shook his head back and forth, "Stay here. I'll be back. Mike don't start *no* shit!"

Once Greg was out of view Nate turned his attention to Mike, "What the hell is wrong with you?"

"Nigga who you thank you hollerin' at?"

"Man you're not going to keep dragging me into this shit. You need to leave other peoples pussy alone for you get us both killed. As a matter of fact you need to cut this shit out all together, you too got-damn old for this!"

Mike stared at Nate dumbfounded before he responded, "Nigga whut you my mammy now? Huh? Just 'cause you bitched up and proposed to that European trick you want me to tuck my dick and bow down to some fuckin' piece o' pussy? That shit ain't phenna happen so you can x that shit dirty!"

"Man screw you Mike," Nate walked away with Mike on his heels, "So you wanna pull it with me now?" he asked without turning around to face Mike.

Mike chewed the inside of his mouth, glaring at the back of Nate's head, his fists clenched, "Man take yo' pussy ass home to that bitch."

Nate walked out the front door while Mike headed back to the bar. He was sipping on a Long Island Iced Tea when he spotted the young woman who'd been giving him the lap dance before the commotion began. He pulled her to him and whispered in her ear. She laughed out loud and nodded. Mike gulped down his drink and set the plastic cup on the bar. The young woman who'd introduced herself as Kelly followed Mike outside the club. They made small talk on a bench in front before Mike guided her to a secluded area. Kelly protested slightly when Mike eased his hand up her short skirt and caressed her nearly naked rear. When he stuffed his tongue into her mouth and guided her hand to massage the swelling in the front of his jeans she relaxed. He unzipped the jeans allowing Kelly access to his stiff penis, which she pulled out before sliding her body down the length of his until she could circle it with her tongue. At that very moment Mike's cellular vibrated inside his pocket.

"Hello?" he answered, his voice gruff.

"Hey Mike, this Janay. You busy?"

"Yea," he said clearly out of breath.

"Well we need to talk."

"What, what you want Janay?"

"Mike, I'm pregnant."

"Congratulations."

"Same to you since it's yours."

"Man, don't be callin' me wit' this bullshit."

"So what you tryin' to say you ain't gone take care of your responsibility?"

"Nay, I ain't got time for this bullshit. Call the nigga responsible," Mike closed the phone and replaced it in his back pocket. He relaxed his body and allowed Kelly to work her oral magic.

12Nate

I sat quietly on the edge of the bed staring blankly out the window before me. My mind and the thoughts occupying its space were in a million different places at once. My mood which had only a short time ago been that of pleasurable bliss had now suddenly transformed into one of anxiety followed by discomfort and unhappiness. The bed shifted under the weight of my new lover as he moved. My lover. I felt a sense of discomfort with that thought but I made no effort to change my reality. The reality of which was that for the first time I had a "lover", a "partner", whatever you want to call it, and it was a male.

I glanced at my wristwatch for the umpteenth time. It was now past eleven pm and naturally was not getting any earlier. Mya had finally stopped ringing my phone or maybe she hadn't stopped. I'd turned it off. I wouldn't further disrespect either of them by speaking with the other while in each others presence. I mustered up all of the courage within me and eased from the bed being careful not to disturb Anthony who was asleep. I felt around in the dark apartment for my clothes and dressed silently. My keys were on the nightstand beside him. I tried to continue my ritual of silence but the darkness of the room made it difficult to do so. My hand bumped an ashtray, which fell off of the edge; its crash to the floor below muffled by the cushion of the carpet.

Anthony shifted under the sheet. I paused for a moment watching for his next move hoping not to awaken him. It wasn't so much that I really cared about disturbing him, what I didn't want was to hear him asking me to stay the night. I secured the keys and crept quietly to the studio apartment door, it creaked as I opened it and light tried to force its way in.

"Nathaniel?" Anthony half whispered.

"Yes Anthony?" I sighed leaning into the door.

"Can't you stay just a little while longer?"

"You know I can't Anthony, Mya's already worried."

"Fuck that bitch! You know I'm not going to keep putting up with this shit!"

"You can threaten me all you want Anthony but remember it was you who pursued me knowing I was engaged to her and I thank you not to speak of her that way."

"Yea whateva. Lock the door behind you," he said bitterly and buried his face back into the pillow. I cut my eyes at him and left not locking the door behind me.

I sat in the driveway staring up at the house when I finally returned home. Mya was still awake and waiting for me. Though all of the lights were off I still had that suspicion and I wasn't really ready to hear it. I took a deep breath and slowly made my way out of the car and to the front door. I unlocked the door and eased inside as quietly as possible. I hadn't taken two steps down the hall and toward the stairwell before Mya appeared out of the darkness. She stood before me with her arms folded swishing the wine around in the glass in her hand. She tapped her foot rapidly against the tile floor. She swayed slightly giving away the fact that she'd been drinking most of the night. In between her fingers a cigarette burned. I made an effort to walk past her but she sidestepped directly into my path.

"So you finally decided to leave the arms of your bitch and come home to me?" she said with venom in her voice.

"Mya please, I'm tired and not in the mood to argue."

"Well too bad Nathaniel because you see I have been waiting up all night to speak with you and am not the least bit exhausted you son of a bitch! Do you realize what time it is? You've been gone all day and all night and now you don't want to talk about it? Have you lost your mind?" she slurred her accented tongue.

"Look Mya you're drunk and I'm tired and-"

"I don't wanna hear that shit Nathaniel!" Mya lunged her glass of wine at my head but I ducked and it smashed into the wall behind me.

"What the hell is the matter with you?"

"Yes, wonderful, Nathaniel, you stay out all night and day screwing around and something's the matter with me."

"You knew I'd be coming home late, I told you, I called you and told you."

"Who is it? And don't give me that crap about needing some time alone," she put her cigarette to her lips and puffed.

"It's no one, I'm a little overworked and pressured that's all."

"Don't lie to me! You know how sick of this lying I'm getting? You're becoming so un-fucking-believable! What is going on with you Nathaniel? Huh? You're shunning me, you're shunning your friends and you leave with no explanation for anyone!"

"Listen I'm not going to stand here and listen to this."

"Sure Nathaniel, run away! That's all you know how to do these days is run away!"

I could hear the tears stuck in the back of her throat as she cursed me and the Earth I walked on. I should have tried to embrace her and look for some words of reassurance but I couldn't or maybe I just didn't feel like it. I turned my back and walked out of the front door with Mya at my heels pleading for me not to go. I debated the issue but my mind was made up, "I need some air Mya."

"You were out all night and didn't get enough air?"

"Yea whatever, don't wait up!"

I screeched out of the driveway with Mya yelling pleas and profanities behind me. I didn't hesitate to take off toward the highway and speed at 100mph with no real destination in mind. When I came upon Sunrise Ave I exited and drove eastbound until I could drive no longer. I found myself a parking space on the oceanfront far from the action. I popped the trunk and reached in and began to stroll along the slim sidewalk. It was a peaceful night; the scent of the saltwater and the sound of the waves lapping against each other were soothing. I wandered slowly across the sand carrying a half empty gallon bottle of gin at my side. I found a dark, quiet, lonely corner and fell to the sandy earth below. I opened the bottle and turned it up; it burned my throat going down. I closed my eyes tight and turned it up again.

Slowly I began to feel myself drift away to a place where the pain was less and less. I'd begun drinking more often to dull the pain I was feeling inside. I wasn't sure how my life, my world had been so completely turned around in such a ridiculously short amount of time. Just a few short months ago everything was as it should have been, my life in complete control. I'd proposed to Mya, planning a baby, living a life that my father was proud of. And now my life was in shambles, the punch-line to a cruel joke; it became more of a lie than it had ever been before. I'm cheating on Mya with Anthony. It hurt to admit but I couldn't stop. She sits home drowning her sorrows in a bottle of wine while I'm interlocked beneath sheets with this man and I cannot tell her, I cannot tell anyone. I'm hurting her day by day, evening by night with no ready explanation; I can barely explain it to myself. It's just that when I am with Anthony something else takes over me and I forget who I am or who I'm supposed to be, what role in life I should be playing. But when it's over and reality resumes then I spend each moment in a regretful state of confusion.

I sat staring out at the ocean as far as it extended or as far as my eyes could see, whichever it was. I'd dozed into a drunken stooper for at least two hours before I pulled myself together enough to drive home. Mya was asleep; an empty wine bottle was at her side in the bed. I almost tripped over the bottle that had been tossed in the middle of the floor. I staggered to the queen-sized bed and fell into it and into sleep fully clothed.

I was in bed alone still fully dressed when I awoke the following morning. My head was spinning and I was going to be late for work. I felt around for the cordless receiver trying not to lift my head too high as it felt like the insides were loose and rattling around. I called my office and advised my secretary that I wasn't feeling well but would be in within the next two hours. I managed to make my way out of bed and pop three aspirin and take a cold shower. Holding my forehead in my palm I wobbled down the stairwell and into the kitchen. Mya was sitting at the table in her business suit sipping what I figured to be sugar free black coffee. She was reading the Wall Street Journal while the small color television on the counter played the early morning news.

"Good morning," I grumbled, she didn't respond to me. I poured myself a mug of coffee and dumped one spoonful of sugar in and stirred before taking a seat across the table from her. My head was still swirling and I prayed that she would continue to keep her mouth shut.

"Sleep well?"

No such luck, "No, not at all."

"So where'd you go last night?"

"To the beach."

"With whom?"

"No one."

The silence returned. Mya downed her coffee and stood to put her mug in the sink. The skirt she wore was very short and her well-toned runner's legs were bare. I turned my attention to the television and an image of Starr Jones. She peered back at me and rolled her eyes but I shrugged it off. She walked out of the kitchen but quickly turned on her heels and came back to face me.

"Why do you do this to me?" she asked.

"I'm sorry," I answered.

"Sorry just doesn't quite cut it Nathaniel. I love you so much it hurts and I would like to know what I've done wrong. I'm standing before you with so much cleavage showing and a skirt so short you could get away with taking my picture for Playboy and you look right through me like I'm wearing a flannel nightgown and avocado mask! You don't come home and don't want to be home when you are home. You would like me to believe that you are not cheating on me yet you can't seem to give me a suitable explanation for your actions."

"I'm sorry honey, you're right. I've been selfish, there's no excuse. But I'm under a lot of mental pressure right now. I just need to sort some things out on my own."

"Well baby talk to me please," she begged. Tears were welling up in her eyes. She knelt between my thighs and searched my eyes for something to make everything right. Feeling self-conscious that she may find the truth of my guilt and infidelities I averted my eyes.

"Come here," I pulled her into my chest and held her tight while she sobbed onto my shoulder, "I'll try to make this right Mya, I promise. Listen, how about Saturday we put all of our work aside and just spend the day together like we used to."

"Promise me," she asked more than demanded through muffled tears.

"I promise, now you better get to the office before Amy runs your business into the ground," I pulled her lips to mine and kissed her as passionately as I possibly could but there was no longer any feeling. I was afraid she sensed it when she pulled away from me with a strange look on her face. But she quickly followed it with a soft smile and final peck on the lips. She stood and grabbed her briefcase and walked out of the front door.

Mya and I made plans to go to the museum on Saturday afternoon. Things in my home had finally been back to normal at least for two days. No swearing, no yelling, no drinking. I was sure my neighbors were relieved that their property value was not going to decrease after all. I stood in the kitchen fixing myself a turkey and cheese sandwich while I waited for Mya to finish getting dressed when my cellular phone rang. It was Anthony. I sighed reluctant to answer the call.

"Hello Anthony," I answered.

"Damn man, what are you still upset with me?"

"Naw, naw of course not. What's going on? How are you?"

"I'm good but I'll be better when you get here. When can I expect you?"

"Huh? You're expecting me? I'm sorry, did we have plans?"

"Uhh, yea. We're supposed to have lunch and then go to the auto show."

"Oh damn I forgot. Hey can we cancel? I'll try to make it up to you next week."

"No way man, I've been looking forward to this for three weeks now. We made plans, I bought tickets and everything, it's a done deal."

"Take someone else."

"I don't want to take someone else, I want to take my man."

I cringed at the reference to me as his man, "I'm sorry, I promised Mya-"

"You also promised me three weeks ago and this is a big deal to me. And I'm not going to-"

"Okay, okay got-dammit okay I'll cancel with her and be there around noon."

"Alright."

"Alright, bye," frustrated I slammed the phone onto the counter just as Mya walked in the kitchen, a cigarette dangling from her lips as she dried her hair with a large bath towel.

"What's the matter babe?" she asked.

I was momentarily amazed at her ability to keep the cigarette from hitting the floor when she spoke, "Nothing, nothing just, uh, work calling."

"Well what did they want?"

"They uh, they want me to come in, they need me to come in and uh check out some purchases."

"What did they say when you told them no? You did tell them no, didn't you?"

I absorbed the expression on her face and felt small in her presence. I felt ashamed of myself for the lies I'd told and was continuing to tell, yet I couldn't seem to find my way out of the hole that I was digging.

"I-I couldn't, I'm going to have to go in."

"Oh this is bullshit Nathaniel," Mya snatched the towel from her head and smacked it against the island, "Well, you can just call *work* back and tell them no can do, you have plans."

"Mya I can't do that-"

"The hell you can't! What, are you just going to break a promise you made to me? Does your word mean anything anymore?"

"Of course it does, you just have to understand-"

"Understand what Nathaniel? I understand that you're constantly lying to me, what else do I need to understand? I understand that was not your fucking job calling you!"

My cell phone began to ring again. I tried to ignore it but Mya pushed for me to answer it. I answered and immediately disconnected but it rang again, "Hello?" I answered becoming angry.

"Well damn, what's wrong with you?" Anthony asked from the other end of the phone line.

"I apologize, I will be their shortly Diane," I spoke calmly trying to convince Mya I was speaking to my secretary.

"Diane? What's going on?" I heard Anthony ask before I hung up on him.

"That wasn't Diane! Who was it?" Mya charged at me in an attempt to take my phone, which was ringing again.

"Mya stop. Stop," I pleaded becoming angered and annoyed with the persistent ringing, "Got-dammit just stop!" I slung my phone past Mya's head full force and it shattered against the wall behind her. Mya froze in her position, her mouth shut with eyes wide. The obnoxious ringing was no more. Beads of sweat popped up on my forehead and my muscles tensed. My breathing was rapid and my flesh red hot, "I'm sick and I'm tired of all this shit. Why can't y'all let me breath? Huh?"

Mya jumped in fear. She was seeing a side of me she'd never before seen, "I gotta get outta here."

I snatched my keys from the table and charged toward the front door. Mya chased behind me tugging at my shirt but I snatched away from her in fury. I struggled against her, trying to open the door while she tried to keep me away from it.

"Please Nathaniel, please don't go! Baby please," Mya begged, tears rolling down her cheeks.

"Mya stop it," I snatched away from her grip and opened the front door. I paused and looked back at her; she stood in the doorway covering her mouth with her hands as her tears streamed uncontrollably. But I couldn't stay; I walked to my car with Mya screaming for me to please come back. Neighbors and their children looked on in shock and disgust. I sped out of our normally quiet neighborhood to the parking lot of the nearest liquor store and there purchased a fifth of Jack Daniels. Back inside my car I cracked it open and turned it up. I held my nose and drank until the bottle was half empty. The fire from the alcohol burned within my chest cavity but that did not stop me from drinking more and more until the contents were no more.

I held the bottle in front of me taking in its emptiness. I tossed it on the floor beside me and sank back into the seat, tears welled up in my eyes and I cried. In the privacy of my car behind dark tint I released all the pain in my soul through a waterfall of tears. I felt like a punk, a sissy, soft. Hell I was a soft punk sissy, I needed to face it. I sit in my car crying and I sleep with a man a couple times a week, that's exactly what I am and my father not to mention Mike would kill me if any of it ever came to light. I slammed my fist against the steering wheel and went back inside the liquor store to buy a bottle of gin.

I stumbled through Sierra's front door sometime in the middle of the night. I didn't know what time it was nor could I recall what had happened between that bottle of gin and that moment. Sierra helped me inside and sat me down on the sofa. She went to the kitchen and returned with a hot mug of black coffee which she forced me to sip on in an attempt to sober me up. I looked into Sierra's eyes; there was so much love in them yet so much neglect in her home. I wished I could love her, could feel for her the way a man should feel for a beautiful, wonderful woman. I wished that life hadn't dealt me the cards that it had and I could be her husband and her children could be mine. All I ever wanted was to make her happy but I knew I couldn't ever make her truly happy by trying to be more than just her friend. Tears welled up again, Sierra wrapped her arms around me and she comforted me.

"What's wrong honey?" she asked. Her tone was filled with fear. I knew that she too wanted to cry for me but she hadn't the ability.

"Si-Si, I'm…I'm," I opened my mouth to confess my sexual sin, my infidelities, my unforgivable lies and betrayal, my inner feelings. I wanted her to, for the first time in our relationship know the real me and at the same time clear some of this baggage, take some of this heavy load off of my soul, "Sierra, I'm uh-"

"What is it Nate? You know you can tell me anything."

"Nothing, never mind."

"Please baby, if you can't tell me then at least tell someone cause it's obvious whatever it is it's too much for you to handle on your own. Baby if you can't turn to man then please turn to the Lord but turn."

"I love you," I said smiling up at her.

"I love you too."

She held me in her arms and stroked the side of my face. She'd love me no matter what and I knew that. She rocked me and she loved me for exactly who I was, into the night.

Sierra & Nate Meet

The noise in the sixth period classroom could easily be heard down the hall. Students who were clearly excited to be reunited once again gossiped and shared their experiences and summertime adventures. Nate entered the room wearing a pair of dark blue sagging jogging pants with a North Carolina tee shirt. He bounced a basketball between his legs quietly staring ahead, not focused on anyone or anything else in particular. He didn't miss a beat in his dribbling and his female peers didn't miss a beat in watching him.

"Hey Nate," one chimed in rising from her seat to reveal a skirt much too skimpy for a high school classroom.

"What's up Tonya? What's with the skirt?" Nate asked continuing to bounce the ball in rhythm.

"You like it?"

"I guess it's cool if you're easy. You easy Tonya?" Nate asked looking directly into her eyes, already fully aware of the true answer to his question. He smiled to himself inside as she shifted with embarrassment.

"Oh forget you Nate, you so crazy," she attempted to play off her embarrassment with weak artificial laughter. She pretended as if her girlfriend's laughter did not bother her though she really wanted to run and hide.

Nate grinned, showing off pearly white teeth hidden behind sexy full lips that drove the young girls wild. They went crazy over him but kept it to themselves. Secretly they assessed their friend's appearance in search of flaws that may put them ahead of the rest in Nate's eyes.

"You know I'm just messing with you girl," Nate said as he turned to walk away. He caught his ball under his arm and grazed his free hand across the young woman's rear end. Her previous embarrassment fled immediately and she was left with an odd sense of power over her peers as they looked on with envy.

Nate took a seat near the back of the class by a slightly opened window. He stared out of it anxious for the period to end so he could get to the local playground for a good game of street basketball.

"Oiga que vamos otra vez."

"Huh?" Nate said turning to face the cute young woman who'd silently taken a seat beside him.

"I said oiga que vamos otra vez. It means here we go again," there was an awkward silence shared between the two, "I'm Sierra Mitchell."

"I'm-"

"Nathaniel Marshall, I know. Who doesn't know who you are? Besides we've been in the same Spanish class for the past two years."

Sierra smiled at Nate, her smile was genuine. She didn't want anything from him and Nate sensed it. He felt good inside as she spoke to him, which also gave him an odd sensation. He felt bad that he hadn't recognized her,

"Don't feel bad," Sierra continued, "I have a tendency to be quiet most of the time. I generally like to keep to myself but I decided that this year would be different. This year I would speak to at least one person in each of my classes, one person that stood out to me and well, you stood out.... to me."

Sierra shifted uncomfortably. Nate simply looked at her speak without contributing anything to make it a conversation. She wished she'd never begun this new routine. She wasn't sure what she was trying to prove with it anyway. She couldn't really expect that she'd suddenly meet and make new friends in her third year of high school. Sierra chewed her bottom lip and shifted around trying to find the best way to get her out of this mess.

"I like that," Nate finally piped up.

"What?"

"What you're trying to do. Expand your horizons so to speak by setting out to meet new people. I admire that."

"Thank you," Sierra responded shyly.

"You're very welcome. You're not like these other females in this school are you?"

"Well, I don't know. I guess not."

"Nah, you're not. That's good, never change that."

The two smiled at each other feeling comfortable in one another's presence. Their moment was brought to a halt when Señor De La Cruz stepped inside and silenced the entire class with his announcement of, "Comencemos," which translated means, let us begin....

13 Sierra

Sierra carefully pulled a hot pan of blueberry muffins from the oven and gently set them on the stovetop. She lifted the top from the pot of boiling cabbage and stuck a fork inside. She took the utensil to her mouth and tasted. She nodded her approval and turned the heat off from beneath it. Bebe and Cece Winans voices flowed smoothly through the small stereo speakers. She hummed along feeling good. Today her spirits were high and she wouldn't allow anything to bring her down. Her baby sister Lillian was returning to where she needed to be. She and her mother together put the finishing touches on a large lunch prepared in honor of Lilly's return. Mrs. Mitchell got her gospel groove on as she set the table for eight. Cousin Junior had gone to pick Lillian up from the airport and a couple other excited relatives would be joining them for the welcome home feast. Sierra and her mother together sat potatoes, corn, pork chops, baked macaroni and cheese and more on the beautiful table.

Sierra checked on her children who were sitting quietly in the family room with her father. Jennifer was curled up in her granddad's arm sucking her two middle fingers as they watched the cartoon version of *Joseph, King of Dreams*. She assessed their appearance without actually disturbing them or making her presence known. Since they were still clean and neat she relaxed and headed to the guest bathroom to fix herself up.

Though Lilly was only her sister, Sierra felt a sense of nervousness as she freshened up. She hadn't seen her baby sis in a year and a half. When her parents celebrated their thirtieth anniversary Lilly had flown in from California to be there. For the most part the visit was decent. Lilly and their mother disagreed a couple times during the week that Lilly and Derek were in town but Mrs. Mitchell's spirits were too high to allow anything, even a sinful daughter, to ruin that for her. Pastor Mitchell was a separate case all together. Lilly and her actions had broken his heart. First her getting pregnant at age 14, then dropping out of school in her senior year and running away to Virginia with her much older boyfriend Lucas, and over the years "shacking up" with different men that she wasn't married to in different states. At some point he ceased verbal contact with his daughter all together. As a result Lilly acted out, even as an adult, in an attempt to gain her father's attention.

Sierra was heartbroken seeing her sister and father in their present state, not associating with one another. She decided that this trip would be different, she'd see to that. She put herself under the pressure of bringing the two back together before Lilly returned to Utah. She figured that if she could manage to keep Lilly and Mother Mitchell from going at each other's throat then her chances would be improved.

Sierra splashed cold water on her face and watched her reflection watching her. She turned at the sound of commotion coming from the kitchen. Anxious, she pulled a hand towel from the bar on the wall and dried her face. She quickly refolded it and tossed it back across the bar and pushed the bathroom door open. She power walked down the hall and to the kitchen where her aunts were busy gabbing away in Lillian's ear giving her barely enough breathing room. Going unnoticed, Sierra stood quietly in the breezeway happily looking over her baby sister. She appreciated Lillian's outer beauty. At 5'7" tall with honey brown skin and round brown eyes Sierra always felt that Lilly could have been a model but Lilly had chosen a different path.

Sierra cleared her throat and she and Lilly finally made eye contact. Their smiles broadened as they ran into each other's arms. They held each other tightly swaying side to side. The sisters, still holding onto one another, stepped back and looked each other over before hugging again. Tears streamed down their cheeks as they touched each other's hair and face and hands.

"Damn girl, I missed you so much," Lilly confessed.

"Oh I missed you too baby girl," Sierra responded while caressing Lilly's rounding belly, "Girl look at you, all of you! Oh my word I didn't expect you to be so big."

"Girl yes, my feet about to bust from my shoes from all the swelling up they've been doing. And I'm 'bout ready for those damn fat-grabber jeans."

"What?"

"Si you know 'em and you know 'em well. The jeans with the big blue stretchable curtain that wrap around a prego's fat ass tummy!"

"Alright nah Lillian watch it. Now y'all gots plenty of time to catch up. Come on now. Lilly baby, I know you hungry so let's all sit at the table and eat," Mrs. Mitchell cut in.

"Okay momma," Lilly agreed, holding her sisters hand like a schoolgirl as they walked to the dinning room table with the rest of the family.

Everyone took a seat, Sierra and Lillian sat side by side waiting as Mrs. Mitchell and her sisters placed the last of the food out onto the table. When they were done Mr. Pete, their parents long time neighbor who happened to be sitting at the head of the table, stood to say Grace followed by a hearty Amen. Bowls clinked and clattered, as plates were prepared with the bountiful meal.

"Momma, where's Daddy?" Lillian asked with a confused look on her face.

"Well, Lilly honey, Daddy's eating his dinner with the children tonight."

"Unbelievable," Lilly banged her bowl on the dining table, "This is so typical of him. This is about me being here isn't it?"

"Lilly honey, you handle my dishes better than that you hear? Now someone needed to mind the children and Daddy volunteered to do it."

"Momma please don't. We could have just as easily put the kids table in here like you usually do. Speaking of which, you mean I have to wait 'til after dinner to see my nieces and nephew just because Daddy's mad at me?"

"Lilly please," Sierra interjected.

"Lillian now is neither the time nor place for this. Now eat and we will pick this discussion up later," their mother spoke with a subtle sternness in her voice.

"But Momma c'mon now. How can you stand for this?"

"Lillian Anne Mitchell that is enough. Now you ain't gone keep on like this at my dinner table. Now like I done told you, we will pick up this discussion later. I mean what I say chile."

Lillian was ready for a verbal fight but Sierra placed her hand gently on her sisters and looked her in her eyes. Lilly was red hot with anger but to appease her sister she calmed. The dinner guests shifted feeling awkward. Lillian and her mother stared at one another for a length of time before Lillian finally respectfully backed down.

"So how's business going Mr. Pete?" Lillian asked while putting a scoop of potatoes on her plate. The tension in the room eased as he answered. Mr. Pete loved to speak about the excited joy he got out of the fishing industry. Slowly others began to pipe up and join the conversation.

After dinner when everyone had gone, the Mitchell women sat around the kitchen preparing themselves mentally for the task of cleaning up after everyone. Lillian bounced Michele on one knee and Lee on the other. She still had not seen her father and tried not to allow it to bother her. The women made small talk while intentionally trying to ignore the one thought that was pressing in their minds. Though this situation was hardly new, something about it rang different in Lillian's consciousness. Mr. Mitchell had begun distancing himself from his daughter ever since she was fourteen and they had to make the choice to take her to have an abortion. And when she ran away and moved in with many different men he hurt more. But though he remained distant from her he'd never outright avoided her before. He'd at least stay cordial speaking a few polite words to her in passing. But this time he didn't want to see her. He hadn't done so much as come out and say hello. She wondered how he was going to get through two months with her there without talking to her or running into her in the kitchen or hallway. She wondered why he'd even okay'd her to stay at the house when it was obvious that he didn't want her there.

"So Lilly," Mrs. Mitchell turned to face her youngest child, her expression stern, "You're pregnant huh?"

"I was wondering how long it'd be before it came up," she answered, "Well yes Momma as you can clearly see there is a bun in the oven."

"So ridiculous. How do you plan on raising a child? I hope to God that's not why you asked to stay here. Daddy and I are not going to take care of you and your baby. Do you even know who the father is?"

Lilly's cheeks were flushed with heat but she remained calm for the sake of her sister's children's tender ears. Sierra, not missing a beat gathered her three and removed them from the potential scene. Once they were gone Lilly continued to remain calm when she answered her mother.

"As a matter of fact mom, no I don't know who the father of my child is since I'm pregnant through artificial insemination."

"What! Cut the nonsense!"

"What nonsense momma? I really wanted to have a baby and since my girlfriend can't get me pregnant, this was the next best thing."

"Girlfriend? Please, what are you talking about chile?"

"Yes girlfriend. Oh, I'm sorry Momma, you didn't know. I'm a lesbian Momma. Yes, gay and proud of it. Why do you think I'm wearing so many different colors? The rainbow. The teletubbies. I'm down with all that," Lilly proudly announced.

"Girl keep your voice down."

"Why Momma, I'm proud of who I am. I have a girlfriend and we're in love and we're gonna have a baby and live happily ever after," Lillian taunted. Angry and speechless Mrs. Mitchell removed herself from the table and scurried out of the kitchen, "Yea Momma, run and tell Daddy that!"

Lillian laughed to herself at her mischief. Sierra rushed into the kitchen after her mother had gone into her bedroom and closed the door. She walked over to Lillian and stood beside her chair with her hands on her hip.

"Lillian what is wrong with you?" Sierra asked sternly.

"Oh Si-Si please. Do not start with me, I have had enough drama for one day."

"Why did you just do that? What possessed you to lie to your mother like that?"

Lilly pushed away from the table with an empty glass in hand and walked to the refrigerator. She pulled out a pitcher of Kool-Aid and poured herself a glass, making Sierra wait for a response.

"My being pregnant is not any of her business."

"Not her business? She's your mother of course it's her business. Why couldn't you just tell her about Stephen?"

"Puh-lease Si-Si, I'm not fourteen and pregnant, I'm twenty-seven and no it is not her business. And besides I would have happily told her about Stephen, would have gladly told her about the move and engagement had she not come to me like that. That's what this is about," Lillian gasped, her eyes widening with discovery, "Daddy's not speaking to me because I'm pregnant and not married. Why that ornery old bastard. That's fine, I'll show his ass."

"And what's that supposed to mean? Lilly don't do anything stupid," Sierra warned.

"Oh you don't worry your pretty l'il head about it. This is between me and Daddy," Lillian pinched Sierra's cheek as she walked out of the kitchen with her head high.

Sierra was worried about what her sister may do but she knew whatever it was there would be no stopping her. She instead decided to call it a night, get her children, and go home.

It was early Saturday morning. Sierra sat curled up on her sofa eating a bowl of Fruit Loops with Lee as they watched the cartoons featured on

ABC's One Saturday Morning. She could hear Darryl in the back of the house getting himself ready for the day. She was sure he was going to see his mistress, the one he continued to lie about. She confronted him about the woman named Victoria who'd called their home. He told her he didn't know any Victoria and accused Sierra of lying. That was the end of that discussion. Sierra never brought it up again nor did she make any other efforts to save their relationship. She knew it wasn't worth saving yet at the same time she couldn't divorce him.

She heard the telephone ring but it stopped before she could make any effort to answer it. She heard Darryl's voice get closer and closer as he chattered on the phone. He told the person on the other end to hold on and sat the cordless on the coffee table and returned to what he'd previously been doing. Sierra rolled her eyes and reached for the phone.

"Hello?" she spoke into the receiver.

"Hey wassup sis, you busy?" Lilly asked.

"No, just watching cartoons and having breakfast with Lee."

"Mmm, sounds exciting. Well get dressed and ride with me up to West Palm."

"What's there to do in West Palm?"

"I just found out an old girlfriend of mine from Chicago is staying there and I wanna see her."

"Girlfriend?"

"Si-Si please, that was all game for momma alright. She's just an old friend of mine, I'm not gay. Strictly-dickly, okay," Lillian laughed into the phone. Sierra couldn't help but join in, Lilly's laughter was contagious, "Just get yourself and the kids dressed. I rented a car. I'll be there in an hour."

Sierra was relieved when they'd finally rolled up to the quaint little street that belonged to Lillian's girlfriend. It wasn't that she didn't enjoy outings; she hated being in the car for extended periods of time. They piled out of the car and to the front door. A short slender Hispanic woman opened it before they had a chance to ring the bell. She and

Lilly screamed each other's name and hugged tightly, rocking side to side. When they were finally done greeting each other the woman welcomed them inside.

"Oh my, I love your home honey, it's beautiful," Lilly exclaimed at its very cultural set up.

"Thank you, thank you."

"And damn girl you lost weight! Look at your ol' skinny self!"

"Girl that's this Florida heat, it'll do that to you. Well I hope it don't do you, you liable to disappear! With the exception of that belly you ain't nothing but a toothpick. Ooh girl but you so cute pregnant!" the two laughed with one another, "Now Lilly don't be rude. Introduce me to your family."

"Oh shoots y'all my bad. This is my sister Sierra and her children Michele, Jennifer and Lee. Si-Si this is my home girl from Chicago, Graciela."

"Just call me Gracie though. It's a pleasure to meet you."

"Same here," Sierra and Gracie shook hands.

"Well hey, make yourselves at home. Here come my babies right now. Lilly you know my son Israel. Izzy you remember Lilly?" The boy shyly shook his head, "You were probably too young."

"Goodness, look how big he is! He's so handsome, just like his daddy."

Gracie shifted uncomfortably and cleared her throat, "Yep, just like him. Anyway, this young lady is Kenya."

"Hi," Kenya waved at the crowd of new faces.

"Oh she is absolutely beautiful Gracie!" Lilly squealed.

"Thank you," Kenya answered appropriately in response to the compliment she'd been given.

"I had no idea you and Kenny had another child. She must've gotten that pretty brown skin from Kenny's side of the family somewhere 'cause she for shole ain't get it from you!"

Izzy eyed his mother quizzically. She smiled and squeezed his hand, "Izzy, Kenya why don't you guys take the kids into the den and let them play with some of your toys."

"Si mami," Izzy answered gesturing for Sierra's children to follow.

Kenya walked up to Sierra, "Can your kids come play with me and my brother?" she asked.

"Yes of course honey," Sierra answered. Kenya took Michele's hand and tried to take Jennifer's but she snatched away, "Jen don't you wanna play with the toys?" Jennifer shook her head 'no' and curled up in her mothers arm. Kenya shrugged it off and took Lee's hand instead.

"To respond to your comment Lilly," Gracie began when the children had disappeared, "Kenya got her color from her mother."

"Oh, I thought she was yours, she looks so much like Izzy."

"That's because she is Kenny's daughter."

"What?" Lilly was in shock.

"Girl so much has happened since you left."

"I see!"

"Lilly girl, Kenny was shot and killed about three years ago now, a couple months after we got married."

"Oh my goodness," Lilly and Sierra clasped their hands over their mouths, "I'm so sorry Gracie, I didn't know."

"I know, I know. You know it took some time but eventually I realized life was too short for grudges and if Izzy couldn't have his father, I could at least give him his sister."

"So that's what led you here, Kenny's passing?"

"That and Kenny's brother Philly got a job out here and since we share custody of Kenya, I came to keep her near him. Girl, it was pure madness but things are looking better now and me and the mom are cool, I guess."

The women continued to chat and reminisce until late in the evening. They decided since the children were enjoying themselves as they also were, to stay the night and ride home the next morning.

"Speak Lord! Speak to me!" The choir sang the church into intermission. Sierra reluctantly waited to be scolded by her mother for being late to church. There was no need to explain to her that they'd just driven all the way from West Palm Beach that morning, as far as her mother would be concerned there was no excuse for not being punctual for church. When the singing ceased she stood with her sister and walked to the back of the church. Sierra eyed Darryl who sat flipping through a Bible and sucked her teeth. Lillian nudged her and pointed inconspicuously at the gathering of church sisters who were known gossips. They shook their heads wondering what evil the bitches were brewing now. It would soon be revealed as they'd set their sights on Lillian and were traveling in her and Sierra's direction. Sierra swung Jennifer around to rest on her free hip and sighed. Sister Betty Wilson led the pack as usual. These women praised louder than everyone else and sinned harder. Sierra hoped they'd keep walking but they stopped directly in front of her and Lilly, fake smiles spread across their painted faces.

"Lillian Mitchell, long time no see," Sister Betty sang out reaching out to hug Lilly.

"Hello Sister Betty, Sisters," Lilly acknowledged.

"So we're expecting are we?"

"Well, I don't know about we but I sure am."

"Hmpf. Well how soon are you expecting?"

"I'm four months now so I'm about halfway there."

"So where's the father? Do we get to meet him?" Sister Betty inquired.

"I'd love to introduce you Sister but I don't know who he is," Lilly replied with sarcasm, "Oh don't look so surprised Sister Betty, see since I'm a lesbian and there's no chance I'll ever sleep with a man again, artificial insemination was the only way my girlfriend Sarah and I could have a child. Oh but don't worry Sisters, we're getting married in a couple months, that way my parents won't have to be shamed, we're going to do it right," Lilly rubbed her belly and smiled, proud of the lie she'd just repeated. Sierra rubbed her forehead and shook it, embarrassed yet humored at the same time.

Sister Betty in awe, was left speechless. She was clearly uncomfortable standing before Lillian. She stammered out a weak "Good luck" before she and the Sisters turned and rushed away. Lilly laughed out loud at their stupidity.

"Lilly, why did you lie to the Sister's like that?" Sierra asked.

"Oh forget those old nosey bitties, they were looking for gossip and I gave 'em some."

"How could you shame Daddy like that?"

"Fuck Daddy," Lillian hissed angrily and stalked away.

Sierra sat on the guest room bed changing Jennifer's diaper when her mother burst into the room, "Where is Lillian?" she asked angrily.

"I-I think she's sitting out back," Sierra answered timidly, "Is everything alright Momma?"

Mrs. Mitchell didn't answer. She charged down the hall, across the family room and out the back door. There she found Lilly sitting within the screened patio at the table snacking on sweet potato pie and talking on the phone. Sierra rushed to finish up with Jennifer's change. She scooped up the dirty diaper and instructed her children to sit still and watch television and not to come out of the room unless she instructed them to. She rushed across the house and to where her mother and sister were already in the midst of battle. Just as she'd suspected it was about the lie Lilly had told the church sisters.

"Lillian Anne Mitchell, what in God's name is wrong with you? Why would you want to bring shame to your father's good name like this?"

"Momma please, everything I do brings shame to Daddy and you always run to his aide. But do you run to my aide when Daddy ignores me, when he treats me like I don't even exist?"

"Why do you think he does that? Look at the terrible things you do to him."

"Do to him? Momma I'm a grown woman now, my life should no longer reflect on him. I haven't seen thirteen in years, my sins belong to me. Anyway, even if I do make mistakes sometimes that's still no excuse for him to treat his own child this way. Why can't he speak to me? Why can't he ever tell me how he feels? Huh? He couldn't even come out here himself and tell me that he was angry with me," tears welled up in Lillian's eyes but she stopped them before they spilled forward.

"You want me to talk to you?" all eyes turned in the direction of the husky voice that'd just spoken. Mr. Mitchell stood with his cane in his hand behind Sierra, "Is that what you want Lillian Anne? Fine. I want you out of my house, you're my daughter no longer."

Mr. Mitchell and Lilly eyed each other angrily before Lillian pushed past him muttering, "I hate you too Daddy."

"Daddy please," Sierra began but was quickly silenced.

"Sierra, no. Get the kids and go home, I need some peace and quiet," Mr. Mitchell turned and headed back to his bedroom. Sierra turned to face her mother.

"You heard your father," was all she said before following behind him.

Sierra chewed her bottom lip as she gathered her children and helped her sister gather her belongings and load them into the car. Lillian followed behind Sierra in her rental car to Sierra's home. Once there she gathered pillows and blankets and set Lilly up as cozy as possible on she and Darryl's sofa. Knowing her sister wasn't in the mood to talk about it she left her be and retired to her bedroom. Darryl was already in bed sleep. Sierra changed out of her church clothes and into her nightgown and climbed into her side of the bed, exhausted and distraught. No sooner had her head hit the pillow before her telephone rang. Darryl groaned so she quickly answered, it was Mya.

"Are you alright? What's wrong?" Sierra asked barely loud enough for Mya to hear.

"Well, I was hoping you'd seen Nathaniel."

"No I haven't, why what's wrong with him?"

"Keep it down," Darryl grumbled.

"I don't know Sierra, I really don't. He just hasn't been himself lately. He's been drinking an awful lot lately and I think he may be doing drugs."

"Drugs?" Sierra exclaimed.

"Ay can you take that noise outta here?" Darryl demanded more than asked.

Sierra eased out of bed and crept to the bathroom, "Nate doesn't get high Mya."

"Yes well the old Nathaniel doesn't drink like a fish and stay gone for days at a time either. I'm very concerned Sierra; I don't know what to do. He won't stay home or sober long enough to talk to me."

"I'm sure he'll be alright Mya. Try to get some rest but be sure to keep me posted alright," she said pretending to be calm.

"Yes, yes I suppose you're right. I'm sorry to have disturbed you this late. I'll call if I hear anything."

"And I'll do the same okay."

The two women said their goodnights and disconnected the line. Sierra held the phone in her hand and continued to sit on the toilet top. She was worried but she couldn't let Mya think that. She had to pretend to be strong so that Mya could be. But Mya was right; his behavior was clearly not normal. She hadn't spoken to him in over two weeks now and had no idea what was going on in his mind and this scared her. Sierra sat the phone on the sink. She slid to the floor and sat on her knees on the mat in front of the tub. She bowed her head and there prayed for Nate, Mya, Lilly, her mother and her father.

14Nate

This must have been what rock bottom felt like. I was nodding off as I sat on the toilet in the bathroom at the end of the first floor hall, a cigarette dangling from between my lips. I could smell the faint stench of something burning floating up and through my nostrils from a distance. My eyes half shut, I thought that it must be a dream, a very vivid dream. They happen to everyone, don't they? I have heard of people dreaming that they were falling and waking up in a cold sweat. That they were being chased by demons and being awakened by their own deafening screams. I strained to push. I couldn't understand how or why women desired to give birth because my ass was hurting like crazy!

I sat upright quickly remembering that I had been cooking something…something…something…what? Eggs! I moved from the toilet as quickly as I could and rushed down the hall toward the kitchen wearing nothing more than boxers and house slippers. Sweat rolled from my forehead and down the bridge of my nose. I held the cigarette between my lips as I scraped the hard burned eggs from the skillet and onto a plate. A couple ashes sprinkled onto them but I brushed them away. I needed to eat and now wasn't the time for being picky. I grabbed a beer from the refrigerator and took a seat on the sofa in front of the television.

I ate my eggs without tasting any of it. The burnt parts, the well-cooked parts, the few raw pieces. I ate and washed it down with my ice-cold beer. I stretched out on my sofa staring at the television with my hands down my boxers stroking myself not for pleasure but for relaxation purposes. My stomach cramped as it had all day. Relieving my bowels hadn't helped and unfortunately neither had eating. I wanted to get up and take painkillers but I couldn't move. I knew what I needed but I hadn't the ability to obtain. I instead rolled over onto my side and pulled my knees into my chest and rocked myself to sleep.

I awoke to the sounds of Mya stomping through the house complaining. She was in the kitchen putting dishes into the washer and slamming cabinets. My stomach continued to cramp but I managed to rollover and change stations on the television.

"This house stinks!" she screamed out as she stalked down the hall. I could hear her fumbling around in the bathroom and then the toilet flushing, "Nathaniel! Oh my God you're so disgusting! Why didn't you go to work today? Huh? Oh now you're not speaking?" she asked suddenly standing above me. My head pounded, I had no desire to talk and so kept quiet, "Aaarrgh! I'm going to shower, you get that piece of shit you call a car out of my driveway, you're making the property value decrease."

I listened to her stomp up the stairwell and slam the bedroom door behind her. I groaned from the noise. My "piece of shit" car as she referred was a 1987 Mercury Topaz. A few months back while hanging out after work with a few co-workers I was introduced to the benefits of cocaine. I had never indulged in drug use previously only recently taking up a habit of smoking marijuana but I needed an escape. Mya was pressuring me into creating a baby and setting a date for the wedding and at the same time I had Anthony whispering in my ear about leaving Mya and spending my life with him. The pressure was too great and I decided to try a few lines in an effort to relieve the mental pressure. It worked for me; it took me away and numbed the pain. It became a sort of medication for me but not wanting my associates in my business I had to get a prescription on my own. I began to cop from Ernie, a dealer from my old neighborhood. Since I naturally wouldn't want to park my Benz outside a dope spot I would rent a car. Soon I bought a car no one would consider stealing.

I mustered up all of my strength and carried my weight up the stairs. Though I'd already lost almost thirty pounds at times my body weight seemed too much for me to handle. I opened the door and stepped inside the bedroom. Mya was unfastening her bra when she noticed me. She rolled her eyes and continued with what she was doing.

"Can I get twenty-dollars?" I asked.

She stopped as if she were in shock. She tilted her head as she looked at me as if she were trying to figure out what I'd said.

"Why do you need my money? You have your own money, don't you?" she asked yet accusing at the same time. She stood staring at me, naked from the waist up, hands on her hips and waiting for my answer.

"Of course I have my own money," I lied. The truth of the matter was I'd already drained my checking account. A chunk of my salary was direct deposited into a joint savings account, which could not be drawn from without both Mya's and my signature, "I just lost my cash card and the bank's obviously closed. I just need some pocket money, y'know, for gas and what have you."

She looked me up and down before sitting on the bed. She crossed her legs and rubbed her forehead as she eyed me. I was uncomfortable and becoming anxious but I wanted and needed the money and thus tried to remain at ease.

"Nathaniel, why don't you tell me what is truly going on with you?"

"What are you talking about?"

"Don't pretend ignorance. What is going on in your head? Why are you behaving as you have been? Allow me to help you."

"Damn Mya, can I just get the money?" I snapped.

"Don't you dare speak to me with that tone. Are you doing drugs?"

"What?" I asked in fake astonishment.

"Are you doing drugs? I want to know."

"Of course not."

"The truth please."

"No I am not doing drugs."

"Well something sure as hell is going on and I want to know what it is. You don't even want to make love to me anymore. I stand before you completely naked these days and you ignore me. But you say you're not sleeping with anyone else. Normally I'd call you a got-damned liar but as shitty as you've looked lately I couldn't see how any other woman could even want you."

"Is that what this is about?" I bellowed, "You wanna fuck? Huh? You mad 'cause you wanna fuck?"

I charged at her. I could see the fear in her eyes as she scurried back onto the bed but I didn't stop. She was afraid, afraid of me. She'd never been afraid of me before. But then I hadn't ever behaved this way before and couldn't stop myself from doing it now. I grabbed her by her ankles and pulled her to the edge of the bed. Her eyes widened and her mouth dropped open. She wanted to scream, I sensed it but I kept going. I flipped her body over onto her stomach and pulled her by her waist to me.

"That's what this is all about? You want to fuck? Aiight then, give that pussy here!" I peeled her skirt from her body and ripped her thong away. I quickly dropped my boxers and roughly rubbed myself against her opening until it was hard enough to force my way inside. I slammed back and forth drowning out her cries of pain or pleasure, whichever, until I erupted. I snatched away and she fell forward onto the bed. She grabbed the quilt from the foot of the bed and scrambled to the corner covering her body, trembling with fear. With the backs of her hands she smeared the tears from her eyes and watched me still appearing afraid but I didn't care. I wanted to get out and somewhere that I'd feel more comfortable.

"Can I get the fuckin' money now?" I hissed. She pointed at her purse, which was set atop her writing desk. I pulled her wallet out. Out of the corner of my eye I noticed her debit card. I slipped it out along with a twenty-dollar bill and returned her wallet. I grabbed a pair of dirty jeans from the top of the hamper and threw a fresh t-shirt over my head. I left her frightened in the corner of the bed and trotted down the stairs and out the front door.

I jumped in my "classic" ride and stopped by the bank. Fortunately at one point she'd trusted me enough to give me her PIN. I withdrew $750 and made my way to South Dade and Ernie's spot. I parked on the side of the house. Valeta, a regular at Ernie's, stood outside the back door shaking and struggling to smoke a cigarette. I didn't think Valeta was much older than 25 but she looked old and worn out. Though she was about 5'6" she couldn't have weighed more than 90lbs. Her eyes were sunken in her head and she had sores on her lips and arms.

"Wassup baby?" she spoke in a strained voice.

"What's up V? Ernie in there?"

"Yea but he in a stank ass mood."

I shrugged my shoulders and tapped three times on the door. Sugey, Ernie's 300 lb bodyguard, opened up and peeked outside.

"Bitch get yo' ass away from dis do'. Whut da fuck wrong wit' you? Don't let me tell Ernie, yo' ass fuck 'round and be cut off," he yelled at Valeta. I was allowed entrance before he slammed the door and turned his attention to me, "What you need?"

"The usual."

"In or out?"

"In."

"Aiight."

I handed him the original twenty-dollar bill I'd gotten from Mya, he reached for my package, "Sugey hold on," I added another twenty for a bigger pack.

He handed me the package and I stepped over trash and junkies and took a seat at a large wooden table in the living room. I took a razor from the table and sliced half the coke into lines. I took a twenty-dollar bill and rolled it tight. I put it to my nose and inhaled. The rest I cooked and injected into my veins. When I was done I fell backward into my seat. My eyes rolled to the back of my head. The needle dropped from my hand and to the floor.

The pressure of kicks in my side awakened me. I groaned and struggled to open my eyes. I looked up to see Ernie standing above me glaring down. He was a short yellow man with a wide nose smashed across his face. His curl was slicked back, surely staining the collar of what he considered to be an expensive suit.

"This place is for payin' customers only," he nodded at Sugey who took the responsibility of making sure that I either bought more or got out. I smeared the slob from my mouth and struggled to get to my feet.

"Wassit gone be partner?" Sugey asked.

"Hit me," I said. I reached in my front pockets for money but came up with lint. In a panic I checked my back pockets. Mya's cash card was there but all of my money was gone, I'd been ripped off. I felt as though someone had wrapped their hands firmly around my lungs, I couldn't breathe. Sugey shook his head and nodded toward the door. Keys in hand, I headed out to my car. I peeled away and parked down the street. My stomach hurt. I jerked open the door and leaned out the car, throwing up dry heaves on the curb. I was sobering, sick and beginning to think. I needed money and quickly.

I looked at the small clock inside the car. It was only 10:15 in the morning. I searched the car finding only five dollars in the glove compartment. I sped back to Ernie's and talked Sugey into selling me a nickel. It wasn't easy but I was a loyal customer and he knew Ernie wouldn't appreciate loosing my business to the competition. Such a small amount didn't get me where I needed to be but it was a band-aid for the physical pain. I knew that wouldn't last long and so drove to the bank to get more cash. I inserted the card and typed the PIN but no cash was dispensed not because I'd withdrawn the max limit but because Mya had cancelled the card. My breathing became rapid as I became distressed.

Angry and anxious I rushed inside of the bank. It was Friday and there were at least ten people in line already. I stood impatiently at the back of the line trying to wait my turn. But I couldn't wait. I pushed ahead of the line of people as they angrily swore and attempted to stop me. I pushed aside an older man who was completing his transaction.

"I need to get cash and my card won't work," I said out of breath.

"That's terrible sir but you see all those people? They were here first," the young lady calmly explained.

"I know but look, my card won't work and I need money now," I reasoned.

"Sir, I'm going to have to ask you to leave," the large security officer that had stepped up beside me demanded.

"Just a minute brother," I turned back to the clerk and attempted to plead my case, "Ma'am-"

"Look sir, you're gonna have to wait."

Angry and impatient I threw my body partway over the counter and lunged at the teller, "Give me my got-damned money now!"

The officer abruptly grabbed me kicking and screaming and threw me out of the bank, "Don't make me call the cops!"

"Alright, alright. I'm sorry, I didn't mean it. I'm sorry."

Broke and in a panic, I strolled back to the car and kicked the tire. I climbed inside and looked at the clock again. My eyes widened and my mind raced. I had an idea and fortunately Mya would already have gone to work. I peeled out of the banks parking lot and drove to my home.

"Mya!" I called out when I entered the house, "Mya!"

I was pleased that there was no answer. I ran up the stairs and to our bedroom. I opened my drawer and pulled out a large velvet case, opening it to reveal my collection of watches. Movado. Rolex. Bulova. I closed the case and jogged back down the steps, stopping in the kitchen to grab a beer before heading out of the door. I made my way to the nearest pawnshop with the velvet case under my arm. The clerk did a double take when he looked at its contents. I was sure he wondered why but he didn't pry, just paid me $982 and I went on my way.

My mind was on Ernie's spot but I knew I may need more money to get by for a while. I stopped at a Texaco to fill up my tank and then rolled up to the liquor store and bought a fifth of Gin. I guzzled it as I made my way to Anthony's house not knowing if he would be home or not. I was relieved when he answered the door. He stood looking at me as if he'd seen a ghost.

"What's up baby?" I asked leaning in for a kiss but he backed away.

"This is a surprise," he said dryly. He stepped away and I followed him inside, "To what do I owe this... pleasure? Oh I see," he said eying the bottle of alcohol in my grip.

"Naw baby. Can't I just want to see my man?" I could feel the Gin begin to take affect. I snorted and rubbed my nose harshly. I took his hand in mine and slowly pulled him to me. I again leaned in for a kiss but he refused me.

"Where have you been Nathaniel?"

"Come on now baby, don't start," I told him turning my bottle up to my lips.

"Naw I'm going to start. I ain't seen you or heard from you in a week and now you pop up at my door drunk and I'm supposed to fall into your arms and say everything's okay?"

"Yep."

"Man, fuck you Nathaniel."

"That's what I hoped you'd do," I snickered, "But I need a favor first."

"What is it this time?"

"I'm in a tight spot and need a couple dollars to hold me over 'til pay day."

"What? Wassup with your bank account?" he lit a cigarette and took a drag not taking his eyes off me as he awaited my answer.

"What difference does it make? I need your help, are you going to help me?" I was becoming angered. I knew I'd soon loose it if he pushed. Anthony tilted his head and looked at me harder. He pushed up from the couch and walked up to me taking my chin in between his fingers. He looked into my eyes until I jerked away.

"Can I get some cash or not Anthony?"

"You're high," he said as though he'd just at that moment realized it.

"Fuck you, I ain't high. Drunk but ain't high."

"Bullshit! That's what you want my money for? To get high? What the hell is wrong with you Nathaniel? I'm not supporting that."

"Man I don't know what you're talking about," I said nonchalantly. I sat on his bed and took one of his cigarettes and lit it. I inhaled deeply and held the smoke in my mouth before exhaling, "So you going to give me some loot or not?"

"Hell naw," he walked over to the window.

My temper was lost. I felt as though he'd wasted my time. How could he tell me "no"? He was supposed to love me yet he could deny me when I needed him most. I'd become this because of him. My life was great, I was relatively happy, successful, and on my way up until he pushed and forced his way into my life and now this is what I'd become and he could fix his mouth to deny me! I pushed up from the bed and headed to the door in a fit of anger.

"Nathaniel," he called after me, "What's up man? Why are you doing this?"

"You don't understand. You...you may try but you won't. There's just too much shit...I mean there's Mya but...you don't know how much I... How I feel about you. How much I..."

"I do know but what I don't understand is why your loving me is so bad. You know I love you Nathaniel but I can't be apart of this anymore, I've told you that. I need it to be you and me, once and for all. You and me only," he was in front of me, holding my hands, "Baby just stay with me. I'll help you get better."

"Anthony I gotta...I need..," I looked in his eyes, saw the love and desire and the hurt. It was the same look I'd seen in Mya's eyes a thousand times but the difference was that I could actually, honestly share in Anthony's feelings. I brushed it off and took my hands from his, "I need to go. I got something to do."

"Nathaniel please. If you leave...if you leave, don't come back," he told me.

Those words pierced my heart. I wanted to curl up in his arms and stay there happy but the urge to curl up in a corner at Ernie's was stronger. I'd become addicted, I hadn't meant it to happen but it had and it wasn't until that very moment that I realized that. That moment when the physical pains outweighed the emotional ones. That moment when anxiety began to set in. That moment when I turned my back on the man I loved, walked away and listened to the door close and lock behind me without looking back.

15Nate & Sierra

Nate's hands were shaking on the steering wheel as he pulled into the empty lot beside Ernie's dope spot. His mind was whirring filled with thoughts of Anthony and Mya and his job and childhood. His body ached and he withheld the urge to regurgitate. He climbed out of his car paranoid looking around before walking to the door. He spotted Valeta standing about a half a block away. Their eyes locked and Nate knew her pain but he couldn't help her. He tapped three times. Sugey opened up and allowed him inside. The stench of the house hit Nate like a brick. He grabbed his stomach and swallowed hard. He shuffled around inside the pocket of his jeans and fished out his money. He handed Sugey forty-dollars and Sugey handed him a package.

Nate took a seat near the back of the room away from most everyone else. He didn't want to snort. He knew snorting wouldn't help him escape. He took a dingy spoon from the table and dumped the contents of the package. He picked up a half a plastic cup of water and put a few droplets inside. He found a lighter in his pocket and lit the flame beneath the spoon until the mixture boiled down to a potent liquid. He patted his jeans, frantically, with his free hand. "Shit," he mumbled. He nudged a scrawny old man named Peppy who was nodding off beside him. The man jumped and glanced around before nodding again. Nate turned up his lip as he reached over and took the man's used needle. He suctioned the drug into the needle and set it beside him. He wound a rubber band tightly around his arm before taking his two fingers and tapping in search of a vein. He found one easily and picked up the needle and carefully slid it in. Blood mixed with the drug before it released the fluid directly into his bloodstream. His body relaxed, tensed muscles eased, he pulled the needle out and set it on the table as he slumped down in his chair.

"Remember this picture?" Sierra asked Lilly. She handed her an old photo bent at the edge. It was one of her and Lilly building a sand castle on the beach when they were quite small. It could have been more elaborate however they'd declined their father's assistance.

"Oh my goodness!" Lilly squealed, "Look at me. I was so funny looking back in the day! I didn't have any teeth in the front, looking like a miniature whino. And look at you with that big ol' forehead!"

The two sisters laughed together feeling happy. They'd been sitting cross-legged giggling at old photos for the past half an hour. It was a relief to Sierra as she'd watched Lilly mope around her house for weeks after their father had thrown her out. She didn't know how appreciative Lilly was of this also. She'd been distressed over the situation between herself and her father and sitting here like this laughing and smiling and reminiscing on easier times felt good.

"Girl I know you not talking about nobody's forehead with that Cro-Magnon dome of yours!" Sierra shot back in fun.

"Whatever! My man likes it though."

"Girl he white, he don't know no better."

"He knows a good thang when he sees it," Lilly laid her head on a large pillow on the floor and flipped through another handful of photos.

"So what exactly are you and Stephen's plans anyway?" Sierra asked twirling the ends of her hair around her finger.

"Well," Lilly began smiling as she sat upright, "He says the house should be completed in about seven more weeks. As soon as the builder's finish and his transfer is complete he'll be down and we'll have the wedding. I'm gonna be an old fat bride. Y'all gone have to roll me down the aisle!"

"Why not go on ahead and get married sooner?"

"He suggested that and sure it would be nice but I really want to get married in front of the family and I-"

"What? You what?"

"I really wanted Daddy to marry us," water began to well up in Lilly's eyes but she immediately wiped it away with the back of her hand.

"Aaaww baby," Sierra crawled to Lilly's side and put her arm around her shoulders, "Daddy will do it, he's just being stubborn like you. But honey you need to let Momma and Daddy know these things. How can they help if you're getting your kicks off of b.s-ing them all the time?"

"I know, I know, you're right."

"That's why I'm, the big sister!" The two laughed in each other's arms, "Oh shoot! I smell the cookies!"

Sierra and Lilly sprang from the floor and hand in hand ran to the kitchen. Sierra grabbed a pair of oven mitts and pulled the cookies from inside the oven and set them on the counter. Lilly grabbed two mugs from the cabinet and prepared to make hot chocolate. They joked and laughed as they bumped around the kitchen. Sierra leaned into a cabinet and pulled out a fresh roll of paper towels. When she stood upright she came eye to eye with Darryl who was standing in the doorway grinning from ear to ear. She immediately began to feel stressed.

"Hey babe," he said as he walked over to her. He put his arm around her waist and kissed her cheek leaving Sierra feeling confused and suspicious, "Lilly. Wassup baby girl?"

"What's up baby?" Lilly leaned in to hug Darryl not noticing Sierra sucking her teeth behind them, "How you doing today?"

"Good, real good. And you? How's the little bun in the oven? You excited you 'bout to be a momma?"

"Yea, looking forward to it. Y'know the whole happily ever after stuff like y'all got going here."

"Nice but you ain't never gone get what me and my baby got, ain't that right Si-Si?" he asked hugging Sierra's shoulders.

"I sure hope not," Sierra replied through tight teeth and a plastered smile.

"Well you girls have fun, I'm going to bed," Darryl kissed both Sierra and Lilly on the cheek and walked out of the kitchen and to the bedroom.

Sierra mumbled incoherently under her breath as she slammed chocolate chip cookies on a paper plate. The nerve of him, pretending that he was happy with her just to have an excuse to get close to Lilly.

"Si-Si. Si-Si!" Lilly called to get Sierra's attention, "You okay?"

"Huh? Oh yes, fine, just fine. Come on. Let's go watch this movie."

"You're sure you're fine?"

Sierra looked at Lilly with sincerity in her eyes, "I'm wonderful."

Nate felt his body being nudged. He swayed back and forth in his chair; his eyes open yet his mind asleep. He thought he was dreaming but the nudging persisted. With all his strength he turned in his seat to face his aggravator. He jumped up and stumbled backwards, tripping over his chair. A look of horror crossed his face. "D-Daddy?" he reached up to touch the face of a man that was leaning over him.

"I ain't yo' damn daddy boy. You gone give me my shooting stick back or what?" the old man complained.

"Huh? I'm sorry, I thought...but I swear..."

"Mmhm, yea, ol' theivin' ass," the man snatched the needle from Nate's hand and hobbled away.

Nate sat in the middle of the filth and looked around the room. The world appeared blurry through his eyes. He looked around, back and forth, nervous and intimidated. He swore he saw Sierra and Mike and his mother and father nodding out, snorting, shooting up, and scratching. He wanted to escape, break away from them all. He shuffled backward until his back was smashed against the wall. Tears streamed down his cheeks and he held his knees to his chest and rocked. Suddenly Anthony and Mya appeared before him staring down angrily, scolding him with words, which were muffled and incoherent. Nate felt a sudden sharp blow to the leg. He blinked and shook his head. When he looked up again Sugey and Ernie were standing above him.

"Man, you gone have to get the fuck outta here wit' dat crazy bullshit," Ernie threatened.

Nate tried to pull himself together in front of his dealer and bodyguard. He brushed the dust off of his already filthy jeans and stood. His eyes were bloodshot and his armpits were sweaty and foul smelling.

"Ernie I need something else. I-I'm freakin' out here, I'm loosing my mind. This shit ain't working any more Ernie!"

"Man, you better back da fuck up and calm yo' ass down," Ernie stepped back and adjusted his collar, "Look dawg, I got sumthin' for ya," Sugey placed a small brown vile in Ernie's palm and he handed it to Nate, "Load dis shit in yo' veins playa. It'll get you right."

"How much?"

"Twenty-five."

Nate paid Ernie his money. He began to walk to the table but going in and out of hallucinations he decided he could not stay. He rushed out to his car in the midst of paranoia and climbed inside. He was anxious to take advantage of this new medication that he'd been given however he was afraid. Everywhere he turned he saw someone that he knew and he was fearful that Mya and Anthony were after him. He drove somehow without seeing the road, without seeing stop signs or signals. He drove in a cold sweat while being chased by his own demons. He drove until he found himself in the parking lot of the Baymont Hotel. He decided it was worth it to get a room where he could be alone, away from anyone familiar to him. He attempted to fix himself up before going inside to try and rent a room. He smeared his face with his palms and combed his fingers through his hair, which had grown wild and wiry. He looked at his eyes in the mirror; they were bloodshot. He fished out a small container of Visine and placed a few droplets into his eyes.

He took a deep breath and reached for the door handle. When he looked up he saw Sierra and Mike walking hand in hand past the car looking into his eyes as they passed. He sat back in his seat breathing rapidly, his pulse racing. Nate remembered the gun he kept under his seat for protection. He'd purchased it when he began scrounging around the underbelly of South Dade County. With Mya and Anthony after him and Sierra, Mike and his parents stalking him he was afraid that someone might try to hurt him. He slipped the .38 from beneath his seat and stuck it down inside his jeans. He stepped out the car and looked around before taking long strides toward the hotel doors and going inside.

Sierra and Lilly laughed so hard their face literally hurt. Lilly slid off the sofa and went to remove the movie from the DVD player. She replaced it in its case and returned it to where it belonged.

"Damn that movie was funny," Lilly exclaimed, "You wanna watch another one?"

"If you can find a good one," Sierra told her as she stuffed the last cookie in her mouth.

"So Si-Si let me ask you something. What's going on between you and Darryl?"

"What do you mean?" Sierra asked nonchalantly.

"I got the impression that uh, y'all ain't all that happy together."

"Is that right?"

"Yes, that's right," Lilly raised her body from the floor and walked on her knees to the sofa. She sat beside her sister's leg and looked up at her awaiting Sierra's response.

Sierra fidgeted for a few moments before she spoke, "He's a no good S.O. B."

"Whuut? Are you serious?"

"Yes I am. Very. All of that in the kitchen, everything he's done since you've been here, was just nonsense. We don't kiss, we don't even talk. If we had a spare bedroom we wouldn't sleep in the same bed at night. Besides that he's got another woman who he sees almost every night."

"Hell naw, please tell me you're lying."

"C'mon, you've been here how long and how often have you seen him? He has a girlfriend, her name is Victoria, and she wants to take him away from me for good."

"How do you know all of that?" Lilly sat herself on the sofa.

"She's called the house, told me everything. He tells me it's not true but it's so obvious that it is ridiculous."

"Wait, wait, wait, hold on. Why didn't you tell me this before? Better question. Why is he still here? Why haven't you divorced his sorry ass?"

"Now there you go," Sierra stood and walked to the kitchen with her mug and empty paper plate in hand. Lilly followed behind her.

"And what's that supposed to mean Si-Si?"

"You of all people should understand that I can't divorce Darryl."

"Why should I understand," Lilly asked dumbfounded.

"Because you were raised with me. I made a promise, a vow to God that I'd stick with Darryl for better or for worse and well, this is definitely worse but I can't bail out now."

There was a long silence between the sisters before Lilly spoke up, "Si-Si no disrespect intended but that's about the dumbest load of bullshit I've ever heard. No, no, no, let me finish. The son of a bitch is cheating, not coming home at night, not kissing you, not holding you, making love to you, not even talking to you and you think God wants you to spend the rest of your days unhappy like this because you promised him something? Let me tell you something, y'all may think I'm the spawn of Satan but I know God and I know He wants us to be happy while we're here. Now you are not the one breaking the promise here, Darryl is. You've stuck it out, you've tried, you want it to work but he has to as well. Besides all that, what about the vow you made to your children? Which vow do you think God is more concerned with your honoring? Your being loyal to a man that is not being loyal to Him? Or your loyalty to those three babies that He has blessed you with?"

"Are you finished yet?" Sierra asked.

"Quite finished."

The silence returned. Sierra was angry but not with Lilly but with herself. Deep down she knew what Lilly said was right. The truth was she was more afraid of how her parents would react than anything else.

"Lilly, I'm sorry. I'm not upset with you, all right. Maybe we should just skip the movie tonight, I'm tired. I think I'm going to go to bed."

"That's okay sis. I didn't mean to come down so hard on you. I just love you and hate to see you get hurt."

"I know. I love you too baby girl," Sierra wrapped her arms around Lilly and they held each other in a tight embrace, "See you in the morning."

"Okay. Goodnight Si."

Sierra released her grip and turned. She walked out of the kitchen and headed down the hall to her bedroom.

Nate released the heroine into his blood stream. The small clock radio on the nightstand played classic R&B music or "dusties". The room blurred before his eyes. He stared at the old bed, used and worn by many previous to him. He stared through moist blurred eyes at the bed with the rumpled comforter with the invisible stains. He tilted his head and watched as Mya and Anthony had sex before him. He endured the sight of Anthony leaning Mya forward on her knees and positioning himself behind her. He watched as Anthony held her rear in his hands and thrust in and out of her. He felt cold and intimidated as they smiled and stared into his soul while they fucked on his rental bed.

"Aaargh!" he screamed out as he flung a lamp at their images, which faded as instantly as they'd appeared, "Where are you? Come back here!"

Nate slid from his chair and to the floor beneath him. He scrambled to the bed and felt around but there was no one there. Tears fell from his eyes. He held his knees to his chest and rocked back and forth fearful that Mya and Anthony may try to hurt him. He peered from behind his knees. Mya sat in the chair he'd previously occupied with her legs cocked opened, pointing and laughing. He charged at her but when he reached out to grab her she was gone.

Nate sat in the chair and scrambled for the brown vile. He turned up a bottle of Vodka and gulped it down. He turned the vile upside down and tapped it against the spoon but alas it was empty. He threw the vile with a mighty force across the room sending it crashing into a wall. He scratched his scalp repeatedly while looking back and forth around the room. His sights landed on the gun, which was sitting on the table. He took it into his hands and aimed it ready to shoot Anthony or Mya if they came back to taunt him. He scanned the room until his eyes landed upon a vision in the dark shadowy corner, much too tall to be Mya or Anthony. He smeared the tears from his eyes with the back of his hand heavy with the gun and then pointed it at it.

"Who are you!" he called out but there was no answer, "Who the fuck are you?"

There was silence in the room with the exception of Luther Vandross crooning about how a house is not a home. But an answer soon came; it came as a voice in Nate's mind.

"Who the fuck are you? Answer me got-damit or I'll kill you!"

You should.

"Excuse me?"

You should. Right between the eyes. The back of the throat. The side of the head. You should shoot me. You should kill me.

"You're crazy."

You're the one talking to yourself.

"I'm talking to you."

And who am I but you.

Nate's eyes widened in horror as the image appeared clearer before him. Standing at 6'4" tall it was none other than his own image lurking in the shadows.

"You're not real."

How can you be so sure?

"What do you want from me?"

For you to do what's right for Anthony, for Mya, for us, for everybody concerned. You're ruining everyone's lives. Why don't you just go away?

"Go away?"

Go away. Let everyone get back to living their lives. Let them live happy-without you. Go away.

"But I don't think I want to go away."

Stop being selfish! Think about Mya and how she loves you so much. You hurt her terribly. She doesn't deserve that. Go away.

"Mya. I made her fear me."

What about Anthony? He wants to spend his life with you but you're too selfish and stubborn and scared to take a chance and be with him, the man you love. Just go away.

"I do love Anthony but…"

You're of no use to Sierra. Because you're a faggot. You can't commit yourself to her and now she's stuck spending her life with Darryl. Nathaniel Lee Marshall, go away.

"Go away. You're right. I'm not helping anyone, only hurting everyone. B-but if I go away then they can all be happy, right? They won't have to worry about me. Go away. I've got to go away," Nate felt around for the phone and dialed.

Sierra groaned as she rolled over without opening her eyes to answer the phone, "Hello?" her voice was deep and groggy when she spoke. There was no answer immediately so she again said "Hello?"

"How you doing Si-Si?"

"I'm fine, who is this?"

"I love you Si-Si but I gotta go away now," Nate's voice came from the other end.

"Nate? Is this Nate?" Sierra whispered.

"I'm sorry Si-Si. I should've been with you. I can't take care of you but I should," Nate began to sob as he spoke, "I'm no good to you."

"Nate what are you talking about? What-where are you, where've you been? We've been worried about you," panic began to wash over Sierra.

"No, no good. Why? You're beautiful Sierra. I gotta go away now Sierra."

"Nate no!" Sierra screamed into the receiver. She felt Darryl shift under the covers, "Where are you baby huh? Where're you at? Let me come and get you."

"You're so beautiful. I gotta go away so everybody can be happy again."

"Nate stop it! Stop it this instant and tell me where you are!" Sierra flung the sheet from her body and scrambled around the room hastily trying to get dressed.

"Sierra shut that fuckin' noise up and take that conversation elsewhere."

"Darryl why don't you shut up and go back to sleep or go back to your whore's house!" Sierra glared at Darryl as if she were daring him, challenging him to say something to her. When he didn't respond she returned her attention to Nate, "Nathaniel baby, I'm on my way to get you. Where are you at?"

"Si-Si I love you. Tell my momma I love her. Tell my daddy I'm sorry. I gotta go away," Nate disconnected the line.

"Nate? Nathaniel? Oh my God, oh my God," Sierra began to panic. She held the phone to her chin and thought for a moment. She turned it on and pressed *69 on the keypad. After two rings a woman's voice answered.

"Baymont Hotel, this is Maggie. How may I direct your call?"

"Yes, can you please connect me to the room of Mr. Nathaniel Marshall?"

"I'm sorry ma'am, Mr. Marshall requested that we not disturb him tonight."

"Listen this is an emergency. I think Mr. Marshall may hurt himself. I'm on my way but I need you to go to his room and check on him."

"Again ma'am, I'm sorry. Mr. Marshall specifically requested that we not disturb him. May I take a message?"

"Look, I don't have time for this *I'm just doing my job*' nonsense! Just go to his room and make sure he's okay. My name is Sierra Douglas and I'm on my way, let him know I'm coming to get him," Sierra slammed the phone back onto its base and scrambled for her keys.

"I know you ain't phenna leave them kids here while you run out wit' yo' little boyfriend," Darryl spoke up.

Sierra stopped in her tracks. She slowly about-faced and came eye to eye with her so-called husband, "As a matter of fact yes I am. It's 4 o'clock in the morning, Lilly is out there asleep, the kids are asleep, and in case you've forgotten they're your kids too!" Sierra opened the bedroom door and charged down the hall and out of the house allowing the front door to slam behind her.

Sierra turned the car into the first available parking spot and ran inside of the hotel. She breathed in and out slowly, trying to remain calm. She walked up to the front desk where a young woman was sitting picking at her fingernails.

"Excuse me," Sierra began, "My name's Sierra Douglas, I just called about fifteen or so minutes ago. Are you the young lady that I spoke with?"

"Uh, yes ma'am."

"Did you go up there? Is he okay?"

"Ma'am I told you, Mr. Marshall does not want to be bothered."

"And I told you- look little girl, I'm not going to argue. You have a manager around here tonight?"

Sierra's blood boiled. She wondered what happened to people's sense of decency. What was more important? A person's bullshit seven-dollar an hour job or potentially another person's life. The young woman answered that question with her defiant attitude and refusal to help her. Sierra waited impatiently as the young woman radioed for her superior to come to the front desk. Moments later a tall, lanky young white male wearing his hotel uniform and small round glasses turned the corner. Sierra rushed him pleading her case before he could comprehend her presence. He immediately denied her request but she remained persistent.

"Let me tell you something. Mr. Marshall is like a brother to me, I know when he's not right. He called me not long ago telling me he has to 'go away'. Now I'm not going to reason those words in my mind as you'd have me to. No. What you're going to do is get a key for his room and take me up there to check on him. If you don't then what I'm going to do is knock on every room in this hotel making your guests quite angry until one of two things happens. Either I'll find his room or the police will drag me out kicking and screaming."

The young manager hesitated before ordering his assistant to make a key for Nate's room. She reluctantly obliged as she thought that Sierra was mentally off. She handed the key card to him and together he and Sierra rushed up the steps to the second floor and down the hall to Nate's room.

Inside the room Nate sat in silence. There were no more voices. No visions. Only a mission, a goal that needed to be completed. Nate sat the pen that he'd been writing with beside his letter. He picked up the gun from his lap and twirled it in his hand. He breathed deeply in and out as he waited for the perfect second. He inhaled deeply and slowly inserted the gun into his mouth, tears rolled down his cheeks and he swallowed hard. All sound was drowned out. All he could hear was his own breathing, the sound of his heart beating its final rhythm and the one thought consuming his brain – *"I gotta go away."*

Outside the room Sierra banged on the door with all her might. Tears rolled down her cheeks and she screamed his name. Her heart raced as she cried out to him but he would not answer. The hotel manager grabbed her and pulled her back from the door.

"Ms. Douglas, please. Maybe he stepped out. I can see you're concerned but there's no sense in disturbing our other guests when he's clearly not in there," he looked nervous as he anticipated angry guests stepping into the hall and having his head for her behavior.

"No, no, no! He's in there, I know he is! You have the key, open the door."

"Ms. Douglas please-"

"Open the got-damned door now!" Sierra glared into his eyes. Several clicks and the faint sound of angry voices could be heard. The manager finally gave up and slipped the key card in the door but it was too late. He opened it just in time for Sierra to witness her best friend pull the trigger, "Nate! No!"

Click. Boom.

16Mike

Sweat beads rolled down Mike's back and sprouted on his forehead. He held a firm grip on the young woman's waist. His eyes were closed and his head tossed backward. He held one of her shoulders as he thrust in and out of her body. He was turned on by her rear end, round and brown as it jiggled from his pounding. He took his hand and smacked it to make it wiggle some more. The woman, Danielle, called out to her maker in ecstasy. This was some of the best sex he'd had in a long time and his cell phone's ringing was driving him crazy. He tuned it out by focusing on Danielle's sweet voice as she sang out his name. He flipped her onto her back and she cooperatively threw her legs open, beckoning him. He slid in slowly, then faster and faster. He was on edge and confused, feeling so good he wanted to burst yet feeling so good he didn't want it to end. But alas all good things must come to an end. He collapsed on Danielle's soaking, sweaty body.

Mike summoned his energy and rolled over onto his back. Danielle huffed, puffed and panted. She was glad she'd met Mike at the grocery store the day prior. Her husband was out of town on business and even when he was home he'd never made love to her the way that Mike had. She rolled over onto her side and rested all her weight on her elbow. She smiled at Mike, a strand of hair plastered across her face.

"Want a beer?" she asked.

"Yea."

Danielle climbed out of bed and walked naked through the dark house to the kitchen. Mike enjoyed the view of her sashaying out of the room. She was gorgeous and exotic. Part Jamaican, part Asian, her skin was smooth caramel and her eyes hazel brown. Her long thick brown hair hung to the center of her back. Her breasts round and perky and that ass, that perfect round ass. And what was better, besides being great in bed she knew the game. She was married and needn't anymore than sex from Mike. That thought eased his spirit. He reached for his phone and checked his messages. He deleted three before he came across one from Sierra left fifteen minutes prior.

Mike felt his heart stop momentarily. He jumped from Danielle's bed and rushed to get into his clothes. He was both pulling his shirt over his head and stepping into his shoe when Danielle re-entered the room carrying a beer and a sandwich for him.

"Where are you going?" she asked.

"I gotta go. I'll holler at you later aiight?" Mike rushed to the front door.

"Oh. Okay. You sure you okay?" that was the last thing Mike heard Danielle say as he rushed out the door. He jumped into his car and revved up his engine. He was sure he'd misunderstood Sierra's message but he wanted to be positive. He tried calling her cellular phone but there was no answer. She'd said she was on her way to Nate's parent's home. Fortunately Danielle happened to live only five minutes away. He ran up to the house and banged on the door.

"Yea, who the hell is it?" Mr. Marshall asked angrily from the other side of the door.

"Wassup Pop, it's Mike, open up!"

"Mike? Boy you crazy or sumthin'?" Mr. Marshall asked as he unlocked and opened the door allowing Mike to enter, "Boy what the hell wrong wit' you banging on my door like that? You know what time it is?"

"Pops, what happened?"

"What? What happened to what? Who? Boy you high or sumthin'?"

"Naw man, I got a message on my cell from Sierra. She say sumthin' happened to Nate and said to meet her here. She ain't here?"

Mr. Marshall became concerned. He hadn't heard anything though. He called out to his wife as he walked to the back of the house with Mike on his trail. He asked his wife if she'd heard from Sierra but she had not. She decided to call Sierra's cell phone to find out just what, if anything was wrong with her only son but there was no answer.

"Michael, are you sure she said something was wrong with Nate?" Mrs. Marshall asked feeling very concerned. What she hadn't shared with Mike and her husband was the bad feeling she'd had all morning. That was why she was up at seven in the a.m. dusting and doing laundry, she couldn't sleep. Before Mike could respond there was another knock at the door. Mr. Marshall disappeared down the hall as quickly as possible and Sierra soon appeared in the living room without him. Moments later he returned with Mya following.

"Sierra what happened to my baby?" Mrs. Marshall questioned, tears already flooding her eyes.

"Umm, I uh-have some very bad news," Sierra searched for the right words and a way to verbalize them.

"Dammit Sierra, what is it?" Mr. Marshall asked impatiently.

"Nathaniel's dead," Mrs. Marshall felt sick whispering those words. She slumped down into a chair and clutched her stomach. She gasped for air.

"What? That's not true baby," Mr. Marshall told his wife, "That's not true, is it Sierra?"

Sierra chewed her bottom lip. She wanted to tell her best friend's parents that, no of course their only boy was not dead. She averted her eyes and fidgeted. She tossed her head back and took a deep breath, "Yes, he is."

"No, no! What happened?"

"He shot himself."

"What?"

"I don't get it Sierra, why would my son shoot himself?" Mrs. Marshall asked, "He wasn't unhappy. Was he? He...he seemed fine. I hadn't spoken to him much for sometime but...but he said he had a lot of work. He seemed fine, why would he do this?"

"Because he's gay," Mya spoke up sounding embittered.

Sierra was momentarily stumped. She wondered how Mya knew that information when she had yet to fill her in on the details surrounding Nate's suicide. Mr. and Mrs. Marshall and Mike's attention immediately focused on Mya. The men were angered and offended by her words. The urge to hit her for saying such a thing was quite strong. Mike jumped to his feet, his fists clenched at his side. Heat radiated from Mr. Marshall's face.

"How dare you," he hissed, "How dare you say such a thing about my son! I don't know what my son ever saw in your uppity ass."

"Mr. Marshall please, don't, she's...right. He is-er, was gay. Nate was gay. Here Mrs. Marshall, he left a note. I stole it from the room. I figured if he hid it from those that loved him most then the last thing he'd want is some reporter advertising it on the local news."

"Good girl, thank you," Mrs. Marshall reached to take the letter from Sierra's extended hand.

Stunned, hurt, and angry Mr. Marshall turned and left the room. Mike sharing his reaction to the news snatched the letter from Sierra's hand. His face became warm as he read Nate's final words and confession to himself. He swallowed hard as if he were swallowing his heart. He flung the letter back at Sierra and charged out of the house. He climbed back inside of his car and peeled out of the driveway. His mind was going faster than his tires spinning. He drove without seeing and found himself outside of his building. He sat inside his vehicle debating whether or not he should go inside. He didn't feel like being alone. He decided to head back south and visit his grandmother.

Mike hadn't seen his grandmother Marie in about eight months. He did not get along with her or his aunt Antoinette who'd lived there with her three children Jean, Claude, and Patrice since he was small. Mike's aunt and grandmother did not like him and vowed never to agree with or accept anything or anyone that he cared for. But his grandmother could not stop herself from liking Nate. She never came right out and expressed it but Mike knew. It was apparent in the way she treated him. She'd be disappointed by his demise. He pulled up and parked his car on the grass in front of his grandmother's home. He knocked on the door and jiggled the handle. It was unlocked so he walked inside.

"Who is dat come in my home?" she asked through her still thick Haitian accent.

"S'a passé, Grandma? It's me Mike."

"What you want Michael?" she asked not taking her eyes off the television.

"Damn, it's still like that huh?" Mike took a deep breath to calm his frazzled nerves. He took a seat on the sofa kitty-corner from his grandmother's sitting chair, "Grandma you remember my boy Nate?"

"Oui."

"Grandma I just found out he's dead," verbalizing that fact left a bitter taste in Mike's mouth.

"Dat what you come tell me? He dead? Well I'm sorry ta hear dat but why ya wanna bring me bad news for, eh? You don't come say hi, you come bring me news somebody died."

"Damn, that's all you can say?"

"What more ya want me to say, eh? You want me to say what I think?" she looked at Mike for the first time but she ignored the pain in his eyes. She ignored the suffering in his heart. She disregarded the longing for sympathy and secret need for an embrace, "What trouble ya done gone an' got dat boy mixed up in what done got him kilt?"

Those words, that accusation hit Mike like a ton of bricks. His face was red hot and his lungs had wound tightly around his heart or so it felt. Grandmother and grandchild glared at one another unflinching.

"You raggedy old bitch, you ain't gone neva change are you?" Mike hissed.

"Why ya come here for Michael, huh? To disrespect me in me own home?"

"Fuck you Marie. I just told you my boy dead and that's what the hell you got ta say behind that?"

"Don't raise ya voice to me boy an' don't you call me by my first name like you my equal."

"All you can do is accuse me? It wasn't my fault Grandma, sorry to disappoint you but Nate shot hisself! It ain't have shit to do wit' me!"

"I want you out me house!" she screeched pointing a bony finger at the door. All the commotion had carried down the hall attracting the attention of Mike's eldest cousin Jean.

"Grandmamma, what's the matter?" he asked coming down the hall. His eyes locked on Mike when he reached the mouth of the living room.

"Damn, I grew up in this joint too, now all of a sudden I ain't welcome?"

"You never been welcome," his grandmother told him.

"What the fuck?"

"Ay man, watch your mouth when you talking to her. Don't be coming up in here disrespecting my grandmamma," Jean threatened.

"Yo grandmamma, huh? Whateva nigga that bitch my momma's momma too. Fuck her old angry ass."

"Man tighten that shit up, Mike."

"What yo' pussy ass gone do Jean but get yo' punk ass whipped?" Mike was up to the challenge. He wanted to take his anger and hurt out. He was just waiting for the right opportunity. Jean knew his limitations. He knew he didn't stand a chance going against his cousin. He just wanted him to leave their grandmother alone. He backed down.

"Mikey come on now man, we cousins. I ain't phenna even go there wit' you. Just chill man, come on," Jean pleaded.

"Nigga fuck you and that triflin' ass hoe you call Grandmamma," Mike turned and walked back out to his car in more emotional turmoil than when he'd arrived. He sat in his vehicle outside the house he'd grown up in. Angry at his grandmother for turning her back on him. More than anything Mike was angry with Nate for leaving him, for taking his own life. Mike was angry with Nate for being gay and having a boyfriend. This whole time he was a fag and hadn't said anything. Had he been putting secret moves on him? "Fuck Nate's sissy ass too," Mike mumbled.

Mike drove about ten minutes further south. He pulled out his cell phone and called Sherika. There was no answer so he called again. Her voice was groggy when she picked up. Irritability caused by being awakened at eight in the morning was evident in her 'Hello'.

"You got company?" Mike asked without announcing himself.

"Naw. Damn Mike what time it is?"

"Eight-fifty-three. I'm phenna come through there. I'a be there in about three minutes," Mike closed the flap on the phone and drove to the duplex Sherika lived in. The door was cracked open when he arrived. Sherika was sitting on the sofa in a pink robe with a scarf tied around her head. She was rolling weed inside the wrapper of a Black and Mild when he entered. He locked the door behind him and took a seat beside her. He picked up the remote and began quietly flipping through channels.

"Okay so you gone tell me why you got me out my bed so early in the mornin'? Shiit, ain't you supposed to be getting ready for work or sumthin' right about now?" Sherika asked. She lit her Black and inhaled deeply. She held the smoke in her mouth momentarily then twisted her bottom lip to blow it out. She kept her eyes on Mike as she passed it off to him. Mike took a long drag and slumped down in his seat.

"My boy Nate shot hisself this morning."

"Whuut? Oh my God! He aiight?"

"Naw. He dead."

Sherika covered her mouth with her hands. She didn't know Nate well; she'd only met him once or twice. She didn't like him very much and he made it clear that he didn't care for her either. However she was aware that he and Mike were very close, almost like brothers.

"Dang Boo, you gone be okay?" Sherika asked genuinely concerned.

"Yea, I'm aiight. Fuck dat nigga."

"Huh? Hold on now, that's yo' boy and he shot hisself and that's what you got to say? Fuck him? What happened that got you talkin' like that?"

"Forget it man."

"Naw nigga, talk to me."

"Sherika. I don't wanna talk about that fuck ass nigga aiight. Why don't you get me a beer or sumthin', make yo'self useful."

Sherika shook her head. She felt sorry for Mike but she knew better than to make mention of those feelings. She instead pushed up from the couch and walked to the kitchen to get Mike a beer as instructed.

17 The Homegoing

Sierra moved at a non-stop pace around the house, trying to keep her mind and her body busy. She was getting herself ready, getting her children ready, straightening up a home that outside of its residents, no one would see. Since witnessing Nate's suicide she had not actually cried. Yes, water had streamed down her cheeks at a snails pace when she'd tried to stop him. But she had not allowed her emotions to take over. She had not actually stopped and sobbed and mourned the loss of her friend.

She smeared the smuck off of Lee's face. She re-braided the braid in Michele's hair. She packed a carryall bag for Jennifer. She rushed around back and forth picking and plucking at her three children until Lilly stepped behind her and gently took Sierra's shoulders in her palms. Lilly was worried about her sister. She hadn't been sleeping but staying up as long as her body would allow doing redundant, repetitive housework. What she didn't know was that every time Sierra closed her eyes she saw Nates' blood and brains splattered all over a hotel room wall. What she didn't know was that every time Sierra closed her eyes she saw her best friend's lifeless body growing cold. Lilly pulled her sister away from retying little Lee's shoe.

"Honey, Sierra, please. You've been moving non-stop for days now. It's not healthy. Go have a seat, I'll deal with the children," Lilly instructed.

"I can't sit down Lilly, there's too much to do."

"The only thing you have to do is mourn the loss of your friend. Si-Si have you even cried once?"

Sierra chewed her bottom lip and stood upright, "I can't sit Lillian, there's too much work to be done."

"Sierra Diane. Go sit, alright?"

Sierra took a breath and left Lilly in the room with the children. She went into the living room and took a seat on the couch. She fidgeted with her skirt momentarily. She was too antsy to sit still. She got up and went into her bedroom where she found Darryl still sitting in his boxers flipping through television stations. Heat radiated from her face. She angrily turned the television off and stood directly in Darryl's line of vision.

"Ay what the hell is your problem?" Darryl asked of his flustered wife.

"Why aren't you dressed? It's about time to go."

"I ain't goin'."

"What? And why not?"

"What for? He ain't like me and I shole as hell ain't like his faggot ass."

Sierra and Darryl glared at one another not flinching nor backing down. Sierra's breathing became rapid and her body began to tremble. Her fists slowly began to clench. Sierra charged at Darryl. She pounced on him and began pounding him with her fists.

"You bastard!" she screamed as she beat his bare chest, "You son of a bitch! I hate you! I hate you, you bastard!"

"Sierra!" Lilly ran to the doorway and saw her sister beating on her husband. She ran into the room and pulled her off of him, "Si-Si come on! Come on, he's not even worth the energy. Come on girl, the kids are out there."

Sierra allowed herself to be pulled away. Darryl was stunned. He raised his hand to a spot underneath his eye. He looked at the blood on his fingertip and then to Sierra who was huffing and puffing and looking like a mad woman.

"You crazy bitch, you cut me."

"I hate you," Sierra spat out.

"Come on honey, let's go," Lilly guided her toward the front door.

"I hate you," she reminded him as she was led away.

Mike dusted a small amount of cocaine on top of the marijuana that filled the emptied Black and Mild wrapping. Sherika watched him prepare his drug of choice and felt sorry for him. He pretended that everything was normal and that Nate's killing himself didn't bother him but she knew that was not true, not at all. All he'd been doing since that day was getting drunk and high and she knew it was all an attempt to cover his pain. She thought his refusal to go to Nate's funeral was the worse thing he could do and would eventually be more damaging to him than anything else but he'd get angry if she tried to make him go. But she was sick of seeing him in his present state. She had to say something.

"Mike, quit it," Sherika told him.

"What? Girl what you talkin' about?"

"You need to stop this bullshit, tryna pretend you ain't sad that your boy gone. You ain't even cried yet have you?"

Mike inhaled a mouth full of smoke and held it momentarily before blowing it in the air, "Sheri stay outta my business."

"Why you don't get off ya ass feelin' sorry for yo'self and go to yo' boys funeral? Tell him how you feel, why you so angry. 'Cause whateva it is that shit just gone keep eatin' at you 'til you get it out."

"Who is you, fuckin' Dr. Phil now? I'a tell you what, I'll holla."

"Oh now you gone put me out 'cause you know I'm right? Fine, whateva 'cause you full of it anyway."

Sherika jumped up and gathered her belongings and left Mike alone in his condo. He took another drag and looked at the joint in his fingers. He couldn't stop himself from thinking about what Sherika had told him. Even if Nate was a secret sissy they'd been boys for nearly twenty years. He owed it to him to at least see him off. He let the joint dangle from his lips as he left his sofa to change into something more appropriate.

"Mya darling, come now. Lift your foot and let Mummy put your shoes on."

Mya's mother Lorraine Engles helped her daughter to get dressed for her late fiancé's homegoing. Tears rolled down Mya's cheeks at an uncontrollable rate. She'd been crying practically non-stop since news of Nate's demise. She seemed to be in a trance, not acknowledging anyone around her. She'd sit in tears rocking backward and forth with a picture of Nate clung tightly to her chest. She had become terribly depressed. Fortunately her parents and grandmother had flown down to help their child through this very difficult time, "Come now Mya darling, we really must go now. Come give Mummy the picture, we'll leave that here."

"Nooo!" Mya cried out startling her mother, "Nooo! Nooo!"

"Honey, it's okay. You can keep the picture okay," Mrs. Engles tried to reason with her unreasonable daughter. She wiped the tears from Mya's eyes. She wrapped her arms around Mya and rocked until she calmed down, "Come baby, you can keep the photo okay? Come now, we must be going. Father and grandmother are waiting."

Mother and daughter walked hand in hand down the stairs and to the foyer where her father stood waiting. He walked over to meet his baby girl with his hands extended.

"Come, let us go now," he said to Mya. Together the family left the house with Mya clutching Nate's photo.

There was no sound in Anthony's efficiency apartment other than the noise he made as he dressed in his best black suit. The quiet began to suffocate him. The confines of the small residence and its walls made him uncomfortable. He was anxious to get out yet not anxious to get to his destination. He spritzed a small amount of cologne on his suit and rubbed it in. He reached to grab his keys from the nightstand. He paused and picked up a picture of him and Nate together that he'd blown up. He felt a tear roll down his cheek, he didn't stop it.

"I'll always love you," Anthony whispered as he held the photo to his lips. He replaced the picture and left for the funeral.

Mrs. Marshall was fully dressed and ready to go. That wasn't the problem. The problem was that she didn't have the energy to get up. Or maybe she didn't have the strength to see her only son lying there in that coffin after only twenty-nine years of living. She never thought that she'd have to bury one of her children. Two of her daughters, Claudette and Natalie sat on either side of her trying to soothe her.

Mr. Marshall had not spoken more than two words at a time to his wife since the news was brought to them. He hadn't put his arm around her shoulder. He hadn't held her hand. He'd sat alone in his basement with the door closed listening to Coltrane, Ellington, or Basie and clutching an old worn, nearly deflated basketball. He sat there taking full blame and responsibility for his son's taking of his own life. That is where he sat while his wife suffered their loss upstairs. In his suit and tie thinking of all the many things he could have done differently which could have kept his son from ending his life.

"Where is your father?" Mrs. Marshall asked her girls.

"In the basement Mama, you want me to get him?" Claudette asked.

"No, let's go. Leave his sorry ass down there. Leave him here to feel sorry for no one except himself. Let him blame himself for this tragedy because Lord knows I blame him!"

The sisters looked at each other and silently agreed to keep their mouths shut and allow their mother to express her hurt as she chose. They helped her to her feet and out the front door.

As the guests filed down the aisle to speak a prayer over the closed casket holding Nate's body, Sierra rushed around the church finding odd jobs to keep her busy. Lilly was worried about her sister and her behavior. She decided to approach her mother for her advice.

"Mom," Lilly took a seat beside her mother, "Mom, I'm worried about Si-Si. She's like a …a robot. She just will not stop moving. She's not sleeping, Momma, she hasn't even cried yet. That can't be normal. I cried and I wasn't nearly as close to Nate as she was."

"Lilly, honey stop. Don't worry about your sister, she's got to handle this in her own way, ok? I hear what you saying. I cried, shoots your father cried and so will your sister. Just be there for her when she does."

Mrs. Mitchell placed her arm around her child's shoulder and pulled her into her breast. She was also concerned about Sierra but she didn't want to worry Lilly. She swallowed her tears and held her daughter tight. She felt for the Marshall's, she couldn't imagine having to bury one of her girls.

Lilly felt a hand on her shoulder. She looked up and into the eyes of her father. Pastor Mitchell pulled Lillian into his chest. Tears spilled from his eyes as he held his baby girl tightly. He took Lilly's face in his palms and looked deeply into her eyes.

"I love you Lillian, you hear me? Lord knows I love you and your sister and your mother. You're my world. Yes, yes you've done thangs that have disappointed me and maybe at times I haven't been the best father. But this tragic situation has reminded me of our own mortality. It's a shame it took something like this but baby girl I want you home for the rest of your stay. I'm sorry, I just want us to begin again baby."

"Yes Daddy, of course and I am so sorry. Really I am."

"Nooo!" a shrill cry came from the back of he church.

Pastor and Mrs. Mitchell and Lillian jumped from their seats. It was Mya and her families turn to visit the casket. Mya had been in a trance up until that point not noticing nor acknowledging anyone that spoke to her. But she sensed what was going on and she didn't want any part of it. She couldn't bear to think of Nathaniel in that box and she did not want to remember him like that. Instead she jerked and screamed until her parents led her to a seat out of direct view of the casket. Mya's body shook violently as her mother tried her best to console her. Sierra ran to her side and pulled her into her breasts. She stroked her curls smooth and whispered words only she and Mya could understand. Mya slowly calmed, she felt safe in Sierra's arms since Sierra was the closest person to Nate. She slipped back into her daze not noticing Anthony slip in and take a seat in the back of the church.

Anthony opted not to visit the casket either. He didn't want to envision what Nate looked like lying inside of a casket. Scanning the crowd he noticed Mya near the front sobbing. He felt bad for her and wanted to offer his condolences but he didn't think that to be a very wise idea. He sat back and watched the visiting line shorten. He smeared a tear from beneath his eyes and waited. A young lady, who he didn't realize was one of Nate's sisters, handed him an obituary. A large man who walked with a cane wobbled up to the podium and began to speak:

"Dearly beloved. Brothers and Sisters. Family and friends, we are all gathered here today...to pay our respects to one of God's beautiful young children, Nathaniel Lee Marshall. Nathaniel was a young man so full of- of life and of love and of charisma. Nathaniel-Nathaniel, he was like a son to me, the son I never had. As you all know the Lord blessed me with two beautiful daughters, Sierra and Lillian but you know most every man wants a son and I was no different. And when Sierra was about, uh, I'd say about sixteen she brought me a blessing which was Nathaniel Lee Marshall..."

Sierra held Mya in her arms and rocked her back and forth to keep her calm. She'd scanned the crowd repeatedly but found no sign of Mike. She was both worried and disappointed. She knew that Mike was upset with finding out about Nate but she didn't think he'd disrespect him and his family in such a way. She sighed and returned her attention to the front of the church.

"Can I share with y'all my fondest memory of Nathaniel? Can I share? Well alright now. It was early on Sunday morning and Nate and Sierra were here bright and early as usual. It musta been about eight-sumthin' 'cause it was right before Sunday service was to start. Nathaniel was eighteen years old. He walked up to me looking clean as always in his blue suit and tie with his hair cut low and he said, 'Pastor, I would be honored if you'd let me do the sermon today.' He'd never done it befo' and I had no idea what he'd say but the Lord come to me and he say, 'Let that boy do it.' So's I stepped aside and that was the best sermon that I'd ever heard."

The door to the church creaking open didn't go unnoticed. Mike slipped inside and took a seat in the rear. He'd decided he'd stay just long enough to pay his respects to Nate's parents and Sierra and then leave. He caught a sight of Sierra signaling for him to join her. Mike gently tiptoed in Sierra's direction. As he reached her row he felt someone grip his arm from the opposite side. When he looked over he saw that it was Mrs. Marshall. She pulled him down to sit beside her. He was very surprised considering that as far as he'd correctly assumed she'd never liked him. He sat beside her and the two held hands through the conclusion of Pastor Mitchell's sermon.

"I'm not here to make you cry, you gone do that anyway on your own time, in your own environment. Naw, naw. We are here to celebrate! Celebrate life! Celebrate love! Celebrate the Lord! We are here to celebrate the homegoing of our son Nathaniel Lee Marshall to the arms of the Lord! Amen! Sang it wit' me, Amen! One mo' time! Amen!"

The crowd was uplifted for the time being. They clapped and praised and called out their thanks through Amen's. They dabbed the corners of their eyes with handkerchiefs and knew in that moment that their brother had truly gone on to a much, better place. The choir hummed softly behind the pastor. Sierra gently moved Mya's head from the security of her bosom and rested her against her mother. Mya was so deeply entranced she had not noticed. Sierra stood and walked up the front of the church.

"At this time brother's and sista's, I'd like to bring my eldest girl up here to say a few words about young brother Nathaniel. Sierra honey, come on up here."

Sierra chewed the inside of her bottom lip softly as she strolled up to the pew. She took a deep breath as she walked up the steps and stood beside her daddy. She took his hands in hers and kissed his cheek.

Pastor Mitchell turned and sat down beside Lillian and held her hand in his. Sierra closed her eyes and breathed slowly toward the heavens.

"I'm sixteen years old and it's the first day of class. I'm terribly shy so I really don't have any friends. This guy walks in the class bouncing this basketball and all these young girls are, are all over him. The sight is pathetic. But I recognize him, not just from around the school. I've been in this class with him since freshman year. I decide right then and there I'm going to make a new friend today and make all these little fast tail gals jealous at the same time. So I speak to him in Spanish and he has no idea what I'm saying, heh, heh! But that was the start of a wonderful, wonderful friendship. And I'm going to miss our times together but I'll never, ever forget the times we shared," Sierra's eyes began to water but she blinked the tears away and continued;   "Now the choir will sing us out."

"Oh Mary don't you weep...Tell Martha not to moan...Pharaohs army...Don't you know that they drowned in the red sea...I'm sangin' Mary...Tell Martha not to moan...Mooan! Humm..." the choir went into an upbeat selection of various popular gospel songs to try to keep the congregation from feeling too down.

When the service was done the guests began to pile outside and the pallbearers carried the casket out to the Hertz. The Florida sunshine felt ironic on such a day as this one. Mya, with photo clutched to her chest, walked out in a trance with the help of her mother and grandmother. When she stepped outdoors her eyes locked on Anthony.

"Murderer!" Mya screamed. She snatched away and ran after him. When she reached him she began beating him with her fists, "You! You killed him! You took him away from me! I hate you, I hate you!"

A crowd gathered separating Mrs. Engles from her daughter. Mike exited the church holding the hand of Mrs. Marshall when from the top of the steps he spotted Mya accusing a guy of being a murderer. He took his hand back and ran to her aide.

"Mya what's goin' on? Who is this nigga?" Mike asked.

"Michael whip his ass! He killed Nathaniel!"

"Mya stop, calm down," Anthony tried to reason, "You are not going to put that on me, now be reasonable," his plea was answered by

Mya spitting in his face. Angrily he took his handkerchief and smeared it away.

"Aaaww, you must be that sissy nigga Anthony," Mike said stepping between him and Mya.

"Who are you?"

"Don't worry 'bout that nigga, alls you need to know is that I'm the nigga that's phenna whop yo' punk ass."

"What is going on here?" Sierra asked cutting between the two pumped up men. Their chests were poked out and their fists were clenched, nostrils flared, "You two ought to be ashamed of yourselves! I-I –I don't know what's going on here but we're here to pay our respects to my best friend and you will not make a mockery of this day in front of his parents, are you crazy? Whatever your problem is you can handle it some other time, some other way!"

Mike and Anthony's glare locked for a few moments longer. Mike's shoulders relaxed. He wrapped his arm around Sierra's shoulders and walked in the direction of his car. He was going to bury his brother but he wouldn't allow himself to forget to blame and punish Anthony for it. His face was now etched in Mike's brain.

Mrs. Marshall sat curled up near the edge of the bed. The room was dimly lit as she rested her head against her daughter Claudette's shoulder. She willingly allowed the tears to roll from her eyes as the two looked through a stack of pictures of their son and brother.

"Mama, are you and Daddy gonna be alright behind this?"

I don't know Dette. Lemme ask you though, have you once seen Daddy wrap his arm around me, console me? Not one time. He's been too busy sitting in that basement feeling sorry for himself because he blames himself as well he should, I blame him. I don't know Dette, I just don't know."

Claudette was concerned that if Daddy didn't get it together her parent's marriage could fall apart. She decided to let it be for the time being. For now she'd just do Daddy's job and be there. After all they'd just buried a child today.

The humidity was thick and suffocating. Anthony strolled slowly along the River Front. All the lights and music and cheer behind him contrasted greatly with his emotions. They sat out here often sharing their thoughts. The very first time he convinced Nate to meet him for a dinner date, afterwards they sat here on the River Front just talking 'til about four in the morning. Anthony smiled to himself as he reflected. He took a seat on a bench still dressed in his best suit. A single rose he held in his hand he tossed in the river as a symbol of his letting go.

"I'll always love you Nathaniel Marshall."

Mya had recovered from her trance but not from her sorrow. The tears continued to flow seemingly non-stop. She slowly walked down the stairwell with the last bag in hand. She stopped midway looking about at the space below. The paintings Nate had auctioned on to have grace the walls. The furniture they'd loved and laughed and spoken on. Her father called to her from the foot of the stairwell and Mya continued on. It would be hard to give up his home, their home and move back to England but there were just too many memories here. Mr. Engles took Mya's hand in his and led her to the front door. He took her luggage and Mya followed. With tears flowing sort of like a river she turned to take one last look before leaving her and Nathaniel's home forever.

Mike pulled up on the run-down grass and parked his car beside a large tree. He'd spotted Sherika amongst a group of several of his homeboys from back in the day. He walked up and slapped palms and gave pounds. Sherika stepped up to him and looked him directly in his eyes searching for a hint of his true emotions.

"So how you feel?" she asked in all sincerity.

"I'm straight."

"You know baby you can be real wit' me."

"I know."

Sherika opened her arms inviting Mike in. He'd tried to be a thug, tried to be hard but he really needed the support right then. He accepted Sherika's love. They'd slept together often over the years but outside of that she was a good friend. Mike pulled back feeling slightly relaxed.

"Yo' lemme hit dat," Mike inhaled the weed smoke which for the time being calmed his spirit.

Sierra washed the last dish, dried it and put it on the shelf. She wiped down the counter and folded the dishrag and hung it across the faucet. She leaned back against the sink and looked around the kitchen. The food had been packaged and put away. The floor had been swept and mopped and countertops and tabletops wiped down. The trash had been taken out back. Lillian and the children were fast asleep as it was about 2 a.m. Darryl hadn't come home. Maybe it was his way of getting back at her for going off on him. She didn't waste too much brainpower wondering. She stood ringing her hands trying to think of something else to do but she came up thoughtless. She'd scoured every inch of her home over the past week.

Sierra reasoned with herself that she should just go to bed; she'd need to get up early to tend to Michele, Lee and Jennifer. She clicked the lights off and walked to her bedroom. She laid her robe across the chair in the corner of the room and crawled beneath the comforter. She closed her eyes but they would not stay shut. She reached over and turned the bedside lamp on. She sat up and picked up her Bible and flipped through for a passage to begin with. She sniffed and turned the page. She swallowed hard and flipped through a couple more pages. She rubbed her forehead and sniffed again, her eyes began to burn. She chewed her lip and tried to blink the tears away. She tried to read but the water blurred her vision. Her lip quivered, her body shook and for the first time in years Sierra cried.

The Letter

Dear Momma,

I'm writing to tell you that I've got to go. Momma forgive me but there is no other way. I love you and Daddy and I only want you to be happy. I only want that Daddy will not ever hit you again like he did when I was little. Momma when you read this letter don't cry for me, this was best. I cannot live two lives anymore. It is eating away my flesh like acid. Not being able to let people see the real Nathaniel Marshall. Two lives too many. Daddy I'm sorry. You told me no boy of yours would be a faggot and I tried to live up to that but I was weak and I disrespected you. I broke the rules of the Lord, I sinned in so many unspeakable ways. I had a boyfriend Momma, his name is Anthony. You would like him. In a lot of ways he's like Mya. He loves me and I love him. Don't tell Daddy that, I don't want him to hurt you. If he tries tell Mike, I mean Michael. I know you don't like him because you think it's his fault I got in trouble but it wasn't. Mike is my best friend but I only imitated him to keep Daddy off track. I'm sorry Daddy, I'm not trying to make you the bad guy. You just did what you thought was best. Please don't be mad at me and don't blame Mom. Momma don't be mad at Michael. He never had anybody but me that's why he's the way he is. He had no love from anybody except me. Please take care of him for me. Don't be stubborn this one time, for me. Oh and Momma tell Mya I do love her and I'm sorry for what I did to her that day and

I'm sorry I cheated. I couldn't give my all to her because I was living a lie. Tell Sierra she's my favorite girl, she will know what I mean. You always liked Sierra and wanted me to be with her and if things were different I would marry her. Momma, make her leave Darryl, he's no good for her. I'd be happy if she were with Mike, she would make him a better person like she tried to do for me. I pray the Father and Son forgive me for the sins I've committed and the one I am about to commit.

-Nathaniel Lee Marshall

(Nate)

Mike & Sierra Meet

Sierra stood outside of the school with her book bag in hand waiting. Her new friend Nate had invited her to go with him to the 163rd Street Mall. She was aware that it was a major hang out for her peers but she had never herself gone, at least not with any of them. There were two reasons for that. One was that she didn't have anyone to go with except her younger sister Lilly and even she had a life of her own. The second reason, which was actually more important than the first was that, her parents had required her to come directly home from school. The only difference between today and any other day was that it was a rare occasion where she would disobey her mother and father.

She was nervous about her decision. What would Momma and Daddy do as punishment? What if Nate stood her up? What if he was just toying with her? After all who was she but a sixteen and a half year old geeky Pastors daughter with bad ends and eyeglasses? The more she thought about it the more she expected him to stand her up. She felt small standing there alone while the other students went home, to the mall or to their young girlfriend/boyfriends house.

Sierra threw her bag on her back and began toward home. She'd reached the corner when she heard Nate calling her name. She shyly turned and saw him signaling for her to come to him. She struggled to keep from smiling too hard and looking foolish. She felt butterflies fluttering within the pit of her stomach. Nate looked so handsome standing there in his baggy jeans and classic Chuck Taylor's. His arms were extended when she reached him and so she happily gave him a hug.

"You were going to leave me?" Nate asked.

"Huh, uh no. Well I thought maybe you forgot. I'm sorry."

"Don't worry about it l'il momma. Ay Si, I'd like you to meet my homeboy Mike."

"Pleased to meet you," Sierra said.

"Yea," Mike seemed to look right through Sierra as if she weren't there. He twirled a toothpick around his mouth with his tongue looking off into the distance, "Damn dog, git yo' l'il hoe an' let's ride."

Sierra's eyes widened in shock from Mike's blatant disrespect. She was speechless as she glared at him. Nate became angered and annoyed at once. He'd been reluctant to introduce Sierra to Mike because he'd expected something like this.

"Mike man, what the hell is wrong with you?" Nate spoke up.

"Why would you say something like that? You don't even know me. I'm not a hoe and I don't appreciate you calling me one."

"Shawty, I don't really give a damn what you wanna be called, just brang yo' ass on if you comin'."

"Nate I thank you for the offer but I just remembered I have homework. Maybe we can go some other time," Sierra said.

"Sierra, I'm sorry. I'll call you."

"Don't reason wit' her ass, be like Moses, let dat bitch go! Ha ha!"

"You need Jesus," chewing her bottom lip, Sierra turned away hot from anger and headed toward home.

"Mike why you gotta be so damned ignorant?" Nate spat out, "Wait up Si!"

"Man, fuck both y'all bitch asses," Mike turned away.

Nate jogged until he caught up to Sierra.

18Mike

Mike was overwhelmed with surprise when he received the telephone call. He didn't even think she knew his phone number. He reasoned that she'd gotten it from Sierra or maybe her husband had it. Either way he seriously doubted that she'd permanently etched it in her address book beside the numbers of people that she actually respected. In the nearly twenty years he'd been close friends with her only son; Mrs. Marshall herself had never once invited Michael into her home. When he'd eaten there or even stepped past her front door it was on the request of Nate or Pops Marshall. It became even more of a challenge to get him past those doors once Mrs. Marshall caught wind of his crush on her young Annette.

Mike normally cared not what others thought of him but for a reason unbeknownst to him it'd always bothered him that Mrs. Marshall did not like him. Maybe it was because he admired her and the mother he'd observed her being to Nate. She was always very attentive and loving toward her family the way he'd secretly imagined his mother could have been. But he was a troublemaker and he knew it and that was all he knew how to be.

Mike smoothed his shirt and tie repeatedly as he drove wanting to make sure that when he arrived he was neat and impressive. He'd gotten a fresh trim though he could have done without one and had his barber's wife manicure his nails. Michael was nervous. Butterflies floated along the border of belly and bowels and no matter how hard he tried his tough act was not going to work for him this time. He kept his eye on the clock as he drove not wanting to ruin this by being tardy. He laughed to himself at his unnecessary panic when he arrived a half an hour early.

For the very first time Mrs. Marshall greeted him at the door. Initially the meeting was awkward. Mike cursed himself internally, "I should have brought a flower or something," he thought. He concealed his self-disappointment with a smile. Mrs. Marshall smiled and pulled Mike into her arms. She held him tight against her breast and rubbed a hand up and down his back. Mike swallowed hard. He felt warm inside, at ease. For the first time in what had to be ever Michael Toussaint felt positive. Mrs. Marshall stepped back and held Mike's hands in hers while she smiled at him.

"I'm glad you could make it Michael."

"Thank you for inviting me Mrs. Marshall."

"Oh boy, call me Momma, what the hell!"

"Yes ma'am – I mean Momma."

The two walked hand in hand to the back of the house where classical music played softly in the background of the gentle chatter. Mike realized that he remembered this as the sound of the Marshall house. Soft classical music and non-stop chatter which over the years would grow louder as newer generations were born unto it. Nate's sisters Claudette and Felice chatted, set the table, and scolded their children, three among them. They welcomed Mike and offered him a seat and a drink. Mike scanned the area for Mr. Marshall but he had yet to make an appearance. Normally he would have been the first to greet Mike with a proud grin on his face and a cold beer in his hand.

Mike watched sisters and husbands and nieces and nephews, grandchildren and cousins enter. He heard the noise level increase greatly and gabbed about sports and such with the men. His attention shot to the young Annette as she entered hand in hand with her fiancé. She was still captivating with her honey brown skin and large round brown eyes, which peered from behind prescription cat-eye lenses. He was a bit disappointed with the short auburn twisties growing from her scalp but he could not deny her beauty. He'd never make a move on her. She was Nate's baby sister and therefore she was a sister to him as well. Mike took her hand in his and pulled Annette into a harmless embrace while jealousy burrowed into the spirit of her man as he watched. Annette threw her arms around him tightly and kissed his cheek.

"How have you been holding up?" she asked holding her palm to his face.

"I've been good y'know. I don't like to dwell on it too much."

"You're still in denial too, huh?"

"Denial? N-naw, just dwellin' ain't gone change it."

"Yea," Annette paused as if her mind had just traveled miles away. She stared past Mike without actually looking at anyone or anything. When she spoke it was sudden, "You look good Mikey, I'm proud of you."

Annette's attitude 360'd as she joined her family in lively conversation. Mike still had not seen Mr. Marshall and it was getting close to dinnertime. Sierra and her family, parents included, rushed into the Marshall home in time for grace. Mr. Marshall wobbled up the basement steps and slipped into a chair barely being noticed.

After dinner Mike took a seat on the sofa beside Sierra. He was stuffed and tired of the same boring male gossip and he didn't feel he fit in with any of the young men present. Of the men that were apart of the Marshall family that he meshed with, one had once again confined himself to grieve in his basement and the other was buried six-feet under. There was an odd awkwardness shared between Mike and Sierra. In all of the time that they had known each other they'd rarely, if ever, spent time together without the benefit of Nate's influence. In all the time they'd known one another they did not have social telephone conversations. Nate was the glue that bonded them together and now that he was gone they were pretty content with the thought that they may see less and less of one another until they stopped seeing each other altogether.

"So, how've you been?" Sierra asked putting her hand on top of Mike's.

"I should be asking you that."

"I've been hanging in there. It's been hard but..." Sierra's voice trailed off.

"Ay, I uh, I got the club. Y'know the jazz club me and Nate was phenna get?"

"Oh yea. That's great."

"Yea, I'm namin' it *Nathaniel's*. Sounds real jazzy y'know."

"That's so nice Mike. Did you tell his mother?"

"Yea, yea, she cried. Ay wassup wit' Pops Marshall? He come up for dinner and don't say nothin' to nobody then disappear down them damn steps again. He ain't even holla at me...nothin'."

"I don't know. I know Claudette and Annette were concerned about him and Mrs. Marshall. I hope they're okay."

The two shared in another moment of awkward silence. Sierra flipped her wrist and eyed the dainty inexpensive watch. She sighed and smacked her thighs with her palms and stood up.

"Well, Mike I'm gonna head home, it's getting close to the kids bedtime."

"Aiight Si-Si, take care."

Sierra paused and turned to face him, "Mike just because Nate's not physically between us anymore doesn't mean you have to be a stranger."

"I appreciate that l'il momma," Mike stood and embraced Sierra. They held one another tighter than they'd expected. As if they were reaching out for one final physical piece of their lost best friend, some sense of relief. They found brief solace in each other's arms before parting ways.

Mike was up bright and early on Monday morning. He was dressed and in his ride on the way to the office. His superior Reginald had approved and made arrangements for Mike to take a couple weeks off to grieve but he made the decision to return early. He found it to be too mentally stressful to sit around his home doing much of nothing but thinking. Though there were a few things left to do on the club before the grand opening, there wasn't nearly enough to keep Nate off of his mind. His soul was conflicted with anger and sadness directed at and as a result of the actions of his late friend. Besides that, his projects had been taken over by Bjorn Zuchovski and the last thing he needed was a white man doing as good as he. There were plenty people who didn't want his black ass there to begin with and were just looking for a reason to get him out.

He was taken aback when he stepped off the elevator at his floor. He found himself face to face with a not so fully recovered Samantha Falls. He hadn't seen Sam since the day of the attack. He hadn't really considered the severity of the punishment he'd inflicted upon her. Mike assessed the damage that he was responsible for. There was a long scar across her left cheek, which would clearly be permanent and her leg was in a cast. It had been a couple months since and she was still a damaged woman. A small part of Mike felt guilt as he realized how terribly Sherika must have beat her. Then he thought of the bogus sexual harassment charges filed against him and grinned. Fearful and uncomfortable in his presence, Samantha rushed away as quickly as her crutches would take her.

Michael settled into his large office chair feeling a bit relaxed now that he was back in his own environment. He leaned back in his seat and felt the leather embrace him. He closed his eyes and swiveled from side to side. He drummed his fingertips along the arm of the chair and tried to clear his thoughts. His mind returned to a couple of days ago. It made him feel good to have had a mother even if only for a day. Mike knew that would not last, he didn't feel he had it in him to live up to the expectations of a good mother. That didn't matter to him. What meant most was that moment in time when Mrs. Marshall held him tight in her arms the way a mother would a child that she loved.

In pleasant spirits Mike turned in his chair to face the desk. He pulled out his appointment book. He had a series of appointments scheduled, which had been turned over to Bjorn. He picked up the telephone receiver and dialed Bjorn's extension, his voicemail picked up the call. Mike left him a message advising of his return and intent to take over his previous workload. Mike decided that before he got to work to get himself a hot mug of Colombian brew. He'd barely returned to his office sipping the strong caffeine and began pulling out paperwork and blueprints when Reginald Tuttle tapped on his door. Mike looked up and signaled for him to enter. Reginald entered gently closing the door behind him. He shook Mike's hand firmly looking Mike directly in the eyes as he did so. The two men took a seat simultaneously. Mike felt comfortable with Reginald and trusted his decisions. He never felt as though there was any malice behind things he said or did and the news he brought on this day did not sway or alter Mike's feelings.

"Michael, glad to see you son but what in the world are you doing back so soon?" Reginald asked folding his hands across his rounding belly.

"Aawww, Reg I just couldn't take sitting around the house. Didn't want to keep thinking about what happened."

"I understand son, I do. When my sister passed last year I was a wreck and staying home didn't do a thing for me but make it worse."

"How did your sister die?" Mike asked surprisingly interested in what his aging boss had to say.

"Cancer," Reginald's mind trailed away momentarily similar to how Annette's had at dinner and it came back just as sudden, "Yes sir, Cindy and I were pretty close so I can relate to what you're saying. And that's what makes this so difficult. Samantha Fall's went to Brad this morning crying that you're back and how she's so afraid. She's a bratty little tramp, a real pain in the ass," Mike was shocked. He'd never heard Reginald be so real. He tried his best to stifle his laughter, "Anyway Brad's having a hissy fit. He wants you fired. Bottom line, as far as I'm concerned the woman has slept around with so many men who knows how many people have her name at the head of their hit list. But – and this is between you and me – she's clearly gotten him hooked on her head and now he's raising hell about this situation. Word came down from the partners that I have to suspend you while this investigation is pending."

Fury gave birth within Mike. If he weren't so dark-skinned he'd have been beet red. His fists clenched involuntarily and his palms were sweaty. The violent thoughts racing through his head were louder than the on-going yet supportive words of Reggie Tuttle. Mike's breathing became thick and heavy as he became separated from the room.

"Michael?" Reggie repeated recapturing Mike's attention.

"Y-yes sir sorry. What was that Reginald?"

"I said take a vacation. They may have their way and get your body out but I made sure they keep money flowing into your bank account that's for damn sure. Burns me up that I'm the oldest fart here and I'm more liberal than these young racist bastards."

Mike forgot about what was happening to him, his life, and his world as he listened to Reggie vent. He'd never in the entire time he was employed with the firm seen this civil rights motivated side of him. Now Mike was certain that the picture of that little sun drenched colored baby on his desk was black. But respect didn't equal job security. Confused and disgruntled and still babbling Reggie shook Mike's hand like professionals do and he left Mike alone in his office disgusted. He leaned back in his chair and stared down at the cars below his window and began to silently count. He tried to mentally drift back to dinner and the hug shared between himself and Mrs. Marshall as a means of embracing something positive. He focused hard and counted. He began to feel the stress washing away. He watched a young woman who appeared to him to be pregnant play 'frogger' through traffic as she darted across the street.

"Damn she look just like Janay," he mumbled to himself. His counting, vibing, breathing then stopped ever so suddenly as a horrific thought passed through his mind. He leapt from his chair and stood close to the window watching the woman quickly jump into the passenger side of a red Honda Civic and watched the car speed away. Mike felt as if his heart had stopped as he swiftly turned and ran out of his office and to the elevator. He banged on the down button as if that would make it arrive any faster. Impatient Mike darted to the stairwell and ran down the four flights of stairs to the parking garage. In Stacy Adams shoes he ran as though he were wearing Nike Tracks until he reached his car.

"Son of a bitch!" his words echoed through the garage, bounced off cars and steel beams and came back at him. Steam, heat, fury permeated through his flesh. He became even more infuriated as he looked at the busted back windshield and the word PUNK that was scrawled across the hood with a key. He decided to take the stairs back to his office doing his best to relax his very tense muscle through breathing techniques. He stood before his windows and tried to count cars again but his mind could not focus and he lost count. He closed his eyes and tried to think back to Mrs. Marshall but all of his efforts were in vain. The only vision was one of his hands wrapped around Janay's neck. He picked up the receiver and dialed the number for the Lexus dealer and made arrangements to bring the car in. In the midst of speaking with Randy the service technician he had a better idea and made arrangements to turn the car in first thing in the morning.

He returned the phone to its cradle, gathered his belongings and locked his office. He took the elevator back down to the parking garage and drove away in his battered vehicle. He called Sherika and asked her to look out for Janay. He let her know not to touch her but to instead call him and he'd shoot down south. He went directly into his bathroom upon arriving home, stripped and climbed into the shower. He stood and allowed the lukewarm water to run down his face over his closed eyes. His muscles were tight and tense and his mind overloaded. He tried to think about a better time, the same thing he'd struggled with at his office. He remembered Annette's beautiful face and her honey complexion as he stood beneath the pounding water. He felt a throbbing between his legs as his penis stiffened. His hand slid down his body and to that hard spot between his thighs and he stroked it slowly as he imagined Annette's small round breast bare and pressed against his chest. He reached for the body wash and squirted it on his hand and stroked with ease. He imagined what her breath would feel like blowing softly on his flesh. He stroked faster and harder as he imagined what she must feel like sitting on top of him rocking slowly back and forth, moving her body up and down. He stroked faster and harder until some of his tension exploded from him and was washed down the drain.

Mike washed his body, dried and walked into his bedroom. He stretched out across his bed on his back with nothing but a dry towel wrapped around his waist. He lay in absolute silence. He hadn't realized that he'd fallen asleep until his home phone rang. He jumped, startled at the sound. It was still early but it was winter in Florida and the sun had already found rest making his room darken quickly.

"Hello?" he answered with a voice thick with sleep.

"Ay boo, that bitch out here," Sherika told him, "She out front of Kia's crib, don't look like she phenna go nowhere no time soon."

"Aiight thanks, I'm on my way."

"What she do? You sure you don't want me to blaze that bitch? I can't stand dat hoe anyway."

"Naw, naw shorty I need to handle this. Hit me back if she leave though."

"Aiight, lata."

Mike dressed quickly in black jeans, tee shirt and sneakers. He slammed a cap on his head and shot downstairs to his battered vehicle. He cut through traffic as if he were trying out for a role in *Fast and the Furious*. He slowed his pace when he reached his old neighborhood and kept a watchful eye out for Janay as he neared the block that Kia lived on. He muttered profanities under his breath when his eyes locked on a red Honda Civic. He pulled along side it and saw Janay, Kia, and Janay's sister Tomiko leaning against a fence passing a joint. Mike leapt from the car with the engine still running. Janay spotted him too late; he was on her with his large hand wrapped around the back of her neck dragging her to his car.

"Look at this shit!" Mike yelled, "This funny to you? You thought I wasn't gone catch yo' trick ass?"

Janay's cries were muffled as Mike pressed her head into the warm hood of the car.

"Mike stop!" Tomiko yelled at him, fearful for her sister, knowing how dangerous Mike's temper was.

"Bitch I should kill you! Makin' me spend all this got-damned money and you just keep fuckin' up my ride!"

The heat from the engine began to burn Janay's cheek as he held her face in a fixed position. He smacked the back of her head repeatedly as he spat threats and curses at her.

"Mike stop!" Tomiko pleaded, "She's pregnant!"

"So I don't give a fuck, it ain't mine! If it was my baby the bitch wouldn't be out here gettin' smoked out!"

"It is yo' baby!" Janay cried out.

Mike pulled her head away and looked her up and down in disgust. He spat in her face, "I oughtta kick you in yo' fuckin' stomach for lyin'. Look what you did to my mu'fuckin' car bitch! Look at this shit!" Mike grabbed Janay by her short ponytail and pulled her down eye-to-eye with the word PUNK that she keyed on the hood. Janay yelped in pain.

"Mike I'm sorry! I'm sorry!" Janay cried, "I'a pay for it!"

Mike pulled her back by the ponytail and threw her to the filthy earth below. Her round stomach was peeking from beneath her button down shirt begging to be noticed. Mike wanted to kick her, stomp her, punch her, damage her the way that she'd damaged his baby, his car. But if he followed his instincts and as a result the baby growing inside of her, the child she claimed to be his died, he could be jailed for murder one. He knelt beside her and held his hands firmly around her neck as he spoke.

"That bastard saved yo' ass! You betta pray I don't see you when you drop dat load, either way bitch you gone regret fuckin' wit' me," Mike jumped back inside his car leaving Tomiko and Kia to console a shaken and battered Janay. Mike sped away leaving the three women to inhale and choke on fumes and dust. He wasn't done with Janay yet; he had a long memory when it came to him being wronged. As soon as she delivered he'd have Sherika standing by to finish what he started.

19 Darryl

The scent of fresh cooked eggs, bacon, toast and hash browns lingered in the air. Darryl caught hold of the smell and followed it like a possessed man to its source, the kitchen. There were no bodies around. Dishes were piled high in the sink. A lit cigarette burned in an ashtray on the small round kitchen table which was otherwise empty with the exception of leftover crumbs and bits of what vaguely resembled scrambled eggs. On the counter were more dirty dishes and half a glass of orange juice with a small roach floating lifeless upside down in it. A pack of cigarettes was set beside the toaster amongst a valley of crumbs. He checked the stovetop and found only a skillet full of fat and another coated with thick caked on egg. Inside the stove he found only a tray with crumbs.

Darryl muttered curses under his breath as he sifted through items in the refrigerator hoping to at least find a Saran wrapped plate which he could stick in the microwave but coming up short he took a seat at the table feeling upset. He removed the burning cigarette from the ashtray and stuck it between his lips. He inhaled and held the smoke inside his already tainted lungs for a few seconds before exhaling slowly. He slumped down in his chair and watched as a lonely cockroach crawled up the cabinet door. Darryl guessed that he was out looking for his friend as well as a bite to eat. He sighed and replaced the cigarette between his full lips. He may not have been in love with Sierra but at least she kept him in a clean home.

Victoria walked in the kitchen, a fresh cigarette dangling from her lips. Her long hair was wild on top of her head. She wore a thinning housecoat, which hung loosely open revealing her lace panties and the design on her small tee shirt. She walked toward the table without picking up her feet, dragging her dirty yellow slippers across the kitchen floor.

"Kill that roach," Darryl instructed, pointing to the cabinet door. Victoria spotted it chilling in a corner surveying the world below, its antenna's moving as though it were transmitting some important information back to its lair. Victoria reached down and pulled a slipper from her foot and smashed it, ending its transmission and its life. She shuffled over to the table and took a seat across from Darryl. She took a final drag on the cigarette before smashing the butt in the ashtray.

"Where the food?" Darryl asked flicking ashes.

"It's gone, the kids ate it all."

"Damn Vicky, why you let them eat all the damn food?"

"Excuse you. It's their damn food Darryl; you're just a guest here."

"Oh now I'm a guest right?"

"Yea you're just a guest," Victoria leaned back in her chair and folded her arms across her breasts. She locked gazes with Darryl unflinching.

"Ain't this some shit. You know you're really trippin' Vicky."

"No Darryl, you're tripping!" Victoria yelled pointing an accusing finger at Darryl as she pushed away from the table and stood upright, "You want to lay around my house and be treated like some kinda fucking king, stick your raggedy dick in me whenever you damn well please but you are not willing to give me what I want!"

"Victoria we've been through this-"

"Darryl please. Save that cheaper to keep her bullshit. I want you here with me and only me. That means not married to another woman!"

"Got-dammit Victoria!" Darryl slammed his fist against the faux wood table and swiftly stood from his chair. He paced around the kitchen scratching his scalp, "Look, I thought you wanted me here. I'm here so why you still stressin' me about getting a divorce?"

"You just don't get it do you? It's not only about-" Victoria paused and picked at her fingernails. She kept her eyes low when she spoke, "I want you to leave."

"What?"

"I said I want you to leave."

"H-h-hold on. All you did was complain that you wanted me to be here with you and now I'm here and you want me to leave? Hell naw!"

"I need my man to be here with me fully and that's not possible if he's married to another woman. And don't give me that bullshit about money 'cause I don't give a damn about that. Believe it or not Darryl I do love you."

"And you puttin' me out 'cause you love me?"

"I'm putting you out 'cause I love me."

Victoria and Darryl stood in silence. Darryl feeling as if Victoria had turned her back on him, rejected him. Victoria wishing she hadn't said what she'd said but still glad she'd said it. Darryl slammed his fist into the freezer door, Victoria didn't flinch. He walked down the hall and back to the bedroom, Victoria's bedroom. He walked through the room grabbing his belongings and shoving them inside the duffle bag they arrived in. He stepped into a pair of loose fitting jeans and pulled a ribbed white tank top over his head. He stepped into his tennis shoes, grabbed his bag and walked to the front door. Victoria didn't acknowledge him. She instead faked emotional strength as she struggled to light a fresh cigarette. Darryl paused silently giving her the opportunity to change her mind and stop him from leaving but she didn't. She kept her back turned as he exited her apartment.

Darryl drove slowly down busy streets as cars blew their horns and shot around him. He didn't know where to go. He hadn't been home in weeks and it was the last place he wanted to be. He drove slowly until he came upon an old bar that was barley noticeable from the street.

With nothing else to do on a Saturday afternoon and nowhere to turn without first making a few phone calls, he parked his vehicle and stepped inside. It was dark and dank inside the bar. A large fat black man who probably bore a name like "Tiny" stood behind the bar top drying out a mug. A scrawny, already drunk Caucasian man sat watching Sports Center and sipping a beer. Darryl took a seat three stools down and ordered an Ice House. He tossed the bottle back and watched the highlights of last nights Heat game. He guzzled two more and ordered another. He wanted to drown his frustration in alcohol. He wanted to go home to Victoria but he didn't want to beg any woman for anything. Equally he didn't want to curl up in bed next to Sierra. He could probably cop a squat at Randy or Bluebird's but a musty pillow could in no way compare to Victoria's warm thickness.

The beer wasn't giving Darryl quite the buzz he was going for. He ordered a shot of Hennessy straight and took it back. The scraggly old white man who had watched Darryl guzzle alcohol since he sat at the bar slid down beside him and ordered two more of what Darryl was having. Darryl didn't want to be bothered though he wasn't about to turn down free liquor. The man smiled at Darryl revealing tiny yellow teeth, the front two were missing. He was balding and smelled faintly of urine.

"So what's a nice young man like you doing in an old rotten place like this?" the old man asked releasing from his tongue the powerful scent of years of alcohol abuse combined with a total disregard of oral hygiene.

"Appreciate the drink but just leave me alone old man," Darryl stated knocking back the free liquor.

The old man jumped off the stool and threw his hands up in a surrendering motion and stumbled backwards, "Whoa young buck, I ain't mean no harm. You look like you got problems and I know you to young to have problems that make you surrender to this kinda place. If you wanna talk about it I'll be right down here."

"Yo' Red! Leave da man alone an' drank yo' drank!" the barkeep yelled.

"Okay, okay but I used to be a shrink y'know. Just offering some free medical advice."

"Yea yea, just have a seat."

Darryl tried to focus on the games highlights but his mind wouldn't let him. He wanted to be with Victoria and as far as he was concerned it was Sierra's fault that he couldn't be happy. The facts didn't matter to him. Not the fact that he'd met Sierra years before he'd met Victoria. Not the fact that he'd proposed to Sierra, not the other way around. Not even the fact that he'd insisted on continuing to have unprotected sex with her even though he knew he couldn't trust her to take her birth control pills. If Sierra was a good wife and took care of him the way a woman should and made him happy by satisfying all of his needs then he wouldn't have had a need for Victoria to begin with and thus would not be getting drunk in a bar at eleven in the morning with an old smelly deadbeat and a Devil's Advocate.

Darryl continued to drink until things began to blur. By the time he stumbled out to his car the sun had begun to set in the west. He scrambled through his pockets in search of his car keys. He finally found them and struggled to put the key inside of its hole. He eventually managed to get the car started up and peeled out into the street causing a lane of traffic to come to a screeching halt. Horns were blown and curses flailed at him as he sped away from the scene of the near accident. He drove like a madman swerving through traffic and running red lights until he eventually screeched into his driveway. The old dented Chevy that he'd bought his wife was there so he knew that Sierra was home.

Darryl unlocked the door and stumbled inside. He threw his keys on the ledge and took what for him became the long walk down the hall to him and his missus bedroom. He thrust the door open and found Sierra sitting on the bed under the sheets wearing a flannel nightgown. A stack of pictures was on the bed before her alongside an open scrapbook that she was working on. She was startled and discomforted by his appearance. Darryl approached Sierra and snatched from her hand the picture that she was preparing to cut. It was one of Nate and her by the ocean years past. Darryl flung the picture to the floor and grabbed the scrapbook from her. He flipped through finding page after page of photos of Nate.

"What are you building a shrine to this mu'fucka?" Darryl slammed the book into the wall.

Sierra began to panic. She could smell the awful stench of the combinations of alcohol he'd been drinking. She was grateful that the children were not home to witness their father's behavior but also upset that Lillian had returned to their parent's home. Her eyes watered and her body trembled as he stood over her with his chest heaving. He glared down at Sierra, proud of the fear that he was invoking in her.

"You bitch, you ruined my life now you gone make it up to me," Darryl slurred, "Come here! Get yo' ass over here!"

"Darryl no! Stop it!"

Darryl ignored Sierra's pleas. He grabbed the bottom of her gown and pulled her, choking, to him. He flipped her over onto her back and fought to get his hand up her gown and grip her panties.

"Darryl, stop please!" Sierra cried out but was answered with a powerful closed fist blow to her right eye.

"Gimme this pussy bitch! You my wife an' from now on you gone fuck me when an' where and however I want you to fuck me, ya hear me? Huh?" Daryl took the back of his hand across Sierra's cheek, "Answer me got-dammit!"

"Yes...yes...I un-...I understand," she cried.

Darryl pushed off of Sierra and stood between her legs with his hands on his waist. He looked down at her grinning, a vicious look in his eyes. One thing he did find sexy about Sierra was the shape of her mouth, the curve of it. Those evil eyes focused on her sensual lips. Darryl quickly undid his jeans and let them drop to his feet. He stepped out and stood with his hard penis poking out of the opening in his boxers. Sierra braced herself preparing to unwillingly accept him inside. Darryl climbed on the bed over her body and to her horror placed his body over her face.

"No...don't," Sierra whispered through rapid breathing.

"Shut the hell up and open yo' mouf. Now bitch 'fo' I hurt you!"

Sierra slowly parted her lips and widened her mouth to fit around Darryl's stiffness. Fresh tears flooded her eyes as soon as her tongue touched the warm flesh. Darryl assisted her inexperience by shifting his body back and forth moving himself in and out.

"Oooh shit," Darryl moaned, "Yea bitch, suck this dick...suck it, yesss. Aawww fuck!"

Sierra closed her eyes tight and tried to accept it. She tried her best to pretend it was normal and no big deal but all she could see was her Uncle Deacon Myron standing in front of her as a child sitting on her knees with his dick in his hand. Sierra closed her eyes tighter trying to pretend that the images in her minds eye did not exist. Her breathing became more and more unsteady from her panic. Sierra clamped her teeth down biting into Darryl's penis disturbing his pleasure.

"Aaaahh!" Darryl yelled in agony. He leapt backwards from the bed and continued stumbling back until he crashed into the wall. He slid to the floor and held between his legs rocking back and forth. Sierra slid from the bed and ran hastily around the bedroom. She grabbed her shoes and a jacket from the closet. She scrambled around searching for her keys, "Get yo' ass back here bitch!" he spat.

"Leave me alone! I hate you! I hate you! I hate you Uncle Myron, I hate you!" Sierra found her keys and ran barefoot from the bedroom as Darryl struggled to get back into his jeans, "Leave me alone!"

Sierra ran out of the house and jumped into her car. Darryl limped after her but she was too fast and he was too hurt. He jumped in his car and followed her. Every street she drove on so did he. Every turn she made he was hot on her tail. Sierra, Lilly and Annette had spent the better of the previous week at NATHANIEL'S helping Mike get the place ready for business. Instinct led her to the Hollywood club. Sierra screeched to a halt in front of the valet just centimeters from a brand new Jaguar that a now angry couple was stepping out of. Sierra jumped from the car and darted into the club paying no attention to the tens of tons of people around her. She didn't make it far before one of the bouncers grabbed her by her waist and carried her kicking and screaming back out front.

"Ma'am you can't come in here like that," the large Trinidadian bouncer, Bear, told her.

"I have to get in there! I need to see my friend Nate, it's an emergency," Sierra looked around nervously.

"Ma'am sorry, I don't know a Nate, now you're going to have to get back in your car and go home."

"Noo, I can't. Look my friend owns this club!"

"Ma'am nice try but the club is called NATHANIEL'S, doesn't mean it's owned by a Nathaniel."

"Listen, my friends Nathaniel and Michael own the damn club. Find them!"

"Alright woman, don't make me get the police involved," Bear threatened. At that moment a message came through Bear's walkie-talkie from Mike asking what was going on out front, "Nothing boss-man, nothing to worry about. Just some lady looking for her friend Nathaniel," Bear chuckled.

"Nathaniel?" Mike repeated.

"Yes sir, she seems to think her friends Nathaniel and Michael own the club."

"What's her name?"

"Ma'am what's your name?"

"Sierra, tell him it's Sierra," she said breathlessly looking around scanning the area for signs of Darryl.

"She says her name is Sierra."

"Idiot! I oughtta fire yo' dumb ass, what the hell you think Mike is short for? Michael! Have Willie bring her to me!"

"Sorry sir, sorry ma'am," Bear mumbled.

Willie ran out the entrance of the club. He paused, momentarily taken aback by Sierra's unusual club attire. She stood before him in her flannel gown, a jacket, and bare feet with a pair of white tennis shoes in her hand. Her cheek was bruised and her eye had blackened. Willie looked at Bear and shook his head and led her inside to Mike who was taken over with the same reaction at first glance of Sierra. He pulled her to him, "Si-Si what happened? Who did this shit to you?" he asked becoming both concerned and infuriated.

"Mike where's Nate? I need to see Nate," Sierra cried.

Mike felt her body trembling as he held her. He swallowed hard and answered carefully, "Si-Si, um Nate ain't here."

"Well where is he? I need him, go get him!"

Mike sighed, "Si-Si, baby girl Nate ain't here. He's gone. Remember? He's…he's dead," Mike's voice cracked as he spoke.

Sierra's heart seemed to have stopped beating, "Oh my God, I don't believe the fool that I'm making of myself. Oh my God," Sierra cried. Mike pulled her close to his chest.

"Sshh… Si-Si tell me who hit you."

Sierra took a deep breath and stepped back from Mike, "It was Darryl. He tried to rape me."

"He did wh-? Son of a bitch! Where that nigga at now?"

"He was following me, I don't know what happened to him."

Mike's name was being called across the walkie-talkie; it was Bear, "Mike some guy is out here acting a damn fool calling for that woman."

"Right on time, I'm on my way," Mike rushed toward the entrance with Sierra. Sure enough Darryl was standing outside of his club yelling Sierra's name and yelling threats. Michael walked directly to him and swung connecting his fist with Darryl's jaw. Caught off guard Darryl fell hard to the concrete.

"What is wrong wit' you nigga?" Darryl spat out.

"Get up and fight a man!"

"Why you don't stay outta this Mike, this ain't got shit to do wit' you," Darryl struggled to get to his feet.

"Michael!" Sierra called out, "Michael stop, please. I don't want you to get into any trouble over him!"

"Fuck this nigga Si-Si!!"

"Mike please just let him go!"

Everything in Mike's being said *whoop this nigga's ass* however out of respect for Sierra's wishes he backed off.

"Yea Mike, listen to that ol' dried up ass bitch!" Darryl retorted.

"What?"

"Michael!" Sierra called. She tried to reach him but Willie restrained her.

"Gone back in yo' club and tend to her silly ass. NATHANIEL'S. Hmpf. Named the damn club after a faggot."

"Punk muthafucka."

Mike charged at Darryl with fists raining down. He spat out profanities as he kicked and stomped, smacked and punched. He didn't notice the police pull up, jump out their vehicles and run at him until one had his arms locked behind his back.

"Why you ain't talkin' now? Huh? Where all that bitch talk at now nigga?" Mike intimidated Darryl.

"Calm down," the officer said into Mike's ear, "Now sir, what the hell happened here?" he asked Darryl assuming him to be the victim since he'd been beaten so badly. After hearing both sides and deciding that he didn't like Mike's aggressive attitude he asked Darryl if he wished to press charges. Darryl contemplated his options.

"Yea, nigga thank on it. Don't make me have them bring Sierra out here."

"Shut your damn mouth," the officer told him.

"Naw I don't want to," Darryl mumbled.

"What? Are you kidding me? Do you want to see what he did to your face?" the cop asked.

"Damn the nigga don't wanna press charges, now let me go."

"You'd better calm down right now, Mr. Toussaint."

"Then get yo' hands off me. I ain't do shit that nigga ain't deserve. You think I fucked him up? You oughta see what the nigga did to his wife," Mike jerked from the officer's grasp.

"That's it, you're coming with us."

"Fuck outta here, I got a business to run."

"You heard me."

"Oh no, no, no! Stop it! Let him go!" Sierra screamed, "It's my fault Officer! Let me go," she tried to release herself but Willie held tighter when Mike gave him the signal not to let her go.

The officer was deaf to her cries. He was determined to arrest Mike and some crazy bitch in a flannel nightgown wasn't going to stop that even if she was clearly abused.

"Sierra stay back!" Mike demanded, "Willie get her home! Darryl don't you even think to go near her, y'hear me nigga?"

"Shut up and get in the got-damned car," the Officer insisted trying to force a cuffed Mike's head down.

"Fuck you cracker! Darryl stay yo' ass away from her!" Mike finally cooperated and got inside of the car. The officers joined him inside and peeled away from the curb.

Willie eased his grip and Sierra pulled away. She stood in the middle of the sidewalk fuming with her gaze set on Darryl. Willie gently grabbed her arm and tried to guide her away but she snatched from his grasp. Slowly she walked to Darryl barely blinking and no longer afraid. She stood directly in front of him and looked into his eyes unflinching. Willie made sure that he was close enough just in case something went down. Onlookers in party wear focused all their attention on Darryl and Sierra rather than trying to get into the new exclusive club. Women ready to take their heels off, men come out of their suit jackets and ties if Darryl made a move on Sierra. The air paused, everyone stood still in anticipation ready to move in unison if necessary. The only sound was music thumping in the various local clubs and the sounds made by approaching cars. Sierra reached back as far as she could and with all her strength smacked Darryl with open palm across his cheek. After the initial amazement the crowd cheered and applauded.

"I hate you. You disgust me."

"Si-Si please," Darryl reached out to take a hold of Sierra, not out of love but out of fear that she'd sic Mike on him again.

"Don't touch me! I hate you and I want a divorce. Stay away from me and my children, that bitch can have you," Sierra turned her back and walked toward Willie, pausing to put her white tennis shoes on her feet.

"Sierra!"

"Go to hell Darryl!" she responded without looking back. In bedtime clothes she walked proudly inside the club that belonged to her best friends, Nathaniel and Michael.

20 Sierra

Monday was the earliest that Sierra was able to bail Mike out of jail. Though Willie was more than capable of taking care of it, Sierra felt consumed by a sheet of guilt and the only way she could find redemption was to take financial responsibility. Mike was surprised to see her there bright and early yet concerned about her spending her much needed money on him. Sierra felt a stronger sense of friendship with Mike than she'd ever had in the past. She wrapped her arms around him and held him tight, joyous and thankful.

"What you doing here l'il momma?" Mike asked, "Willie was supposed to come handle this."

"I couldn't let you pay for it. You wouldn't have even been in here if I'd have kept my dirty laundry at home where it belongs."

"Si-Si don't even try it. I'm gone take care of you regardless. I woulda been more mad if you didn't come to me."

Sierra blushed but felt good and safe, "Hey, why don't you come by the house? Let me fix you some breakfast. It's the least I can do."

"Don't worry about that Si. Come on now, you still my girl."

"Please Mike, it would make me feel better about all of this."

Mike absorbed the innocence of Sierra's face. He really wanted to go home and shower but he couldn't deny Sierra.

"Alright you got me. What you cookin'?"

"Whatever you want."

"Shit, don't get me started. I'a have you up in there fixing me some boiled fish and grits, some cheese eggs, all the good shit."

"If that's what you want."

"Aiight, let's get outta here then. Being around too many crackers with guns make me uneasy."

Sierra drove Mike to her still empty home while he called Willie and let him know that he was straight. She set him up in the guest bathroom to shower and took his clothes and placed them in the washer. While he bathed she prepared a hearty southern breakfast. Once Mike was done showering he wrapped the large soft bath towel around his waist and joined Sierra in the kitchen.

"Need some help?" he asked stepping through the archway.

"Huh? Oh uhh...no, n-no. I'm okay. I uh, I got it," Sierra tried to ignore the fact that Mike was standing in her kitchen nearly nude. His strong chest speckled with fresh water. She swallowed hard and forced herself to return her attention to the pancake batter that she was preparing, "You can uh, go in the kitchen – er, I mean the living room and watch television if you want."

"Yea aiight," Mike was tickled by Sierra's obvious discomfort. He laughed internally as he thought about how she might react if he snatched the towel from his waist. He turned and went into the living room as he'd been invited to do.

Sierra put all of the food on and took a seat at the kitchen table. She felt silly sitting there, being nervous around a man she'd known half her life simply because he was nearly naked and she was alone with him.

"Si-Si!" Mike called out startling Sierra.

"H-huh?"

"I know you about done putting that food on. Don't be a rude hostess nah!"

"W-would you like something to drink?"

"You got some juice?"

"Orange or cran-raspberry?"

"Orange!"

Sierra inhaled deeply and rose from her seat. She fixed Mike and herself a tall glass of OJ and carried them to her living room. Mike was stretched out comfortably on the sofa. Sierra handed him the juice and went to sit on the chair but Mike stopped her. He sat upright and tapped the spot beside him. Nervously Sierra accepted the seat.

"Si-Si you know you ain't gone go to hell just 'cause a man naked in your house especially if you ain't phenna do shit with him," Mike said trying to relax her nerves.

"I know. I'm just being foolish," she sipped her juice and smiled, the butterflies easing slightly, "Mike, again I am so sorry I got you in trouble with the police."

"Man, Si don't worry about that, I told you I'm here for you. Them crackers wanted to take me in anyway, it ain't have shit to do with you. Besides that I only did what Nate woulda did and I don't regret that shit."

"Yea, he would have. He never did like Darryl."

"Punk ass. I know I ain't the best nigga out there y'know but I ain't never hit no bi-I'm sorry. I mean I have never hit a woman," Mike shifted a bit becoming slightly discomforted himself. He'd never bit his tongue or adjusted his speech for anyone.

"Mike, I miss Nate so much but whenever I close my eyes at night all I can see is…is the way I found him in that hotel," there was an awkward moment of silence shared, "He was always there for me. He was so supportive of everything. When I married Darryl, when I told him about what happened to me when I was a little girl."

"You mean with your uncle?" Mike asked softly.

Sierra paused and blinked rapidly, repeatedly, "You know?"

Mike nodded, "Nate told me. You know how I used to be an ass with females back in the day. I think he thought by telling me about what you was going through I'd be, y'know, better around you. I ain't neva say nothin' to nobody and I know he ain't tell nobody else," Mike shifted again and wondered if maybe he should have kept his mouth shut.

"He was a good friend," Sierra whispered.

"Yea. He the reason I'm here and not locked down or dead. I'm who I am today because of Nate. I ain't neva told nobody but him about my past and what was really goin' on wit' me," Mike chewed the corner of his mouth and looked away as the wheels in his mind churned, "My umm…my moms was a prostitute. She was out hoein' and shit when she got pregnant wit' me. My grandmamma ain't like her 'cause of that shit but she let her come home when she was getting too big to be walkin' the streets. They say she planned to put me up for adoption as soon as she had me but my grandma took custody and my ol' girl just up and left."

"Oh my goodness, that's awful. Have you ever seen her?"

"Nah. My grandma and auntie raised me but them bitches ain't neva like me 'cause of all the shit my momma did."

"No, maybe they were just hard on you because they were afraid that you may turn out like she did," Sierra reasoned. She found it hard to believe that a mother could not like a grandchild.

Mike felt a rage begin to boil within as he listened to Sierra attempt to defend his aunt and grandmother but he took a deep breath and calmed, "I know you grew up kinda sheltered so you probably have a hard time believing somethin' like that but naw, they just ain't like me 'cause they ain't like her. My auntie had three kids livin' with us and I watched her and my grandmamma cater to they spoiled asses. I'a bring home good grades and they would blow me off. My cousin Jean would bring bullshit ass grades to the crib and they would be rewarding his ass. Talking about he needed it so he could do better. Whatever. They ain't give a fuck, so I stopped givin' a fuck and they ain't care one way or another.

"Nate ass was always getting good grades an' shit, even though he was runnin' wit' me. He just told me one day straight up that if I kept fuckin' up an' goin' to jail and getting sorry ass grades all I was gone do was prove them right and that made sense to me. That was the first thing that made sense to me. That's why I say he the reason I am who I am today," Mike's voice cracked slightly as he blinked away tears, too proud and too afraid to express his emotions in that manner. He coughed a couple times to clear his throat and continued pretending to be stronger than he actually felt.

"Man, I ain't tryin' to sit here and feel sorry for myself, y'know what I'm sayin'? But nobody gave a damn about me when I was a shorty growin' up, not even my own blood. Nobody but Nate. Even as men you and him were the only people in this world that cared what happened to Mike, how Mike was livin'. Wit' odds like that I can't afford to loose nobody. And Nate going like that, it's like a part of me is gone. Know what I'm sayin' shorty? I was fucked up to begin with so where does that leave me now?"

Mike tried his best to swallow his emotions but his pain escaped. His expression remained stern as a few tears rolled forward. Not for his own past and sorrows but a thug tear for his homeboy. Sierra slid beside him and took his hand in hers. She wanted to hold him but she knew Mike well enough to know that this was hard enough for him, the last thing he wanted was to be babied. Instead she rubbed the back of his hand softly just to let him know that they didn't need Nate there in physical form to hold them together. She would always be his shoulder no matter what. Mike shook his head a couple of times feeling like a soft punk. He hadn't cried since he was a small child and to now sit here as an adult, as a man and cry in the presence of a woman was difficult for him.

"Damn, I know I look like a pussy sitting here crying and shit," He tried to laugh it off.

"No, it's good to let things out sometimes. I'm just now able to cry after fifteen years of silence," It was now Sierra's turn again to feel uncomfortable, "Hey, I'm going to check on the food and grab your clothes out of the dryer ok?"

Sierra stood to walk away but Mike grabbed her hand and stopped her. She turned to face him and he stood before her. Without a second thought he placed his hands on Sierra's waist and eased her against his body. Mike looked into Sierra's eyes; he embraced their softness and sincerity. He was intoxicated by their innocence. A feeling washed over him unlike any feeling he'd ever experienced. He looked at her lips, noticing for the first time just how sexy they were. He gently touched the side of her face. He was slightly amused by her inability to conceal her discomfort. He desired to kiss her but he respected her too much to disrespect her. He instead wrapped his arms around her and held her tight. It felt so good that he did not want to let her go. Unbeknownst to him and to Sierra's surprise, she was feeling the same.

Sierra and Lilly stood together at the county courthouse. Lilly rubbed her belly while observing the expression on her sister's face as she looked over the form the impatient young clerk had given her to fill out.

"Step aside ma'am please," she scolded.

Sierra hadn't heard her, her mind was still focused on the forms she'd been given to fill out. Lilly gently grabbed her sister's arm and eased her away so that the next person in line could be serviced. Sierra's face was without expression but the tears flowing gave her emotional status away. She'd prayed repeatedly over the past few weeks and the answer always came back the same. Guilt washed over her. Her marriage had failed. Her husband made a home with another woman. She herself had been spending much of her time with Mike. Although nothing romantic had occurred, she was still guilty of having romantic feelings toward him. Not only that, she'd not been honest with her parents. She kept quiet about her plans to divorce Darryl, as she knew that they would not accept it. It wouldn't matter if she told them that Darryl had in her eyes, raped her. They would find it impossible to believe.

"Oh my goodness Lilly, Daddy's gonna kill me then momma's gone dig me up and do it all over again."

"Si-Si, calm yourself. It's going to be alright. You're a grown woman entitled to make your own decisions. They'll have no choice but accept it, it's your life not theirs. Besides, what he did to you is unacceptable and you don't need to stay married to someone as disrespectful as that."

"I know but-"

"But nothin' Si. Fill out the paperwork, start this process and end this pathetic marriage, please. You deserve so much better than him."

Sierra knew that Lilly was right but she was also aware that her parents wouldn't see it that way. If anything went wrong in a marriage then it must be the fault of the woman. And if Darryl was willing to grant her a divorce that meant that she was not living up to her end of the relationship. Sierra closed her eyes and said a silent prayer for forgiveness. She took a deep breath and signed by the X.

Sierra sat by the living room window breathing in and out slowly. Jennifer was stretched across her mothers lap sound asleep with her two middle fingers in her mouth. Butterflies fluttered about inside of her belly as she waited while wondering if she'd done the right thing. Would she be denied access at the pearly gates for breaking a vow that she'd made to the Good Lord? She felt strong hands on her shoulders attempting to massage the tension away. She rested the back of her head on Mike's arm and tried to relax. She was happy that he was there to provide moral support.

Darryl had readily accepted Sierra's request for divorce. He didn't question it, consider it, nor did he have any intent to fight it. He happily took the news back to Victoria and she was thrilled to hear it. She accepted him with open arms as she'd regretted putting him out as soon as she'd done it. Now he was on his way to what was once "their" home to pick up some of his things. Sierra and Lilly together had packed his bags and sat them at the front door for him to remove.

Sierra felt as though someone had wrapped their hands around her throat cutting off all access to oxygen when she finally saw Darryl's car pull into the driveway. She considered for an instance changing her mind and maybe offering again to try and work things out. That instance ended as soon as she made out the face of a woman sitting in the passenger's seat. A woman with a brown face and long curly hair that sat stroking the scalp of a small child that was sleeping in her lap with her face buried in the woman's breasts. Sierra's blood began to boil. She hadn't known before that the mystery woman was also a mother and that her husband was playing daddy outside of the home.

Sierra stood and gently placed her daughter over her shoulder and followed Mike to the front door to let Darryl in after he'd discovered that his key no longer worked. Sierra enjoyed the surprised look on his face when Darryl saw Mike answering the door. She watched him shift with discomfort at the sight of him. Mike silently stepped aside and allowed Darryl indoors.

"Couldn't wait to get me out so you could move him in huh?" he commented once he noticed his bags neatly packed and placed at the front door.

Mike smirked, Sierra sneered, and Jennifer shifted slightly from the sounds and the light.

"So can I expect you to provide support for your own children or will all of your money go to her child?" Sierra asked bitterly.

Darryl glanced at Mike then rested his gaze on Sierra, "I'll take care of my kids, you just remember whose kids they are."

It took every bit of effort for Mike to exercise restraint and keep silent. He realized it wasn't his place to comment; he was only there for support. He walked over to and stood behind Sierra massaging her shoulders but never taking his gaze off of Darryl. His awkwardness humored Mike.

Sierra straightened her spine and held her head high when she spoke, "I am only going to say this one more time, Darryl. Take care of your children."

With her free hand she touched Mike's and turned to walk away leaving Darryl alone to remove his belongings from their property.

Celebrate Good Times

Mike struggled to make the last bit of fluid in the lighter create a flame from a spark. With one hand he protected the cigarette that dangled between his lips while struggling with the other. Hurricane-force winds whipped overhead as he stood in front of the school waiting for Nate to join him. He was always waiting, as Nate never left a class early though with Mike's influence he may have been persuaded to miss one occasionally. He sat on the steps listening to four brothers rhyming in a cipher. He and an acquaintance of his sat bobbing their heads to the sound of the beat-boxing.

"Yo, yo, yo, yo, I'm the one and only brotha, super dope coochie lickin' lova, I'll stick yo mutha under yo own damn covers, beat it up, eat it up, den grab my joint an' stick anotha..." One lyricist sang out with pride as his peers rocked back and forth laughing.

Mike laughed and shook his head as he blew smoke from between his lips, "This nigga talkin' about eatin' coochie. You know dis nigga way out there. Neva dat."

He looked up and spotted Sierra exiting the building shortly after the bell rang and called over to her. She'd known him for quite some time but she'd only associated with him in the presence of Nate and she didn't see him around. She tried to fake relaxation as he scanned her body. She felt as though he were judging her nonchalant fashion statement. As long as she was comfortable in ponytails, ankle length skirts and dresses that came past her knees, she didn't care what anyone else thought.

"Dayum Si-Si, why you 'on't neva show no skin?" Mike asked before taking another drag from his cigarette.

"Because I don't need to get naked to meet quality people."

"Mm is that right? Yea that's why I like you," he chuckled as Sierra raised an eyebrow in amazement, "Yea, for real do'. Nate always sayin' for me to give you a chance. Said you was different than them otha hoes 'round here but I wasn't hearin' dat. But yea, you different. You, uh, classy."

"Well thank you. Wow. That means a lot coming from you," Sierra shifted slightly as she blushed.

"So ay gurl, you going to that pre-graduation party?"

"No, I don't think so. My daddy is not having that."

"Aww yea, yo' daddy a Pastor ain't he? I feel for ya shorty. I still think you should try to make it tho'. Tell him you staying at one of ya girlfriends house or sumthin'."

"Nah, my daddy won't go for that," Sierra said shaking her head.

"We'll come up wit' sumthin'. I think you should come an' I know Nate want you there," Mike began to light a fresh cigarette but opted to wait when Sierra cringed.

"I'll see what I can do," she assured.

She smiled and waved goodbye. Mike lit his cigarette as she walked away. He returned his attention to the young brothers in the cipher.

21 Sierra

Sierra's hands trembled as she washed the dishes. She attempted to focus all of her energy on cleansing the pot that the devoured roast had been prepared in but it continued slipping from her grasp and crashing against the dishwater. Sierra swallowed hard and blinked back tears. Though she wasn't up to it she pushed herself to keep at her motherly duties. She smiled weakly at the sound of her children at play with their "Uncle" Mike.

Sierra found herself suffocated by her depression and Mike's continual presence calmed her nerves and eased her spirit. But other circumstances caused her to yet again become rattled and even Mike's being there would possibly not be enough to soothe her. Under the circumstances she was facing she needed Nathaniel. Nate would be the only person who would be able to help her fight the demons that had resurfaced as of that afternoon and she was uncertain if she'd be able to handle it without him.

The day had begun like any other Florida day. The sun was high and shining bright and the birds were singing their sweet love song. A soft warm breeze rippled the pond in the back of Sierra's Miami home. The day was in direct contrast with the news that was to be delivered.

It was a Saturday and she was expecting Mike for lunch. He was due to arrive near two but he seemed to be running late. The telephone rang. With a smile as broad as the day was long Sierra answered. She made the incorrect assumption that it was Mike and hoped that he was not calling to cancel.

"Hello Michael," she answered with a deliberate tone in her voice.

"Michael? Girl, this your mother. Michael who? If it ain't bad enough that you done gone and betrayed the Lord by putting your own husband out, now you have some sinful man calling for you?"

Sierra felt like a child with being scolded as she was, "Sorry ma'am. Michael is just Mike, Nate's friend from high school. You know who he is. Well I just invited him over for lunch and I thought you were him calling to cancel."

"Hmpf. Well that ain't much better. Yea, you right. I remember that little sinful boy and I remember how poorly he treated that boy at the funeral. I remember clearly how he disrespected the Marshall's, that's what I remember about that boy."

"So Momma what's going on?" Sierra asked anxious to change the subject.

"Hm? Oh yes, I have wonderful news. Your Uncle Deacon Myron has decided to move back to Florida!"

Sierra's eyes opened wide and she was dizzy. Her face became flushed and her palms sweaty. Soon her body weight was too much for her to bear and she slid to the linoleum below. She realized that she'd have to face him again sometime in life but she was hardly looking forward to it. He'd been gone for so many years. He'd disappeared shortly after Lilly's abortion and now for reasons only he and God knew he'd decided to return.

"Isn't that great news?" Her mother continued.

"Uh, yea ma it is. Just…uh-wonderful," Sierra's mind drifted to a place her mother wasn't invited to visit. She barely heard how wonderful it was that her husband's brother was returning to his roots. "Momma. I'm sorry to cut you off but Jen is crying."

"Oh okay. Well go on and tend to my grandbaby. Remember your Uncle will be here the Friday after next. Write it down 'cause I'm gonna want you here early to help prepare dinner. You understand?"

"Yes ma'am. Bye Momma."

Sierra jumped forcefully at Mike's touch. The pan that she'd spent the last half an hour trying to wash slipped from her grip and splashed into the water. Droplets of water speckled Mike and Sierra.

"Calm down l'il momma, it's just me," Mike assured. "Damn whatever it is must be hectic."

"Whatever what is? What are you talking about?"

"Whatever's on your mind that got you so jumpy this evening. Giving a nigga a shower in the kitchen and shit. Talk to me."

"Oh my God, I'm so sorry. I didn't mean to," Sierra babbled while dabbing his shirt with a dry hand towel.

"Si-Si stop. Stop, stop it. It's just a little water, it won't kill me."

"Sorry," Sierra fidgeted with her apron hoping that Mike wouldn't notice that her hands were trembling.

Mike became greatly concerned for Sierra's mental well-being, "Sierra why don't you come and sit down."

"No, no, I've really got to finish these dishes."

"But you been in here doing the dishes for almost and hour and the dishes still dirty. Why don't you just take a breather?"

"I know, I'm sorry."

Mike tried to figure his next move or words of encouragement. He didn't know how to handle her or anyone so vulnerable. His thoughts were interrupted by the sound of tapping against the linoleum tile floor.

"Come on Mike," Lee called.

"Hold on l'il homey, let me help mom's with the dishes first."

Sierra broke from her trance, "I got it really. Go ahead in the living room."

"Are you sure you're okay?" Mike tilted his head sideways as though that would help him see clearer what was bothering her.

Sierra offered a rehearsed closed mouth smile and nodded. Mike hesitated for a moment but Lee's persistence won out. He took the child into his arms and carried him back into the living room to play.

Sierra sat alone on the front stoop. It was well past evening and the sun had settled for the day. The children were fed and sound asleep. Mike had gone hours ago and Sierra was enveloped in loneliness. She held the cordless phone between her palms hoping for something that would never again come to pass. Hoping that phone would ring and Nate's voice would be on the other end of it. The last time it rang it was her mother calling to provide Sierra with her uncle's flight information. Sierra felt like the devil was rubbing it in that her past was coming to haunt her. Sierra's nerves were shot and she had nowhere to turn. Of course Lilly was still staying with their parents and she'd be more than happy to receive a call from her but Sierra didn't want to burden her. Besides she would not be able to be real with her sister. Her sister didn't know anything about their uncle's dirty little secret and there was no need to break it to her now.

Heat and humidity consumed Sierra's being but she didn't budge from her place. The startling sound of the telephone ringing caused the hair on her arm to stand and she felt as though she were choking on her own heart. Nervously she answered.

"Hello?"

"Hey l'il momma wassup? I'm just calling to make sure you alright."

"Mike?"

"Yea, what's the deal?"

Sierra shrugged off the chill which had overcome her. She felt foolish, "Oh nothing. I'm fine."

"I don't think so. You don't sound fine to me."

"No really I am," her voice cracked but she didn't cry.

"Ay I'm phenna come through."

"No, no don't do that. I mean I appreciate it but really I'm fine."

Deep down Sierra longed for the companionship, needed it more than anything but there was no way that she would allow herself to become a burden on Mike. She didn't want to take advantage of his kindness toward her. Her issues were hers to deal with. But alas Mike was stubborn and anyone that was remotely familiar with his personality was aware that once he set his mind to something there was no changing it. Sierra locked her knees together and placed her elbows solidly against the bone. Salty tears streamed down her brown cheeks. She sniffled as quietly as possible and smiled weakly.

She asked, "Have you had dinner yet?"

"Dinner? Girl I'm still full from that lunch you cooked. But if you got something there I'a eat again."

Sierra chuckled and dried her tears. After disconnecting she went inside and warmed up a plate of collard greens, macaroni and cheese and meatloaf. At the sound of the doorbell she subconsciously smoothed her hair and her dress. She smiled and the two embraced when she opened the door.

Mike cleared a plate and worked diligently on his second one. Sierra felt a thrill at having a man around who actually appreciated her good down home southern cooking. The two sat without speaking in one another's company in front of the television while Mike finished his dinner. He glanced at Sierra and saw the distant look in her eyes. He placed his palm on Sierra's thigh and gripped it firmly with his thick fingers. Sierra jumped slightly but relaxed quickly.

"You don't seem yourself. Talk to me."

Sierra fidgeted with her fingernails and shrugged her shoulders, "I'm okay. There's nothing to talk about."

"There's nothing to talk about," Mike sucked meat from his teeth and set his plate on the coffee table. "Stop bullshitting me Sierra, I ain't trying to hear that. Y'know what I'm sayin', I know you betta than that so why not just quit frontin' shawty. Spill it. Get that load off yo' chest."

Sierra looked at Mike then at the space between them. She scratched her forehead and chewed her bottom lip. Mike, she'd known for the greater portion of her life and he'd become a pretty good friend but she wondered how much she could confide in him. She cleared her throat and looked past Mike focusing her attention on one of Lee's toys.

"My Uncle, Deacon Myron Mitchell is moving back to Miami," she spoke just above a whisper.

Mike exhaled and steadied himself, "Is that the nigga that put his hands on you when you was a jit?"

Sierra nodded. Mike sighed and sulked into the sofa cushions. He hadn't had much experience in being someone's support system. Normally he was the one secretly needing it while publicly turning it down. He looked at Sierra's face and spied the water pooling in the brim of her eyes. He bit his bottom lip and leaned forward resting his elbows on his knees.

"Why don't you tell me about it?"

Sierra's heart paused and a feeling of amazement swept through her being. She was surprised Mike wanted to hear of her troubles. Sierra's legs trembled violently.

"My uncle would um, he'd take care of me and Lilly when my parents were away on church business. He said we were like daughters to him and every time he was in charge he'd just…" Sierra's voice faded. She cleared her tears from her throat and stood abruptly. She paced the floor, "At night after dinner he'd send Lilly to bed then he'd call on me to help him with something. Wash dishes, clean the bathroom, anything he could think of. While we're washing dishes he's finding excuses to touch my body. Soon he's taking me by the hand to my Daddy's bed and climbing on top – on top…

Sierra's words caught in her throat. She squeezed her eyes tight and continued, "I was only a baby. Six when he started, thirteen when he stopped. But he never really stopped. Every time I lay in that bed with Darryl he was there. Touching me and putting his mouth on me. For twenty-two years I've smelled his stench on my pillowcases and now I have to smile in his face all over again while everyone talks about how wonderful and blessed the good Deacon is. Well I didn't think he was so wonderful when he was putting his hand up my skirt and I didn't think he was so wonderful when he threatened to touch Lilly if I didn't cooperate. I don't think he's so wonderful after he ruined my marriage and my life! He's not so wonderful…he's not so wonderful."

Mike sat in quiet horror, his appetite long gone. Tears streamed from Sierra's eyes, a vacant expression on her face. Sierra swallowed hard and her shoulders shook. Her body fell to the floor. She clamped both hands over her stomach and rocked back and forth. Mike eased to her side. He placed an arm around her shoulder and awkwardly rubbed. He didn't know what else to do and at the moment wished desperately that Nate were there to take care of it.

Sierra struggled to clean the tears and mucus from her face without Mike seeing. She was embarrassed. She struggled to find her voice. Mike interjected before she could speak the word he knew was coming.

"Don't worry about it l'il momma, I got you. But you should probably get some sleep now. You had a hard day," secretly Mike was anxious to escape.

"Yea, I think you're right. I'm so tired. I'm sorry about all of this. Let me just throw some foil on that plate so you can take it with you."

Mike nodded and helped Sierra to her feet. She took the plate and wrapped it tight. Sierra walked Mike to the front door. She kissed his cheek and thanked him kindly for being there for her before locking the door behind him.

The doorbell rang while Sierra listened to the ringing of the phone on the other end. She shuffled quickly to the front door and smiled when she heard Mike's voice travel through the receiver.

"Hey there," she said. She opened the door allowing LoriAnne entrance. She held a finger to her lips to hush her rapid fire tongue. "Did I wake you?"

"Hey baby girl. Yea you did but don't worry about it."

"Sorry. I'll make this brief. I just called to thank you."

"Thank me for what?"

Sierra fell into the sofa, "For being such a great friend. For being there and looking out for me. For the first time in a while I slept through most of the night. That's thanks to you."

"I think you givin' me too much credit shawty but don't worry 'bout that, I got you."

Butterflies blossomed as she listened to Mike's morning voice, "Well thanks again. Hey, LoriAnne's here now so I'm gonna let you get back to sleep."

The two expressed their goodbyes and Sierra terminated her end of the connection. She held the phone to her heart smiling and feeling much better than she had the previous evening. Her thoughts were interrupted when LoriAnne entered the living area speaking with a cold drumstick in her mouth.

"Ooh girl, what nigga got yo' panties moist?" she asked.

"What? Oh chile whatever," Sierra stood from the couch and replaced the portable phone in its charger.

After a filling lunch at Rain Forest Café, Sierra and Lillian took a seat on the bench near the mall's play area while Michele, Jennifer, and Lee enjoyed their time. Lillian rubbed her belly and tilted her head sideways looking at her sister with great interest.

"What?" Sierra chuckled, "Why are you looking at me like that?"

"I'm not looking at you like anything. I think you're just feeling guilty."

"What exactly do I have to feel guilty about?"

"What's up between you and Michael? LoriAnne told me you was all cheesy when you got off the phone with him the other day."

Sierra dropped her head and laughed. She spied the play area quickly to ease her motherly nerves and make sure the children were out of earshot. Smiling she returned her attention to her younger sister, "Mike and I are just friends that's all, bonded by an equally great loss in our lives. We need each other to get through this. Doesn't mean anything is or will happen between us."

"And that's all? Really I understand that you guys lost someone special and each is being a shoulder for the other but on the same token I've seen you two together. I see how you look at each other and I see more than just friends of circumstance."

"Lilly stop over analyzing the situation," Sierra adjusted her eyeglass frames on her nose.

"Fine, fine. I'll take your word as bond but I personally would like to go on the record as stating that you and Michael Toussaint would make a wonderful couple. You'd be good for each other."

"Me and Mike?" Sierra shook her head in disbelief, "Are we talking about the same Mike? Women-ain't- nothin'-but-h's-and-b's Mike?"

"Yes. Suck-my-dick-in-a-Burger-King-bathroom Mike. You don't get it do you Si-Si? You're each strong where the other is weak. You balance the other out. But hey, like I said I'm letting it go. You'll just have to see for yourself."

Sierra thought for a moment but shrugged it off. It was a ridiculous notion that she had no business entertaining. She opted to change the subject rather than dwell on potential that was non-existent.

The children slept soundly on the ride home as they'd had a long and active day. Together Lillian and Sierra tucked the children in for the night. Lillian kissed Sierra on the cheek and headed for their parents home. Sierra sighed from exhaustion. She removed the big brown bobbie pins from her hair and tussled it with her hands. She took a seat on her sofa and with the remote control flipped through until she came across the gospel station. Sierra nestled into a corner with her feet tucked beneath her. The light on the answering machine flickered. She reached over and hit the PLAY button. The first message was one from her mother checking up on Lilly. The next was from Darryl,

"Ay wassup Si-Si? This is Darryl. I –uh, I got the divorce papers and like I told you I don't have no problem with signing them. I am gonna warn you though; if you try to get alimony from me then I will fight for custody of my kids you better believe that. And don't think for a second that a judge won't award them to me. All they have to do is look at your boyfriend's police record to see he's unfit and so are you for having him around. He assaulted me, remember? Anyway, I'll call you back tomorrow so we can discuss how we gone handle things."

Sierra sat in shock and her body trembled. She was equally angry and afraid. She wondered how much truth was present in his words. Could he really take her children away, would he, and if so how would she go on if he did? She would forgo spousal support if necessary but how would she survive? Darryl may not have been the most emotionally supportive husband but he was a good provider and she'd not worked outside the home a day since they married.

Sierra clicked the television off and slammed the remote onto the wood coffee table. She took a few relaxing breaths before she stood and tiptoed down the hall to her daughters' bedroom. She peered inside and looked upon their sleeping faces, they were at ease completely unaware of the turmoil that was brewing. She pulled their door to and stepped across the hall to where Lee was resting. She blew an imaginary kiss in his direction. Sierra was hurting but she didn't cry. She rested her weight against the door jamb and slid to the floor. She pulled her knees to her breasts and wrapped her arms around, rested her head and quietly rocked her body back and forth.

21 Mike

Mike finished his hearty breakfast and washed it down with a tall ice cold glass of OJ. He eyed the pretty young waitress who was now taking the order of an older couple seated some rows away from him. Her nationality could not be easily determined. Her caramel colored complexion was free and clear of smudges and imperfections and her long and healthy mane was wrapped in a bun and pinned to her head. She had eyes as large as saucers and full kissable lips but none of that was what caught Mike's attention. The small waistline and pronounced round rear is what captivated him.

Mike licked his lips and finished the last of his juice as she walked in his direction. She had a seductive stroll that Mike was sure she invented just for his pleasure, eye candy for him. Her mutual attraction to him was evident but she kept her desires secret. She smirked and flaunted her feminine sexuality as she handed him his bill. Mike was amused and intrigued. Enough was enough. He ate breakfast in this restaurant at least once a week and the game had been fun but now it was time to declare a victor.

"You need anything else?" she asked in an inappropriate and suggestive tone.

"Nah, I'm strizzle," he stated. He watched her switch away before he stood. He strolled up to the counter to pay his debt, Sindella the waitress looked up from what she was doing and waved goodbye.

Mike was busy studying the blueprints on his desk when his secretary buzzed him and informed him that Reggie wished to see him in his office. Although the case with Samantha Falls was impending Mike had officially been allowed to return to perform his hired duties thanks to great persuasion by Mr. Tuttle. The three weeks that he'd been back seemed to go well. He was unconcerned when he passed by Samantha in the building. It was as if he did not even know who she was even though she was clearly intimidated by him. Not only her but also many colleagues expressed discomfort when he was near, a discomfort solely based on Samantha's accusations. Mike did not care what others thought of him. All that concerned him was doing his job to the best of his ability and pleasing his clients and that he did without fail regardless of the office place conundrum.

Mr. Tuttle was in the midst of a conference call when Mike tapped on his door. Without loosing a beat he signaled for Mike to enter and have a seat. Mike carefully spied the office décor while patiently waiting for his turn to be attended to. He took a deep breath and wondered what this impromptu meeting could possibly be about.

"Yes I understand. Okay…goodbye," he spoke into the phone before hanging up the receiver. He closed his eyes and took a deep contemplative breath while shaking his head from side to side. He folded his hands and placed them on his desktop in front of him then looked up at Mike and smiled, "These folks really know how to stress an old guy out. That was Joe Thornton, wants me to fly out to Phoenix for a conference tomorrow because some guy got sick. Never mind the fact that I'm up to my bushy eyebrows in hot sticky shit around here."

"I hear ya," Mike said beginning to feel anxious.

"So how are things m'boy? I talked to Larson and he said that the plans are looking great, he's feeling a great deal of confidence in your abilities. That's wonderful."

Mike nodded, "Well you know I always do my best."

"Yes that you do. Michael, I'm not going to bullshit you, it's not looking good right now. Yes I pushed and fought to get you back in here but Samantha's crying to Brad that she's uncomfortable and that you're looking at her in a threatening manner and she can't work under these conditions."

"What?" Mike's face became flushed and his body tensed.

"Yes I'm sure it's all a crock, this isn't the first time that spoiled bitch has pulled some crap like this but she's Brad's girl and Brad is Thornton's boy. Those bureaucratic sons of bitches have to go through the motions so they come out shining and fair but bottom line is its Brad's call. If Brad tells Thornton he wants you out then young man you're on your ass on the curb with your blueprints by your side."

Mike took deep easy breaths as Reginald returned to his seat. He leaned in closer and his tone was low when he spoke, "Get out of here Michael. Don't let these pompous bastards name you a harasser and violent and toss you like day old chutney. Consider this your resignation. Get the heat off you and shine the spotlight on them. I will give you my utmost recommendation but act now. Thornton's going to drag this on as long as he can so to the untrained eye it appears that he gave you every possible benefit of the doubt. Truth is he's not interested in hearing the facts. Soon he's only going to be interested in pulling the plug on your career here. Do you understand me young man?"

"Yea, yea, I hear you. I hear you loud and clear. My color got me in here and it's my color that's getting me tossed out. May I be excused now?"

Reginald Tuttle closed his eyes and nodded his head. Mike rose quickly from his chair and exited the office. Samantha worked in Brad's office only a couple doors down. There was a bitter taste in Mike's mouth. He walked in that direction considering giving them a reason to fire him. Save everyone some time and trouble, beat the hell out of Samantha himself and then turn to kick Brad's racist ass. But Mike instead stopped mid-stride, "fuck 'em," he mumbled to himself before turning on his heels and heading back to his own office space. He closed and locked the door behind him. Fuming he sat on top of his desk and stared out the window. He needed a friend more than anything else right now but his had selfishly taken his own life. Mike's body became consumed with rage and he so desired to about face, grab the blonde bimbo by her hair and drag her kicking and screaming across the floor.

Mike removed the phone cord from the base and with all his might slammed it into the wall. Within minutes there were voices on the opposite side of his door and the knob twisted back and forth as someone tried to enter. Mike stood still and silent with gritted teeth and mounting anger. His shoulders were tense as he stared at the scarred wall before him. He took deep shallow breaths and his heart raced. The phone on the clip of his belt vibrated. Slowly he removed it and consulted the caller ID. It was Sierra.

"Yea?" he answered with an excess of bass in his voice.

"Hey Mike, how are you?" she asked timidly.

"It's not a good time right now Si," Mike answered plainly.

"I'm sorry to disturb you. You okay?"

Mike paused for a moment and thought before he spoke. He rubbed his temples and let his shoulders fall, "I'm straight. I'll holla at you lata on aiight?" Mike immediately closed the phone and slumped down into his chair.

Sherika sat in short terry cloth shorts with her legs crossed exposing slightly scarred brown flesh. A large tattoo that read "Lakeside Girl" covered most of her right calf. A cigarette dangled between her fingers and she bobbed her head up and down to a beat playing from a car down the street. Mike's temperature rose slightly at the sight of her. He scratched his temple and coaxed himself into remaining calm. He strutted to where she sat in front of his building and stopped beside her. The two eyed each other but moments passed before one actually spoke a word to the other.

"What's up l'il momma? You know you can't be poppin' up at a nigga crib unannounced and shit."

"Calm down boy. I was just in the area. Tay ran into some fool down at Wet Willie's and it just so happen homeboy stay up in here so I thought I'd just check up on you. Ain't heard from a nigga in awhile. Wassup? You straight?"

Mike's nerves relaxed and he took a seat beside her, "Crackers trippin' that's all."

"Yea? That ain't nothin' new, shiit. White man always got his foot on a nigga neck," Sherika laughed and took another drag on her cigarette, "So wassup pimpin'? You got a shorty up in da crib or somethin'?"

"Naw I'm flying dolo."

"So since when I gotta ask if I can come up?"

Mike paused momentarily as if in serious contemplation. He nodded and stood. He walked to the front entrance to his building with Sherika on his heels. She took a final drag on her cigarette and flicked it into the air as she blew the last of the poison to mingle with the polluted night air. The couple rode the elevator together in silence. For the first time since she'd known him Sherika felt awkward in Mike's presence. The ding announced their arrival to Mike's floor and they walked to his condo. She was taken aback by its appearance, as it was not as neat and orderly as it normally was. Without a word Mike disappeared into his bedroom leaving Sherika behind to make herself at home. She took a seat in front of the flat screen television, which was already set to BET. At the close of the third consecutive music video the fact that she was alone began to set in. Sherika wondered to herself why Mike had even bothered allowing her up to his place if he was going to behave as though she were not there.

"Mike!" she called out, "Ay Mike!"

When she received no response she decided to take the initiative to go after him. She stood and walked down the short hall to his bedroom and tapped on the door. Still without a response she slowly eased the door open and at that moment realizing she may see something on the other side that she was not interested in seeing.

"I'm coming in," she announced as she pushed the door open further. Mike, dressed in nothing more than a pair of boxers lay stretched out on his back with a t-shirt lain across his chest and his eyes glued to the television set. With attitude Sherika fully opened the door and stood beneath the archway with her hand on her hip, "Wassup? You invite me up here and you just gone leave me out there to entertain myself?" she asked with just enough hostility.

"You invited yourself," Mike answered plainly.

"Oh so it's like that nah, huh? Well how about I invite myself to be up outta here," Sherika turned to leave but Mike stopped her.

"Don't do that l'il momma. Come lay with me."

Sherika pursed her lips but obliged his request. Inside she was relieved and excited that he'd asked her to stay. She stretched her body beside his. Mike sat the remote control on the nightstand and rolled his body over hers. His tongue found hers and entangled in thug passion. His blood made its way to the family jewel and hardened as the pre-set of children sprouted on the tip glistening like a diamond. Sherika reached out to touch it, massaging it and offering silent praise. Mike pulled the tank top over her head. With no brassiere to shield them, her hard nipples stood at attention. Mike touched her body in a way he hadn't before. He was gentle and attentive to her needs. Sherika couldn't help but be curious as to why he was being so easy with her, offering for the first time, a sweet prelude to love making but not wanting to damage this opportunity in anyway she rather just relished in the beauty of it.

Mike closed his eyes tight and tried hard to pretend the body he was kissing didn't belong to Sherika who often times was more mannish than he. He wanted the figure he was caressing to embody all the love and innocence and purity he needed. He embraced that feeling tightly but the illusion began to fade away as the ringing of his phone became louder and louder. Mike tried as he might to tune it out and recapture the moment he was blessing Sherika with but alas it would not happen for them.

His cell phone beeped signaling that a voicemail waited. Mike pushed his body off the bed and away from a thoroughly disappointed Sherika and dialed in to retrieve the message, "Hey Mike, it's Si-Si. Just calling to check on you, make sure you're okay. You didn't sound so hot earlier. Well, hope everything's good and uh, just call me later."

Mike stopped all movement abruptly. He stepped away from the bed and backed up until his body was against the wall. "Fuck," he mumbled to himself. Sherika sat up aroused and confused. She stared helplessly at Mike who stood naked with his palms covering his face and his erection virtually non-existent. She eyed the phone curiously then returned her attention to him.

"That was a bitch huh? Who was the bitch?" Sherika asked.

"Nobody."

"Must be somebody, she got you all distracted and shit," she pointed at his diminishing erection.

"I said nobody now mind your own fuckin' business. Why don't you come over here and get me right, worry about that."

Sherika was vexed. All that passion he'd had for her was gone in a heartbeat and the Mike she knew best had returned. She sighed and dropped to her knees before him.

Mike hadn't felt himself in some time. Just as things seemed to be looking up things seemed to go further south than he was living. Mike found himself conflicted emotionally. He longed for his friendship with Nate. No longer was there anyone for him to turn to when things were wrong. He was angry to have learned the things that he'd learned but at the same time there was a void that only the type of love and unconditional friendship that Nathaniel Lee offered him for many years could fill. There were sensitive feelings filtering through his soul but he didn't know how to handle them. He had a standing date with Sierra for that evening. It wasn't really a date, the two had just made plans to hook up and hang out no differently than they'd done in the recent past.

Mike grabbed the jeans he'd worn earlier in the day from the bedside chair and reached inside the pocket. He felt around until his fingertips grazed the edge of paper. He pulled out a small wad of bills. He flipped through it until he found what he was looking for. He pulled out the small corner of paper he'd torn from his bill earlier in the week. He picked up the phone and dialed the number written on it; Sindella's number. He sat on the edge of the bed and waited for her to answer.

After the third ring he decided to disconnect when a voice came through from the other end.

"Hello? Can I speak to Sindella?"

"This is Sin, who is this?"

"Mike. One of your regulars at the restaurant. I was in there this morning."

"Oh chocolate thunder."

"What?"

"What up shorty? I didn't think you'd call."

"Quit frontin', yes you did."

"Yea, you right," she laughed.

After a brief conversation Mike invited Sindella to accompany him at his club that evening, an offer to which she of course agreed.

The music was loud but the grooves were mellow and Mike was comfortable in his element, high off herb and drunk off Henny. His eyes were half closed and he nodded his head to the music. Sindella was looking sweet. The mini a-symetrical skirt exposed her solid thighs. Her breasts were round and perky in the sexy midriff top. A small Japanese tattoo etched near her belly button flattered her tight tummy. Big curls flowed down her back and landed above her rear end. She was older than Mike and business-like in her demeanor. She swayed her hips from side to side and held the glass of sparkling champagne in the air. Mike looked forward to having her in his bed. He smiled to himself as he thought of the many things he'd do and the many ways he'd have her.

"Mike!" a voice called above the music.

Mike opened his eyes and sat upright. His pulse quickened when he saw Sierra standing before him. He averted his attention. He reached out and took the half empty bottle of Hypnotic from the table and filled his glass. He reached for Sindella and placed a hand on her waist. She took a seat on the plush sofa beside him laughing and smiling unaware of any potential problem. He pulled her to him and kissed her lips.

Mike leaned back and again locked his gaze with Sierra's. Sindella's expression slowly changed from one thrilled to be having such a joyous night out to one of discomfort and discontent as she became conscious of what Mike was up to. Her eyes shifted from Mike to Sierra and back. Sierra chewed her bottom lip and abruptly walked away.

Mike blew air from his lungs and looked into Sindella's face. She rolled her eyes and stood and stalked away. Mike was unfazed by her actions. He was however disturbed by Sierra's presence and reaction. He eyed Sindella's frame as she leaned forward conversing with the girlfriend he'd allowed her to bring with them. He licked his lips and imagined what it would be like to have her naked ass smacking against his body while tugging at her healthy mane. Mike stood and looked her body over. He took the bottle of blue alcohol and headed for the door. He walked out into the night air ignoring the voices of the people vying for his attention. He signaled to the valet to bring his car around.

Mike turned the radio off and drove silently, thinking. He pulled his car into Sierra's driveway and parked it behind her old Chevy. He looked at his wristwatch and saw that it was past 2 am. Mike stepped from his vehicle and walked to Sierra's car. He touched the hood; it was warm. He knocked softly on her front door. When there was no answer he knocked harder. Moments later the door unlocked and Lilly stood with a smirk on her face.

"Sierra," she called softly, "You have a visitor," Lilly stepped aside and allowed Mike entrance.

"What are you talk – what are you doing here?" Sierra asked.

"I'll leave you two alone," smiling, Lilly disappeared into the living room.

"I could have asked you the same thing," Mike replied with a slight slur giving away the fact that he'd had a lot to drink.

"Oh goodness, you're drunk. You stood me up. I was in the mood to have some fun tonight so I thought I'd try the club. I wasn't looking to start trouble with you, I wasn't even expecting to see you."

"Can I holler at you?"

"Talk."

"In private."

Sierra fidgeted with the belt on her robe. She sighed and reached for the front door handle.

"We can't just talk in your room?" Mike exhaled and followed Sierra outdoors accepting that as her answer.

The only sound was that of the night creatures. Many minutes passed before Mike finally spoke again, "How you feeling?"

"I'm well. I should really be asking you that question."

"I'm good. I'm straight."

"So you say."

"And what the fuck is that supposed to mean?"

"Mike please don't curse at me."

"Damn that goody-goody shit gettin' real old real fuckin' fast."

"So why are you at my house at two in the morning then?"

"Why? Dawg, you been stressin' me for weeks. Now you stalking me at my club an' shit. I just wanted to see what the hell you wanted."

"If I've been bothering you I'm sorry. I was only concerned about you. Mike I'm not sure what I did wrong but I promise I'll leave you alone if that's what you want," the brims of Sierra's eyes began to fill with water. She felt her heart crumble inside her chest cavity. She fought a loosing battle with being an unfazed bitch. She mumbled a sorrowful good night and turned away.

"I'm sorry," Mike mumbled.

Sierra paused, her door partway open. Her tears began to escape. Mike carefully walked behind her and gently placed his hands on her waist. He leaned close to her ear and repeated, "I'm sorry." Mike turned her slowly to face him. He was angry with himself when he saw the river of tears he'd inflicted. He leaned forward and kissed Sierra's lips softly. In shock she was stoic but soon responded. The two kissed softly and sweetly, Sierra becoming drunk off the combination of intoxicants embedded in Mike's tongue and the warm sensation that was overwhelming her. The feeling captivated Mike; never had he felt so connected and so weak emotionally. His mind could not process what his heart was feeling. Slowly Mike backed away. No words were spoken as he walked backwards and out the gate to his car not taking his eyes off of Sierra. He dropped his head and entered his car, backed out and drove away.

23 Sierra

Sierra returned the phone to its cradle. She sat still and quiet on her living room sofa. She chewed the corner of her lip and thought hard but her mind came up blank.

"Sierra are you okay?" Pam asked. She stood above Sierra in her paint-stained coveralls with a hand on her hip.

"I'm fine, why?"

"I don't know. Girl you just look funny. Doesn't she look funny Lilly?"

Lilly was seated on the floor in the corner of the room. With a small brush she painted the base board off-white. She turned to look at her sister's face.

"You okay Si-Si?" she asked through her protective mask.

"I'm fine, why do y'all keep asking that?" Sierra chuckled uncomfortably.

"Who was on the phone?"

"Nobody, just Mike."

Pam mumbled, "Uh oh."

"What?"

"You jonesin' for this guy now?"

"Girl naw."

"Yes she is," Lilly interjected.

"No I am not. He just invited me out to dinner."

"Heyy," Pam swirled her hips and snapped her finger. She sashayed to the bucket of peach colored paint she'd been using on Sierra's wall and dipped her brush inside.

"It's no big deal Pamela. This won't be the first time we've gone out to eat. It doesn't mean anything."

"You need me to sit with the kids?" Lilly asked without stopping what she was doing. She looked back at Sierra who nodded, "Where are you crazy kids going anyway?"

"Nowhere that special. Just to Ruth's Chris."

"To Ruth's Chris? Damn that sounds more like a date."

"That's what I'm afraid of especially since he kissed me the other night."

Silence blanketed the room. Simultaneously Pam and Lilly dropped their brushes and rushed to Sierra's side. They took a seat on the hot plastic that was spread across the floor and furnishings. Sierra dropped her head low and the three women chuckled.

"Why the shit you didn't tell me?" Lilly asked with wide eyes, "Details quiet one."

Sierra explained what had happened that evening on the front stoop between her and Mike, "But I'm sure its nothing. I ain't even Mike's type. I'm not gonna spread my legs so what do I have to offer him? Please. I'm sure it's just us hanging out same as always."

"Hanging out at Ruth's Chris? You tell me who just hangs out at Ruth's Chris?" Pam asked.

"You really need to quit it," Lilly stood and scratched her round belly. She continued to talk as she walked toward the bathroom, "It's a date and you *are* his type. Don't kid yourself. Mike needs a person like you in his life. You'd be good for him."

The bathroom door closed. Sierra's mind drifted back to Nate's letter and those final words he'd left for his mother. He was high, he was drunk but he was only expressing everything that was in his heart. He wanted Mike and Sierra together because he thought she'd be good for him.

"Girl, Mike is fine. You betta throw that coochie on that nigga. Heyy!" Pam moved her body down low and jerked it back and forth. Sierra laughed and resumed painting while still wondering if there was any meaning behind that kiss.

Sierra sat nervously in the passenger's seat of Mike's car. Every now and then butterflies would multiply and flutter throughout her belly. Her palms were sweaty and she inconspicuously took quiet deep breaths. For the first time she couldn't think of anything to say. Pam and Lilly had taken time to help her get ready for her date. Her hair was done in a stylish flip and her make up was made to flatter her skin tone and complexion. Her nails were trimmed and painted and Pam lent her one of her sexiest dresses, a red knee length spaghetti strap with heels to match. Mike's expression gave away his shock and amazement when she came to the door.

She glanced quickly at Mike. She thought about how handsome he was, something she'd never paid attention to before. His skin looked so smooth she wanted to graze her fingers across it. She closed her eyes and inhaled the faint aroma of his cologne. She felt a touch of shame at her reaction to Mike on this evening; after all she wasn't yet divorced from Darryl. Mike cut the wheel and turned into the parking lot of the restaurant. He didn't move immediately after turning the engine off. He leaned against the steering wheel with the keys dangling, eyeing Sierra. Her nerves were frazzled and she felt moisture form in the pits of her arm.

"Wassup l'il momma?" he asked. Sierra shrugged her shoulders and rubbed her sweat filled palms together, "Bring yo' fine ass on."

Sierra smiled broadly and exited the car. She met Mike on the passenger's side and together the two entered the restaurant. Mike advised the Maitre'd of the reservations he'd made and they were seated at a nice secluded table. Unsure of where to look, Sierra opted to remove her eyeglasses. If she could not see clearly the person whom she was engaged with she couldn't feel quite as subconscious. She listened to her own breathing and heartbeat as Mike ordered for the both of them. Once the waiter had taken their order and disappeared Sierra felt the tension return full force.

"Sooo… how's work?" she asked.

"Man, a bunch of bullshit and politics," Mike sighed, "This female is accusing me of sexual harassment."

There was a pause. Sierra's eyebrows raised and she leaned back in her seat.

"I know you think I did it."

"No, no I didn't say that."

"You ain't gotta say it, it's all on your face."

"Well…"

"Well," Mike laughed, "I'm not sexually harassing the girl. Now before the night is over if you ain't careful I might sexually harass you."

Sierra only blushed and smiled.

Full from her meal and not quite ready to go home she expected that the night was coming to an end. She was boring and predictable and didn't expect Mike would want to spend too much time with her. So she was surprised when he parked the car across the street from Bayside. He took her hand in his as he guided her past the vendors and shops and toward the water where they took a seat side by side.

"Back in the day me and Nate used to hang out here and pick up females. I don't know why. There's Spanish chics all over the M-I but whenever we had a craving for one we would always come here," Mike looked into Sierra's face, "My bad, I ain't mean to make you uncomfortable."

"No, I'm not uncomfortable. It's a memory of your time together. I just hope it was before Mya."

Mike chuckled, "Yea of course it was. Nate was too into that girl to do anything I was doing. You cold?"

"A little chilly."

Mike wrapped his arms around Sierra's shoulders and pulled her into him. He rubbed his warmth up and down her arms.

"Thanks," she whispered.

"You're welcome. Nate was always telling me how much he loved Mya and how I needed to know how it felt so I would understand. Now I know he was lying."

"I'm sure he did love her."

"Not like he claimed to. Don't get me wrong l'il momma, I think he probably wanted to believe that shit but it wasn't true."

"But it seems he did know love because he really was in love with this Anthony."

Mike's face became flushed, "Sierra I don't wanna hear about that. I ain't able to process that shit," Sierra swallowed hard and wished she'd kept her mouth shut. Mike gently pressed her body against his, "He was right though, that I need to know how love feels. I just hope you have enough patience to let me find out."

Mike locked his eyes on Sierra. Her heart seemed to jump from her chest and paused in her throat. Her eyes widened. With his free hand Mike tilted her chin so that she was facing him. She tried to divert her eyes. If she didn't look directly into his she'd be less nervous. Mike leaned forward and gently pressed his lips against hers. They kissed slowly and then with more passion. Sierra forgot about her shyness, she forgot that her divorce with Darryl was not final. She didn't jump when their tongues met and she didn't want him to stop – not ever.

Sierra and Mike chatted and laughed all the way home. Their social noise stopped abruptly when his wheels stopped spinning in her driveway but their smiles remained.

"So that's it huh?" Mike spoke up.

"What's that?"

"I'm in a relationship now."

"Yea, I guess you are. Whoa, Michael Toussaint is my boyfriend. Romeo," the two laughed, "It's late, I should be getting in."

"Yea you should," Mike leaned forward and engaged Sierra in a welcomed goodnight kiss. Feeling excited and happy inside, Sierra practically bounced through the gate and to her front door while Mike watched. After she was safely inside she listened to his car pulling from her driveway. Sierra sighed and rested her back against the door. She never thought she could feel the way Mike made her feel. She'd never thought Mike could make her feel that way.

She removed her heels and tiptoed down the hall to her bedroom. Lilly was sound asleep with the television on displaying the latest infomercial. Sierra pressed the power button ending the blabber of yet another nighttime techno geek. Lilly shifted beneath the sheet and blinked her eyes open.

"How was the date?" Lilly asked in a low gruff and sleep filled voice.

"It was wonderful. I think I have a boyfriend."

"What? You for real? What happened?"

Sierra smiled as she reflected on the passion on the docks, "Go to sleep baby sis. You and the baby need your rest. I'll tell you everything in the morning."

Lilly didn't argue. She turned her head and easily returned to her slumber. Sierra walked into her bathroom to get ready for bed. Before she proceeded to do anything she dropped to her knees beside the tub.

"Dear Lord, it's me. You know why I'm here. I need to know if I'm doing the right thing. I'm not even divorced from Darryl yet and I'm kissing Mike. Somewhere inside I know that's wrong, I just don't understand why it feels right...so right and so natural. But if I'm following the wrong path I won't hesitate to cross the street no matter how I feel. Just please, Lord let me know if where I'm headed is your

will. Thank you. In Jesus name, the Mother, the Father, the Creator.
Amen."

24Nate's Family

Mrs. Marshall's home was quiet, too quiet. In soft cotton pants and an oversized long sleeved shirt she shuffled down the hall and past the six body-length mirrors to the sitting room. She walked to the classic record player in the corner and stooped down low and flipped through the selection of jazz, blues, and classical albums. She carefully eased Ella on the turntable and placed the arm on it.

"At last...our love has come along...," the classic diva crooned. Mrs. Marshall stood with closed eyes. She inhaled and exhaled deeply several times repeatedly. When she opened them her eyes landed on the face of her dead son. She shuffled to the mantle where she'd created a shrine to her child. An enlarged photo of Nate was the centerpiece. His smile was broad and to someone who didn't know any better he appeared to be happy. She used to be one of those unsuspecting fools but now his mother knew the truth, he wasn't and it was too late for her to step in and make a difference.

A pillow was permanently set before the unused fire place. Mrs. Marshall knelt and bowed her head low, her eyes closed. She sent a silent message to her son as she'd done every morning since his funeral. When she was done she stood and turned the volume up on the stereo so that the sound would be a whisper on the wind through the rest of the home.

The sound of the telephone's ringing caught her attention. At a quickened pace she rushed to a desk midway through the hall and answered it.

"Hello Mother Marshall, it's me Mya. How are you?"

Mrs. Marshall smiled broadly. She placed her hand over he heart and took a seat in the solid wooden chair, "I'm fine darling. It's so wonderful to hear from you. How have you been? When are we going to see your lovely face again?"

"Well actually that's what I am calling you about."

"Really?"

"Really. I just touched U.S. soil and I was, well hoping, if you're not too busy, to come by and see you."

Mrs. Marshall sank back in her seat and blinked away the tears that blurred her vision, "If I had anything to do consider it cancelled. Come. Hurry. Wait. Do you need a ride?"

"No, no. I've got a car waiting. I'll be there shortly."

Mrs. Marshall nodded and placed the phone in its cradle. She sat with her hands clasped smiling and allowing joyful tears to fall freely. She smeared them away with the back of her hand and walked across to the bathroom. She stood before the mirror and looked hard at her reflection. She lightly ran her fingers across the gray hairs overtaking her mane. The soft bags beneath her eyes appeared more pronounced than they in reality were. She reflected on the early years of life when she was a classically trained beauty with the world at her feet. At nineteen she was a brilliant dancer with a bright future. She legally changed her name from Hattie Louise to Brigitte Simone and with eleven dollars in her pocket she escaped the small Louisiana town that she called home in search of the bright lights and fame which she was sure awaited her in New York City. But along with the memorable meetings with the stars of the time there was the meeting with the wanna-be jazz manager James Marshall. And after a careless night of passion Brigitte's life was instantly altered. Mrs. Marshall didn't regret changing her last name and hanging up her dancing shoes in exchange for a stable life and six children. But she was drawn to Mya because in her she saw everything that was familiar and after months without having her son, she was glad to soon have Mya in her home.

Mrs. Marshall changed her clothes and attentively touched up her long brown hair. She was surprised at how quickly her doorbell was ringing. She paused to look herself over in the mirror then like a sixteen year old anxiously anticipating her first date she rushed to answer the door. Her eyes widened and glistened with water and she covered her mouth. She gasped and allowed Mya entry into her home. Smiling and overwhelmed with emotion Mya nodded repeatedly. She handed the pink bundle to the grandmother and followed her to a spot on the sofa in the sitting room.

"She's tiny, oh but she's beautiful," Mrs. Marshall spoke about the newborn baby she held in her arms.

"She's but a month old. Her name is Nathalia Piper Marshall. Adorable isn't she?"

"An absolute doll," Mrs. Marshall spoke softly not taking her eyes off of Nate's daughter. Mya, smiling warmly, took a seat beside her reaching over and adjusting the lightweight soft pink blanket.

Mrs. Marshall turned to face Mya, "Why didn't you tell us?"

Mya sighed and stood. She walked to Nate's shrine and was momentarily speechless. She swallowed the lump in her throat and turned away.

"I'm so sorry Mother Marshall. I couldn't speak to you or anyone here for that matter, I was just too distraught. I realize that was selfish, I truly do. I...I just don't know what to say."

"Mya. Did my son know...that he was going to be a father?"

Mya's expression changed. She smeared her tears away with her thumb and shook her head, "I wasn't immediately aware. By the time I found out Nathaniel was so far gone I was afraid if I said anything it would only make matters worse. Believe me I struggle every day wondering whether or not telling him about her could have tempted fate. But I'll never have an answer to that and if you're angry with me I completely understand."

Mrs. Marshall took a deep breath and glanced at Nate's photo, "I'm really not sure how I feel about your choice but I can't consider the alternative, I just can't do that. I am however ecstatic that you brought my granddaughter to my attention and she's all I need to get through."

Mya nodded and bit down on the corner of her lip. She wanted to assure Mother Marshall that had she known that Nate would have even considered suicide for a tenth of a second she would not have hesitated to share the results of her EPT with him. She took a seat beside Mrs. Marshall who was learning all of the identifying marks on Nathalia's tiny cream colored face, completely oblivious to anything around her.

Mya slept soundly in the spare bedroom that once belonged to three of five of the Marshall daughters. She was exhausted from her motherly duties and international travels. The better part of Mrs. Marshall's morning had been fulfilling and joyful. She'd tended to little Nathalia feeding her the bottled breast milk and disposing of dirty diapers. While rocking the baby to sleep and gaining ideas from HGTV she was struck with sudden inspiration.

She telephoned her daughters, Mike and Sierra and her husband inviting them all to her home for a celebratory dinner. As far as they were aware it was merely a welcome home to Mya. She'd wanted to inflict the same surprise upon them that had been done to her, just to see what her face must have looked like.

She pulled an old basinet from the basement and sanitized it, one that previously belonged to one of her other grandchildren. She placed the sleeping child inside and set her right outside of the kitchen so that she could monitor the rise and fall of her back. Mrs. Marshall diced vegetable and boiled water, she tenderized and marinated meat. She prepared a meal and her home in anticipation of the gathering. It was just past six pm when family began to arrive and Brigitte Marshall was more than ready answering her front door with a mother and daughter by her side armed with an old Polaroid camera.

Mrs. Marshall's soul was filled with joy and with spiritual wings she floated to a heavenly epitome. The void wasn't completely filled, only a fool would mistake a joyous band-aid for an emotional antidote. When she rose from her bed the next morning the routine would be similar. She'd place a classical or jazz 45 on her turntable and kneel in prayer before her son's image. Where it would differ is on that occasion a basinet with Nathalia inside would accompany her.

It was getting late into the evening and Mr. Marshall hadn't yet shown. Mrs. Marshall suspected that her husband held some resentment towards Mya for not being able to "turn him straight" but she didn't expect he'd be so disrespectful as to transfer his blame and responsibility to her by not showing up.

Mrs. Marshall looked into the faces of her children as they exited her home. Delight lived in their eyes and they felt as though they'd gotten a part of their brother back, maybe even a second chance. When everyone had gone she ran a warm bubble bath for Mya to relax in. Nathalia grew fussy so she took her in her arms and rocked her gently singing Italian words softly into her ear. She sat in the old scarred wooden chair beside the phone and lifted the receiver. She dialed her brother in law's phone number and asked to speak to her husband.

"Where were you?" she asked as soon as he picked up the line.

"I can't face that girl right now Brig."

"How can you be this selfish? It's this selfishness that-" her accusation caught in her throat.

"That what Brig? Come on nah, don't bite your tongue, say what you thankin'."

"Don't push me James."

There was silence on either end as the two carefully contemplated their next words. Nathalia again began to fuss as she fidgeted on her grandmother's shoulder. Mrs. Marshall kindly shushed her as she rocked faster.

Mr. Marshall asked, "What grandbaby is that?"

Mrs. Marshall paused, "Nathaniel's daughter. Your newest grandbaby."

Mr. Marshall's heartbeat paused and he couldn't think. His son was a father. Why didn't he know this before? Did it really matter? He looked at the ceiling holding the fluid back in his eyes. He didn't know if he should be angry that no one had told him or just let it go and be happy that it was true, "Brig...why...?"

"I didn't know either James, I didn't know either."

"But why wouldn't that girl-"

"Does it really matter now? Believe me honey, I know where you're headed but James baby I'm going to have to ask you to come back. Just please, come back. It isn't worth getting angry over at this point. Won't do either of us any good. You have to pick your battles honey and believe me when I tell you; this one is not worth fighting."

On the other end of the line, Mr. Marshall rubbed his temples with his free hand. He wanted to be defiant but what good had it done him thus far? He sighed, "What she name it?"

"Nathalia. Nathalia Piper Marshall. Isn't that beautiful?"

"A baby girl. Yes Brig, it sure is beautiful. What she look like? She favor my boy?"

Mrs. Marshall relocated Nathalia to the crook of arm so that she could see her face clearly. She swiped her tears away so that they would not leak onto the child, "She looks just like him."

"Is it too late Brig? Can I come see my grandchild?"

"Y'know James, you don't need to ask my permission. This is still your home too."

Two hot cups of coffee sat cooling and untouched on the kitchen table. Mr. Marshall held his sleeping granddaughter in his arms studying her face the same as his wife had early that morning. Mrs. Marshall watched. She wasn't angry anymore. She stopped blaming. She moved her chair closer and smoothed Nathalia's fine dark hair. Mr. Marshall softly touched her hand. Their eyes met and all of the questions were present. *Do you forgive me? Do you still love me? Can I make it up to you? May I come home?* Brigitte Simone Marshall leaned into her husband's personal space. She kissed his lips tenderly and he understood it to mean *"yes"* to all of the above.

25 Mike

For yet another morning in a three-week time span Mike rolled from an empty bed. He'd almost forgotten how good it felt to sleep through the night. To his surprise he didn't really miss sharing his bed with a stranger though he couldn't deny the occasional urge to please himself.

It was already past eleven when he staggered slowly to the bathroom to relieve his full bladder. He no longer rose at 5am, not since Sierra convinced him to follow Reggie Tuttle's advice and quit the firm two weeks prior. Though it was arguably foolish for him to have quit his job without another lined up he decided it was a break well deserved. Besides it gave him more time to invest in securing his clubs position as the hottest spot in town for people of color.

He felt good. It was a new experience and he wondered how he'd lived without it for so long. Nothing bothered him. Not the thought that Nate slept with men before his passing, not his mother's lifetime absence, not his grandmother's indifference toward him. He'd found a family with Sierra and the children. He'd found a mother in Mrs. Marshall and to have learned that Nate had given him a "niece" was just the icing. The only element of disdain was Mya's return to England with Nathalia and Mrs. Marshall's choice to join them permanently. His loss compared not to Mr. Marshall's who'd only just come home to work things out with his wife when Mya put the invitation on the table. The invitation extended to the both of them but he was not comfortable with the idea of leaving his home...the United States. Whether he changed his mind or not, his wife was leaving and soon. He had his daughters but he was alone without his wife and son so Mike spent as much available time as possible trying to somehow fill his void.

Mike washed his hands. He splashed the cool water on his face and looked at his reflection in the mirror. He then blotted his face on the large bath towel that hung from the wall and returned to his room to take a seat on his bed. He dialed the digits to the Marshall home but after four rings and no answer he determined that Pops Marshall was not home. He called Sierra and told her to get dressed, he'd be there for her within the hour.

Mike allotted Sierra an extra thirty minutes to dress the children. She answered the door in traditional Sierra form, ankle length skirt sprinkled with flowers and white cotton blouse. She smiled broadly when she set eyes on his face. He leaned in and softly kissed her lips placing his hand on her waist but being careful to be respectful. She invited him inside. The look of the freshly cleaned little faces happy to see him made him exude with a fatherly joy. Michael focused on his new girlfriend and shook his head at her age old ritual of not showing any skin. He walked to her and lightly brushed his fingers across her hair. He kissed her forehead.

"Come on. I wanna take you to get some new clothes. We need to be done by 4:30 though cause my home girl gone hook your hair up," Mike announced with great pride. He turned to head back to the door but Sierra didn't budge.

"What's this all about?" Sierra asked becoming apprehensive.

"What? You my woman now and I wanna do something nice for you. Is there something wrong with that?"

"Changing me? You knew me before you got into this. You can't just make me over into one of your rump-shakers 'cause you don't like my style."

"Ay, ay calm down Si-Si," Mike exhaled slowly and counted backwards from twelve, "Believe me I don't wanna change you, that's the last thing I'd ever wanna do."

"Well I have enough skirts and blouses that you don't particularly care for so what type of clothing are you planning to purchase?"

Mike wanted to throw his hands up defeat and forget the entire thing. But then he realized that Sierra wasn't exactly challenging him but rather was against being forced to change anymore than he'd want to. He took her hands in his and gave her the respect of looking her in the eye.

"I don't necessarily wanna change you l'il momma but I do want you to live for you sometimes. You cover yourself 'cause your daddy raised you too. I want you to see yourself in a different light. If you don't like it you can go back to your paisley prints and rose petals, I promise. I promise."

Sierra cracked a smile and laughed, "I'm trusting you."

"That's all I ask," he leaned in and kissed her lips softly.

Mike was pleased at Sierra's receptiveness to his choices. Her leeriness began to fade the moment she saw what her body looked like in a pair of jeans. She couldn't keep her eyes off the French manicure and pedicure she'd been pampered with. And with her first ever hair relaxer and highlights her attitude changed as her self-esteem immediately blossomed. Michele applauded and Mike was amazed at all of the length previously hidden which now swept across her back when she moved. Mike found keeping his hands off of her lower back and waistline nearly impossible. He wished Nate would have been able to see her this way with such happiness and confidence. He'd be proud that Mike of all people, who hid behind money and used material possessions to disguise his insecurities, was the vessel that brought out the best in Sierra.

Mike pulled his car in front of NATHANIEL'S and turned the keys over to the valet. It was still early in the evening and not many people were present. He did a double take as he headed to the front door. Sherika was approaching in the distance. There was no sense in continuing as though nothing changed; she'd already noticed him notice her. He stopped and waited for her and the women she was with to catch up to him. Mike sighed and awaited the tongue-lashing.

"Wassup Mike?" she said without stopping.

"Damn it's like that?"

"It's however you want it to be."

Mike rolled his eyes to the back of his head but shrugged it off and walked inside the club.

From when Mike was a child until he was old enough to be independently defiant his grandmother Marie dragged him into church. He hated he experience and often found himself sitting up fast asleep. His grandmother had hoped to save his soul and spare him from a life like the one his mother had. Forced religion didn't feel good to Michael. It didn't take long for him to mysteriously disappear before Sunday services were to begin. He turned his back on church early in life and decided that he controlled his own destiny. There was nothing, not a man, a book, nor could a cynical grandmother tell him about the future of his existence and eternal spirit.

Sierra asking Mike to church was inevitable. She wanted him to join her family for Sunday service to hear the good Pastor speak. When the time arrived he was unclear as to how he'd handle it. But when that day came he decided it just wasn't for him and he told her so. He felt he hadn't tried to change her just turn her on to new things and he didn't appreciate her trying to make him into a man he was not. But it was deeper than that. Her uncle, the "good" Deacon, after postponing his trip had finally flown in that morning. She'd very soon come face to face with him and she needed support.

So Mike dressed in brown slacks and a faint yellow button down with a tie and reluctantly drove himself to the Mitchell family church. He found himself a parking spot and settled into it. He chuckled to himself as he thought about how his grandmother would react if she knew he was about to make his way inside a house of God of his own free will.

Mike sighed and exited his vehicle. He adjusted his tie and headed to the church. He immediately felt out of place after he walked through the large doors. He'd only been on the other side of those great doors once before and that was for Nate's funeral service. He'd never intended to run. He stood in a safe position near the door and looked onto the sea of people seated throughout the hall. It was a full house. He looked around at the religious art. His eyes lowered and landed on the top of a Bible peaking from behind a seat. Small beads of sweat popped out on his forehead and he felt anxious. He decided he cold not stay, it just wasn't for him. He didn't know how he'd explain his absence but he'd come up with something.

"Good morning young brother, I haven't seen you here before. Are you a guest?"

Mike turned to come face to face with a heavy set fair-skinned woman. Her warm smile was infectious but not enough for Mike to stick around.

"Naw, I can't stay."

"You sure about that? You're going to miss a wonderful service if you leave."

"I'll check it out some other time."

"Okay brother, I shole hope to see you in the front row next week."

Mike reached out for the door handle.

"Michael?" a voice came from behind him.

His eyes grew wide and he turned slowly, "Hey, how ya doin' Momma Marshall?"

"Wonderful especially now that I see you in the house of the Lord. To what do we owe this honor?"

Mike grinned and scratched the back of his neck, "Si-Si invited me."

"Oh well this is a blessing son, a real blessing. Praise be to God, your child has come home."

Mrs. Marshall reached out and wrapped her arms around Mike's body. She held him close and rubbed her hands up and down his back. She pulled back and held his hands in hers.

"It's really good to see you here," Mrs. Marshall stared quietly at Mike's face. She reached up and caressed his cheek, "I don't know if you've heard but I'm moving to England in a couple weeks with Mya and my granddaughter."

Mike nodded, "Yea Sierra told me. What about Pops Marshall? How he gone handle that?"

"He's not. But I need to do this for me. I have to make things right between my son and me. Look baby, I don't expect you to understand anymore than James. I let my son down and now I've got a chance to in a sense make things right and I intend to do that with or without my husbands support."

Mike nodded and smiled but if he were honest with himself he'd have admitted the great loss that he himself was feeling by her decision to leave. He felt as though somehow he too was being left behind and it hurt his soul to see her go. Hell, who looses two mothers in one lifetime? But one day he'd rejoice in the fact that this mother he'd, if nothing more, had the opportunity to know. He'd had the chance to love and be loved by her even if only for a little while.

He moved his eyes from Mrs. Marshall's face and watched as Sierra nervously rushed down the aisle toward him.

"You made it," she smiled. She kissed Mike on his cheek.

"Michael, you come see me next week sweetheart. Okay?" Mrs. Marshall gave his hand one final squeeze before she turned to walk away and give him and Sierra brief privacy.

A concerned look washed over Sierra's face, "Thank you so much for coming. I was afraid you'd change your mind. I mean I realize that this isn't the most comfortable place for you."

"Naw, I couldn't do that to my girl," Mike fibbed.

Sierra smiled shyly. She took Mike by the hand and led him to the front of the church. He was apprehensive but he followed through with the precedent he'd set of being a good friend. Lilly, pleased as well by his presence, smiled brightly and gently squeezed his arm. Mike could smell the stench of doubt coming from Mrs. Mitchell but he easily brushed it off suddenly feeling more encouraged to see it through. Mike watched as the three rows of patrons cloaked in purple robes danced onto the stage singing about joy and victory. He nodded his head slightly to the upbeat rhythms.

Pastor Mitchell hobbled to the podium and sang strong and proud in unison with the choir. Mike glanced around at the church goers observing the clapping, chanting and stomping of feet along with the beat up until the Pastor signaled for them to cease.

"Hallelujah! Glory to God, glory to God! Amen! Whew! I feel good this morning. This morning I feel uplifted! The Holy Ghost done took over my body and I welcome him in! Y'all had better tell that Devil to get back...'cause I got the Word as my sword and shield and victory is mine! Say it with me y'all, victory is mine! Victory is mine! I say victory is mine! Praise the Lord, hallelujah! Y'all in y'all seat sayin' the Pastor up there actin' a fool today. Let the church say Amen. Ha ha, I know.

"I'm gone talk to y'all today about joy. Yes joy. Real joy ain't merely 'bout a smile or a simple laugh 'cause somebody told you something funny and now you thank you happy. Naw, happiness is fleeting, it comes and goes in and out of your life but not joy. Uh-uh naw, not joy. Joy never leaves you! Joy is commitment. Y-you could be lying on your sick bed with tubes coming out your nose and toes, you gone be happy 'bout that? I don't thank so but if you got God in your life and joy in your heart then your soul will go unaffected. With joy in your heart you will shout out, by His stripes I am healed! And so you shall...."

Mike glanced about in an awkward motion. He watched the congregation raise their hands to the sky in praise while expressing their agreement with what the good Pastor was saying through their Amen's. As the service continued the intensity in the church heightened. Tears streamed down Sierra's cheeks freer than they had before. Mike thought that must be the joy that Pastor Mitchell was speaking of and he could admit to himself that he wanted a dose. He was touched by all that he saw and all that he heard but was uncertain how he should react.

The Pastor continued, "Now if it's alright I want to bring my baby brother up here. We all know him, we all love him and the Lord has seen fit to return him to us. C'mon up here Brother Deacon Myron."

An old fair-skinned gentleman with an awkward walk climbed the steps. A wide smile stretched across his face as he accepted the love and praise of his brother's congregation. There was nothing unusual in his appearance; he looked the part he played which was as the distinguished and respectable good Deacon. And it was clear his return came at the delight of almost all when the people of the church rose from their seats clapping and thanking God. Nothing about his appearance accused him of being a child molester and Mike would not have ever suspected him to be capable of such a thing. But Sierra's mood had changed nearly instantaneously. She looked small in her seat, almost childlike and Mike knew that there was no denying those allegations. He gently squeezed her knee.

When the Deacon spoke the words, "Jesus be my light cause I walk by faith and not by sight", the congregation rejoiced and sang out. The feeling that Mike had only moments earlier been relishing in dissipated as he listened to the words that escaped the lips of the baptized pedophile.

Hours after the service had begun it came to a close. Members of the church shook hands and intently discussed the values that they'd learned that morning. Many gathered around waiting to shake the hands of the Deacon and welcome him back. Sierra silently shrank into the background. Mike felt terrible watching her so timid and unable to hold up her head.

"Michael," the Pastor broke through the group and walked to Mike with his hand extended, "It's wonderful seeing you here son. I am so glad that you took the time out of your busy life to come and praise with us. Did you enjoy the service?"

Mike shook Pastor Mitchell's hand firmly, "Yes sir."

"That's great to hear. Excellent. Son there's someone that I'd like you to meet. This here is my brother, the good Deacon Myron Mitchell. I'm sure Sierra's told you all about her uncle."

"Yep, she sure has. All about him," Mike glanced at Sierra who shifted uncomfortably.

"Good Deacon this is Sierra's old high school buddy Michael."

"Michael, pleased to meet you son," the Deacon extended his hand as a gentlemanly courtesy but Mike could only look at it. Shake his hand? What he wanted to do was go head up with the Deacon but he held back out of respect for Sierra. However he would not shake the hand of an incestuous child molester. All eyes were on him, Mrs. Mitchell's in particular were boring in the side of his head but Michael would not flinch and would not remove his gaze from the man who was this church's pride and joy while also being responsible for much of the misery in Sierra's life. Mike stood tall and clasped his hands in front of his body.

"Sorry man, I'm uh, gettin' over a bad cold and y'know I don't wanna spread my germs. Don't wanna get you sick and you just got in town."

"Oh. Well uh, yea that makes sense," a feeling of confusion took over the Deacon, "At least you look healthy though."

"Yea. Ay Si-Si you 'bout ready to ride out? I'm starting to feel a lot less healthy."

Mrs. Mitchell pushed her way past the members and positioned herself in Mike's path, "Sierra has lunch with the family after Sunday service. Every Sunday after service and with her uncle being in town it's very important that my daughter not miss this lunch. Now I do thank you for joining us but you're right, if you're ill you should be home in bed."

Mike's blood pressure rose and he struggled to control his breathing. He looked past Mrs. Mitchell to her timid daughter, "What do you want to do?" he asked firmly.

Sierra sighed and fidgeted, "Momma's right, we can't miss lunch."

Mike eyed Sierra closely. He looked directly into her eyes when he spoke, "Are you sure? Do you want me to stay? I won't leave you if you need me to stay."

Sierra paused and swallowed hard. She quickly darted her eyes to her uncle and then back to Mike's face. She slowly looked toward her mother, "I'm okay, thank you. Go on home and rest. I'll call later and check up on you."

Mike nodded. He was disappointed that Sierra gave in to her family and chose to spend the afternoon unhappy and uncomfortable in her uncle's presence but he chose to respect her wishes and quietly back away.

26 Sierra

Sierra sat curled in the corner of her sofa with her feet tucked beneath her. The television aired an episode of Clifford the Big Red Dog in the background. Michele lay stretched out beside her mother with her thumb in her mouth. Her eyelids were heavy but she was determined to focus on her favorite program. Sierra gently caressed the side of her daughters face as she chatted with Lillian on the phone.

She was happy despite some of the tough issues she was dealing with. Having her sister in her life daily, less than two months away from being an aunt, her relationship with Mike, not to mention her three beautiful children, it was all enough to keep her face lit up most of the time.

Sierra was startled to hear the doorbell ring. She wasn't expecting any company. Mike had only just called after dropping her and the children off back at home. She stood with the cordless phone in hand and walked down the hall to answer the door. She stood on her toes and peeked through the peep hole. She gasped and her eyes widened. She no longer heard any of her sister's words but rather only the questions forming and racing through her mind. She pressed her back against the wall and sighed. The doorbell rang once again.

"Lilly. Lilly I have to call you back," she disconnected the line before Lillian had an opportunity to say anything else. Sierra sat the phone on the ledge and unlocked the front door pulling it toward her slowly, "Hi Darryl. What's going on, what are you doing here?"

Darryl was stripped of all his words. He'd heard the rumors about his soon to be ex-wife but he had to see for himself whether or not they were true. He absorbed every inch of her new look. Her once plain and kinky brown hair that she kept pinned to her head was now highlighted with golden streaks and straightened so that it hung past her shoulders. Her eyeglasses were now thin and barely noticeable and her lips glossy. His eyes traveled down the length of her frame. Her body looked curvaceous in her dull yellow tank top and jeans, something that she'd previously never be caught in. Her finger and toe nails were French tipped. She definitely was not the woman he'd walked out on only a few months earlier.

"Wassup Si-Si? Damn girl, you look good. Real good. Guess life's been treating you well."

"I guess it has."

"Can I come in?" Darryl asked. Sierra chewed her bottom lip discomforted. Darryl threw his hands up in surrender, "Come on now, I come in peace. Si-Si please, I'm still your husband and technically this is still my home."

Sierra stepped aside and allowed him entrance. Darryl slow strolled down the brief hall to the living room. He stopped and looked around. He nodded at all the changes Sierra had made, from the new peach walls to the relocation of the furniture to the absence of all wedding photos.

"I see your look ain't the only thing that changed."

"Nope."

The two stood awkwardly in silence. Sierra fidgeted with her finger tips as Darryl assessed everything that had changed since his departure. He admired how she'd handled herself and envied the cleanliness of her home. He couldn't admit how he'd been less than a man looking for love outside of his house. A love he was sure he'd found with Victoria but living with her full time only made him realize how fallible his theory was. Of course he could not confess these private thoughts to Sierra.

He couldn't tell her how quickly things changed when his mistress officially became his woman. How the things that should've changed didn't.

"Daddy," Michele's soft voice traveled from the spot she'd been resting in on the sofa.

"Hey baby girl," he wished the hellish children he now lived with day to day were more like the angel's that bore his name and resemblance.

Michele shuffled from the couch and ran into her fathers arms forgiving and forgetting any past lacking. He lifted her and held her close. He didn't know what her favorite color was, didn't know the program coming to a close on the television was in her eyes the greatest show on TV but he did know that she was his no mater what and that she loved him unconditionally.

"So you wanna tell me why you came here Darryl?" Sierra asked.

"I came to get Lee," he lied, "I wanted to have a guy's day out. Where is mini-me anyway?"

Sierra rolled her eyes discreetly, "He's sleeping."

"Oh. Look Sierra, I know we ain't had the best marriage, I mean we both coulda done some things different but we're still married and we got these kids together. Don't you think maybe we should be trying to work things out?"

Sierra blinked rapidly. She couldn't believe what she was hearing. After all, she'd fought so hard to keep her family together and he'd denied her at every turn.

"Why are you doing this? Why now? I thought you were happy with that woman. Doesn't she make you happy? Doesn't she give you everything you want?"

"Man she straight but she ain't my wife. Come on Si-Si, God don't want this and you know it."

Sierra reached and took Michele from Darryl's arms and instructed her to go to her room. While waiting for a private moment she contemplated what Darryl, her husband, was suggesting. Her provider and father of her children, now that he'd seen what could be was proposing that they become a family once again. She considered her love for Mike who was not her husband, who she'd never made a vow of commitment to. She gasped for air and turned to face Darryl.

"My God how I've longed to hear you say those words. Let's work it out. Let's start over. Let us be the family we were meant to be. I always thought they'd sound much more beautiful than that though. I mean Darryl, seriously I can't go back to that. It took so much for me to get emotionally where I am today and I still have a long, long road ahead of me. But I am not going to be right in my heart nor any good to our children if I allow myself to turn around and undo all the good that I have done."

"So this ain't got shit to do with Mike? What he sexin' you that good now?"

"This has nothing to do with Mike. This is about Sierra and Michele and Jennifer and Lee. This is about being right with God and being right with self. Darryl you don't even love me."

"You don't know how I feel. You don't know what's going on in my head."

"You're right I don't but it's alright. If it wasn't her then it would be someone else and I am not about to set myself up for failure again."

"So that's it shorty? That's how it's gone be? You just gone turn your back on our family just like that?"

"Would you stop? Yea. Y-yes, that's how it has to be."

Sierra and Darryl stopped speaking. They eyed one another moments more before Darryl backed away, "Aiight then but you gone regret this. You just remember I tried to give you another chance."

Sierra nodded calmly and opened the front door. She thought of her love for Mike and though it was true that he factored into her decision not to give Darryl a second chance, it was more about her and the renewed sense of love and self respect she'd acquired that kept her from letting him back into her life.

Sierra closed the door behind Darryl and leaned against it staring at the ceiling with a broad smile across her face. "Aaaaaah!" Sierra called out at the top of her lungs while she ran in place. Her arms flailed wildly at her side and she shook her head vigorously sending hair slapping hard against her face. The sound of tiny footsteps traveled down the hall in her direction.

"Mommy!" Michele called as she fearfully rushed to her mother's aide, "You okay Mommy?

Sierra reached down and lifted her daughter into her arms and held her tight, rocking from side to side. She rubbed Michele's thick ropes of hair. A broad smile spread across her face.

"Oh my sweet angel, I'm good. Mommy's better than good, she's great and she's happy and she loves you guys so, so much."

"I love you too Mommy. Where's Daddy?"

"Oh honey Daddy had some things to do and so do we. We need to be at Grandpa's tonight for his birthday dinner. So how about you come and help me wrap his present? Okay?"

"Okay."

Sierra dressed in a knee length blue dress and low heels. She placed her hand to the gold cross that dangled from her neck and held it tight. Sounds of happy children echoed throughout the home as Lee and Michele played 'Tag' in the living room. She took a few deep breaths to ease her nerves but she was frazzled and the teachings she'd learned from Lamaze were not helpful in the least. She was beyond nervous about the upcoming dinner with her family – her entire family, Deacon included. She intended to pray for solace but to her dismay could not come up with one word or one scripture.

The sound of the doorbell ringing startled her. She closed her eyes and sighed and walked down the hall to answer its call. The side of Mike's face could be seen through the peephole. Sierra rushed to undo the locks and let him in. She accepted his embrace and held his body much tighter than she'd intended. Mike squeezed back and rocked gently. He pressed his lips to her forehead and kissed her softly. Sierra's muscles eased.

"Are you gone be able to make it through the night l'il momma?" he asked. Sierra smeared a stray tear and nodded. She backed away and blinked a few times. Mike wiped her eyes dry, "Now don't start that cryin'. You know you ain't cute when yo' face be all balled up and stuff."

Sierra chuckled softly while rubbing Mike's arm, "I didn't get this flustered when I was a little girl and Uncle Myron would come to dinner."

"And don't let that junk bother you now. You gone go there and wish your daddy a happy birthday and then we can break out wheneva you ready. Just holla at me."

Sierra nodded and went to gather her children. Mike took Jennifer in his arms but she struggled to get to her mother. He instead took Michele and led the group out the front door and to his car.

"Hello Michael," Mrs. Mitchell spoke in a matter-of-fact tone as she opened the front door.

"How you doin' Mrs. Mitchell?"

"Just fine young man. Surprised to see you here at a family function with my daughter."

"Momma please," Sierra pleaded.

"Please what Sierra? Is there something more going on here that your father and I should be aware of?"

"Mikey you made it!" Lillian cut through ending the potential verbal assault that her mother was preparing to launch. She hobbled over, her round belly peering from her white button down maternity shirt. She approached Mike and gently rubbed his arm curbing his rising tension, "Momma, Auntie Tessa is looking for you."

"What the devil that woman want now? Ooh she shole know how to work my nerves," Mrs. Mitchell forgetting all about Mike and Sierra's appearance together huffed her way back into the living room.

Directing her words at Mike, Lilly spoke, "Tessa is my dad's sister. She and Momma do not get along. So sorry about that less-than-a welcome. Come on inside and let me fix you up a plate of hot food. And I have a surprise for you Ms. Sierra. Stephen's here."

"No! Why didn't you tell me?"

"Well he wasn't sure if he'd be able to make it. I didn't want to get folks hopes all up for nothing. But everything seems to be settled which means we can get married now," Sierra wrapped her arms tight around her sisters neck and congratulated her. Mike stood aside feeling like the odd man out and ready to eat. Lilly took Mike's hand in hers, "Come y'all, let's get our grub on. You know Momma done put her left and right food in it, bunions and all!"

Sierra was on pins and needles. She chewed without actually tasting her food and though she'd been formerly introduced and shared polite words with Stephen, she didn't actually know what he looked like, only that he was White. She was distracted and through mouthfuls of chatter she only heard the words her uncle the Deacon spoke. She'd managed to keep her children distanced despite his obvious attempts to connect with them. The last thing she needed was for Jennifer and Michele to grow up with tormented souls just as she had.

With the Deacon moving back to Florida for good it would be quite the challenge keeping her children away from him but she would even if it meant cutting back on the time her parents had with them. Sierra was antsy and she wanted to leave but her father had yet to open his gifts and she did not want to be rude especially on his special day. She kept Jennifer in her arms and Lee and Michele close by her side, her eyes following every move her uncle made.

Aunt Tessa's booming voice traveled into Sierra's mind shattering her train of thought. Moments passed before she realized her elder was speaking to her.

"You gone deaf girl?" Aunt Tessa asked Sierra.

"No ma'am. I'm sorry my mind was elsewhere. What did you say?"

"I asked if you can show your Auntie to the bathroom."

"Aunt Tessa you've been here plenty times before. You know where the bathroom is."

"Girl don't get quick with me. I ain't seen the inside of this house in over six years thanks to yo' mammy. Now I don't remember, come show me."

"Yes ma'am," Sierra took Jennifer up in her arms and called out to her others to follow her but they pretended not to hear. With a half drunk aunt tugging at her sleeve she decided the children would be just fine if she walked away for ninety seconds. Sierra had forgotten how rowdy her Aunt Tessa could be particularly after a few hits from the flask of whiskey she kept stashed in her purse. It was that addictive habit and an unfortunate publicized romp in the Pastor's bed with a drunk named Spanky that had Tessa black balled for six years. But Sierra's most powerful memory of her Aunt was not of her crude act in the place where she and her sister were conceived, it was her final words. The last thing she said before she was tossed out on her behind was *'You trust that ol' Deacon Chester in your home but not me!'*

Before disappearing down the hall she glanced back and saw her uncle standing at the counter catching up on old times with her father. She turned and guided Aunt Tessa to the restroom before turning quickly on her heels to walk away.

"Si-Si now hold on for a sec, I just want to talk to you," Aunt Tessa reached out to take Sierra's hand in hers, "You grew up to be such a pretty young lady, you know that."

"Thank you Auntie," Sierra tried to pull away but Tessa held firm.

"I just wanted a chance to apologize to you Catnip."

"You didn't do anything to me Auntie."

"Naw, nah I ain't been a good auntie. You're all grown now and got your own kids and now it's a little too late. I never took you to the Fair that time when you was little. You was like seven weren't you? You used to love to go to the Fair."

"Auntie, Auntie, it's okay. Really. I think you're a great aunt. Now go on to the bathroom before you wet yourself."

"Oh yes. Hey. I love you Catnip."

"I love you too Auntie," Sierra answered hastily.

Sierra stood impatiently as her aunt pressed her lips against her cheek. The door had barely clicked closed before she turned and headed back to rejoin the family. Her heart skipped a beat and she paused as she reentered the family room. She saw her daughter being bounced on her uncle's knee as her father stood idly by chatting and smiling. Sierra couldn't breathe, she couldn't think, she could only react. She rushed into the room pushing her way past relatives until she was within arms reach of Michele.

"Michele, come to Mommy now. We're going home, it's past your bedtime," Sierra commanded breathlessly as she took Michele's small hand in hers and pulled her away from her great-uncle.

"Sierra why are you in such a hurry? It won't hurt you to stay longer," Pastor Mitchell instructed more than requested, "Michele go on back to your uncle and Si-Si just relax. The kids have stayed up past their bedtime before, it won't hurt them occasionally."

Sierra looked at her dad, then her uncle and then daughter. She stooped low and smoothed Michele's skirt assuring it extended to its full length, "No Daddy, I really think we should be leaving now."

"Sierra Diane, what is wrong with you?" Mrs. Mitchell stepped in cutting off her husband before he could say another word, "That's your uncle, not some stranger. You and Lillian haven't seen him in years. Now he deserves to have time with his nieces and nephew without you behaving all neurotic like you have been. And you will not walk out on Daddy on his day."

"Yes ma'am I understand. I just don't want them up too far past their bedtime. It throws off our schedule."

Mr. Mitchell said, "Sierra honey talk to Daddy. Why so early? Are you okay?"

"Yes Daddy, I'm fine."

"She is not fine Robert," Mrs. Mitchell interjected, "She's been behaving like a raving idiot ever since she started seeing that boy out there. Sierra, sit your tail down and enjoy Daddy's party. Spend some time with your uncle. Michele go back and sit with your great-uncle Myron."

Panic consumed Sierra. She felt as if the walls were closing in on her. She didn't know what to do or what to say to get her children out safely without being inappropriately touched by the so-called "Good Deacon". All eyes were on Sierra as everyone wondered what she was making such a big deal about and what her next move would be. The sounds around her had been reduced to nothing more than mumbles. She could make out no sound but the beating of her own heart as she watched Michele in seeming slow motion return to her uncle's personal space. She couldn't think nor breathe and she knew that she was for sure going to collapse with Jennifer in her arms until Mike appeared suddenly and carried the small child to the safety of her mother's side. Relieved she took her daughter against her body and caressed her sweetly.

"Wait a minute, now just hold on one second. What is this about Sierra?" Mrs. Mitchell shouted, "This is about your uncle? Why Sierra, why would you dare treat your uncle in this manner? She trusts this criminal around her girls but not her own flesh and blood who practically help raise her? Is that what I'm to understand? You don't want your children around your uncle? What kinda foolishness is this? See what happens? You disobeyed the Lord and now you walkin' around here paranoid 'bout nothing. Michele get over here."

"Man naw, you ain't phenna send jit over there to that child molesting ass pervert," Mike interfered. It didn't matter to him any longer that this was family business and he was definitely not considered family. All that mattered was Sierra and her immediate family.

"Excuse me boy," Mr. Mitchell stepped forward until he was chest to chest with Michael, "You care to repeat that?"

Deacon Myron stood at his brother's side, "Son I don't think you should speak about family matters you know nothing about."

"Nigga I ain't yo' son," Mike was enraged and there was no way that he was going to bite his tongue now, "No disrespect intended Pastor but I recommend you watch this cat around your grandkids, especially yo' granddaughters."

"Boy, I haven't been a Pastor for my entire life. Now what I recommend is you get out of my home right now!"

"You ain't got to tell me twice. Come on Si, we phenna bounce."

"My daughter is not going anywhere with you," Pastor Mitchell raised his cane in an aggressive manner, "Oh now I see what is going on here. You're filling her head with all this nonsense. You're trying to brainwash my child!"

"Old man I don't want to disrespect your daughter but homey I'mma suggest you back up with that cane. Like now."

Sierra blinked back her tears and swallowed hard. She opened her mouth to speak but the she couldn't find her voice.

"Sierra apologize to your uncle and then the both of you sinful heathens can be gone from my home permanently if you're going to allow this thug to disrespect me. Your own father."

"Sierra you betta not apologize to that nigga. Damn that, tell 'em what he did," Mike demanded, "Tell 'em now. Right fuckin' now Sierra 'cause if you don't I'm tellin' you, I shole the fuck will."

The Deacon, younger and stronger than his brother the Pastor stepped forward mentally preparing himself to throw down with Mike if it came to that, "Young man you do not know me or my family for that matter. And whatever it is you think I did to my niece I will suggest you keep it to yourself before you make a bigger fool of yourself than you already have."

"Oh word?" Mike smirked at the Deacon and nodded his head. He made direct eye contact with the Pastor when he spoke, "Your brother, the fuckin' no-good Deacon, put his nasty hands up your little girls skirt when she was growing up."

Pastor Mitchell lunged for Mike's neck, "You little nigga!"

Mike swerved and backed out of reach, "Nice try pops. Why don't you ask her? Ask your daughter if I'm lying. That's it, just ask her. Real simple my nigga. What you afraid it might be true?"

"I am a man of God but nigga don't you forget I am a man first and I ain't afraid to take your little narrow ass-"

"He did it," Sierra's voice was barely audible.

"Sierra Diane Mitchell how dare you say such a vicious thing about your uncle!" Mrs. Mitchell raised her voice.

"Momma I'm sorry," Sierra cried, pleading for forgiveness through her tears. Forgiveness for what she didn't know. The truth was finally out and she should have felt relieved but she rather only felt guilty. She felt as though she'd been the one to betray the family, particularly her father. She listened as her mother and father ripped into her. She listened as Mike argued her defense to no avail. Sierra dropped her head as she listened to her frightened children cry and reach up to be held by her. Those angry voices and accusations only rose louder and louder.

"Daddy stop it! All of you, stop it!" Lilly's voice traveled from the kitchen. The angry tones calmed and all eyes were on Lillian. She appeared weak and fragile, a position she'd not been seen in practically since she was in diapers. A disturbed Stephen stood by his fiancée's side and held her up. He tried his best to guide her to a seat but she only snatched away. Tears poured down her face and she held the underside of her round belly, "All of you just stop it. Now Daddy you say it every Sunday, the Devil is a liar and he's stood right here in your home, eating your food, drinking your wine, and touching your daughters!"

Mr. Mitchell, forgetting about Mike, anxiously hobbled over to his pregnant baby girl. He took her hands in his and looked in her face, "Baby girl. What are you saying?"

Lilly took a deep breath and quickly swiped the tears from her eyes, "I remember like it was yesterday. Being fourteen and pregnant and how disappointed in me you were, you both were. Truth is I was so terribly disappointed in myself cause I hurt you and you gotta believe me Daddy when I say that I never in my life intended to do that."

"Baby I know that. I have forgiven you of that and so has the Lord-"

"But as a Christian must I forgive the man that caused me to betray you in the first place?"

"Okay now Lilly, I don't understand. Help me understand. What is this all about?"

"You and Mom were so angry with me when I refused to tell you who the father was. And you were so hurt how could I possibly hurt you more by telling you that Uncle Myron was the father? He promised me that if I didn't say anything then he wouldn't touch Si-Si. You promised! You liar! You touched her, how could you! You said you wouldn't touch her!" Lilly tried to attack but Stephen confused and concerned about the well being of his unborn child held her firm in his arms. Lilly sniffed and vigorously rubbed the mucus that was running from her nose with the back of her hand.

Pastor Mitchell's temples hurt and he was disoriented. He looked from his daughters to his brother for final clarification.

"I'm sorry Bobby," the Deacon whispered confirming his daughter's allegations while answering his brother's unspoken question. Pastor Mitchell's face became red hot and he forgot the vow he made as a cloaked man of God. He forgot about commandments and could only remember vengeance as he reached out to attack his flesh and blood. But he was stopped short when his heart attacked him instead.

"Daddy!" Sierra called out. She passed Jennifer off to Mike and rushed to her father's side. The family became panicked, heartbeats heightened, and mouths dropped open wide.

"Lillian call 9-1-1!" Mrs. Mitchell instructed. She fell to the floor beside her husband and held his head in her hands, "Come on baby, don't do this to me."

Lillian tried to steady her shaking hand long enough to make the life saving phone call. Stephen snatched the phone away and dialed for her. Lilly buried her head in the crook of his neck and cried hard as Stephen stated their emergency.

"Michael, get my grandbabies outta here, please," Mrs. Mitchell pleaded. She smeared beads of sweat from her husband's forehead. Mike was shaken from his trance and awe at the turn of events and jumped into action gathering the horrified and crying children. He, for a quick moment, observed the Deacon sitting quietly in the midst of all the commotion. He'd been forgotten about for the time being. He sat staring into the distance with a vacant expression. Mike hadn't forgotten about him and he hadn't forgotten why his girl's father was lying on the floor on his birthday and he wouldn't forget why he was carrying three hysterical children out to the car when all they really wanted was to be with their mother. He glanced back to see Sierra and Lillian who were wrapped in their mothers arms looking as infantile as the children he was struggling with. He didn't have time to wonder if he'd done the right thing. He took the children home.

27 Sierra

The ride home from the hospital was silent with the exception of the sound of the engine purring. Lilly and Sierra sat in the vehicle together with Stephen at the wheel yet alone in their own related thoughts. Each found it unbelievable that they'd both gone through the same torment with their uncle and had been completely oblivious. He'd made the very same promise to the both of them and they believed that they were protecting the other. They questioned the premise of their relationship. Sierra wondered what kind of big sister she'd been and how she could have not suspected, not known exactly what her uncle had been up to. She wondered if she'd abandoned her baby sister. She too had been quite disappointed in Lilly when she turned up pregnant at age fourteen but now she wondered whether or not she was part to blame. She wondered if there were maybe someway she could have prevented Lilly from going through such psychological torment and utter humiliation.

The car slowed to a stop in front of Sierra's home. She paused and thought about what words she wished to part with. She tried to find the best way to apologize for not being there for her sister. She looked up at the dark sky that daylight would very soon be breaking through. She blinked a few times and twisted her lips. Lilly leaned forward and placed a soft kiss on Sierra's cheek. She stroked her hair.

"I know what you're thinking Si-Si and now you just need to stop that. You are and always have been a great sister."

Sierra rested her eyes on Lillian's face. She caressed her hand and smiled. She reached for the door handle and climbed out of the backseat. She walked to the passenger side and leaned in to embrace Lilly and kiss her on the cheek. She offered a good night to Stephen and rubbed Lilly's belly and whispered, "Goodnight Lilly and Stephen junior."

Sierra turned and walked to her front door, stopping long enough to dig the spare key from the side of the large potted plant. She listened to the sound of the car pulling away from the other side of the door. She leaned and pressed her back against it. The house was dark and quiet. She questioned everything she'd been raised to believe. She'd deprived herself of so many of life's little pleasures and she wondered if it had in fact been pointless.

She looked in on her sleeping children and contemplated whether or not adjusting some of the values and beliefs she'd been instilling in them was in order. She kissed each one gently before walking to the opposite end of her home to her bedroom. She carefully eased her door open. Mike was stretched out across the bed sleeping soundly. Sierra stood quietly watching. She was happy to have him as a part of her life and couldn't stop wondering what might have been had she seen the beauty in him earlier in life. Had this Michael Toussaint always existed? Maybe that's what attracted Nate to him in the first place. Sierra crept to the television and turned it off. She carefully sat on the edge of the bed.

"How's your pops?" Mike asked in a groggy tone.

"I'm sorry, I didn't mean to wake you."

"I'm straight. What happened? What the doctors say?" Mike struggled to sit upright.

"He's going to be just fine. They're keeping him for observation but otherwise he's okay, physically anyway."

Mike observed Sierra's body language, "You gone be alright?"

Sierra sighed and sucked her teeth. She turned to face Mike, "Yea I think so. I think I'll be just fine."

The two watched each other in the semi darkness. There were things they'd wished to say but chose not to. Mike stood from the bed and stretched. With his foot he felt around for his shoes.

"Well why don't you get some rest. I'm gone head up outta here."

"Yea. Sure. Thanks."

Mike leaned in and kissed Sierra's forehead, "Anytime shawty," he said before turning to leave the room. He'd barely moved two steps when he felt Sierra take hold of his arm and ease him back toward her.

Sierra asked, "Actually...do you have to go? I mean it's so late...early...well you know."

Mike scratched the back of his head and looked down at Sierra's face. Sure he wanted to stay, the Magnum living a comfortable life in solitude in his back pocket could attest to that. However he didn't want Sierra to make hasty decisions based on pure emotions, the type of decisions that she may regret when the sun rose over Miami. Sierra stood in front of Mike, she leaned forward and kissed his lips first soft and gentle but progressively with more passion. She took his hands and guided them to her body and allowed them to explore all the secret places she previously deemed off limits. Taking her cue, Mike kissed her deeply, entangling his tongue with hers. He carefully sucked the air away then slowly blew it back. Michael held Sierra tight and massaged her rear. He grasped her firmly around her waist, lying her down on the bed on her back. He hovered above her body kissing her lips then moving his lips to her neck. He nibbled softly while his hand caressed her frame. Sierra breathed heavily, her breasts rising and falling and her hips voluntarily gyrating against his.

Mike placed his hand against the warm flesh of her leg then slid it beneath her dress to discover the inviting moisture forming between her thighs. Sierra gasped and backed away slightly. Her breathing became ragged and unsteady. She struggled to relax her body. Mike moved away and observed her face. He nibbled her bottom lip and caressed it with his tongue. He smiled, "I'm gonna gone ahead and get up outta here now."

Sierra thought for a moment but tightened her grip on him, "No. Stay with me," she whispered.

"Are you sure? You ain't got to do this l'il momma."

Sierra paused to think. She chewed her bottom lip and looked past Mike at nothing in particular. She then returned her gaze to Mike's face. Salt water pooled the brim of her eyes. She took a deep breath then closed them as she went in for another kiss. The signal was given clear and was accepted. Mike was free to be himself and do all the things that Darryl wouldn't or maybe even couldn't do.

Michael sat Sierra upright and assisted her in shimmying out of her dress. She sat feeling shy and intimidated in her bland white bra and panty set. She'd wished she'd thought to wear her pair of satin underpants. She folded her arms around her body attempting to conceal the stretched out flesh. Mike knelt before her. He carefully eased her arms away from her body and placed them at her sides. His lips gently caressed the soft flesh that was a constant reminder that three beautiful children had once resided, been nourished, and grown inside of her. Her shoulders slowly relaxed as her tension evaporated. Mike coaxed her onto her back then guided her fully onto the bed. He kissed every inch of her body from her temples to her fingertips to her toes.

A tear of joy rolled down the side of Sierra's face. She'd never had anyone be so attentive toward her. When Mike's warm breath was felt against the moisture between Sierra's thighs she gasped. She wondered if she should stop him but it felt too right for him to stop. Self-conscious and embarrassed about enjoying such an act, Sierra gently but forcefully pushed Mike away. He obliged temporarily. He lifted his body above hers and whispered softly into her ear, "It's alright for you to feel good." He then returned to make love to her with his tongue.

Sierra closed her eyes and blocked out all the barriers and over-the-top standards she'd set. Her hips began to gyrate and moans that had been rooted somewhere deep down in her soul escaped through her parted lips. She stretched her arms above her head and arched her back. The feeling becoming intensified, Sierra found herself helping Mike along by gently pressing on the back of his head. Her legs opened wide and her knees fell apart. She saw ribbons and rainbows as her blood river rushed from her toes to her brain. Euphoria was the word to describe her new experience. She collapsed breathless and sensitive.

Sierra felt drunk and a pleasant smirk emerged on her lips. The warmth of Mike's body hovering above enveloped her. She felt comforted, safe and secure with him. Michael caressed her opening with the tip of his penis ever so gently before easing himself inside of her body. He moved in slow motion, he didn't want to hurt her at all. He only wanted to make her feel good, sorta like she'd done for him. He lay above her feeling connected through more than just a sexual organ but more through their soul and their love for one another. A feeling Mike knew nothing about washed over him. The feeling clashed with everything he'd been taught and known about manhood. He swallowed the urge to reject the emotion but rather stared deep into Sierra's eyes that were filled with salty fluid. Michael kissed Sierra's lips and for the first time in both of their lives the two made love.

Mike slept soundly in Sierra's bed. She lay beside him wide awake and unable to catch any sleep herself. She could only sit with a long-term grin plastered on her face. She reminisced about the way Mike's hips rotated when he was inside her and the passion emitted when his tongue explored the curvature of her spine. A tingle and chill shot through her body and she wanted more of him but didn't want to disturb his slumber.

The air in the bedroom was thick. Sierra slipped from beneath the sheets and wrapped her robe around her body. She crept down the hall to the thermostat to cool things down some. Sleep just wasn't with her. She walked to the living room and took a seat by the window and watched the stillness of the morning sky. She wanted to talk to someone but alas it was barely six in the morning and everyone she knew would be asleep. Sierra picked up the cordless phone and dialed Lilly's cell phone number. After only one ring Lilly's voice came through clear and alert.

"Lilly? What are you doing up? I thought I was just going to leave you a message."

"The same reasons you're up I suppose. I got a lot on my mind," she answered with a sigh.

"Is everything alright? Stephen okay?"

"Yea, yea it's all good. Just...y'know, trying not to think about everything that happened yesterday. Aw man, why did Stephen have to see that? He is not going to wanna marry me now that he sees just how much baggage I really come with."

"Oh Lilly please, I bet you Stephen has all kinds of drama in his family too. Any fool can see the love in that man's eyes and he is not going to leave you over that."

"Yea you're right. He ain't crazy," Lilly chuckled, "Oh girl, I am so glad Daddy's okay but I think I'm a bad daughter after all."

"Why would you say something like that? "

"Well while Daddy's laid up in the hospital I'm sitting here at the house nervous and wondering whether or not he's going to be able to marry Stephen and me."

Sierra laughed out loud at her sisters acknowledged selfishness, "No, it's actually kinda sweet. You want your father to marry you, that's special."

"Yea, yea well don't get all sappy on me girl. God, this baby is due, shoots any day now. And the wedding! The wedding is only a few days away. I hope the damn crane I reserved is still available cause how else am I gonna get down the aisle?"

"Chile you are insane," Sierra scratched her scalp as she fought a yawn.

"So that's my story of franatic worry."

"Franatic?"

"Yes franatic. That's how far gone I am. I'm making up my own words. If Mary can do it, well dammit so can I," the sisters enjoyed their laugh together, "So what's on your mind this time of morning?"

"Mike," Sierra answered honestly.

"Oh really? Sounds like things may be getting serious between my big sis and the big sinner."

"You could say that but add one more sinner."

"No! You didn't!" Lilly squealed, "Shit girl you did!"

"Keep your voice down before your mother hears you."

"Oh screw that Sierra, Momma still at the hospital anyway. I want details. Was he good?"

Sierra twirled her hair around her index finger, "Now Lillian, you know a good girl never tells."

"That's cause you ain't never had anything worth telling before. Now stop beating around the bush. How big was his sack of groceries?"

"Oh you are too foolish. But it was Cosco size girl."

"He packin' like that?"

Sierra smiled broadly, "Mmhm. Oh my gosh Lilly, I never knew love was meant to feel that way."

"Damn, he put it on you like that?"

"Lillian I cried. And not like I've cried with Darryl. I cried because I felt so good, I was so happy."

"Whaat?" Lilly whispered.

"He touched me in ways Darryl never did. And-and he made me feel beautiful in my own skin. I swear I did not mind being undressed in front of him."

"Damn. Well alright then. G'head Mikey."

"Yes Lord," Sierra sighed and sat quietly momentarily, "Hey, get your rest Lilly but I'll see you at the house in a few hours."

"Okay sis but hey, do me a favor please. Don't feel guilty and don't blame yourself for any of this. Not about me, not about you and Mike. Can you promise me that?"

"Yes, I promise."

Sierra blew a kiss into the receiver before placing it on its base. She stood before the window and watched the sun break through the leaves of the palm trees. She yawned and scratched the base of her neck. Sierra turned and headed back to bed.

The church was decorated beautifully. Lily's hung from every archway and decorated every bench. Sierra walked through and oversaw every detail. She wanted to be sure that Lilly and Stephen's marriage would start off on the right foot. A few people who were responsible for the decorations, including her mother, were scattered about. A few guests who had arrived early mingled and discussed the beauty in the church. Sierra smiled to herself pleased at all she'd accomplished and grateful that things were ultimately going to work out for Lillian.

Feeling satisfied with all of the preparations, Sierra made her way to the back of the church. She approached a lone door and tapped it twice before easing it open and stepping inside.

"Hey girl," she sang out.

"Hi Si-Si," Lillian responded. She was seated in a chair in front of a vanity and beneath a hot curling iron that their hairstylist cousin was in control of. Another cousin, the beauty consultant of the family, sat quietly on an ottoman intensely selecting the perfect combination of blushes, shadows and glosses.

Sierra flashed back to her day in that chair, The Lady Chair as it was dubbed. Every woman to ever be married in the Mitchell's church had her time in The Lady Chair. Despite the outcome of certain aspects of her personal life she had no regrets about that day and smiled fondly as she recalled it. After all, her marriage hadn't started out bad. Actually Sierra and Darryl's wedding was quite lovely. During that time she was happy and pleased with life and hindsight being twenty/twenty she at that moment realized that her joy was more a result of pleasing her father as opposed to a woman's expected thrill of becoming a missus. But Sierra wasn't disappointed by this nor was she saddened, not the slightest. She snickered at first then laughed as though she'd just caught the punch line to a Bernie Mac joke.

"Sierra!" hairstylist-cousin snapped, "What in the devil has gotten into you? What you don't like my work all of a sudden?"

"Huh?" a puzzled look washed over Sierra's face, "Well no, as a matter of fact now that you mention it I really don't too much care for it."

Lillian gasped, "Girl are you messing up my hair on my wedding day?"

"Too poofy. You trying to make her look older than she is. What you trying to do, make her look like you?"

Lillian's eyes became wide as saucers and she fought the urge to break out in hysterical laughter. Her cousin however finding no humor in Sierra's words quickly turned resting all of her weight on one foot and landing a hand on her hip. She clicked the curling iron a couple of times before she spoke, "Girl, I did your hair for your wedding and you ain't have no complaints then."

"You're right, I didn't say anything. I just hide the pictures."

"Sierra Diane!" Lilly blurted out giggling ridiculously.

"Well then Ms. Thang you think you can do a better job than me then here you go," she outstretched the hand she held the hot utensil in toward Sierra.

"No, no. I'm only teasing. You're doing your thang, seriously," Sierra said smiling. She laughed inside as her cousin rolled her eyes and in slow motion returned to what she was doing.

"Sierra get out of here before you have me messed up on my wedding day for real," Lilly teased.

Laughing about nothing and everything simultaneously Sierra practically skipped to the door. She stopped and looked behind her, "Lilly."

"What chile?"

"You look simply marvelous darling."

"Why thank you darling."

"Congratulations."

Lilly blew a kiss in her sister's direction. Sierra stepped out the room and firmly closed the door behind her.

The feast at the reception was heavenly, catered by the glorious sisters of the church. Sierra sat in front of a Styrofoam plate filled with bare-naked chicken bones, cornbread crumbs and collard greens juices. She smiled and rocked in her seat as she watched Lilly with her big belly groove with her new husband. She hoped that the excitement of the day didn't cause her water to break. Mr. and Mrs. Mitchell sat holding hands looking more relieved than anything else. The DJ switched to Michael Jackson's *Rock With You* causing a soul stir within the guests. Sierra mumbled a soft "hey" and snapped her fingers and swayed her head side to side.

A pair of strong hands caressed her shoulders. She looked up and her eyes met with Mike's. She smiled and flirted with her eyes. He reached out to take her hand in his and led her to the dance floor. Mike wasn't known for his dancing skills, outside of the simple two-step and finger pop that he was oh so skilled at he was rhythmless. This dance was no different. Sierra dropped her head and laughed as she imitated his moves. She thought about Nate and wished that he could've been there to share in this happy occasion. She chewed the side of her lip carefully but then sighed and smiled. She knew her wish had come true and although she could not see him nor feel him or hear his gentle tone, she knew without a doubt that Nathaniel Lee Marshall was near in her heart and that he was happy for her.

28 Mike

Mike sat in the car behind the steering wheel looking over at the house. He took several slow breaths in and out, his nerves frazzled. Several times during this trip he contemplated turning the car around and driving back home but he knew that dealing with his grandmother was something that he had to do. He needed to lift that four-ton weight off of his shoulders and move on with his life. Yep. He'd just go inside and speak to her in an easy, gentlemanly manner and then be on his way. No problems. And when it was all said and done he'd feel less burdened and free to be happy in his youth. He had even dressed up for the occasion leaving most of his jewels on his nightstand giving her one less reason to look down her nose at him.

"Forget it," he mumbled under his breath. He pulled the handle and pushed the car door open and climbed from behind the steering wheel. He pushed his hands down inside his pockets and taking long strides walked to his grandmother's front door. He reached for the doorknob but then instead decided to knock. He stood beneath the hot Florida sun patiently rocking back and forth on his heels. He could hear the sound of heavy footsteps approach the door then stop abruptly. He knew he was being watched from the other side of the peephole. He could make out the voice of his aunt announcing to his grandmother in

Creole news of his unexpected, unwelcome arrival. The sound of her voice dropped back as she walked away cursing his name.

Frustration crept through his spine and Mike fought to remain in control of his emotions. He was determined not to let anyone or anything bring out the beast, not today. He inhaled deeply and knocked once more, this time with a touch more force than his previous effort.

"What?" his aunt called to him.

"Open the door!"

"What do you want Michael?" she asked suspicious. Her accent was much stronger than it should have been for someone who'd lived in the United States for more than half of her life, "You only come here to start trouble and upset mother."

"Man I ain't come here lookin' to start trouble with nobody. I promise, just open the door."

She hesitated, contemplating the choice presented but soon though reluctantly obliged, "What do you want?" she again asked.

Mike walked past his aunt ignoring her question. He rolled his eyes to the back of his head and counted silently as he listened to her curse and complain about his presence in her family's native tongue while she stomped to the back of the house. He took long languid steps toward the sofa nearest his grandmother and took a seat. For a period they sat in silence, she did not acknowledge his presence in her home. Mike decided that it was best to tell her what he'd come to say and quickly be gone.

He began, "Look man, I know you don't really want me up in your crib so I'm gone make this short. I just wanted to let you know that I'm doing okay, I mean if you care. I've been seein' this shorty I used to go to school with named Sierra for awhile now. She makes me happy. She got three kids so I guess I'm kinda a step-daddy and sh- uh, stuff."

Without turning to look directly at him she asked, "Why you want to ruin a girl and her babies' life too?"

Mike smiled and chuckled to himself, "No ma'am, I am not going to ruin nobody else life. I don't know if Jean told you 'bout my nightclub but it's doing real good and I got a job interview on Wednesday so I plan on getting back into architecture. I even go to church on Sunday's. Well not every Sunday but y'know I do try. That junk be feelin' weird as hell for me but maybe it'll...y'know, make me a better person or somethin'."

Mike paused to think about what he was saying, to make sure he didn't miss anything, "So yo, that's basically it. Just wanted to come here and tell you thanks man. You know, for keeping me...for not leaving me out there with my momma. So, uh, I'mma gone 'head and bounce but if you need anything y'all know how to get in contact with me."

Mike stood and fidgeted for a moment. He moved his body toward the front door then back. He shrugged his shoulders and walked to the chair his grandmother was sitting in and leaned forward and kissed her on the cheek, it was a gesture he could never recall doing before. He turned and walked out the door not looking back and closed it behind him.

Walking to his car he realized that his expectations had in fact been quite realistic. In that moment he felt better, much better about everything in life. His outlook was brighter. He knew he could be a better, happier and more fulfilled person. He did a double take before entering his car. He was almost certain he'd seen Janay in the distance pushing a stroller but when he looked again she was gone. After a quick mental calculation he realized that she would in fact have already delivered her baby. He looked at his baby. She hadn't laid a hand on it since he confronted her that night but it didn't mean all was forgiven. He jumped in his ride and peeled away. He sped toward home, he had to change and make an urgent phone call.

"You want me to do what?"

Mike held the phone to his ear with his shoulder while he pressed a fresh out the dryer pair of jeans, "Come on girl, don't start judgin' me now. I gotta settle this once and for all."

"Well why didn't you tell me before that you had a baby on the way?" Sierra asked feeling frustrated with the news.

"I ain't neva said shorty was mine. I just wanna find out for sure. She say it is mine but that bitch be sleepin' around with so many niggas-"

"Michael!"

"What? That hoe is a bitch. Aiight, my bad. Look man, my bad I just gotta see what's what, that's all."

"And you want me to go with you to meet one of your ex-girls?"

"Quit makin' it sound so scandalous. Come on shorty, I need you," Mike sat the iron down and waited for her answer.

"Okay, okay, I will go. I'll be there for you."

Mike thanked Sierra and informed her that he'd make the arrangements and get back to her. He was nervous when he hung up the phone. What if the child was his? Sure he was ready and able to financially support a child but the parental buck stopped there. He didn't think that he was hardly mentally equipped for fatherhood. He was there with Sierra's three often but he was more a cool uncle and not hardly a dad. His own dad was probably a pimp or a pusher or maybe some five dollar trick who was taking a late night hiatus from his missionary position wife when he got a hooker pregnant.

He contemplated calling Janay to make an arrangement to meet but realized he'd put a lot of fear in her, there was no way she'd trust him not to lay a hand on her. He dressed and chose to take a drive into the city anyway hoping to bump into Sherika. He hadn't spoken to her in quite some time and with the way they'd left things he felt out of place calling her.

He cruised down the street that she lived on. A black new model F150 was parked in front of her home. Mike pulled up behind it and parked with the engine running. Not wanting to mess up her game he called her phone and asked her to come outside. He hadn't realized how much he'd missed her until he saw her. Her twisted lips were maybe meant to show much attitude but only served to conceal a smile. Sherika walked to the driver's side of the car and stooped down to a squatting position.

"Don't tell me that's PhilMo ride," Mike opened. Sherika nodded, "You got that nigga up in yo' crib?"

"Don't even trip. You know PhilMo paid out the anus these days. I can swallow my pride and entertain him for a little while."

"I ain't hatin', I heard dog big time now. Must be if he sniffin' those panties."

"Y'know," Sherika smiled. There was a twinkle in her eye and it was clear that all had been forgiven, "So rumor has it that Big Mike is a big Poppa now. Any truth to that?"

Mike shrugged, "I guess anythangs possible. I did hit it 'round that time. I was twisted dog, I don't even know if I wore a raincoat. You seen shorty?"

"Yep. It's a boy. It's cute. Big. Dark-skinned, look like it could be yours. But then she been fuckin' Smooth for years so you never know."

"What she name it?"

"Shandrake."

"Yo, what's Smooth real name?"

"Shaundray. I wouldn't even put too much thought in it, that bitch dumb. I asked her how she going around sayin' you the baby daddy and she named it after Smooth. That hoe gone try and tell me she ain't name it after him. That Smooth and her baby got two totally different names."

"How she figure? What that nigga Smooth say?"

"Smooth ain't tryin' to claim that hoe shorty whether it's his or not. That nigga got too many kids as it is. I'm tellin' you dog, I'a blaze dat hoe for tellin' niggas its yourn if it turn out it ain't."

"My nigga," Mike gave Sherika a pound before she stood upright.

Sherika rubbed the kinks out her legs and began to walk away, "Well let me get back up in the crib before PhilMo start gettin' nosey and come out here and see you. Can't have you fuckin' up my money, you know that nigga never did like you no way."

"Man tell *Phillip Moore* I said fuck his sorry, pussy ass!" Mike reversed and pulled away. He drove past Janay's house. He thought about stopping, going inside and finding out just why she was telling people the baby was his if she named it after Smooth. Knowing he wouldn't be able to be that polite about the situation on his own he kept on driving.

Mike hadn't realized he cared so much or would be this happy to hear news of Lillian having her baby. Maybe it wasn't even so much about that but more feeling good about being included in such an intimate family event. After receiving the call from Sierra saying that Lilly had gone into labor and delivered a baby girl Mike made his way to the hospital. He was instructed to follow the path up the elevator and down the halls to the nursery. The Mitchell family was gathered outside the large window smiling and pointing. Mike walked up to the new proud father and shook his hand, congratulating him. He stood behind Sierra and rubbed her shoulders.

"Which one is it?" he asked.

Sierra sniffed back a tear and pointed, "Right there, Girl Vance. She named her Alichia. Alichia Shawntelle. Isn't that just beautiful?"

"Yep baby, it sure is," Mike kissed the back of Sierra's head and whispered, "I love you Si."

Sierra turned and looked Mike in the eyes, smiling and softly kissed his cheek, "I love you Michael." She turned and wrapped his arms tightly around her waist. Looking up to the heavens smiling she whispered softly, "I love you too Nate."

Happily Ever After...

Sierra stood nervously outside of the school. The Pre-Grad jam was in full effect but she was afraid to go inside. What if her mom and dad found out that she wasn't at Tracy's house studying for finals but was rather out with heathenish children listening to *Ready for the World*? Her father particularly would be displeased by her actions. Lilly was inside. Although she wasn't graduating her boyfriend Monty was a graduating senior and she'd come as his date also against her parent's will. And Nate, he'd asked her to come but she told him that she wouldn't be able to make it. He was probably already inside with Carla Dobbins on the dance floor grinding and feeling on her booty.

Everyone had come with someone, even she. She'd come with Lilly and Monty but her bold rebellion parked at the front door. Deciding she wouldn't have much fun anyway she turned and headed down the dark street toward home. It was foolish of her to come anyway. She'd just go unnoticed by most and be the butt of a joke for others. She kept her head low and walked as fast as she could, following the shadows so that no one would recognize her. Not watching where she was going as she turned the corner she bumped into a firm chest.

"Sorry," she mumbled embarrassed while trying to quickly step around and get away.

"Yo Si-Si, what up?" he asked.

Sierra's heart paused. She turned slowly and found herself face to face with Michael "Romeo" Toussaint. She thought about running away but she was seventeen years old and such an act would be more ridiculous than her sneaking around corners to escape children she'd gone to school with for the past four years.

"Hey Mike," she answered shyly.

"Where you phenna go? The party's that way."

"No, I'm not going to the party. I told you, I can't."

"So what you doin' by the school in what's clearly yo' party dress this time of night?"

"Cause…well," she stammered, trying to find the right words and find them quick so that she could get out of there, "Well I thought about going. I changed my mind, I don't wanna get in trouble."

Mike pulled a pack of cigarettes from his pocket and pounded them against his hand. He head nodded and slapped palms with a couple of guys that walked past. He smirked at Sierra, "Nate already there."

"With Carla."

"So fuck Carla. He'a be happy to see you."

"Thanks but I'm going home. Besides everyone has a date and-"

"Well just say you my date."

"You're kidding right?"

"What? You too good for a nigga? I know you saved and Ms. Goody-Goody and all but dang, you neva know. I just might surprise you."

"Well you've already done that."

"Yea? Well, I gotta watch myself around you. You'a mess around and make me wanna be a better person an' shit."

Sierra shook her head and smiled. She thought how crazy it would be to go to the party as Mike's date. She decided to entertain it, have some fun for a change. It would give her something juicy to write in her journal. How she went on a once in a lifetime date with a guy that she had absolutely nothing in common with and would likely never associate with again after graduation. Sierra smiled and followed Mike back to the party.

Acknowledgments

From the top of the dome...

The story you just read is a work of fiction and my favorite story to date. People always assume that the stories told by authors are somehow directly (or indirectly) related to ones own life. I suppose there is a degree of truth in that belief. I've never been through any of the situations that the characters experienced. I don't know any of them. I've never met Nate or Mike or Sierra personally but rather others over the years that left behind bits and pieces of their personalities for me to do with as I pleased. So I suppose, in that sense, there is a level of truth to everything I write. Ticks and habits, catch phrases, reactions...every character is founded on the reality of the many people that I have encountered in my life over the years. Friends and family, those I've met in passing...and those I've observed from afar.

With that being the case, I owe many thanks and acknowledgments to the plethora of individuals who inspired the characters that I love and adore so much. The ex-boyfriends, the friends of friends, the cousin, the colleague, the talk show guest, the character in that movie, the great people of London with their really cool accents, the people of different cultures and the people of my own ethnicity, the individuals, the followers, the dog boyfriend that somebody nearby complained about, the character someone else created, the sexually perplexed, New Yorkers and Floridians, artists and visionaries, hookers, Sunday Christians and

acknowledgments

full time prayer warriors, hypocrites and those that speak their mind, the list goes on and on...and I thank you all!

I thank you God and Christ for the blessings that you've bestowed upon such a cynical, analytical believer who frequently forgets to have faith (Father please forgive me)...and I thank you for the blessings that await me of which I cannot fathom even exist!

I extend my gratitude to those that love and support me and ride with me no matter what. And I acknowledge the importance and impact you've all had on my life. As I type this off the top of my head (a big deal 'cause I always gotta write it out first!) I consider and acknowledge my husband Glorius and my sunn Storm, my mother Dawn, my sister Trina and my brothers Leslie and Christopher, my step-dad Kevin, my spiritual sis Maggie Jean and her Beenie baby, my niecy Lady Bug, my aunts Mildred, Delores, Ernestine, Berta, my uncles Mike and Bud, Grandaddy and Momma (RIP), my Granny (RIP), my cousins Diane, Lisa and Nick (RIP), Eric and Jenni, Shelly and Lich, any relative that adored me enough to call me Bunky, my boys Juan, Dre, Kin and Sid, the Gallery 37 alumni, Dem Gurlz Clique, the entire Pack fam and affiliates, the Martin fam and all the Johnson fam, friends and special people from Chicago to the Twin Cities to South Florida to L.A. and back.

Naming names is probably a bad idea! I do acknowledge anyone that I missed.

Love always,

Miki Starr